I0761066

THE GHOST WOMEN

Also by Jennifer Murphy

Scarlet in Blue

I Love You More

THE GHOST WOMEN

A NOVEL

Jennifer Murphy

DUTTON

An imprint of Penguin Random House LLC
1745 Broadway, New York, NY 10019
penguinrandomhouse.com

Book design by Kristin del Rosario
Interior art: Tree art © ekosuwandono / Shutterstock;
Texture background © Dmitr1ch / Shutterstock

Library of Congress Cataloging-in-Publication Data

has been applied for.

ISBN 9780593474365 (hardcover)
ISBN 9780593474372 (ebook)

Printed in the United States of America
1st Printing

The authorized representative in the EU for product safety and compliance is Penguin Random House Ireland, Morrison Chambers, 32 Nassau Street, Dublin D02 YH68, Ireland, https://eu-contact.penguin.ie.

During the early modern period, between 1400 and 1775, an estimated 40,000 to 60,000 women were executed for witchcraft throughout Europe and America. Many were burned at the stake. I dedicate this novel to all the women who died in such heartless and brutal ways, in many cases merely for being seen as independent or defying traditional gender roles, and I can only hope that their ghosts have found peace inside a magical tree located deep in a lush forest.

By faith Abraham, when he was tested, offered up Isaac, and he who had received the promises offered up his only begotten son.

—HEBREWS 11:17

And though documents indicate that the tarot deck was used for game playing from the fifteenth century, there were no records that specifically detailed the rules of play.

—HELEN FARLEY, *A CULTURAL HISTORY OF TAROT*

THE GHOST WOMEN

Six Centuries Before the Murders

I am surrounded by darkness. The air is cold and damp. I cannot say how long I have been in this dungeon. Sleep—and the dreams inside it—is my only refuge. Dreams of a magical tree located deep in a forest.

A tree that sings.

I was but fourteen years old when the abbot sent his henchmen to my village to take me. My last clear memory is of the men in red robes ripping my infant sons from my breast. They wailed, like I do now, their pain as great as my own. The men held their shiny crosses to my face. "You have been accused of witchery," the tall one said. They read a proclamation made of lies, sordid accusations they deemed proof of my transgressions. I had sinned against God and the Church. I was seen in the forest gathering poisonous plants that I used to make devil's brew. I stole into the abbot's chambers while he slept and added it to his tea. I beguiled him with my fire-red hair and the sway of my hips. I was never to hear what happened to my infant sons.

Now I hear the pounding of boots descending the dungeon steps, the same boots that came for others before me, but this time, it is my name they call. They lead me through a maze of dank corridors and stone stairwells until we reach a heavy door that opens to the sun. I raise my face to its warmth, adjust my eyes to the light, and breathe in the crisp air. Hot sand burning my feet as I approach the wooden cross, ropes cutting into my skin as they bind me. The sound of splashing waves draws my attention to the sea. The sun reflecting upon its glass, the cerulean sky so bright and clear.

I smell my burning flesh before I feel the knives of the fire.

Then something miraculous occurs. I hear the song of the tree, the one from my dreams, sweet and inviting, and I see three wispy, translucent figures swirling and circling above the water, above me, their pale gowns shimmering, their arms beckoning. And so I rise from a body that is no longer mine and follow them into a lush forest. Deeper and deeper we go, the heady and resinous scents of pine and spruce and fir luring us toward a clearing, and that is when I see it. So lush and plentiful, its magnificence undeniable. And in that moment, sight and knowledge wash over me and I understand that I am not alone, that there have been many who came before me, and many who will follow. For we are a sisterhood of the unjustly murdered, and together, one day, we will take our revenge.

On the twenty-second day of September in the Year of Our Lord 1437, my earthly body was burned alive and my soul came home.

PART ONE

The Hanged Man

Then one of the twelve, whose name was Judas Iscariot, went to the chief priests and said, "What will you give me if I deliver him over to you?" And they paid him thirty pieces of silver.

—MATTHEW 26:14–15

Day 1

THE AUTUMNAL EQUINOX
FRIDAY, SEPTEMBER 22, 1972

LOLA

Dead man in forest. East entrance. Meet you there?—Colin

"Brutal" was one of the words heard most often that September of 1972. Brutal murders. Brutal hurricane. Brutal temperatures. In the Deep South, Septembers were notorious for scorching heat and fierce storms. Those of us born and bred on Waverly Island understood how to handle temperatures well into the hundreds. As children, we were raised not to light matches too close to the forest, play high-energy sports outdoors for more than twenty minutes at a time, or lean our bare thighs against shiny automobiles. As adults, we knew to have extra fans on hand to cool our homes in the event one or two conked out, cover our necks with cold, wet rags if we felt heatstroke coming on, and board our windows at the first mention of a hurricane. But what we didn't anticipate that autumnal equinox of 1972 was that we'd be cutting a dead body down from a tree.

I had just stepped foot in my office at the Waverly Island Police Station and was turning up the air-conditioning window unit when I saw Colin's note on my chair. I'd barely finished reading it when the phone rang.

"Lola," a frantic voice said, "it's Alice Landry, from St. Luke's.

I've been trying to reach you. One of our students, Abel Montague, was found dead in the forest. He was a Second Year, only nineteen years old. So tragic."

Founded in 1948, and named for Saint Luke, the patron saint of painters, St. Luke's Institute of the Arts was a privately endowed visual arts college that ran like a secret society. The members of its board of directors weren't disclosed. Its location wasn't listed on any maps. Students didn't apply—they were recruited. Attendees were guaranteed fame and success and promised a significant stipend upon graduation. Tuition, room and board, and all other living expenses were covered. Past instructors were rumored to include the likes of Larry Rivers, Mark Rothko, and Willem de Kooning. I myself had spied such greats as Lee Krasner and Helen Frankenthaler visiting the island. Though if you researched any of these artists, there was no mention of them having knowledge of St. Luke's existence.

"I just saw Colin's note," I replied to Alice.

"Yes, I understand he's on the scene. But I want you there. It's delicate. The victim—oh, I hate calling him that. Anyway, his father is the chairman of our board of directors."

"I'm on my way."

Waverly Island was located a few miles off the coast of South Carolina. While South Carolina's barrier islands were primarily sand and sediment, Waverly Island was formed by uplifted bedrock, a remnant of ancient geological activity. St. Luke's was situated on the island's highest elevation. A wall of large boulders stepped down to the ocean and the sandy beach below. The water could be angry there, crashing against the rocks with a force that sent it thirty feet in the air. The main campus was surrounded by a twelve-foot-tall, ivy-covered brick wall, a veritable fortress. Classes were held in the mammoth, four-story stone monastery where the monks had once lived and worshipped. In fact, that was what the students called the building: the Monastery. A covered walk, known as a cloister, formed a quadrangle around the Monastery. Also inside the brick wall were the Tower, the ancient monks' sepulchers, and a row of newer storage-unit-type buildings complete with garage doors. These were the students' art studios. There were rumors that a series of underground tunnels had once connected all the buildings, but I had never personally seen them. Six additional cottages were located outside the brick wall. These were granted by lottery to a select few. St. Luke's went to great lengths to present itself as just another expensive private school, but curiosity about what went on behind the redbrick fortress abounded. More than once, island kids, motivated by rite-of-passage dares or juvenile curiosity, had tried to climb the ivy walls and test these rumors, only to be met by men wearing dark sunglasses, carrying two-way radios, and clad in black suits bearing only the school's insignia on the lapels. These men, generally referred to by students as "Luke's Lackeys," or "Lackeys" for short, were the Institute's security detail.

Per Colin's note, I parked in the lot closest to Dead Witch Forest's east entrance. The forest encompassed about a quarter of the island's land and had four designated entrances, north, south, east, and west. While my house was north of the forest, I generally used the east entrance on my morning runs so I could avoid the Garden of Angels, an ancient cemetery with squeaky iron gates, creepy and crumbling tombstones, and a reputation for being haunted. As I neared, I eyed the two student cottages situated near the entrance. I had passed by them many times on my way into the forest, pausing to admire the garden of the one closest, but never took notice of their residents. I made a mental note to find out which students occupied them. Perhaps they'd seen something.

A few of my guys and some Lackeys hovered at the opening to the trail. "He's at the Ghost Tree," one of my guys said. "Follow me."

I thanked him even though I and every island resident knew exactly where the Ghost Tree was located. Deep into the forest we went, steering off one path onto another. I felt the same foreboding sensation I had the first time I walked this particular path as a child with my father years earlier, his idea of how to dispel my fear. The Ghost Tree was the stuff of legend and folklore. It was said that the spirits of the burned witches had flown to this particular tree to rid themselves of the cruelty of their deaths, and in so doing had infused the tree with magical powers. Dead-witch stories were told at slumber parties, over campfires, and in barbershops and hair salons. At night, children and teenagers grabbed flashlights and snuck out of their homes in search of the tree, and the Ghost Women who were said to still live inside it. There were those who insisted they had seen the wispy specters walking or flying in the forest, but most spoke of *feeling* their presence or *knowing* unfortunate happenings were attributed to them. Everything from missing pets to unexplained deaths to financial problems were blamed on the Ghost Women. The local Gullah population, who practiced a form of folk magic called hoodoo and were highly superstitious, believed that dead witch sightings foretold good fortune.

I tried to contain an audible gasp when we arrived at the tree. The entire scene looked like something out of a demonic ritual. The tree was surrounded by a circle of black candles that had obviously burned for a while. The wax curled like waves over the edges. A handmade burlap poppet, roughly six inches long, had been placed on the ground directly under the victim. A black pearl–tipped pin was stuck into its red-painted heart. But it was the repugnance of the victim's pose that stole my attention and curiosity. The body was hanging upside down, the rope attached only to the ankle of his right foot. His left leg was bent at the knee and fashioned into a ninety-degree angle by tying his left calf behind his right knee. His hands were tied behind his back. His feet were bare. A mane of blond hair hung from his head. Flies buzzed about his face.

I smelled death as I approached. Up close, his face appeared even more grotesque, lips blue, face and neck swollen, skin discolored, most likely due to blood pooling in the head. He had been there for a while. I put on my gloves and crouched down to take a better look. The tongue was protruding and dry. Lifted his eyelids. Eyes bulging, pupils dilated, corneas clouded. Who shut them? That was usually a sign that the murderer cared for the victim. I rose. Rope burns were present on the left ankle and wrists but not as apparent as those on the right ankle. Hanging by one foot would be particularly painful. Death would be slow, and joints would get dislocated, akin to the body being stretched. I checked his mouth. No signs of a gag. Even this deep in the forest, someone might have heard his screams. I would have to rely on Rebecca to determine the exact cause and time of death. Rebecca Beach had only recently taken over as the island's medical examiner following the death of her father, Winston. This would be her first murder autopsy.

"Hey, boss," I heard someone behind me say as I stood. "What do you think?"

Colin was my second-in-command. When I took over as lead detective of the Waverly Island Police Department two years earlier, I worried Colin might have wanted my job, which could have made our relationship uncomfortable, but he dispelled my concerns immediately. "My wife and I are busy having babies," he'd said. "The last thing I need is any more pressure than I already have."

"Interesting choice of location for a murder," I said. "Not to mention the theatrical staging."

"Yep," he replied. "We found some fake coins, and this in the kid's back pocket."

"The Hanged Man," I said. While the card was in good

condition, its larger size, gilded imagery, and lack of an identifying number or name indicated it was from a very old deck. "You said you found coins?"

"A bag of fake silver ones," Colin said. "Like something you'd find at a five-and-dime. We didn't see it at first." He pointed at a small black velvet pouch three trees away. I squinted.

"Judas Iscariot," I said.

"The disciple?"

"The story goes he hanged himself after being paid thirty pieces of silver for betraying Jesus. Some say he was found upside down in a pose very similar to our victim's, and that the illustration on the Hanged Man card was originally based on his suicide. I wonder why all these disparate clues. Sure seems like the killer was trying to overwhelm us."

"I was thinking the same thing," Colin said.

"Who found the body?"

Colin checked his notes. "A student named Karla Gardyn. She's a Third Year. Lives in that cottage closest to the forest's east entrance. She was also the victim's neighbor. Said she was going for a morning walk through the forest when she came upon him. She ran all the way to the administration building to tell Dean Landry. Apparently the cottages don't have phones."

"Our victim lived in the cottage next door to her?"

"Yep," Colin said. "Weird coincidence, don't you think?"

"When will Rebecca be here?"

"She's on her way."

"Make sure she takes lots of pictures. You okay to manage the scene? I'm going to go talk with Dean Alice Landry, and hopefully this Karla Gardyn. Radio if you need me?"

"Will do. Take care of yourself, okay? Whoever did this is a brutal SOB."

PEARL

I knew from a young age that I had the gift of sight. I could perceive truths beyond what was apparent to the physical eye. And yet I was blind to you. It took seeing you and her together to discover your deception.

The morning sun is streaming through the blinds as I lie in bed. I keep playing it over in my mind. I didn't plan to confront you. Not yet. I needed to think it through. We were so entwined. The cottage. Our stuff. Our routines. Our love—I thought. I wanted so badly for it not to be true. And so I waited and I pretended. But then you said you were working late in your studio. You'd said that before, but this time it was different. A stiffness. A dismissive tone. And I heard myself blurting it all out. "I saw you," I said. "You were holding her hand, touching her cheek, kissing her." I was losing control, asking why, why her, telling you to leave, my heart and body shaking at that thought, crying, whining, then forgiving you, begging you to stay, to love me again.

And then you left. You didn't say anything at all. You just turned away from me and walked out the door.

That's when my gift of sight returned. After you left, I *saw* you lying dead on the floor of your studio.

I hear someone knocking on the front door of the cottage. I know Karla's knock. It's urgent. Insistent. Everything about Karla is urgent and insistent. Karla is the type of person who isn't afraid to take up space in the world. "Pearl, are you awake?" she asks. "It's early. Something has happened." I hear the turn of the doorknob, the creak of the door opening. There are no locks on doors at St. Luke's. The buckle of the wood floorboards. She enters the bedroom, sits beside me on the bed, starts blabbing about finding you, about your face and your hair. "Pearl, did you hear me? Abel is dead."

"Did you say the Ghost Tree?" I ask, and for a moment, I'm confused because that's not what I *saw*.

"Yes, it was just awful," she says. "The police will want to talk to me, won't they? I won't say anything about your poppets."

"Poppets?"

"There was one lying on the ground under the body," she says. "More like carefully placed. Just because you make them doesn't mean it was one of yours. Anybody can buy one at Priscilla's. Are you okay? Can I get you anything? I have some valerian root. It will help calm you. I'll bring you some tea."

After she leaves, I pull the bedcovers over my head and try to sleep. *Maybe it isn't real*, I tell myself. *Maybe it's all a bad dream*.

LOLA

The murder weighed on my mind as I turned onto the drive that led to St. Luke's. Its brutality was disturbing enough, but the fact that it had happened at the Ghost Tree felt like a warning. Security was tight at St. Luke's. I waited for the guard who regularly manned the iron gate to verify whether my name was on the VIP list, which it always was. Finally, the gate opened. I drove through, parked in the Monastery's guest lot, and went inside. Christine, Alice's secretary, nodded when I walked into the school's main office.

"Go right in," she said. "She's expecting you."

Alice was on the phone arguing with someone about the air conditioning not working. As usual, she seemed oblivious to my arrival. The students at St. Luke's often referred to Dean Alice Landry as Alice in Wonderland. She considered it a term of endearment, completely missing the term's derogatory implication. I sat in the chair opposite her and waited. I had forgotten she was a chain-smoker. The ashtray on her desk was overflowing with cigarette butts, and the room was so thick with smoke and the scent of tobacco that I coughed, a few times. Alice was one of the first women I'd met when I moved back to Waverly Island. We were both members of the Waverly Island Women's Club, a luncheon group that hosted "powerful women speakers" on a monthly basis. Neither of us were regulars. Alice continually referred to me as a good friend, but I had never felt close to her. She wasn't the type of woman other women got close to. She was competitive where men were concerned. The type of friend who dragged you along to parties, only to leave you behind when a man caught her eye. I had read somewhere that she was thirty-four years old, just two years older than me, which felt young for a person, especially a woman, in her position. She looked much younger than her years. With her slight frame, wavy dark hair, and youthful energy, she could easily pass for one of St. Luke's students.

"Sorry," she said as she hung up the phone and stood to greet me. "We just had those air-conditioning units installed. It's a mother out there, isn't it? I hear we broke a heat record. Did you know that all the fans in town are sold out?"

I didn't bother to say they sell out every year. It was often like that with Alice. Random thoughts. Questions that rarely required answers. The truth was I hadn't been listening too closely because I was busy trying not to stare. Normally, Alice was very polished, her white blouses always steam-ironed and neatly tucked into her signature pencil skirts, but now a strand of her tight ponytail hung loosely over her ear, and her eyes were puffy and bloodshot like she'd been crying. I had never seen her this disheveled.

She sat back down, grabbed a pack of Virginia Slims off her desk, tapped it, but nothing came out. "Damn." She tossed the empty pack into the wastebasket, opened the top drawer of her desk, rooted through it, pulled out a single cigarette. "There you are," she said to the cigarette, then lit it, leaned back in her chair, and slowly inhaled.

"What a morning," she said. "I just got off the phone with

Monty Montague, Abel's father. Well, not *just*. I was talking to him right before I called the air-conditioning people. I told you he's one of the school's founders, right?"

"You said he was chairman of the board of directors."

"He's both, actually, but he doesn't like it advertised that he was the founder. It's some sort of family name thing. Don't tell anyone that, okay? Anyway, I could tell from his voice how *very* upset he is about Abel's death. He adored that kid. We were working out the details of how he and his third wife are going to get Abel back home. *Third*, do you believe it? By the way, the new Mrs. Montague is not that much older than Abel. She just had twin boys. Geez, it's probably two years ago now. Apparently twins run in the Montague family." She paused. "Oh, Lola, I'm so sorry. I didn't even say hello. How are you?"

"I'm fine," I said.

"Really? You look tired."

"It's been busy," I said. "The tourists have discovered us, it seems. Ever since we got a chamber of commerce. I keep telling Colin we need to run them out of town."

"The tourists?" she asked.

"The chamber," I said.

She laughed, which I hoped would help release tension. For both of us. I was having difficulty getting the visual of Abel Montague's dead face out of my mind.

"How can I help you?" she asked. "Oh gosh. That's a stupid question. You're here to talk about the murder. It is a murder, right?"

"It appears so. But we need to wait for Rebecca's report. You know Rebecca Beach, right? Our new medical examiner?"

"Oh yes, from Women's Club. So sad about her dad's cancer. I hope she's doing okay."

"Do you know if Abel had enemies?"

"The instructors all despised him," Alice said. "Many of the students did too. Abel is—I mean *was*—sorry." Her voice shook slightly. "I still can't believe he's gone. Abel was arrogant, argumentative, disrespectful, and he cheated on his girlfriend. But he was an amazing artist. One of the best we've ever had."

"Who was his girlfriend?"

"Her name is Pearl Calhoun. She's a Second Year. So was Abel. They lived together in one of the cottages."

I wrote Pearl's name on my notepad. "Is it common for students of the opposite sex to live together?"

"I wouldn't say common, but it isn't against the rules. I think it happened gradually after they started dating. Abel still has, I mean *had*, his own room here at the Monastery."

"The choice of tree was interesting, don't you think?" I asked.

"What do you mean?"

"The Ghost Tree."

"*The* Ghost Tree?" She noticeably shivered. "I had no idea which tree he was hanged from. The whole thing is just so upsetting. And scary. To think we may have a murderer loose on the island."

"You said Abel cheated on this, um, Pearl?"

"According to my liaisons, everyone knew that about him," Alice said.

"Your liaisons?"

Alice immediately straightened, her body language shifting from fear and concern to self-importance, as school dean.

"Yes. I select one student from each incoming class to act as class liaison. That student's job is to ensure all the other students in their Year have what they need, and to keep me abreast of anything or anyone that could become an issue. I run a tight ship. And of course rumors do fly."

I briefly pictured speech bubbles with wings crisscrossing the sky.

"What about Pearl? Do you think she knew Abel was cheating on her?"

"I can't say for certain, but I'd guess not. Pearl is the opposite of who Abel was. She's a sweetheart, universally liked. Esme Li, the Second Year student liaison, and all Pearl's instructors are very fond of her. They describe her as diligent, kind, studious, passionate about her art, and caring. The type of person who brings out people's protective natures. I doubt anyone shared Abel's sexual escapades with her. They most likely went to great lengths not to. You see, Pearl's background is different from our usual recruits. First of all, she's from around here. Not the island, the mainland. Her mother overdosed soon after Pearl was born. She was a sickly child who spent a lot of time in orphanages and foster homes. Our scout first saw her artwork at a statewide high school art competition. A sister from the convent where she was living had entered a painting of hers, and it won first prize. I believe she was just a freshman at the time. Amazing that she emerged so talented with no formal education to speak of. You'll have to see the paintings she's working on for her thesis. They'll take your breath away. She calls them Fairy Paintings. But don't get me wrong. Pearl is no shrinking violet. She's a smart cookie, and very intuitive. Spiritual, I guess you'd say. She dabbles in the occult. Magic spells and the like. She's gotten some of the other girls involved in it. They light candles and incense, smoke pot, read cards. I'm sure it's all quite harmless."

"Tarot cards?" I asked.

"I believe so. Why?"

"Just wondering," I said. Alice didn't appear to be aware of the victim's pose, and I wasn't about to share that information now.

"These other girls that Abel had sex with, do you think there might be any jealousy there?"

"Jealousy?" Alice shifted in her seat. "You mean as a motive for murder? Oh, no, I don't believe one of our girls would be involved in that."

I had considered the possibility that more than one person carried out this murder but decided not to mention that to Alice. Instead, I said, "I need to look into every possibility. Do you know the names of any of the other girls he may have been seeing?"

"It was common knowledge that he hooked up with girls and women outside the school, which is strictly forbidden. He bragged about it. I have no idea who they were. As far as campus goes, most recently he'd been screwing a First Year named Jeannine Hart. But I'm pretty certain that had ended."

I checked my notes for the name of the Second Year class liaison. "Did Esme Li tell you that? About Abel and Jeannine Hart?"

"Actually, it was Jeannine who told me. She set up a meeting with me to discuss her dissatisfaction with something or other, a usual occurrence for her, and started gloating about having sex with Abel."

"Why do you think she told you that?"

Alice rolled her eyes. "Jeannine is arrogant and entitled, but she is also aware that all the instructors think she's a shit artist and is only here because her grandmother sits on the board and donated a very large endowment to the school in exchange for her acceptance. I imagine she believed having sex with Abel, the handsomest and most talented boy at St. Luke's, and the son of the chairman of the board, would elevate her in my eyes and everyone else's. I'm sure I'm not the only one she told."

I was curious why Alice's tone was so disapproving. She seemed angry. Was it directed at Jeannine or her grandmother? I noted it on my pad and switched the subject back to the murder. "I understand the student who found Abel ran here to tell you? What time was that?" I knew from my morning runs that it took at least twenty-five minutes at a fast clip to get from that part of the forest to here.

"I believe it was around seven," she said.

"Do you usually get here so early?"

"Not always, but I had an eight A.M. board meeting I had to prepare for. A conference call. They're all conference calls. After what happened, I canceled the meeting, of course."

"I'd like to interview Karla Gardyn and Pearl Calhoun as soon as possible. Can you help me set up those meetings? Is there anyone else you think I should talk to?"

"Esme Li could be helpful. Given her role as class liaison, she might have insight into the other students' opinions of Abel. As I mentioned, she's also a good friend of Pearl's."

"What about Pearl's other classmates?"

"Maybe hold off on others for a bit? I'd rather keep this quiet as long as possible. I don't want to alarm students."

I doubted she'd be able to keep a murder quiet very long. "Can I get a copy of Abel's student record?"

"Christine will send it right over."

"It would be helpful to have Pearl's, Karla's, and Esme's as well."

"I'm going to need to run that by the board. We have a strict policy about sharing student files. Of course it's different with Abel. Would a picture of the girls do in the meantime?"

"Sure," I said.

She turned her chair around, perused the many photographs on the bulletin board behind her, and unpinned one. "This is from an event we had at the Monastery earlier in the summer. That's Pearl there. Karla is to her right, and Esme is on the end to her left."

"Who is the girl between Pearl and Esme?"

"That's Hazel Donovan. She's also a Second Year."

"Thank you," I said as I stood. "I'll keep you updated."

"I have every confidence in you," she said.

It was half past eleven by the time I finished making and eating a Lowcountry tomato sandwich and sat down on my sofa to study the photograph Alice gave me. I had decided to stop at home to take a shower and do a load of laundry to get the cigarette smell out of my hair and clothes. Joni Mitchell's *Ladies of the Canyon*, played on my stereo, her melodic swoon both comforting and relaxing. In the photo, the four girls stood with their arms around one another. While the other three wore wide, happy smiles, Pearl's mouth was closed, the edges of her lips curled up ever so slightly. I found her eyes the most telling. Alice had used words like "sweetheart" and "kind" to describe her, but also "smart cookie." That was what I saw in those eyes, a combination of discernment and circumspection. This was a girl whom life had scarred. Alice had also said she doubted Pearl knew about Abel's sexual escapades, but the girl in this photo appeared anything but naive. I pulled out my notepad to review Alice's words: *She's a smart cookie, and very intuitive. Spiritual, I guess you'd say. She dabbles in the occult. Magic spells and the like. She's gotten some of the other girls involved in it. They light candles and incense, smoke pot, read cards.*

Read cards.

A picture of the Hanged Man tarot card we'd found on Abel's body flashed through my mind.

Are you a good witch or a bad witch, Pearl Calhoun? I wondered.

PEARL

This is what I remember about the first time I saw you.

It is in that initial life drawing class in the Monastery's chapel, the room where the monks once worshipped but where now drawing and painting classes are held during the day, and school functions are held in the evening. The class description says we will be sketching a "nude model," my first. I hope it will be a woman. It is hot, the air fuggy and stagnant due to the lack of fans. Six of us, three young women and three young men, straddle our wood drawing horses, fidgeting and sweating, our charcoal sticks in hand, our 18-by-24-inch newsprint sketch pads flipped to the first blank page, as we eye our competition or worry we are poseurs. Everyone except you, that is. Not a bead of sweat on your brow or an impatient shake of your foot. It is hard not to stare at your proud, fearless confidence and your utter perfection—chiseled features, strong neck, bushy blond hair, and piercing blue eyes. The kind of eyes that suck you inside them, capture you. Beautiful boys are freaks of nature, I remember thinking. They exist outside the realm of possibility for the likes of me.

Periodically, I check the big clock above the four sets of heavy oak and beveled glass doors that lead to the courtyard. Twelve minutes past the hour. Fourteen minutes past the hour. Seventeen minutes past the hour. Beyond those oak doors are the Tower, where the monks paid penance and plotted the witch burnings, and the sepulchers, where several generations of monks are buried. And then there's the ocean. Twenty minutes past the hour. Twenty minutes of trying not to look at you. Of trying to act cool, as if I belong here, as if I see and draw naked people all the time.

Then: chaos.

A group of people dart into the room. Too many to count. No time to try. There are men and women of all ages. They wear revealing black leather leotards, carry whips and batons and pom-poms. The sounds of bare feet sliding and jumping and slapping the concrete floor as they snap and twirl and toss their props. A troupe of deviant dancers. A man comes into the room, tall and thin with long, stringy dark hair. He wears black leather pants, a black silk shirt unbuttoned halfway, chest hair exposed, and combat boots. Carries himself with a kind of nonconformist nonchalance. Stands in the center of our circle.

"Draw them," he says.

Only you obey this command. While you sketch, our heads dart back and forth, spying one another's reactions, our jaws dropped, our eyes wide, our arms and hands stiff and frozen, our hearts racing.

"Don't think," the instructor says loudly. "Draw."

And then time pauses, and I enter another dimension where there is only me, my body, my space. My hand tightening around the charcoal stick, moving furiously up and down and around the thick drawing paper, trying to capture what I see. Light and shadow and density and white space.

"New drawing," he commands.

The ruckus of readjusting the awkward sketch pads. Sounds of pages peeling and flipping and tucking. My charcoal moving over the entire surface, sometimes hitting the edges, more than once snapping in half, fragments dropping or flying. Becoming unwitting extras in the raucous production.

"New drawing," he repeats again and again. Every few minutes a fresh white sheet.

One by one, the dancers exit the room, the precarious tumult gradually abating, until only one is left. A voluptuous woman with long, flowing black hair. The man helps her out of her costume, slide of zippers, slap of leather. He stands where she did. She walks gracefully to the center of our circle and poses, her nakedness so pure. I feel no discomfort, no embarrassment. She is no longer woman; she is shape. Our sketch pads flip. Sticks rub and scribble. Creating music unto itself.

And then a harsh awakening, like a bird crashing into a window. "Stop," he shouts. "That's all for today."

It takes a few moments for the sweeping motion of my arm to slow and stop. I uncurl my fingers, stretch out my stiff charcoal-stained hand. Roll my shoulders and neck. Check the clock. Two hours have passed. The man walks toward the woman, hands her a silk robe. "I'm Mr. Smith," he says to us as she dresses. "Make sure you bring extra charcoal and sketch pads with you tomorrow. And please dispose of your discarded drawings. There's a trash can in the corner. Class dismissed."

I look at the floor. It is a sea of black-and-white drawings. Five of us gather and toss them. You are already gone. Unencumbered by the rules of life. The others are already talking about your arrogance and unhelpfulness, their complaints edged with envy.

I look toward your drawing horse. It is the first time I will feel your void, the first of many such times, and each time I do, the knife will twist further and further into my gut.

Until I bleed out.

LOLA

I knocked on the door, but there was no answer. Just this morning, I had noted the cottage's proximity to the forest's east entrance and pledged to question whether its occupant had noticed anyone unusual or suspicious. Now I was preparing to interview the student who had discovered the murder victim's body. Carl Jung might call that synchronicity, a meaningful coincidence. But as a detective, and nonbeliever in coincidence, I now considered Karla Gardyn a suspect.

I knocked again. Still no answer. I decided to sit on one of the rocking chairs and wait. I had run by this cottage many times on my way in and out of the forest and sometimes paused to admire the garden—an overgrown jumble of flowers, vegetables, and herbs—and the living-room-type setting on the front porch. Two rockers at one end, a long wooden bench with peeling paint at the other, hanging plants, and several indoor-outdoor rugs. The entire ambiance was soothing and inviting. I found it surprising that someone so young had created such a welcoming home. I caught a whiff of marijuana, noted a pipe and ashtray on the table between the two rockers.

Maybe fifteen yards away stood the cottage where Abel Montague had lived with Pearl Calhoun. I had decided to interview Karla Gardyn and Esme Li before Pearl. According to Alice, Abel Montague slept around. It was a standard detective tactic to profile the most obvious suspect prior to questioning them. Jealousy was a strong motivator for murder.

A handsome young woman exited Pearl Calhoun's cottage and walked toward me. From a distance, she appeared more mature and poised than her years. Tall, with straight shoulder-length strawberry hair. She waved and smiled. I waved back. As she climbed the wooden stairs of her porch, I noted a youthful face, freckles, and green eyes. She reached out her hand to shake mine. I found the gesture refreshing. It exhibited a level of self-comfort and confidence uncharacteristic of women of her age.

"You must be Detective Germany," she said in a lovely British accent. "Dean Landry told me to expect you. Sorry I wasn't here. I was sitting with Pearl. We won't be too long, will we? I don't like leaving her alone."

If Karla was any indication, Alice's assessment that the other girls were protective of Pearl was correct.

"It shouldn't take long."

"Would you like some tea? It's hot, I know, but the fans should help. I can add ice if you'd prefer."

"I would love some *hot* tea," I said. "Milk and sugar?"

"A woman after my own heart," she said, and walked into the cottage.

I took the opportunity to observe Pearl Calhoun's front porch. It was a complete contrast from Karla's. No chairs or tables, and no garden. Not even a single potted plant.

Karla returned with two steaming-hot mugs, placed them on the table between the rockers. They were beautiful, obviously handmade.

"Did you make them?" I asked.

"I did. The school has a kiln. Pearl and I make pottery together sometimes. It's freeing, an escape from the seriousness of painting."

We took a sip of our tea in unison.

"It's good," I said. "Thank you."

"It's a rooibos tea from South Africa. My mum sends it. It comes from this amazing tea store in London. That's where I grew up. Henley-on-Thames, actually. She's always sending me fun and interesting teas. I've been trying to grow the rooibos. Do you see that bush with yellow flowers?" She pointed to her garden. "It's called *Aspalathus linearis*. It's struggling a bit, but I'm determined."

"You're a long way from home," I said.

"It was a difficult transition at first. I miss my mum and our matriarchy. We are an entire family of women, governed by my mum's great-aunt. She's one hundred and six years old and looks no older than eighty. Hard to believe, I know, but not unusual for a Gardyn. My mum has four sisters, and between them, they have six daughters, my five cousins and me. But St. Luke's is an amazing school."

"No fathers, sons, or brothers?"

"Nope."

"How is that possible?"

Her lips curled into a sly smile. "Magic," she said. A slight breeze caused the trees in the forest to shimmy.

"Must be lovely living so close to the forest," I said.

"I do love this cottage," she said. "I feel blessed to have gotten it. It's a lottery, you know."

"How does that work?"

"Kind of like bingo. When a cottage comes available, everyone puts their names in a jar, and at the Fourth Year graduation afterparty, Dean Landry chooses names. I assume you want to know about finding Abel," she said, abruptly changing the topic.

"Yes," I said. "What were you doing in the forest that early?"

"I'm an early riser and often walk through the forest at dawn. Before classes and life begin. It's such a magical place, don't you think? There's just something about listening to all the whistling birds and croaking toads. It's like being inside a fairy tale. But I imagine you already know that. I've seen you there."

"You've seen me in the forest?" I say, shifting slightly.

"Entering the forest," Karla said. "You run nearly every morning. I mean, I didn't know that you the runner and you the detective were the same person until I saw you just now on the porch. Your hair color is distinctive. The color of chestnuts. And your walk. The way your legs and feet turn out. You danced—ballet, right?" She paused. Had she noticed my discomfort? "I'm so sorry," she continued. "That must seem unsettling that someone knows your routine."

I hadn't told a soul on the island about my old life, and I didn't intend to. "I've never even taken one ballet lesson," I lied. She cocked her head, adopted a polite but doubtful smile, but didn't challenge me. "Seems odd I never noticed you sitting on your porch when I ran by," I added.

"I'm there, but I'm not surprised you didn't notice me. I leave the porch light off. I like sitting in the dark. It is nice to know that someone enjoys the forest as much as I do. Sounds as if you could be part of our coven."

"Coven?" I asked.

"It's not what you think. We just have fun. Light candles, burn incense, drink wine. It's all quite harmless. St. Luke's can be grueling. We call ourselves the Weird Sisters, an homage to Shakespeare. He was interested in the supernatural, you know. There are references to magic and the occult throughout many of his works, most notably, of course, *Macbeth*."

A phrase from *Macbeth* came to my mind: *Fair is foul and foul is fair.*

"Do all of you frequent the forest?" I asked.

"Mostly Pearl and me. Esme and Hazel aren't particularly fond of the forest. They're city girls."

"Esme Li and Hazel Donovan?"

"Yes. Will you be talking to them?"

"I will be going wherever the investigation leads," I said, attempting the same polite smile Karla had given me previously. "How did you happen upon the body? That tree is quite far off the main path."

"The Ghost Tree was actually my destination," Karla said.

The admission surprised me. "Why is that?"

"I go to visit my aunt Matilda. She was burned at the stake here on Waverly Island in 1437. That's one of the reasons I came to St. Luke's, to learn more about what happened back then. Our matriarchy had been following the school for a long time. We learned of its existence through Aunt Matilda."

Aunt Matilda? "I'm confused. I thought you said she was burned at the stake."

"She was," Karla said, and smiled. "But her spirit is still alive."

"So you believe the stories of the witches flying to that particular tree after their executions and still haunting the island?"

"The first part, yes, of course," she said. "But the Ghost Women don't haunt the island. They protect it. You don't believe that?"

The question caught me off guard. Everyone on the island had heard the stories about the Ghost Women, but that didn't mean we all believed them. To many, like me, they were simply local legends, which, depending on the context and narrator, took the form of either fairy tales or cautionary tales.

"I'm not a believer," I said.

Karla's smile appeared sweet on the surface, but her eyes were laced with sadness and condescension.

"1437," I said. "I didn't think the island was inhabited back then."

"Oh yes," Karla said. "According to one of my mum's sisters, Aunt Agnes, who keeps the histories of our matriarchy, Waverly Island was home to Indigenous cultures thousands of years ago, before Spanish colonists even selected the islands for their Christian missions, and definitely before the territory was ceded to Great Britain. But you aren't here to talk about my lineage. Perhaps we can do that another time. You want to know about my finding Abel."

"Yes, could you tell me more about that? It must have been rather upsetting to come upon a body. Especially the body of a fellow classmate. What was your initial reaction?"

Her body language changed. She shivered, drew her arms tightly together, and clasped her hands. "Shock, of course," she said. "That he was dead, I mean. That it was Abel. And fear. I thought maybe the killer was still there somewhere. I remember I froze and I held my breath. I was afraid to move because someone might hear me. I worried they might think I saw them. I tried to look away but couldn't. You know how people always say something made them feel like time stopped? Well, I never really understood that before, but that's exactly how I felt. Like there I was, all alone with this dead man, just the two of us, neither of us moving. I don't know how long I stood there motionless staring at him before I ran to the Monastery."

"Did you know it was Abel right away?"

"Yes."

"Did anything else stand out to you?"

"The position of the body, of course. It was just like the Hanged Man card in the Tarot."

I felt that feeling coming on, the one I got when I believed I might have accidentally happened upon a clue, that chest-tightening, that anticipation. I wondered if she knew about the tarot card left at the scene. But that didn't seem likely. It was in the victim's back pocket.

"You know what the Hanged Man card looks like?"

"Of course," Karla said. "I thought I mentioned that. The Weird Sisters. The four of us do readings."

"You only mentioned incense and candles."

"I didn't mean to leave it out. Tarot is Pearl's contribution to the coven. She's very attuned to the cards and their meanings. I lead our spells. My matriarchy has engaged in spells and green witchery for years. We are healers. Did you know that most flowers have healing properties?"

I noted that Karla said she led the spells. Alice indicated Pearl did. The discrepancy felt important, but I decided not to pursue it at this point. Instead, I said, "I didn't know that."

Karla's body immediately relaxed. "Take geraniums, for instance," she said while pointing to a pot on her porch. "They're a common front-porch plant, right? But historically, it was witches who began using them on their front porches to protect their homes. The red flowers carry strong protective powers and promote courage. Our coven sometimes uses them in our spells. Different colors have different meanings. White geraniums promote fertility. Remember what I said about magic? To this day, my mum and aunts put white geraniums on their porches to ensure their babies will be female."

"Has that worked?"

"Well, there hasn't been a male born in our matriarchy for six centuries. My aunt Matilda was the last. She had twin boys."

"And the Tarot?" I asked, growing a bit impatient. "What does your coven use it for?"

"To tell our fortunes, of course. Lately, the cards have been telling us that Pearl's paintings will catch the eye of the critics and make her famous beyond her wildest dreams. I guess that makes sense now."

"How so?"

"Well, Abel's dead, so now Pearl is the best artist at St. Luke's. Have you seen her paintings? They're amazing."

"I haven't," I said. "But hopefully I'll get the opportunity. You mentioned the positioning of the hanged man on the card. Do you know the original meaning of the card?"

"Of course," Karla said. "Betrayal."

"Did Abel betray Pearl?"

"Abel betrayed practically everyone," Karla said. Her words were clipped, her lips pursed. She raised her voice. "He was a dick, a total chauvinist pig, and a serial cheater. He screwed anyone who would have him and some who wouldn't. He had no respect for women. Especially Pearl. He walked all over her emotionally. He deserved to die." She took a deep breath. "Sorry. I shouldn't have said that."

"What did you mean by 'some who wouldn't'?"

"Let's just say he was notorious for taking advantage of vulnerable situations. Early on, before he and Pearl were officially together, he came on to me at a party while I was wasted. He was drunk and high, got aggressive, but it was a pretty public situation, so I was able to walk away."

"Abel did drugs?"

"Yes, psychedelics mostly."

"Have you told Pearl what happened?"

She looked immediately concerned. "No. I didn't want to hurt her. You won't tell her, will you?"

"It's not my place. May I ask how you came to be friends with Pearl?"

"I met her the first day she started at St. Luke's. Second Years are each assigned a First Year to watch over the first week they're here, to help them acclimate. I watched over Pearl. We had an instant connection, like we were soul sisters. Then, when she and Abel moved into the cottage next door, I heard them fighting one night. There was a knock at my door. It was Pearl. She was crying. She said he could be cruel, especially when he was drunk or high. She spent the night. After that, whenever they fought, she'd come over and we'd smoke on my porch, listen to music, or just talk."

"Did they fight often?"

"Toward the end, yes."

"Was it ever violent?"

"You mean, did he ever hit her? Not that she said. And I never saw any bruises or anything like that, but abuse isn't always physical. I'm not sure Pearl would ever say this because she was inside it, and she's Pearl, she sees the best in everyone, but I think sometimes mental abuse is just as bad as physical abuse. He wore her down to the point where she continually doubted herself. Believed his toxic bullshit."

Her words were very astute. I felt the hatred inside her. Did she hate him enough to kill him? I noted the information on my pad, finished my last drop of tea, and rose. "I need to get going. I appreciate your time. I'll be in touch if I have more questions."

"Would you like to see some of my paintings?" The request sounded somewhat desperate, as if she were trying to prolong my visit.

"You paint here and not at your studio?"

"Yes. Since I got my own cottage. It's somewhat of a social club over at Studio Row with everyone continually stopping by each other's spaces."

I followed her inside. The smell of turpentine permeated the cottage's interior. I nearly gasped when I saw her paintings. They were strewn throughout her cottage. Obviously, Pearl wasn't the only exceptional artist at St. Luke's. They were stunning. Figurative and eerie and cruel and dark and gorgeous all at once. The exaggerated faces and bodies reminded me of the paintings of Alice Neel, only Karla's paintings were more sinister, and all her subjects were naked men with distorted faces. One resembled Abel.

When I looked back at Karla, she was staring at me, her head cocked, a mischievous smile on her face. "All artists work out their emotions on their canvases," she said. It was as if she'd gleaned what I was thinking.

I thanked her again for her generosity.

"You're welcome," she said, and smiled widely. "Feel free to stop by anytime."

She walked me to the door. As I headed to my cruiser, I thought about the words she had used when I asked her if Pearl and Abel fought a lot: *Toward the end, yes.* I wondered what Karla considered Abel's end.

LOLA

I checked the time when I got into my cruiser. It would be dark soon, but I wasn't ready to go home. I was wired, and the forest always calmed me. *Just a short walk*, I told myself. I noted how cool, quiet, and still it was as soon as I passed through the east entrance. I paused to breathe in the fresh scents of dirt and pine, hear the song of the birds and the scurry of the forest creatures. Then I walked, my mind emptying with each step, the trees getting denser and denser, until I realized I was lost. I stopped, tried to orient myself. An owl hooted. Coyote howled. I didn't recognize anything around me. I took a deep breath and then another. *I know the forest*, I told myself. I saw a glow up ahead and headed toward it. The moon shining on a clearing. There, inside it, stood the Ghost Tree. I shivered.

How did I get here?

I couldn't remember the last time I had really looked at the Ghost Tree. When I inspected the murder scene this morning, my attention had been on the victim, not the tree or its surrounds. As a child, like all children, I had been terrified of the tree. According to island folklore, if the witches who lived inside it saw a child standing near the tree's perimeter, they would either eat it or sacrifice it to the devil in exchange for a second chance at life. Perhaps it was the stillness of the air and the pale bluish tint of the moon, but the scene felt nearly ethereal. I looked up. The tip of the tree appeared to reach beyond the stars. This time of year, deciduous trees would have begun shedding their leaves, but all but one branch of the Ghost Tree remained lush. The branch from which Abel Montague's body had hung was pure white and stripped of foliage, as if it had been struck by lightning. I was certain it hadn't been bare this morning. But there had been no storm, no rain, no thunder or lightning between then and now.

Then something odd happened. A brief wind interrupted the stillness. The leaves on the tree fluttered for several seconds and then stilled again. Had I imagined it? And then I heard a voice inside me say, *Follow the path that leads to the beach where the shore is deep, the sand is white, and the water splashes against rocks as large as buildings.* I knew the path in question but hadn't walked it in a long while. I had no idea why the words had come to me or what I was looking for, so I resorted to doing what my father had taught me. Tracking.

I pulled out my police-issue flashlight and shined it on the path ahead. *Search for bent or snapped branches*, I remembered my father saying. And so I kept walking while shining the light until I saw what looked like some sort of cloth stuck to a thorny branch up ahead. *Cloth comes from fabric. A piece of someone's shirt?* I trained the flashlight on the branch, walked toward it, and there it was, a piece of thick white wool with a frayed red edge. A blanket. It looked very similar to the Pendleton wool blanket I kept at the foot of my bed. Why would someone carry a blanket in thick brush, where it could easily get caught, instead of on a path? *Perhaps to hide a body?* I heard the sound of waves in the distance, followed it until I found myself standing on the island's southern shores, an area of the beach rarely visited due to its shallow shoreline and rocky terrain. I knew high tide would have washed away any tracks in the sand by now, but that was okay. My quest had paid off. Because I was pretty certain that curled inside my hand was evidence that Abel Montague didn't die in the forest.

Day 2

ONE DAY AFTER THE AUTUMNAL EQUINOX

SATURDAY, SEPTEMBER 23, 1972

LOLA

My father always said that everything would be better in the morning. But murder wasn't a skinned knee or a bruised ego. I had gone to bed early, hoping that a good night's sleep would, at the very least, help ease the feeling of impending doom that seemed to be chasing me. I'd felt it at the murder scene. I'd felt it on Karla's porch. I'd felt it when I found the piece of white wool in the forest. But rest seemed determined to elude me. And as the brain so often does inside the fits and starts of interrupted sleep, it conjured dark, weird dreams. Someone had wrapped *me* in a white wool blanket and was carrying me through the woods. I was trapped and suffocating. I woke coughing, trying to catch my breath. I checked the time on the alarm clock beside my bed. Three A.M. Wormed my way out of my actual twisted blanket and sat up. My entire body was soaked in sweat.

I decided to stay awake. The familiar surroundings of my home felt safer than my dream world. I went into the kitchen, filled a glass with water, sat down on the living room sofa, and turned on the TV. Our local all-night news was reporting a "brutal" murder in Dead Witch Forest. They mentioned a male victim but didn't give his name or affiliation with St. Luke's Institute of the Arts. So much for Alice trying to keep students from learning about the murder.

It was still dark when I left for my run. The news was forecasting rain. I tied a light rain jacket around my waist and grabbed the trusty tampon-size flashlight that I got at Galen's Hardware. Galen Jr. and I had dated for a few years in high school before I got accepted to Juilliard, before I danced for the New York City Ballet. I heard that he got married and moved somewhere out West. I had figured Galen would be the one to live out his life on Waverly Island. And yet here I was carrying a badge like my father. I swore I'd never be a cop. I swore I'd never return to Waverly Island.

The air was thick, the heat stifling. When I first returned to the island, I both welcomed the heat and missed the snow. I missed the hustle and bustle and chic sophistication of the city. I missed socializing with writers and actors and musicians and artists. Going to the theater and opera and, of course, dancing. In the city, you could choose to be anonymous; on Waverly Island, anonymity was not an option. I had forgotten what it was like to live in a small town, how everyone knew your routine and your name whether or not you'd shared it. How everyone attended the same nondenominational church, drank at the same local bar, and left casseroles on the doorsteps of folks going through hard times. How people took care of you. How that kind of care could help you heal.

I decided to brave my way through the Garden of Angels. I hadn't been to my parents' graves in a while. Island residents insisted the cemetery was haunted by the restless dead. Sightings of a set of twin boys, a nun, and a lost little girl carrying a doll were the most frequent. They were accompanied by tales of their unfortunate demises. The Waverly Island Library had several books on ghosts that included summaries of their lives and deaths, and the circumstances believed to have caused them to wander the earth forever. Today most people chose to bury their dead in the newer cemetery behind the church, but my father had wanted him and my mother to be buried near our ancestors, which he said went back "centuries." I remembered Karla saying Indigenous cultures had inhabited the island thousands of years ago. I had never thought to ask my father how many centuries. Given this case and its ghosts, real and imagined, I wished I had. The wrought iron gate squeaked as I opened it. Inside, the canopy of ancient live oak trees cast dark shadows beneath the full moon. The cemetery's resident raven, a rare species in the Deep South, perched on one of the tombstones, its piercing eyes following me as I passed. I crossed my heart when I got to my parents' graves and said a short prayer. Then I continued toward the back gate that led to the forest, passing the oldest tombstones in the cemetery along the way, while the raven followed me, as if to make certain I understood I was inside its territory. Something caught my eye. Two small burlap poppets with black pearl–tipped pins stuck in their red hearts rested atop the cemetery's Unmarked Tombstone. Just like the one positioned under Abel Montague's hanged body.

Is there a connection?

The Unmarked Tombstone was said to be the burial site of a great hoodoo root doctor. *Her* name had been left off the grave so boo hags and haints couldn't locate and desecrate her spirit. Though it wasn't unusual to find evidence of Gullah rootwork ceremonies at the Unmarked Tombstone, the poppets made me feel uneasy.

Thankfully, it was still dark when I got to my destination inside the forest, a tall goddess of a tree on a cliff-side mound overlooking the ocean. Watching the sunrise from the mound of this tree was *my* magic. From the time I was a child until the day I left for Juilliard, I had greeted the sunrise on this very mound beneath this very tree every morning, and when I returned to Waverly Island as an adult, I resumed this practice. I had always known that Waverly Island was special, that there was an essence I couldn't singularly define, but it wasn't until I left, until I saw its entirety from my memory, that I understood why. Magic was everywhere. In the uniqueness of the varied cultures, their practices, identities, and belief systems. In the historic architecture, cobblestone streets, and haunted cemeteries. In the blue ocean, wet marshes, and white sand. The island wasn't special because it contained one magic. It was special because it contained *many* magics.

I looked over the cliff's rocky edge. The motley crew of disparate creatures that shared the sunrise with me was starting to gather. Creatures of all sizes and shapes: egrets and herons and pelicans and turtles and frogs. I hovered in my usual spot with my back against the tree. As I waited, I swept my flashlight through the woods. A set of eyes paused my exploration. A deer. Frozen in place by the focused light. When I moved it, the deer trotted away.

Just then, I heard a sound that was *wrong* for the forest. A nearby rustle of leaves followed by a thud, like a shoe slipping on a rock, and a brief audible gasp. My heart pounded. I stiffened. Calling out could be considered either brave or stupid, perhaps a bit of both. "Is anyone there?"

Then the sound of shoes slapping the dirt of the trail as they hurried away. I waited until I could no longer hear steps and was confident that whoever had been there was gone. Slowly, I rose—I realized I'd been holding my breath. I twisted my flashlight to its highest point and aimed it through the trees. Nothing. I was spooked.

Someone had been watching me. But who and why?

PEARL

It's pouring outside when I wake. I'd fallen asleep on the green leather sofa I got at Priscilla's Antiques. I had been so excited to show it to you. A green leather sofa was indeed a special find. But you were offended by its failing springs and occasional rips. That was how it went with us. You preferred the cold, sleek modernist aesthetic of Mies van der Rohe, Le Corbusier, and Walter Gropius, while I preferred unique vintage pieces. I feel your presence as soon as I open my eyes. And I *see* you on one of the chairs. Not *actual* you, but a kind of haze, a grouping of shimmering molecules that are swirling through and around themselves. Periodically, they take shape and form. I've been feeling your presence since Karla told me you were dead. Karla. I see her physical body sitting on the other chair. It's an odd juxtaposition. Warm and sprightly *alive* Karla and shadowy *dead* you. I realize she's staring at me.

"You slept through the night," she says. "How are you feeling?"

"I'm fine," I say.

"You are not fine," she says, and opens the blanket I keep on the sofa, attempts to lay it over me.

"Don't," I say. "I'm getting up." She looks hurt. "Sorry. I didn't mean to snap at you."

"No need to apologize," she says. "It's understandable that your emotions would be all over the place."

The truth is I didn't sleep through the night, but I don't tell her this. I don't tell her that I went to see the place where everyone *says* you died. But I knew immediately you didn't die there. There was nothing of you there at all. No molecules. No haze. No residue of your life. No shadow of your death. So I'd doubled back through the forest to my usual hiding spot behind a different tree, one with a wide trunk that provided me cover and a direct view of the tall, imposing tree that overlooked the ocean. I opened my sketchbook and waited for my ballerina detective to arrive.

"How was your interview yesterday?" I ask Karla.

"With the detective? Good. She doesn't know anything. We talked about Abel mostly. How well I knew him and you. I was careful not to say too much. She seems nice enough. Like she could be one of us. She did tell one lie though. She said she was never a ballerina."

"Maybe she just didn't want to talk about herself," I say. "What else did she ask about?"

"Nothing important," she says. "Do you want some tea?"

It isn't the first time I get the distinct impression Karla is keeping secrets from me. "No," I say. "If you don't mind, I'd like to be alone.

With Abel." She gives me a worried look. "I know he's dead, Karla. It's just that I can still feel him, and he wasn't all bad, you know."

Her worry turns into a blank stare, the same stoic, noncommittal face I get every time I say something positive about you. Probably she thinks I'm foolish and naive. She thinks I didn't know you slept around. Everyone thinks I didn't know. Everyone underestimates the emotional strength of an orphan.

After she leaves, I stare at your molecules. Watch as a ray of light sneaks through a window and captures them. And then, for a brief moment, I feel you, all of you. You slowly wrap yourself around me, one electric touch at a time, making me tremble. Then it's over and I realize I am sobbing.

LOLA

"Good morning, Friday," I said as I closed my umbrella. Her real name was Denise, but we all called her Girl Friday, Friday for short, because she was that rare employee who could fill in almost anywhere, which she did, but mostly she manned the phones. Initially, I made the mistake of assuming she just wanted a summer job on the island to be near the ocean. She had that open smile, white-blond hair, and forever tan often associated with beach bums and surf junkies. It didn't take long to discover how whip-smart she was. She could do cartwheels around most of my guys when it came to psychological profiling and forensic criminology. But due to a combination of understatement and unabashed femininity, even I missed the extent of her knowledge. An entire year went by before I learned her winter breaks from us were spent studying psychology and criminal law at Harvard. Having graduated in June, she was now doing a yearlong internship with us as part of her graduate studies. I doubted we'd be able to keep her after that. She'd go on to the big league.

"Good morning," she said. "Colin is looking for you. He told me about the murder. How awful. How are you?"

"I'm fine. How about you?" Chitchat had never been my thing, but I was making a concerted effort to be more personable with my staff.

"Good," she said. "Oh, and Alice Landry called. I wrote it down." She handed me a pink note. It read: *Wants to know how the investigation is going. Knew you talked to Karla Gardyn. Give her a call.*

"Thanks." I wouldn't be jumping on it, I thought to myself.

Colin was waiting for me in my office. He was drenched. "Got a minute?" he asked.

"Don't you own an umbrella?" I asked.

"The dog ate it," he said.

He noted the doubt on my face. "I'm not kidding. We got a yellow Lab pup a few weeks ago. I've also lost two pairs of socks, a left slipper, and a wallet. Jody says he's teething." He waited for me to get situated before he handed me a clear plastic bag.

"Is that . . . ?"

"The Hanged Man card we found in the victim's back pocket. I asked Rebecca to take a look at it. She said the card wasn't just wiped of fingerprints, it was cleaned with soap and disinfectant. But that's not all. It's from a really old deck. At the scene, you mentioned the card's gilding and its lack of a name or identifying number. The gilding is real gold leaf, and you were right. Today's cards have a roman numeral or number on either the top or bottom of the image. They are also smaller and thinner, easier to shuffle, and most are reproduced from older decks, so the pictures aren't as crisp. Apparently cards this old are really valuable on their own but can be astronomically pricey if sets are intact. Oh. We got the tox report. It wasn't heroin in the kid's system. It's hemlock."

"Hemlock?"

"Apparently that's what killed him. Rebecca said he was dead before he was hanged."

"Why kill him, then hang him?"

"I asked the same question. I did a little research on hemlock. According to Christian mythology, during Jesus's crucifixion, there was hemlock growing on the hillside, harmless pretty little white flowers, and then, after he died, the plant miraculously became poisonous. It was also the poison of choice in Shakespeare's plays."

I thought about what Karla Gardyn said during our interview. *We call ourselves the Weird Sisters, an homage to Shakespeare.*

"Where would someone get hemlock around here?" I asked.

"It seems there's a lot of it in the Lowcountry. It grows wild in forests and marsh areas, and it also isn't that unusual for people to grow it in gardens."

"What about the rope? Did Rebecca find any fingerprints or fibers?"

"No fingerprints," Colin said. "Plastic fibers, yes. Like from rubber gloves. Yellow kitchen-sink variety."

I proceeded to tell Colin about my visit to the Ghost Tree the previous evening and my belief that Abel Montague didn't die there. He listened intently when I told him about finding the piece of white wool, nodding here and there. After he left, I considered what he'd said about the tarot card's age. Given its seeming rarity and artistic quality, it appeared plausible there might be a Tarot expert somewhere out there who could help us. Associated with a museum or library possibly? I looked at the clock. I had an interview with Esme Li soon, and after that Pearl Calhoun. I put on my raincoat and grabbed my bag and umbrella. On the way out, I stopped by Colin's desk and mentioned my thoughts about the Tarot expert.

"Yep," he said. "I was thinking the exact same thing. I called the Metropolitan Museum of Art in New York, who told me the card sounded like it might be from the Renaissance period, so I should call the Uffizi Gallery in Florence, which has one of the largest collections of Renaissance art in the world. They're six hours ahead. I called, but the person who answered said while the museum was open on Saturdays, the office wasn't. So I left a message."

Colin flashed an impish, dimpled smile. He was a good-looking guy, adorable, actually, and when he smiled, you couldn't help but smile too. He was that rare combination of unaffected and extremely competent. Everyone loved him. On more than one occasion, these attributes had helped solve cases.

While Studio Row was located inside the brick wall surrounding the school, it was at the farthest end of the campus, near the forest's east entrance. A tall wrought iron gate and a keypad with a private code allowed access to the entrance from the student cottages. Students had the code, but I didn't. I would have to park in the Monastery's lot and go through security. Luckily, the same guard was still on duty. He recognized me from my visit with Alice the previous morning and waved me through. I parked and took the path to the line of tall garage-like structures that made up Studio Row. It was a hilly but pleasant walk, perhaps a mile or so from the Monastery. I was always taken with the picturesque view that fronted the studios. The vast and pristine green lawn was encased on either end by tall arborvitaes that extended all the way to the edge of the rocky cliff that fronted the ocean. I could hear the water crashing against it from the walkway. The garage doors to the storage-unit-type buildings were generally open, but due to the rain, they weren't today. I could hear music coming from inside Esme Li's studio. The Beatles. I knocked on her side door.

"This rain is crazy," she said when she opened it. "You must be Detective Germany." She quickly shut the door behind me. "Here, let me hang up your raincoat." She was lovely, with delicate features, straight dark hair, and brown eyes. She wore loose-fitting black cotton clothes and ballet slippers.

"Is this their final album?" I asked.

"Yes," she said. "*Let It Be.* So sad they're splitting up. I keep hoping they'll get back together. Let me go turn the music down. Go ahead and sit." She pointed to a small seating area that included two metal folding chairs and a rust-colored loveseat-size sofa that had seen better days. I sat on one of the chairs.

She sat on the sofa when she returned. I waited for her to get situated and said, "Dean Landry speaks highly of you."

Her eyes lit up. "Really?"

I understood immediately that Esme was the kind of person who craved approval.

"Yes, she said you're an exemplary class liaison."

Her smile was sweet and shy. "Would you like something to drink? I only have water or green tea."

"Thank you, I'm fine."

"It's horrible what happened to Abel," she said. "Do you have any suspects? Dean Landry told me about the staging." She looked down for a moment, as if she realized she said something she shouldn't have. I was surprised Alice had been so indiscreet. Perhaps because Esme was a class liaison, they had a closer relationship? I made a mental note to look into this.

"It's an ongoing investigation," I said. "I hope you understand that we don't want to alarm anyone until we know what we are dealing with."

"Of course. Mum's the word." She pretended to zip her lips. "How can I help you?"

"Perhaps we can start by you telling me what a class liaison does?"

"I interface between my fellow Second Years and school administration. Mostly my communications are with Dean Landry."

"Do you ever join in on conference calls with the board?"

"Oh my, no. No one is allowed to talk with the board except Dean Landry." She paused, lowered her voice to nearly a whisper. "The members are completely anonymous."

I was somewhat surprised by her secretive tone. Was the attempt at familiarity personal, meant to gain *my* trust, or was it a tactic she used regularly, to gain the trust of her fellow classmates?

"Could you give me some examples of some issues you might liaise?"

"It could be anything. If one of the students is concerned about a particular instructor or feels they are being mistreated by another student. That sort of thing. But also event planning. Probably one of my most important duties is interfacing on the thesis process. Ensuring our class is meeting all deadlines, including identification and development of their thesis and body of work."

"Did you ever forward complaints about Abel Montague?"

"I did." She shifted in her seat, avoided my eyes, and unsuccessfully attempted to wind a lock of silky hair around her finger. She was obviously considering her words carefully. "Abel was not a considerate person. He could be insensitive when discussing the creativity and art of others."

"In what way?"

Her eyes found mine again. "I'm not the only one who knew how competitive he was." Her tone was defensive.

"Could you perhaps give me an example?"

"Well, when anyone else received compliments or recognition, he diminished it. Maybe it came from a place of insecurity. But even so, it wasn't my job or anyone else's to psychoanalyze him at our own expense, was it?"

Was she seeking my approval? "Of course not," I said. "And I apologize. I know it's difficult to say negative things about someone who is dead, but it will help me to understand who may have killed him and why. Do you feel comfortable continuing?"

"Okay," she said as her shoulders tightened.

"Dean Landry mentioned that he was promiscuous?"

She looked away. "I wasn't personally aware of that. And I doubt Pearl was."

I could tell she was lying. Instead of looking directly at me when answering, she had briefly looked down and to the left. I wondered why she'd not only felt the need to say she didn't know but also to state that Pearl didn't.

"Are you and Pearl close?" I continued. "Karla told me about your coven."

She rolled her eyes. "That's Karla's word. We just have fun. But in answer to your question, yes, Pearl and I are close. She is one of my favorite people in the world. She's a quiet soul, sees the best in people. Is easily taken advantage of."

"Did Abel take advantage of her?"

"Always and completely." She'd straightened her shoulders again when she said it, and her facial expression was stern.

"You disapproved of their relationship?"

"I disapproved of Abel."

I decided to capitalize on the moment of honesty. "Did you ever wonder why Pearl stayed with Abel or advise her to leave him?"

"It was not my place to judge Pearl's choices. It is not my place to judge anyone's. She told me she loved him. I told her I was there for her. End of story."

"I understand they fought a lot?"

"Did Pearl tell you that?"

"Karla Gardyn mentioned that she heard them fighting from her cottage. Does that surprise you?"

"Only in that Pearl never told me that. But I suppose that would be like her. She isn't one to complain, especially about people she loves. Pearl is forever supportive. Of all of us."

I wrote those words down on my notepad: *Pearl is forever supportive. Of all of us.*

"Were you surprised he was murdered?"

The question seemed to catch her off guard. She shuffled in her seat, looked away, bit her bottom lip. Esme was definitely not good at hiding her feelings.

"Not really," she finally said. "No one liked Abel."

"But there's a big difference between not liking someone and murdering someone, don't you think?" I kept my voice gentle.

"Yes, I suppose. But you'd have to know Abel to understand. He pushed limits. He was mean and cruel. He found people's weaknesses and played into them. Maybe he was cruel to someone he shouldn't have been."

"That's helpful to know," I said, and closed my notepad. "Thank you for your time. I think I have what I need for now. I'll let you know if I have more questions later. I would love to see your work. I don't see any on the walls."

She straightened, attempted a smile. "I'm a miniature artist." She rose, walked over to a large table on the opposite end of the room. I followed. It was covered with small jewel-toned paintings of both day and night skies and flying creatures I couldn't make out. I looked closer and then understood. I hoped she hadn't noticed my surprise. Was that the goal? To shock? Hundreds of small penises flew. Their wings dazzling and brilliant. Some traveled through dark, starry nights. Some through billowy white clouds. Some dodged rain and lightning streaks. They were exquisite. The detail sharp, the execution flawless. The colors highly saturated. My eyes returned to the one with lightning streaks. It felt off, and then I realized why. It wasn't bolts of lightning and rain. It was jagged knives and blood.

"I was going for a gemstone-inspired palette," I heard Esme say. "Rubies and emeralds and sapphires. I want them to feel precious. My advisor suggested the gilding. What do you think?"

"They're gorgeous." I wanted to ask why the subject matter, and why miniature ones at that? But I couldn't figure out how to phrase a question without sounding provincial. So instead, I asked, "Why do you choose to paint miniatures?"

A slow curl formed on her lips as our eyes met. Her look mischievous. Then she laughed. And I laughed too, but mostly out of nervousness. While there was beauty in the paintings, there was also danger. It was the painstaking detail, the tediousness, each deliberate stroke of the slim-haired brush. All of it required extreme patience and a kind of obsessive devotion. An image of Abel Montague hanging from the Ghost Tree flashed through my mind. The specificity of the scene. The careful positioning of the body, the orderly circle of the black candles, the exacting placement of the poppet.

I felt uneasy when I left Esme's studio. When I got back to my car, I radioed Colin and asked him to do some digging into Esme Li's past.

"What are you looking for?" he asked.

"I'm not sure," I said. "I just feel like there's something there. This could be a stretch, but maybe a past trauma that had something to do with Abel Montague." After I hung up, I opened my notepad and read what I had written. It was as if the Weird Sisters had gotten together in advance and decided what to say and what not to say. As if they were all painting a picture for me. The question was, was any part of this painting true?

PEARL

Two more life drawing classes pass before you approach me again, in between which you never so much as glance in my direction. I am sitting at a table in the library studying *History of Modern Art*, by H. H. Arnason, in preparation for an upcoming art history exam, when I hear someone say, "I'm Abel." It is the first time I've heard your voice. Deeper than I'd expected. The voice of a man, not a boy. "Abel Montague. You're Pearl, right?"

I can't find my words, feel my cheeks flush, which I know means my face is turning bright red. My face flushes easily. With exercise. When I'm nervous. When I'm warm. Sometimes just because.

As if this is a reaction you get often, you—the handsomest boy on campus, the boy all the other boys follow, the boy whose every movement is both confident and leisurely—*you* smile. At *me*. And of course your smile is perfect.

I remember blurting something about being late for class and racing from the room. Plopping on the bed in my Monastery dorm room.

Burying my head in my hands while chastising myself for being an idiot. Swearing I would die from embarrassment. And wondering if that was it, if I blew it, if I would never get an opportunity to talk to you again. Then thinking that would be for the best. Because no matter what you might have thought of me, or are thinking of me now, it is surely better than what you will think of me after you get to know me. But I don't get a chance to think about any of this for long, because the next day in life drawing class, you make a point to look my way and smile again. And after class is over, you linger. You even help the other five of us gather all the discarded drawings. And then you walk over to me. My entire body freezes. My heart starts beating fast, so loud I'm certain you can hear it.

"Do you want to go and get a coffee with me in the cafeteria?"

I can't find my words, so instead, I merely nod.

You walk with me out of the classroom, the palm of your hand on the small of my back. Out of the corner of my eye, I see Esme and Hazel staring, both with their mouths open in dismay.

And that is the moment when everything changes, the moment *I* end and *we* begin.

LOLA

The rain had stopped by the time I got to Pearl's cottage. A winding cobblestone path connected her cottage to Karla's. They were far enough apart and situated in such a way as to allow some visual privacy, but close enough together that I could hear the low beat of music coming from Karla's stereo. I climbed the stairs and knocked.

"It's open," a soft, youthful voice said.

Chamber music played quietly in the background. Vivaldi. I closed the door behind me and noted the surroundings. I could see all the way through the living room to the kitchen and dining area. A pine table and four chairs sat in front of a large picture window, which featured an unobstructed view of the distant ocean. Whereas Karla's interior, like her porch, had been warm and busy, Pearl's initially struck me as cold and sterile. Most of the surfaces were hard: wood floors, no rugs, white walls. But then, surprisingly, as if a cloud had tumbled by, I felt softness. It came from the makeshift altar immediately to my right. A grouping of lit candles multiplied by the mirror behind them gave off warmth and the scent of vanilla. Pictures of Abel and what looked like objects meant to represent him created a personal tribute: a watch, pocketknife, bottle of Old Spice cologne, paintbrush, and paint tubes, among others. And in the middle of all these was a Mojo bag and a handmade burlap poppet that looked just like the ones I saw at Abel Montague's murder scene and atop the Unmarked Tombstone in the Garden of Angels. Though instead of black, the pearl of the pin piercing the painted red heart was pink.

I rubbed my hand across the sideboard's shiny surface. While an antique, it was beautifully polished, obviously well cared for. A subtle movement, like a sheer curtain trembling in the breeze, drew my attention to a shadowy figure seated on a green leather sofa to my left.

"I got the sideboard at Priscilla's," she said, her voice soft and placid. "Do you know Priscilla's? That shop on the marsh? She has quite a fine collection of occult items, tarot cards, books, candles, and she's an expert on the witch trials and burnings that took place on the island centuries ago. Her family has lived on the island for generations. The altar is a tribute to Abel. I made the poppet and the Mojo bag. The pink pearl means love. The bag contains herbs, crystals, and talismans that are meant to protect his transition to the afterlife."

Here was the young woman whom everyone was praising. The most talented artist. The perfect friend to her peers and girlfriend to Abel Montague. She was not what I'd expected. She was slight, fair, and looked younger than her years. In the right clothing, she could pass for a twelve-year-old. Her fine hair was the color of bleached straw. It was cropped at her chin and tucked behind her ears, which accentuated her delicate features and large blue eyes. Her skin was pale and unblemished, her cheeks pink in what looked to be a constant flush. But what I did not see was a victim. She appeared fragile, yes, but also proud. Pearl Calhoun looked nothing like the picture in the photo Dean Landry had given me. She was the girl you didn't see until you did. And that made her dangerous.

"I've heard of the shop, but I've never been," I responded. "I'm Detective Lola Germany."

"I know," she said. "I was expecting you. I'm Pearl. I just made a pot of tea. Please. Sit." She motioned me toward a pair of modern chrome-and-black-leather chairs opposite the sofa. Her greeting was, like Karla's had been, that of a grown-up, a contemporary.

"Your coven appears to be tea drinkers," I said. "As opposed to coffee or soda, I mean."

"'Tea' is a generalized term. When witches say 'tea,' it can mean anything from witch's brew to potions to green teas to plant and herbal teas. What else can you mix the ingredients of healing or magic in other than hot water? Certainly not coffee. Though, speaking for myself, I do, on occasion, drink coffee if someone else makes it. Abel made an excellent cup. He would make it for me sometimes in the morning. You might not believe this given everything I'm sure you've been hearing about him, but Abel was a total romantic."

She was right. Given what I'd heard to date, I wouldn't have thought of Abel as a romantic. I wondered if she was being totally truthful, or if Abel had been acting. Narcissists, as I was beginning to think Abel was, were exceptional at adopting personality traits that aided in accomplishing their chosen quest. I sat and watched as she poured the tea from a floral porcelain teapot into matching teacups. An odd feeling came over me, a brief moment of recognition, but it quickly passed.

"The chairs and coffee table are Mies van der Rohe," she said. "Abel was a collector. The sofa is vintage. I picked it out. Poor Abel, it really offended his sensibilities. He wasn't too keen on my mismatched china either. He preferred a set of plain white Vietri his father purchased in Italy. He was stunned I'd never heard of Vietri. And then there was my altar. A constant source of disagreement. He would organize and line items up. I would push items ever so slightly askew." She smiled. "We both enjoyed the game of it."

I was tempted to ask if she would get rid of his belongings now that he was dead, as I had once done in similar circumstances, but instead said, "I admit I like the sofa better than the chairs."

She furrowed her brow as if wondering if I were being honest.

I took a sip of tea, jasmine, and became immediately uncomfortable. Did she know that jasmine was my favorite tea? That jasmine was also my favorite scent, that I wore it daily? I chastised myself. Of course she couldn't know that.

"Karla grows it. She says that jasmine is a very feminine tea." A thin smile formed on her lips. "As *you* know, it's associated with the cycles of the moon and promotes harmony and balance."

As I know? I decided not to bite. "Dean Landry mentioned that you practice hoodoo? Where did you learn it?"

She looked surprised. "How odd," she said. "I've never told Dean Landry that. But I guess I shouldn't be surprised. She makes it her business to know everything about us. Did she mention I was an orphan?"

"Yes."

"Someone I knew at the orphanage taught me. But I wouldn't call myself a practitioner. I'm not sure I can be since it's not in my blood. But I am intrigued by it and its people. I love their gentleness and spirituality and I'm fascinated by their healing practices."

I wanted to tell her that my best friend growing up on the island was Gullah, but I was not here to bond with her. She was a murder suspect. Instead, I said, "She said the school was very impressed with how talented you were given you'd had no professional training to speak of."

"I imagine you are here to talk about Abel," she said, ignoring Alice's backhanded compliment.

"Yes, if that's okay. I'm very sorry for your loss."

She nodded and looked away.

I took the opportunity to assess her grief, my eyes peeking over the rim of my cup. It was difficult to tell whether she'd been crying, but crying wasn't the only indication of grief. Shock can sometimes cover emotion for a period of time, and then, one day weeks, even months later, the dam would burst. That was how it had worked with me when my father died.

Her eyes returned, again burned straight into mine. "What can I help you with, Detective?"

I pulled my notepad and pen from my bag, steeled myself, and asked my first case-related question, one that I had both considered and rehearsed.

"Did his death surprise you?"

PEARL

I knew her first question would be considered, but its brilliance surpasses my expectations. I don't want my carefully crafted image of her to suffer even the slightest crack, but I also need to stay a step ahead of her. It's an awkward position that I'm in. I want to tell her I know who she is, or at least was, that I saw her dance, but neither the timing nor the circumstances are right.

"No," I say to her.

She cocks her head, adopts a quizzical stare, but doesn't ask me why not.

"How did you find out he was dead?"

"Karla told me."

"When was that?"

"Yesterday. Around seven thirty A.M. or so. Early. She said she went to the forest to visit her aunt Matilda. It was the anniversary of her death. She was burned at the stake in 1437 during the first witch trials."

"*First* witch trials?" she asks.

"Not on Waverly Island. The others took place in 1792 in Winnsboro, South Carolina, about a hundred fifty miles from here. The women were persecuted and hanged, not burned. Those are the witch trials Southern historians write about. A lot of people don't know what happened here. It's like this secret history that only descendants of those affected, like Karla and her family, know about. Maybe because it happened before the area was colonized by the Europeans. Or maybe because the Catholic Church would prefer no one knows. Around that same time, the Catholic Church in Rome was launching inquisitions and prosecuting heretics. Those convicted were either imprisoned, executed by fire, or banished. Some believe this island was one of the places where convicted men were banished. History books mention that Indigenous cultures settled here thousands of years before the first Spanish colonists arrived, but they don't get more specific than that, which I find interesting. According to the history recorded by Karla's ancestors, in the mid-fifteenth century there was only a small village and a house of worship here, a crude structure that over the years grew into a larger monastery."

"How do you know all this?" she asks, clearly interested.

"In addition to Karla? I mentioned Priscilla at Priscilla's Antiques. You should talk to her. And of course Matilda is a wealth of knowledge."

"Matilda talks to you?"

"Yes, of course. Me *and* Karla. But I imagine you want to talk about Abel."

She writes something down on her notepad, then looks at me. "You said his death didn't surprise you. Why not?"

"I *saw* it," I say.

"Saw it?"

"I've always had the gift of sight, but where Abel was concerned, my sight was limited. It's hard to explain. I didn't see him hanging from the Ghost Tree, but when I woke up yesterday morning, I knew he was dead. I also felt it coming. It was a kind of escalation, like a wind that gets stronger and stronger. Abel pissed off a lot of people. Worse, he didn't care that he did."

"Did he piss you off?" she asks.

"I'm sure, if you haven't already, you'll find out that Abel slept around. The night before he died, we had a fight. I found out he was sleeping with someone new. I was upset."

"Do you know with whom?"

"Her name is Hazel Donovan."

"Hazel? Karla mentioned that Hazel Donovan is part of your coven."

"She is."

"You must have felt betrayed."

"I did, and I told Abel so. Well, actually more than told. I screamed and cried and begged. I was pathetic. I hate that that was his last interaction with me before he died. He said he couldn't help it. That she came on to him. Typical guy statement. Blame it on the girl."

"So you didn't believe him?"

"Abel liked the chase. I'm not saying that excuses Hazel. But once I calmed myself and analyzed it all—that's what I do, I analyze—I realized that I shouldn't have been surprised. Hazel has her own insecurities. She's absolutely beautiful, but she thinks that's *all* she is. St. Luke's is competitive and Hazel is not the best artist. I mean, she's okay, but nobody, including her, thinks she'll make it to graduation. Abel Montague lusting after her wouldn't just feed her ego, she probably thought he could help keep her at St. Luke's. His father is—I mean *was*—well, I guess he's still the school's founder and chairman of the board." Her eyes tell me that she heard my voice crack when I used the past tense. I quickly look away from their compassion. I don't want to cry in front of her. That's how crying works for me. If someone feels sorry for me, that's when I lose it.

"I heard Abel did drugs," she says. "Is that true?"

"Rich-boy drugs mostly," I respond. "Heroin, cocaine, some hallucinogenic substances. He believed drugs opened his mind and fueled his creativity. He said all the New York abstract expressionists were using drugs. He wanted to experience what they did. To, as he said, have his mind blown. But sometimes he went too far."

"How so?" she asks.

"A few times, he saw demons. They set him on fire or pulled his body apart. Horrible things. One time, he insisted the Ghost Women were coming after him, seeking revenge, that his ancestors were somehow to blame for the witch burnings. That he feared his own mortality. When he sobered, he didn't remember any of this. But he would sleep for days, miss classes. I believe he had a difficult upbringing. His dad was hard on him, and he didn't have a mom. He was like a little boy who just needed to be held. And so I would. I would hold him and he would sob so hard his tears would soak my blouse." I pause, look away. "Sometimes I think I had it better than he did. Having a bad family seems worse than having no family." I hear her tap her pen, wonder if she's looking at me. I fear looking at her, fear her judgment. I shouldn't have said that last part.

"What about you?" she finally asks.

"Me?"

"Do you do drugs?"

"I smoke weed, but nothing harder than that. I don't like feeling out of control."

The pen tapping again. It makes sense I'd be the prime suspect. You were sleeping with one of my best friends. I admitted to feeling betrayed. All these questions she's asking are leading to that. She's just waiting for me to trip up. I notice an ever so slight movement coming from the empty Mies van der Rohe chair. Your molecules, which have been relatively sedate during the interview, are fluttering oh so softly. Then they shift, spread farther apart, and leave the chair. And as if they have become a flock of starlings, they begin whirling and spinning and twisting through the cottage, flying in and around and through themselves in ever-changing synchronic patterns, a murmuration, and I know the performance is for me, that you recognize my discomfort, and I remember what it was that attracted me to you, your fluidity, your pure elegance in all things, and especially your perceptiveness. You *saw* me. I remember that time we went to the mainland together and a Sister and a group of orphans walked by. It was the look on their faces, as if they were lost to the world, as if they didn't even have one another. I didn't know I had started to cry until you grabbed and held me. *I'm here*, you'd said to me. *I will always be here*.

"Are you okay?" I hear her ask. I wonder how many times she asked this question.

"It's strange, isn't it?" I ask.

"What is?"

"How someone is here, filling a room, moving through space, and then they aren't. And the room. I mean, he's been gone for two days, but I still feel him everywhere."

"You think he's still here?" she asks.

"Not him. His essence. It's as if he isn't ready to leave." I pause. "Do you feel him?"

Her eyes meet mine. I wonder if she realizes what I am doing. Me asking the questions. Purposefully flipping our power balance.

"I don't," she says. "But I believe there's some truth to what you're saying. Especially how someone's energy takes time to fade away." She looks at her notepad. "Did Karla tell you how the body was hanged?"

"Yes."

"She said you are an expert on the Tarot. What does the Hanged Man card imply to you?"

"Sacrifice," I say.

"Not betrayal?"

"According to some scholars, the card's image references Judas Iscariot, the disciple who betrayed Jesus Christ. But Judas Iscariot's choice to hang himself was a form of repentance, wasn't it? A self-sacrifice. I think the card is telling the querent that they must make a sacrifice in order to right a wrong. Wouldn't the picture on the card, an upside-down man, seem to imply a need to right oneself?"

"Do you believe Abel needed to right a wrong, that that's why he was murdered?"

The question is overly simplistic. My ballerina detective obviously doesn't understand the richness and nuances of the Tarot, and I certainly can't teach her. The Tarot can't be taught. It can only be practiced. I note she is studying me. You used to say you could always see my brain working. "Abel had many wrongs to right," I say. "Some that go back generations."

"Generations?" she asks.

I find it odd that she hasn't done her research. I decide to throw her a bone. "I only meant that his family has roots here."

She picks up her pen and writes on her notepad again. Then she closes the notepad, returns it and the pen to her bag, and rises. "I apologize for asking all these questions," she says. "I know it must be hard. Here is my card. I've written the name of someone on the back. Someone you can talk to. If you want."

"Thank you," I say. But I won't be talking to anyone. I have no desire to dissect myself or my past. I definitely don't want to dissect you and me. There's no need. *You*, just as you were, were enough for me.

"My direct line is there too. You can always call me. Do you paint here? I thought I smelled turpentine. I'd love to see your paintings. I was able to see both Karla's and Esme's work. They're both exceptional artists. I've been told you are too."

Her back is inches away from my *Fairy Painting No. 1*, the first of my series. That's why she smells the turpentine. Oil paint can take months to fully cure, and longer still for the scent of the paints and solutions to fade. Should I point the painting out to her? Tell her it isn't the first time we've met?

"I paint in my studio," I say. "It was hard with Abel here. He was forever interrupting."

"Another time, then," she says. "Thank you for your time."

My eyes follow her out the door.

I breathe in, hold my breath for a moment, and let it out slowly. Study my painting. A willowy figure stands beneath a tall tree in a dense forest. She, my ballerina detective, looks up to a new blue sky, her hands in prayer. Below her is the ocean. Part of me wanted her to see it. To see herself looking up to that tree, talking to it, praying to it. To know I've been watching her. To understand that, from the time I open my sketchbook and apply the first scratch of my charcoal to the paper, she exists for me only.

I own her.

I'm tempted to look out the window, to watch her walk down the path, but that's what she expects me to do. At this very moment, she is gauging my level of curiosity. Chasing me. But I am anything but a mouse.

LOLA

I didn't feel Pearl's eyes on me as I descended the front porch steps. Not yet. She was waiting until I was farther down the walk, closer to my car. She was bright, obviously intelligent, perceptive. She knew I'd expect her to watch me. It wasn't lost on me that she'd asked those questions about whether I felt Abel. The questions themselves, not the context, were a subtle attempt to take control. I kept walking, periodically looking over my shoulder, but I saw no face in her window, no shadow. I reached my car, got in, sat for a while waiting, watching from behind the sun's reflection on the windshield, but still no sign of her.

"I'm the cat," I said out loud.

I told myself to calm down. That competitive energy would cloud my judgment. I took a few deep breaths and ran the interview through my mind. She wasn't what I had expected. She was direct and unapologetic. She answered my questions thoughtfully and efficiently. Based on my discussions with both Karla Gardyn and Alice Landry, I had anticipated someone timid, more subservient. She was obviously grieving, as exhibited by the slight shake of her hands as she poured the tea and her moments of reflection in the midst of mostly unwavering eye contact. Sometimes the way she looked at me felt as if she were studying me, learning me.

I'd added exclamation points to three things in my notes. The first was the brown burlap poppets on her altar. The second was her belief that the Hanged Man card at the scene of the murder meant sacrifice. *I think the card is telling the querent that they must make a sacrifice in order to right a wrong.* What was the wrong that required righting? The third was her admission that she had known Abel and Hazel Donovan were sleeping together. Everyone else I'd interviewed all but insisted Pearl didn't know Abel slept around. I'd noted that her demeanor had changed. She'd shifted in her seat. Her leg started shaking. She avoided my eyes. What was it she had said about Abel's culpability? I pulled out my notepad, read, *Abel liked the chase.*

Looking back, I thought she sounded more like a scientist than a victim. As if she had studied the relationship from all angles. Something someone might do when considering how to exact revenge.

Something a murderer might do.

PEARL

The Weird Sisters are at Karla's cottage. She decided we should give you a Farewell Ceremony, which is pretty magnanimous of her, given the way you treated her. Esme insisted you didn't deserve a Farewell Ceremony. But it was just like Karla to rise above. "A soul is a soul," she said. "And how we choose to send it off may determine the quality of its next life." She is busy preparing. Esme is attempting to help, but Karla keeps shooing her away. Poor Esme. She doesn't get Karla like I do. The two of them approach things completely differently. Esme is a consensus builder, which makes her perfect to be class liaison. Karla is a caretaker. She perceives well-meaning helpers as challenges to her space and judgment. Hazel is trying not to look me in the eye. Her eyes are swollen. She's obviously been crying. When I first met her, I saw her as one of the wide-eyed figures that innocently, and naively, romp through the scenes of her paintings, childlike and curious. But now I see her as one of the evil beings that lurk in the shadows of those same paintings. Karla verified that I was okay with Hazel attending the ceremony prior to inviting her. I wanted her to come. I wanted to watch her. The thought of making her uncomfortable, of seeing her squirm, gave me great pleasure.

Thick white column candles and daylily petals, which represent the afterlife and rebirth, are spread throughout the cottage. Karla is smudging the room with sage. "Aunt Matilda reminded me," she says. "It's for our protection. I hope you all don't mind that I invited her." Hazel rolls her eyes in Esme's direction, which I see but Karla doesn't. Hazel and Esme don't see the Ghost Women. We've consumed way too much wine, the cheap dime-store variety, as we've gone through the rituals of flooding you with love and burning pictures of your father. You called him the devil incarnate. He came to our cottage a few times, you said to check me out. I initially took that to mean he was a caring father who just wanted to get to know his son's girlfriend. But he did that thing that asshole men do, ran his eyes over my entire body. Other than that, he treated me better than he did you. I never saw him beat you, but I saw the bruises, and I heard him diminish you. Esme told us that Alice in Wonderland told her that your father had your body sent to the mainland, that it was whisked to California on his private jet for a burial befitting a wealthy business magnate's son. *You* weren't inside the coffin, of course. Your body might be, but *you* are everywhere but that coffin. In the air, in the sky, in the water, in the trees. Spirits seek space, not confinement.

Karla stops smudging. She places the cast-iron pot that has been in her family for generations (now our cauldron) in the center of the "mystical blanket" she made, followed by the witch's hat she used to wear only on Halloween (now she's often seen wearing it for no apparent reason as she rocks on her front porch), a large section of broken mirror ("It needs to be broken so it doesn't trap things inside it"), and a box of matches. The mystical blanket's detailed embroidered images are expertly crafted and stunning against the deep blue velvet background. Karla's multitude of talents never cease to amaze me. Quilter, embroiderer, master gardener, green witch, and gifted painter, with a knack for making a home beautiful and welcoming.

"Please form a circle and hold hands," Karla says.

I sit on the blanket's sun, Esme on the moon, Hazel on the star, and Karla on the planets. I make a point to blatantly stare at Hazel as we reach for each other's hands, but her eyes still don't meet mine.

"Repeat these words after me three times," Karla says. "We declare the space within this blanket to be the entire universe. Whatever happens here shall reflect off this mirror and shine upon every ray of sunlight, every beam of moonlight, every sparkle of starlight, and every planet of the solar system."

We repeat the words.

"It's time," Karla says. She passes the witch's hat. Inside it, we each place the two folded scraps of paper we wrote on when we first arrived. The point is to randomly choose one from the hat without knowing who wrote it. "Remember," Karla says, "only the reader talks. No comments, no sounds or other displays of approval or disapproval from the rest of us. We are here to honor and cleanse this soul's passage from the earthly plane to the astral plane."

Esme offers to go first. She reaches into the hat, retrieves one of the folded papers, and reads: "'He scoffed at critiques.'" She opens the matchbox, strikes one of the matches to the sandpaper on its side, holds the fire to the paper, and drops it into the cauldron.

"Watch it completely burn before continuing," Karla says.

The paper curls and then turns to ash.

We go clockwise from there, making Hazel next. "'He took no interest in our work. Only his own.'" She strikes the match and tosses the burning paper into the cauldron.

Then Karla: "'He was arrogant.'"

Me: "'He was the most talented among us.'"

Esme: "'He believed our bodies were objects of beauty, not shame.'"

Hazel: "'He said our discomfort with nakedness during those initial life drawing courses was the product of our parochial minds.'"

Karla: "'He could be kind and considerate.'"

Only one note remains. I unfold it and read: "'I'm happy he's dead.'"

LOLA

There was a note from Colin on my chair when I got back to my office: *Student named Hazel Donovan wants to meet. She'll be waiting at Joe's tomorrow at 9 AM.*

The request surprised me. Obviously, Alice hadn't set it up, so it stood to reason Hazel herself wanted to meet. Given what Pearl had said about Abel and Hazel seeing each other, the request was even more intriguing. Everyone I'd interviewed thus far had described Pearl in a very positive light. Surely these girls didn't all adore Pearl, or each other. In fact, none of the three had said one single snippy thing about the other two. It was clear that St. Luke's had set up a competitive environment, a consistent culture in arts schools and institutions. It was similar when I danced for the New York City Ballet. Add that to a dynamic where two women were vying for the love of the same man. I was reminded of something I'd heard someone say a long time ago: *What are the lengths to which a woman will go when shunned by a man she loves? What is her breaking point?* What was Pearl's breaking point? What was Hazel's? Would Hazel describe Pearl in a positive light as Karla and Esme had? I knew from experience that jealousy was not an emotion as much as it was an unexpected spiral that you unwittingly found yourself inside.

I paged through my notepad, reviewed what I'd written so far. An outsider might say the case was going as expected, but I was impatient by nature, as most type A overachievers are. This slow rollout of acceptable interview subjects from Alice was more than frustrating. The students were all adults; I didn't need her permission.

I decided to grab dinner at Helen's Greasy Spoon. I had been picking at food since Abel's body was discovered, but my appetite had come roaring back. Most of our local establishments were named for their proprietors. Helen's made the best hamburgers on the island. I ordered my usual—heavy on the mustard and pickles—and topped it off with a basket of fries and a Coke.

It was dusk when I left. I'd meant to drive home, but instead, here I was parked near the north entrance to the forest, though I had no intention of walking through the Garden of Angels this time. I could go around the outside edge of the cemetery until I was past it, then follow the path that led to the east entrance, where Pearl's and Karla's cottages were located. That way they wouldn't see me approaching. I knew every inch of this part of the forest. Not just from my morning runs, but also from bow-and-arrow hunting with my father as a child. Except for the one he needed to carry as a cop, my father got rid of his guns after my mother shot herself. I have no memory of my mother or her death—I was just eight weeks old—but people who lived on the island back then still talk about "how sad it all was" and the "tragic effects of postpartum depression." Folks said my father changed after that, but I wouldn't know. I only knew him as the center of my world.

I sat in the car for a few minutes and tried to convince myself to leave. What did I think I would accomplish by spying on these young women? The plan was ludicrous, juvenile even. Yet I grabbed my tampon-size flashlight, got out of my car, and followed the plan I'd devised. I loved the forest at night. The hoots of the owls, the howls of the wolves, the chirps of the crickets, the occasional scurry of a squirrel. I switched on the flashlight, turned it to dim, and shined it on the trail instead of the trees so as not to attract bears or accidentally trip over a branch or rock.

Pearl's cottage was dark except for a porch light. Karla's porch light was off, but the rest of the cottage glowed like a lava lamp. I saw shadows moving back and forth and heard the muffled sounds of high-pitched voices. I turned off the flashlight, moved in closer, and then did something really stupid. Something an amateur teenage sleuth like Nancy Drew might do. I tiptoed up the porch stairs, crouched below the window, and slowly raised my head until my eyes were just above the window's wood encasing. I decided I should come up with a believable story for why I was there, just in case, but I didn't have time. Their ceremony was already starting. I was taken aback by what I saw. The four girls wore red robes and sat cross-legged in a circle on the floor, a plethora of white candles and flower petals surrounding them and a huge cast-iron pot in the center. I watched and listened as, one by one, they each took a piece of paper from a witch's hat, unfolded it, read its contents, struck a match to it, and threw it into the cast-iron pot. It was Pearl who read the last paper. "'I'm happy he's dead.'"

Just after the word "dead" left her lips, a large and untamed wind emerged from the forest. It spiraled and swirled its way through the trees, skipped over the open space and through Karla's garden, and then something unexplainable occurred. Something I never would have believed if I hadn't seen it with my own eyes. The wind took the shape of the devil, horns and all. It blew toward the cottage and up the porch steps. I curled into a ball against its intrusion, but it stopped just before it reached me and crashed into the cottage's door. I peeked through the window, saw the girls' robes flapping and billowing and the candle fire dancing. Then a large bird came flying toward me, landed on the porch rail, made a hooting sound, and stared directly at me. I gasped, and not only because it was a huge great horned owl, larger than any owl I'd ever seen, but also because of its eyes. They were red.

"What was that?" I heard Karla ask.

"Some kind of bird," Esme said.

"It sounded bigger than a bird," the voice I didn't recognize said. I'd been so unsettled by the red robes I hadn't looked closely at the fourth girl.

"It sounded like an owl," Pearl said.

"An owl? Are you sure?" I heard someone say. But I couldn't tell who because now they were all talking at once, and I, as quietly as possible, was inching my way back across the porch in a state of fear. When I got down the stairs, I ran, and didn't stop until I was safely inside the forest. I looked back toward the cottage, but the owl was gone.

And there was Pearl's face looking through the window I had just left.

PEARL

It's late when I wake, past two A.M. My head is pounding, and my insides feel as if they are trying to push against my flesh. Something very bad is going to happen. I can *see* it. Fire. Chaos. Death. At first, I'm confused why I'm on Karla's sofa; then I remember the Farewell Ceremony. Karla is passed out on the floor. After Esme and Hazel left, she and I kept drinking wine and talking about the devil wind and the big bird that flew away before we got a good look at it. I worried it was an owl. "Owls are harbingers of death," I said.

I tiptoe over Karla and, as quietly as possible, open the front door and close it behind me. When I get back to our cottage, I take off the robe, fold it neatly, carefully return it and the others to the secret compartment in the antique sideboard, and reach for my special deck of tarot cards.

I was drawn to the sideboard the moment I saw it at Priscilla's Antiques. "I saw you admiring it," Priscilla said when she walked over to me. "It's special, isn't it?" She proceeded to tell me a mesmerizing story about its origin. The sideboard was once a prayer altar, a forgotten relic that the monks used to pray away their sins. St. Luke's had been stripped of most of its ancient furnishings and artifacts centuries earlier, but this piece was among those left behind. Priscilla said that Alice in Wonderland had hired her to clean out the buildings. They made a trade. Priscilla would do it for free as long as she could keep anything she found. The sideboard was found in a crawl space beneath the Tower. "It's yours," Priscilla said before I even asked the price. When I argued, she said, "The Ghost Women always meant for it to be so. That you alone would set in place a series of events that will heal the past." I said I didn't understand these words. "You will soon," she said.

It was Karla, not you, who helped me drag the sideboard into our cottage. She helped me remove its cobwebs and polish its every nook and cranny. Imagine our surprise when we discovered the secret compartment and the four blood robes inside it. "One for each witch in our coven," Karla had said. Then we saw the tarot pack. The cards were larger than cards are today and the imagery stunning. Ancient and gilded and utterly exquisite. I had never seen a deck like it.

Now I light the candles on my altar and sit on the green sofa. I call to the Great Priestess as I unwrap the silk cloth covering the cards. As Sister Winnifred taught me all those years ago, no matter how many times I've read a given deck, prior to every new reading, I must reestablish a connection with it. I close my eyes and hold the cards in my hands, immediately feel their energy. I shuffle the deck, cut it, place it face down on the coffee table, and silently ask the cards to tell me I'm wrong, that everything will be okay. There are a variety of spreads that can be used to do readings. I prefer the Celtic Cross spread, which is considered the oldest and most classic. The spread is said to derive the shape of its layout from ancient cross structures in Ireland. A total of ten cards are used. Two crossing cards form a mini cross. Four surrounding cards form a larger cross. Together they represent the feminine. Four additional cards stack to the right. Often called the staff, they represent the masculine.

Starting with the mini cross, I lay out the *first card.* The Star. As I am the querent, this card refers to me. The Star is considered one of the most positive cards in the Tarot. It heralds joy, good fortune, and a positive outcome. I immediately feel lighter. The *second card* is called the crossing card, that which crosses the querent for good or bad. I am consumed by fear when I see the Ten of Swords. It is one of the most negative cards in the minor arcana, the very antithesis of the Star. It heralds ruin, pain, affliction, anguish, and possibly death. I remember the vision I had when I woke up in Karla's cottage. Fire, chaos, and death.

"What is it?" I ask out loud. "What am I seeing?" I want to stop the reading, stop the future, but it's too late. The cards are merely the messenger. The future has already begun.

I place the *third card*, the foundation or basis of the matter, below the mini cross. The Lovers. A man and a woman hold hands beneath the winged figure of Cupid. You and me?

My recent past is represented by the *fourth card.* I place it to the left of the mini cross, another minor arcana, the Three of Swords. Not surprisingly, it warns of a past betrayal, a broken heart, absence, loss.

The *fifth card* is the crowning card, what I will likely achieve if I continue on my current path. I place it above the mini cross.

Justice. A female figure holds the scales of justice in her left hand and a sword in her right, indicating that the eventual outcome, whether favorable or unfavorable, will be fair.

Finally, I place the *sixth card*, that which lies ahead, to the right of the mini cross. The Wheel of Fortune. The winged female figure located in the center of the wheel is the same one depicted on the Lovers card. The card's message is that the wheel is still spinning, that destiny and fate will have a hand in my question.

I pause. The air around me is thick. I feel the darkness of which the six cards warn. I feel the passage of time and a profound sense of helplessness. I take a deep breath and continue.

The four cards that make up the staff are meant to provide more information. I place the *seventh card* at the base of the staff. It reveals my role in the question, my hidden psychological reaction or unrevealed destiny. The Six of Swords. I always think of it as a bridge over troubled waters, or better days ahead. An actual or spiritual journey will follow the darkness that is in store.

I place the *eighth card* above the seventh. It represents the role others will play in the question. The Five of Swords. It warns of deceit, dishonesty, and backstabbing. *Trust no one*, the card says.

The *ninth card* represents my hopes and fears. The Three of Cups. It is a card of celebration. While the minor arcana in this deck don't include images, most contemporary decks include a visual of three women celebrating a great victory. They dance and hold chalices of wine. Is it us? The Weird Sisters? But there are four of us, not three. And why would I celebrate darkness and evil?

The *tenth card* represents the final outcome. I look at the card lying face down on top the deck. It beckons me to flip it over and add it to its rightful place at the top of the staff. But I fear the outcome. Fear the events that your death has set in motion. Events that I caused. I shouldn't have made the poppets. I shouldn't have offered them to the Unmarked Tombstone. I hold my breath, turn over the final card. Judgment. At the top of the card, a godly, bearded man wearing a crown holds a sword in his right hand and a cross in the other. He is Judgment. Before him, two angelic figures blow trumpets with hanging banners while two other figures rise from a rose-colored tomb. The head of an old man sharing the tomb with them seems to imply that Death has already visited them. I don't understand. Who has death visited? Abel?

A whisper in my ear. *Count the cards.*

I gather the cards and count them. Then I gasp. There are seventy-three, not seventy-eight. I rise, search the sideboard to see if they were left behind. Nothing. I return to the table. Look through the deck to see which cards are missing. Gone are five of the major arcana cards: the Hanged Man, the Tower, Death, the Fool, and the Devil. It can't be random. Nothing is ever random. Fear consumes me. I realize I am shaking.

A flickering light from the picture window in the kitchen catches my attention. I'm not even all the way there when I see it. There, in the distance, above the ivy-covered brick wall, I see an orange glow. Fire lights up the night sky. I put on my sneakers, grab a light sweater and flashlight, and run to St. Luke's Tower.

PART TWO

The Tower

What if the Tower was in fact hell itself?

—LAETITIA BARBIER,
TAROT AND DIVINATION CARDS

Day 3

Two Days After the Autumnal Equinox

Sunday, September 24, 1972

LOLA

The Tower was burning out of control when I arrived on the scene. Flames shot into the night sky. Bricks tumbled down like a stack of toy blocks, thudding and smashing as they hit the ground. Men shouted and hoses sprayed. Waverly Island's only fire truck was parked on the grass between the Monastery and the Tower. Six of our island police cruisers parked every which way, their light bars still flashing, the streams from their headlights crisscrossing the night sky. In the distance, the faint sound of a siren. Waverly Island's ambulance. Like me, Barney Cougar, part-time ambulance driver, part-time retiree, was likely awakened to the news from a deep sleep. Like me, he wouldn't make it on time to save the victims. Like me, he was merely a supernumerary in a tragic stage production.

Colin saw me and jogged over. "This was found outside the belfry," he said, his voice breathless, barely legible over the chaos.

A plastic bag with two burlap poppets and a tarot card inside it. Trump 16, the Tower.

I felt my chest tighten. Fear and dread washed over me. Similar to the poppet left at the Ghost Tree, these poppets had pins with black pearl tips stuck in the red hearts. I turned my focus to the tarot card. The card appeared to be from the same deck as the one left at the Ghost Tree. Same size. Same rich color palette and shiny gilding. No name, number, or roman numeral. The image was eerily similar to the scene before me. A redbrick tower was in the process of burning. A dark billowy cloud behind it engulfed a blazing purple sun. In our scene, it was the moon. There was one other horrifying difference. On the card, two figures, a male and a female, dived headfirst through the air like unwitting acrobats, forever frozen in midair with their arms outstretched over their heads. But in the scene before me, the victims had hit the ground.

"Are the victims students?" I asked.

"Yep," Colin said. "Appears so."

"Arson?" I asked.

"They're still working on that, but it looks that way. The belfry door was locked from the outside with the kids inside. They couldn't get out. They were screaming. Reggie's guys said they reached the door before the kids jumped. The guys shouted for them to hang on, that they were trying to break down the door, but it was an inferno in there. Don Walters said he saw the girl fly by one of the windows after she jumped. She was on fire. Can you imagine having that image in your head for the rest of your life? What a horrible way to die."

What a horrible way to die. I remembered Alice using those exact words when she took me on a tour of St. Luke's two years ago. I mentioned I had visited the Monastery when I was a child as part of a third-grade field trip. It was before St. Luke's Institute of the Arts officially opened. Right after the huge renovation turning the dilapidated Monastery and grounds into a state-of-the-art school was completed. Most, if not all, residents of the island had visited St. Luke's Tower at one point back then. Before the renovation, anyone could just walk right through the rusted-out iron gate and crumbling Monastery and Tower. We did so at our own risk. As the place where the witch trials took place, it appealed to our fascination with the grotesque. And as much as we feared the possibility of seeing the Ghost Women, who were said to regularly return to the place where their trials occurred in hopes of exacting revenge, we also wanted to be a part of the elite club that insisted they'd seen the specters wisping about. During her tour, Alice had made a point to comment on the age of the interior wood, the heaviness of the iron doors, and the bronze padlocks. "We replaced the door," she said. "Students were forever sneaking up here in the middle of the night to drink and build campfires. Campfires, can you imagine? Yes, the Tower exterior is made of brick and stone, but that doesn't mean it's fireproof. One of these days, they're going to burn the thing down, and themselves in the process. *What a horrible way to die.*"

"How did they get in there in the first place?" I asked Colin. "I thought the doors were kept locked."

"I'm checking to see who had access to keys," he said.

"What started the fire?"

"We aren't sure. We think some sort of accelerant. We're checking burn patterns. We also found broken glass. Looks like alcohol bottles. Doubt we'll get any fingerprints, but we're checking regardless."

"Were they able to ID the victims?" Stupid question, but I felt the need to ask anyway.

"Girl and guy is all they know. They're burned over most of their bodies. And it was a long fall, so they're pretty banged up. Are you certain you want to see them?"

My body said no. "Yes."

I followed Colin to the body lying on the right side of the Tower. It was covered in a police-issue blue wool blanket. I crouched down next to it, curled back the edge of the blanket. Shuddered. A wave of nausea rolled from my belly to my throat. I gagged, swallowed vomit.

The body was beyond "pretty banged up." It was mangled, distorted. Limbs bent in unnatural positions. Head twisted all the way around.

"The other one looks worse," Colin said.

"Is there any chance it wasn't murder? Alice told me once that students were always sneaking up there at night to basically camp."

"It seems unlikely given the tarot card." His face registered compassion. For me. He knew I didn't want to believe what increasingly appeared to be true. That Abel Montague's murder was no longer an isolated incident. That now there were three murders. And given the tarot cards, someone at least wanted us to think there could be more.

Something was nagging at me. "How did the fire department know about the fire before the kids jumped?"

"Reggie said someone called the station to tip them off."

"Male or female?"

"He couldn't say for sure. The voice was muffled."

"What did they say?"

Colin grabbed a folded piece of paper from his pocket and handed it to me. "Reggie wrote it down verbatim. Said he knew something wasn't right. That he wished he hadn't answered the phone so the caller's voice would be on the machine."

I opened the paper and read. *There's a fire in the Tower. You better hurry. There are students locked inside.*

"How could the caller know they were students or that they were locked inside unless the caller saw them?" I asked Colin.

"Or was with them," he said.

I shivered.

The arrival of Barney Cougar's ambulance, a 1950s light blue station wagon with wood side panels, stole our attention. I saw he'd brought two of his grandsons with him. He had several, all talented varsity athletes. They removed two stretchers from the station wagon, put on gloves, and ventured toward the bodies. I watched as the boys carefully placed the victims onto the stretchers and loaded them into the ambulance. After they closed the door, Barney made his way to me. He was carrying a clipboard.

"Need your signature," he said. "Are you ready for me to take them to the morgue?"

I checked the time on my watch: 4:23 A.M. If I hurried, I could get in a run before sunrise. I knew that sounded heartless, but I needed to get centered. To, as much as possible, wipe the gruesomeness of the scene from my mind before I headed to Alice Landry's office.

"Yes," I said to Barney. "Rebecca usually arrives around five thirty. Do you mind waiting a bit?"

"I got a key," he said. "But I'll wait. These poor souls deserve some caring company. In the meantime, my grandsons and I will pray for them."

"Looks like a crowd is gathering," Colin said.

He was right. A group of students stood on the terrace of the Monastery. My eyes swept over them. I didn't recognize anyone. I looked farther, beyond the terrace, and there, standing apart from the crowd, was Pearl. Our eyes met. For a moment, we were two helpless deer, each caught frozen by the eyes of the other.

Was it you? I silently asked. I took a step in Pearl's direction. She took a step back. And then she turned and ran.

LOLA

My need to run felt primal. I hardly remembered leaving the scene, getting home, or changing into my running clothes. I ran faster and faster, trying not to think about the fire or the two dead souls or the brief encounter with Pearl. Generally, I could lose myself in the rhythmic sound of my shoes slapping pavement, but not now. I was exhausted. I hadn't slept. My mind was swimming with questions. What was Pearl doing at the Monastery? Who had keys to the Tower? I could tell by the chirps of the birds that sunrise was just minutes away. Up ahead, *my* tree, a regal goddess located on the opposite side of the forest from the Ghost Tree. Her height soaring above the surrounding canopy, her trunk triple my width. When I reached her, I put my hands on my hips, bent forward to catch my breath, then rose and looked over the cliff edge to the ocean below. On the water's edge stood my fellow worshippers, egrets and herons and geese and ducks and tortoises. And together, as we did every morning, we watched as the slim orange line appeared on the horizon, slowly formed into a sphere, and rose into the sky.

I sat, leaned back against the tree, closed my eyes. "Just for a moment," I said.

It was my father who told me that trees were alive. Perhaps he only meant they were alive in the sense that nature is alive, that plants are alive, but as a little girl, I had internalized the statement to mean trees were alive and conscious like me. Nearly every day, like I still do, my father and I watched the sunrise from the mound of this particular tree. One day, as we sat in this very spot, my father said, "This tree is special. Would you like to know why?" He told me the tale of the tree princess. A poor man had promised his beautiful young daughter to the town's mayor in exchange for a loaf of bread. The daughter, having overheard the conversation, ran into the forest, sat beneath this tree, and prayed to the gods: "I want to live my life right here in this great forest on this very mound." That night, while she slept, the gods sent her a dream. She saw herself standing on the very same mound, felt her legs fusing together, becoming strong and sturdy, and her arms multiplying and sprouting leaves. "Are you sure this is what you want?" the gods asked. "Yes," she said. "At this moment, I feel happier than I've ever felt before. I want to stay in this dream forever." And the gods granted her wish.

Now it was I who was inside a dream, and I was telling my tree about these new savage murders, asking her to protect the innocent souls in the murderer's path.

Heed the signs, I heard her say.

I woke, looked at my watch. Only five minutes had passed, though it felt much longer. I rose, stretched my legs, and ran along the forest path. When I got to the east entrance, I saw Karla rocking on her front porch, music blaring from inside her cottage. "Black Magic Woman."

"Care for some tea?" she yelled over the music. "It appears you could use some."

I checked my watch.

"Come on up and rock," she said. "I'll be back in a flash."

The music softened. I could have left, but I was tired, Karla's porch so inviting.

She emerged holding two of her handmade mugs, placed them on the table between the rockers.

I grabbed the one nearest me, blew on the hot liquid, sipped. "It's good. Thank you. Are you a Fleetwood Mac fan?"

She squinted her eyes in confusion. "Oh, my cassette player. Sure, but this tape is a compilation of witchy songs. 'Season of the Witch' by Donovan, 'Strange Brew' by Cream, 'Voodoo Chile' by Jimi Hendrix. I put it together. Isn't it fun? I just heard a new song by the Eagles called 'Witchy Woman.' I need to add it when I make a new tape. Witchcraft is popular right now. Women are coming into our power. Burning our bras at universities and elsewhere all over the country. The Supreme Court is considering that abortion case, *Roe v. Wade*. Can you imagine what it would be like if we could make decisions about our own bodies?" Her eyes were wide, her passion and excitement palpable. "I just read this book called *Power Through Witchcraft*, by a woman named Louise Huebner. She's the official witch of Los Angeles. It's amazing. I have a copy if you'd like to borrow it. My mum sent it."

"Maybe later?" I said.

"Oh my," Karla said. "Of course you are busy right now. Well, it's here when you're ready. I was waiting for you, you know. I figured you'd need to fortify yourself after such a dreadful morning. This is the perfect tea. Black with a touch of cinnamon, rosemary, saffron, and honey. This particular recipe also promotes wisdom and cognitive well-being. Which I'm sure will come in handy in the days ahead."

"Days ahead?"

"While you look into these newest murders," she said. "They are murders, aren't they? Have you and your colleagues considered they might be somehow related to the fifteenth-century witch burnings?"

"Why do you think that?"

"My aunt Matilda mentioned it."

Aunt Matilda mentioned it? I tried to hide my dismay.

"I know, I know. You're not a believer. But just think about it for a moment. First you find a body hanging from the Ghost Tree, the tree the Ghost Women flew to after they were burned. And now two more victims have been burned alive in the building where their trials were held. I suppose it could be a coincidence, but I've never put much stock in coincidence. It feels more like a message to me. Have you identified the bodies yet?"

I thought about all the students standing on the veranda outside the Monastery. It wasn't even eight A.M., but of course word had already spread. "No," I said. "How do you know your aunt Matilda was burned at the stake? Was her story passed down through the generations?"

"It was passed down, yes, but not just verbally. In writing. Our matriarchy keeps tedious diaries of our lineage."

"What was she accused of?"

"Gathering plants in the forest that she mixed into devil's brew to seduce the abbot of the monastery. But that was a lie. He had been lusting after her since she was a child. When she matured, he had his henchmen bring her to his bed. Then, after she gave birth to twin boys, he feared his actions would come to light, so he had her arrested and burned at the stake. For two years, the villagers hid Aunt Matilda's mother, Mary, and younger sister, Grace, as they recorded not only the history of our matriarchy but also the historic events of Aunt Matilda's murder. As more and more innocent women were arrested, fearing her remaining daughter could suffer the same fate, Mary urged Grace to stow away on a boat headed to England, where they'd lived before Mary's husband got the itch to travel with a group of people looking for opportunity in what they were calling the New World. He was killed soon after their arrival. Interestingly, according to records, he was the last husband or brother in our line. Grace settled back in England and gave birth to many daughters, who gave birth to many more, all of whom have added entries to our diaries throughout time. Grace is considered the original Mother Aunt of our matriarchy. She was a healer and a green witch, and she had an herb and flower garden that was admired by many. That was where our surname, Gardyn, came from. I could find no record of a family surname prior to that, either for Mary, her husband, Matilda, or Matilda's twin boys." She paused. "You know, if the witch trials were held today, you and I would most likely be burned. Or at least I would be." She smiled.

"That's quite a family history," I said. "And that's why you came to St. Luke's, because of your aunt Matilda?"

"Yes. Members of our matriarchy tried for years to get recruited so we could learn more about Aunt Matilda and the Ghost Tree. We are all artists as well as healers, but only my work caught the school's attention." She paused. "You asked me earlier about St. Luke's selection process. It wasn't mere luck or even unique talent that got me here. When I was still in England, one of my aunts learned something new about *Atropa belladonna*, the magical plant also known as deadly nightshade. While we were aware of the plant's use as an effective poison, she discovered that when soaked in fat and applied externally, it induces a sensation of astral projection or flying. So when a St. Luke's scout showed interest in my paintings, they applied deadly nightshade to the insides of my wrists every night so I would imagine myself flying across great bodies of water and landing on Waverly Island. My dreams were crazy during that time, or at least in my feverish state I thought they were dreams. I saw myself attending St. Luke's Institute of the Arts orientation, various classes, living and painting in *this* cottage, even doing spells with a girl with large blue eyes, whom I would later recognize to be Pearl. And then, when I got the official invitation, my mum and her mum and all our cousins and sisters and daughters gathered to do one final spell, in which they introduced me to Aunt Matilda. It was she who told me what I needed to do once I got here." She paused, smiled. "The funny thing is, while I know I must have flown here on an airplane, the only journey I remember is standing in the center of several hundred women, spreading my wings, and taking off."

"What was it you needed to do?" I asked.

"To seek revenge, of course." Karla smiled that same smile I'd now seen several times. A combination of secrecy and condescension. As if she'd just remembered that I was a detective looking into now three murders, she added, "There are many ways to seek revenge that don't involve murder. Would you like another cup of tea?"

"Oh, no," I said, and rose. "Thank you though. I need to get going. I've got a full day."

"I imagine," she said. "By the way, did the scene look like a painting?"

"What do you mean?" I asked.

"When I discovered Abel's body, I was struck by not only how theatrical the entire scene appeared, but also how compositionally balanced. As if it was what Pearl calls a 'painting in space.' She's always making a square of her fingers when sketching in nature. She says she's looking for the best painting in space. I just wondered if this new scene was similar."

There was no point in trying to hide the physical appearance of the Tower scene. Too many students, including Pearl, had witnessed it. "I hadn't thought of it as a painting, but I suppose one could say that."

She nodded. "I'll be here tomorrow if you have time to stop after your run. And, of course, if you need some support or relief between now and then, my tea recipes and I are here to help."

I smiled, descended her steps, and continued my run while wondering about the conversation I'd just had. It had certainly piqued my curiosity. *There are many ways to seek revenge that don't involve murder*, Karla had said. I wondered what she'd meant by that. Had she wanted me to ask? Is that why she said it? Was I underestimating these girls and their spells?

When I got home, I wrote down as much as I could remember about Karla's and my conversation in my notepad. But what intrigued me most was her use of the phrase "painting in space."

LOLA

"She's running a tad late," Christine said sheepishly when I got to St. Luke's administrative office. I'd called ahead to say I would be there at eight. "It's just horrible what happened. Everyone is so upset. The phone has been ringing off the hook. Word has obviously gotten out. Colin told me to refer them to your office. Can I get you something? I just brewed a fresh pot of coffee."

"I'm good," I said, still buzzing from the tea Karla gave me.

Ten minutes passed, the tap-tap-tap of Christine's typewriter adding to my annoyance.

"Do you think she'll be much longer?" I asked Christine, loud enough so she could hear me over the typewriter.

She stopped typing. "I'm sure she'll be here soon. As you can imagine, she's been very busy dealing with the board over all this. It seems word about the first murder has gotten out despite our best efforts. I imagine now with this second incident things will get worse."

Right then, in her normal chaotic state, Alice came flying through the door. Gone was her rumpled appearance and puffy eyes. She looked her usual perfectly coifed self. "I am so sorry, Lola. I've been a mess all morning. Do you know anything yet? Oh my, of course you don't, or I would have heard. Come into my office. Tell me everything."

I followed her inside. The room still smelled of cigarettes, but not quite as bad. I noticed her windows were open a few inches. Probably Christine's doing. Alice sat behind her desk, opened the top drawer, and began shuffling through it. "Take a seat."

I was already sitting.

She located a long, thin cigarette, closed the drawer, and lit it. She looked at me. "I do hope I have more somewhere. I seem to be running out of them more often than usual. It's hard to find Virginia Slims on the island. I buy them on the mainland, several boxes at a time. So, what've you got?"

"Nothing at the moment," I said. "Colin said he called you at home this morning? To update you? I didn't see you at the fire."

"He did. But I'm afraid I rushed him. Please apologize to him for me. I was indisposed." She flashed me a gloating smile. "Have you identified the unfortunate victims? This might sound heartless, but you have no idea how many times I've told students not to sneak up there. They just don't listen. It was an accident waiting to happen."

"We don't believe this was an accident. We think it was murder." I wanted to mention the tarot card, but for now, we needed to keep that information close. Alice wasn't known for her discretion.

"*Murder?* Why would you think that? I'm sure the fire was just an unfortunate accident. Students are always sneaking up there. They were probably burning incense or candles, and you know how easy it would be for that to cause a fire in a building as old as the Tower. The wood in there is basically kindling."

"We're looking into all possibilities," I said, and kept probing. "How do you think the victims got inside? I thought the Tower doors were kept locked."

"They are. But being the bright, resourceful students they are, I'm not surprised they were able to find alternative methods to get inside."

"Alternative methods? Do you mean they picked the locks?"

"I mean, I'm not the only one with keys. Groundskeepers, custodians, and the campus police detail all have keys."

"I'm going ahead with interviewing the other Second Years. Is there anyone else you think might be able to provide further information? You mentioned a First Year named Jeannine Hart." I had purposely not asked her permission.

She didn't answer right away. She pretended to be busy organizing some paperwork on her desk.

"I'll need to get with the board on that," she finally said. "We wouldn't want anyone misinterpreting what happened."

"I don't need the board's permission," I said. "It's a murder investigation. My job requires me to find whoever is committing these murders with or without your help."

"I told you that we have student interview protocols here at St. Luke's. I would say the same to the press." Her tone was curt and authoritative.

"I'll let you know if I need your help contacting any of the students," I said, and rose.

"What happened at the Tower was an *accident*," she said, this time firmly.

"Thank you for your time," I said. "I'll keep you informed." Then I left.

When I arrived at Joe's, I was still fuming. Alice was infuriating.

"Your usual?" Joe asked when I got to the counter.

I hated being predictable. "Actually, I was thinking hot cocoa."

"Ahh, changing it up." A big Joe smile. Joe is one of those forever jolly people who can immediately alter your mood. My father was the same. I always wondered how he did it. His life didn't warrant constant happiness. He worked hard. He tried not to show his pain about my mother's suicide, but I found him crying once when he thought I wasn't home. Deep guttural hopeless wails. I had no memory of my mother. I only knew what she looked like because I found a picture of her in my father's desk. In the picture, she was holding me as an infant. She wore a smile, but her eyes were sad. I used to wonder if their sad appearance was a genetic trait or if my arrival had caused it. My ex would have said her sad eyes were a sign of intelligence. He insisted that happy people were simpleminded, but if my father and Joe were any indication, that wasn't true. Joe had a PhD in industrial design. He worked for years designing cars for the Ford Motor Company in Dearborn, Michigan. His wife died of breast cancer a year after he retired. They never had children. Rather than stay in the place where he had lived his entire life, he moved to Waverly Island and opened Cup of Joe, or Joe's, as the islanders called it. He was brave and kind, like my father had been, and his eyes, like the rest of his face, forever smiled.

I returned his smile. "I'm meeting someone. A St. Luke's student named Hazel Donovan. Hopefully I didn't miss her? I'm a bit late."

"Name doesn't ring a bell, but I don't know all the students from St. Luke's by name."

"Pretty, slim, long dark hair."

"Sounds like the girl who sometimes came in with that boy."

"What boy is that?"

"That one you all found hanging in the forest?"

"Abel Montague?"

"Customers have been talking about it for the last two days. Not every day someone is found hanging from the Ghost Tree." He lowered his voice and leaned toward me. "Well, I'm not one to talk out of turn, but that kid was a two-timer if there ever was one. All lovey-dovey, the two of them were. It was like he thought I was blind to what he was doing. Playing them both."

"What do you mean, 'both'?"

"Pearl and that other girl. Sweet kid, that Pearl. The other one was trouble."

"Why trouble?"

"Just the way she was. Slim like you mentioned, but shapely in all the right places, and she used it, if you know what I mean."

"But you knew who Pearl and Abel were?"

"I only knew that was his name after Colin told me what happened. He came in asking questions about the boy. Who he hung out with and all that. I told him about the shapely girl."

"And Pearl?"

"Pearl was my wife's name. I told her that—the kid, I mean—when she introduced herself, and after that, whenever she came in, she asked about my Pearl. What she was like. Most people don't ask about people you lose. They think it makes you uncomfortable. But I enjoy telling stories about my Pearl. That kid, she's special. She always looks me in the eye. Really listens. That Abel was a fool. He had someone special right in front of him. I don't like speaking ill of the dead, but I got to say, it seems to me that Pearl dodged a bullet."

"Had it been going on for a while? With Abel and this other girl?"

"Seemed so. I told Colin all that. You know, I heard on the news this morning there was a fire at the school last night. They said there were two victims?"

"Yes, at the Tower," I said. "Two students died. We haven't identified them yet."

Joe grabbed the rosary he kept beside the register and crossed his heart. “God bless them,” he said. “And you, Lola. I don’t envy your job.”

“Thanks, Joe.”

“Go have a seat. I’ll bring your cocoa to you. And how about a jelly donut on the house. Baked fresh this morning.”

I made my way to my usual booth, sat, and reviewed my case notes, specifically what the girls had said about Abel. Only Pearl had had anything positive to say about him. I assumed the girl that Joe saw Abel Montague with was Hazel Donovan. I was surprised by how angry and protective of Pearl I felt. Of all the negative things I had heard about Abel, I found his openly showing up at Joe’s with a girl other than his live-in girlfriend not just extremely insensitive but also mean and arrogant. It smacked of narcissism. I stopped myself. Was it Abel I was angry at or my ex? Whatever the case, I was looking forward to talking with Hazel.

I checked the time. It was half past the hour. Had I gotten the time wrong? No, Colin had specifically written nine A.M. Maybe Alice had gotten in touch with Hazel and told her not to talk to me? I was beginning to understand why the students referred to Alice as Alice in Wonderland. Nothing was ever what it seemed where Alice Landry was concerned. What was up was down. What was down was up.

Joe’s jelly donuts were out of this world. Goopy and messy and just the right amount of sweet. This one was strawberry. I saw that a drip of pink jelly had landed on my black pants. Thankfully, it had skipped my white blouse. I reviewed the list of suspects I’d made the afternoon that Abel’s body was found. No matter what Joe said about her, Pearl was still on top. The collective of the Weird Sisters was a close second. I checked the time again: 9:50. I was supposed to meet Colin at Rebecca’s at ten to discuss her thoughts on the two

Tower victims' autopsies. I closed my notebook, shoved it back in my bag, and took my empty plate and cup up to the counter.

"You didn't need to do that," Joe said. "Cleanup is my job."

"You'll have plenty to clean up," I said, and smiled. "I'm afraid I made a mess of the table, and my pants. The donut was heavenly as usual. If a girl shows up looking for me, will you tell her to call me?"

"Sure will," he said. "You enjoy this beautiful day. Looks like it's not going to last."

"More rain?" This time of year, Waverly Island caught the brunt of a lot of weather fronts, the downside of being a small island in a large ocean.

"You haven't heard? News is saying a hurricane is headed our way. Course you can't always trust those weathermen. Mother Nature is a fickle one."

I looked up at the sky when I got outside. Clear and blue. It was habit. I knew that what the sky looked like now was no indication of where or when a hurricane would hit. I remembered what the voice in my dream had said: *Heed the signs*. A storm was brewing, and with storms came trouble.

PEARL

I am in my studio waiting on Mr. Smith.

I don't believe you ever asked me about my critiques with my assigned advisor. That said, I don't think I asked you about yours either. Odd, don't you think, that individuals in a boyfriend-girlfriend relationship, a *live-together* boyfriend-girlfriend relationship, wouldn't discuss what is arguably one of the most consequential relationships at St. Luke's? According to Mr. Smith, his job is to guide me through my entire artistic journey "at St. Luke's and beyond." He sees himself as my mentor, advocate, and "holistic" teacher. Fourth Years graduate in May, and new First Years start at the beginning of June. Advisors make their selections at an official ceremony. A rite-of-passage party follows, a drunken, drug-filled event. Selections are meant to be a surprise. I was totally surprised when Mr. Smith announced my name, as I was when all the boys hooted. I should have known then what that hooting meant, but I've been told, *by you*, that I can be dense where it comes to male interest.

Looking back, there were clues, one in particular, that preceded my official selection. It was my first drawing class critique. Mr. Smith and I were in the hallway outside the Worship Room. He was flipping through my drawings, commenting on such things as form, style, application, white-space-to-dark-space ratio, when Suzanne Little walked by. You remember Suzanne, don't you? When you boys were drunk or forgot we girls were there, you assigned her all sorts of sexually derogatory names. We girls, at least those of us trying not to stand out or get labeled prudes, mostly tried to ignore these sorts of comments. But there were some, like Karla, who made a point to publicly chastise all of you. The truth was, Suzie appeared to enjoy her notoriety. "Hi, Mr. Smith," Suzie had said with a syrupy, inviting lilt. "Hello, Suzanne," Mr. Smith responded. When she was out of earshot, he said to me, "That girl is going to be fat by the time she's thirty. You, on the other hand, will always be willowy and beautiful." "Willowy" and "beautiful" were not adjectives I had ever heard assigned to me. But it wasn't just his words that startled me. It was the way he looked at me, with a kind of hunger.

Now I wait for him in my studio for my official monthly advisor critique. He will be late. He's always late. He'll bring a bottle of expensive wine and flowers. I have never understood why he bothers with the flowers. For a leather-jacketed, long-haired, toxically masculine, combat-boot-wearing guy nearly twice my age, both the flowers and *expensive* wine seem out of character. And unnecessary. I mean, it's not like I can turn him down. Maybe all that seduction is some kind of fantasy for him? We will go through the critique of my most recent paintings. He seems to genuinely appreciate my work. He will comment on the *willowy* woman, whom he also calls a forest nymph; will say how she intrigues him, how adept I am at making her appear mysterious, how she will fascinate every viewer, how men (he never says *women*, as if he's oblivious to the fact that there's a sexual revolution going on) will want to run their hands over her entire body, how brilliant my career will be, how he will make certain of that. He will find some things to criticize, of course. That is his job. I admit that his criticism is mostly useful and does sometimes make my work better. By the time the critique is over, we—well, mostly he—will have consumed the entire bottle of wine. I'll be looking closely at something he pointed out in my painting, an errant brushstroke or questionable color choice, when I feel his finger brush my cheek. The finger will trace my jawline down to my neck and over my breast. I used to fight my body's desire, thinking if it felt good, then he and I must be *something*. It is who I am. My mind is always trying to make sense, to fit things inside a definition. But really, what was the use? What would happen next could not be defined. It was merely inevitable.

I hear the knock at the door, check the time. Just so you know, he's earlier than usual. Are you watching? Do you see me take the deep breaths, see me shake my shoulders, see me walk to the door, see me cross my chest (*forever the good Catholic girl*, you used to say), see me invite him inside?

LOLA

Rebecca worked out of a renovated garage behind what was once her father's house. She'd inherited both after his death. Colin was already there when I arrived. I was forever amazed at how a man with a pregnant wife and three young girls, not to mention a new puppy, was able to beat single me, with no human or canine responsibilities, to every single meeting and crime scene. I read somewhere that sometimes the busier you are, the more efficient you become. Which I liked to believe, but the truth was the busier I got, the more scattered I became.

"Hey, boss," he said. "Rebecca was just filling me in on when she'll be done with the autopsies."

"I'm waiting on St. Luke's to get me the dental records they promised," Rebecca said. "Lucky for us, medical records are a requirement of final admission to the school. But who knows when I'll see them. Dealing with Alice in Wonderland is maddening."

"Yep," Colin said.

Two gurneys sat side by side, the bodies beneath them covered in white sheets. She carefully removed the sheet from the body closer to us. Even though I'd known what to expect, seeing the body in the bright light was jarring. It was burned so badly, a visual identification wasn't possible.

"This one is female," she said. "As you can see, the fire was kinder to the bottom half of her body, so her sex is obvious. But you can also tell by her bone structure. She was petite with dark hair."

"Did you say dark hair? How can you tell?" I was reminded of the conversation I had with Joe about Abel seeing someone with dark hair.

"There are hairs stuck to her body in various places," Rebecca said. "There's also a surgical scar on her back. Not huge. About two inches in diameter. Could be from an accident of some sort, or a mole removal. The worst of her burns are on her face, neck, chest, and upper arms. It appears a fire accelerant was poured over her head. You said they jumped, right? I'm not surprised. Fire is a horrible way to die."

"Do you know what kind of accelerant?" Colin asked.

"Gasoline would be my bet."

"So not alcohol?" I asked.

"You mean like whiskey or something? No. It was definitely some kind of intentional accelerant. They were both heavily doused with it. The other is male. I've nearly completed his autopsy."

She covered the female and pulled back the sheet on the other body. Like the female, he was slit open from the neck to his privates; what skin was left had been pulled to the sides, his organs removed like a gutted deer's. But unlike the female, his head was wrong.

"His neck broke in the fall," Rebecca said. "I have his organs in formalin—over on that table, if you want to examine them—but they tell me he was once a healthy boy between the ages of seventeen and twenty-two. His skin didn't fare as well as the female's. Nearly every square inch of it was burned off. I'd guess the accelerant was doused on him first and what remained went to the female. I did find hair follicles though. He also had dark hair, brown or black. He has caps on his two front teeth, which means the original teeth were knocked out at some point. Maybe an accident or sports injury."

"How can you tell?" Colin asked.

"The color differentiation," Rebecca said. "When burned, depending on temperature and length of time, original teeth turn shades of brown. His front teeth are lighter with a grayish cast, indicating ceramic crowns. The female's teeth are all original, no cavities or chips. I already mentioned her scar. Medical and dental files seem our best shot for IDs."

"Fingerprints?" Colin asked.

"Burned off."

"You said you found hemlock in both of their systems?" Colin asked.

"Yes, just like Abel Montague. It was enough to kill them pretty quickly."

"How quickly?" I asked.

"Generally, once ingested, severe symptoms will develop within fifteen minutes. But within five minutes or less, victims can feel dry mouth, faintness, and fatigue. Then suffocation, dyspnea, muscle spasms, and total paralysis will occur. Death will follow shortly thereafter."

"But they would have had to jump before total paralysis?"

"True," Rebecca said. "But if they were already in those final stages, they might not have been able to fight whoever was pouring the gasoline on them."

"Do you think they understood what was going on?" Colin asked.

"Hard to say," Rebecca said. "I hope not."

"Alice Landry is convinced the fire was an accident," I said. "Is there any way that could be true?"

"This was no accident. Even if the gasoline was poured as a joke or was unintentional, which I doubt, the victims couldn't have locked themselves inside the belfry. It's my understanding the door only locks from the outside. Did anyone find the gas can?"

"Nope," Colin said.

"Gasoline cans don't walk away on their own," Rebecca said.

"The perp must have taken it with." Colin furrowed his brow like he did when something didn't sit well with him.

"What are you thinking?" I asked him.

"The timing is off. Our guys got there before the kids jumped. The kids were pounding the door and screaming to get out. Where was the killer all that time?"

"Watching?" I suggested.

"Oh geez," Colin said. "So let me get this right. The killer gets the victims up to the Tower. Some amount of time passes as they party. Then, when the victims are sufficiently wasted, he or she spikes their drinks with the hemlock and goes to call the police. By the time the killer returns, the kids are feeling the effects of the hemlock. The killer douses them with gasoline. Strikes the match. Takes the gas can. Leaves the room. Locks the door from the outside. Hides somewhere and watches the cops try to break down the door while the kids scream and finally jump. The windows are just openings in the brick. Someone must have heard them screaming."

"You're right," I said to Colin. "The Tower is pretty far from the Monastery, but it was a nice evening. We need to check which of the students' dorm rooms face the Tower. I know it was the middle of the night, but someone might have seen something."

"Do you want me to look into that?" he asked.

"No. I'll do that. I was planning to pay another visit to Studio Row anyway. But maybe you could follow through with Reggie on the timeline and the caller?"

"Will do," Colin said.

"Rebecca, do you have any idea where the killer might have gotten hemlock?" I asked.

"It wouldn't be that hard to get your hands on. Hemlock grows wild in the forest," she said. "My grandmother used to grow it in her garden. She liked the pretty white flowers. You'd be surprised at how many garden-variety plants are poisonous. Oleander, lily of the valley, foxglove, rhododendron."

My mind flashed to Karla's garden. "You said you could have an ID within a couple hours once you get the files?"

"Yes," Rebecca said.

"You know," Colin said. "This is kind of off subject, but I took this class on ancient Greek philosophy in college. I needed to fill a humanities requirement, but it turned out to be interesting. Socrates never authored one text, and yet he is credited as the founder of Western philosophy. But what made me think of him was that he was accused of corrupting youth and was sentenced to death by ingesting hemlock. I wonder if our murderer is trying to make a statement. Everything else about these murders seems so didactic and intentional."

"It's really not that far off subject," Rebecca said. She walked over to her desk and came back holding a plastic bag that she handed to Colin. The Tower card was inside it. "Speaking of didactic and intentional, the card was completely cleaned, just like the Hanged Man. No fingerprints or smudges. By the smell, it appears the same cleaning solution was used, some kind of detergent with ammonia in it. Whoever did the cleaning was painstakingly careful not to harm the image."

"What do you think that means?" I asked.

"We're dealing with someone who either really cares about tarot cards or was trying to erase all traces of the card's past," Rebecca said.

"Or the owner's identity," I replied.

PEARL

A girl is running through the forest of my canvas, her dark hair on fire, her clothes hanging in rags from her burnt body. In the distance, my subject, the willowy woman, stands on the mound beneath her tree, her chestnut hair hanging long and loose about her waist, her white gown sheer and sparkling from the new sun's light. She is unaware of the girl or her screams. The orange glow has purloined her eyes. The song of the birds, croaks of the frogs, and grunts of the turtles on the beach below have stolen her ears. In my imagination, the girl cries louder, runs faster, but in the world of my canvas, she is frozen in lost hope. She will never reach the willowy woman. In my canvas, she lives between two worlds, that of life waning and death calling.

"Who is the girl running from?" Mr. Smith had asked.

"Me," I said.

"You the person or you the painter?"

"Aren't they one in the same?"

"What's that?" he asked, while pointing to something pink on the ground behind the girl.

"Her headband."

I put down my brush, walk past the sofa where Mr. Smith and I had lain, where despite my mind's confusion, or perhaps because of it, my body shivered. Where are you? Did you see? I flip through my stack of recently stretched canvases to the two finished paintings I've hidden behind them. The ones I have no memory of painting. These I have not shared with Mr. Smith. These I cannot share with anyone. The first, like most of my series, is set in the forest. But this forest is deeper and darker, and there is no willowy woman. There is a tree with a heavy branch. Tied to the branch is a rope. Suspended from the rope is a boy. The second is set in a large grassy field. A tower burns. On either side of the tower, a man and a woman fall headfirst to the ground. Both are on fire.

I knew from a young age that I have the gift of sight. Knowledge comes to me in visions. Disparate lines and colors and shadows seeking the form they will ultimately take. It is the same with my paintings. I see them before I paint them. See them building in my mind. But that didn't happen with these two paintings, or the one from last year.

I was frightened that first time it happened. When the painting of a boy tied to a wooden cross showed up in my studio. A boy on fire. I recognized my brushstrokes, my color palette, my style and form, but I had no memory of painting it. Two days later, a Fourth Year student named Joseph Covington, who was considered the best artist at St. Luke's, disappeared. The student body was told he moved to Italy, but there were whispers. Remember I asked you what I should do with the painting? Remember you didn't respond? But then the very next morning the painting disappeared, and you said perhaps I had imagined it? No other mysterious paintings appeared after that one. Until now.

Now these two recent paintings hold me hostage. I fear destroying them. I fear not destroying them. But I trust what the Great Priestess told me when I asked her why I was painting these murders.

There is a story is unfolding. A story that must be told. A story that will lead to an ending that began a long time ago.

LOLA

Colin was already sitting at our usual table at Maria's when I got there. He had suggested we meet for a late lunch so he could catch me up on his research into the two tarot cards found at the scenes. Maria moved to the island from northern Italy a year before I returned. She made a mean osso buco, and her Bolognese sauce was out of this world. The restaurant was intimate, with only eight tables, all covered with fine white linen tablecloths and small wrought iron sconces. The menu changed daily.

As soon as I sat, Maria came over. She wasn't one to waste time with pleasantries.

"It's mushroom risotto today," she said. "I also have a nice prosciutto-and-melon salad. The cantaloupe is perfectly ripe. And I have a lovely Barolo. A case just arrived this morning."

I rarely declined one of Maria's Barolos. "Sounds perfect," I said.

"Ditto," Colin said. As Maria walked away, he jumped in with an update.

He proceeded to tell me about Joe seeing Abel Montague with a dark-haired girl, which I already knew. Then he segued to what he'd learned about the tarot cards found at our murder scenes. "I heard back from the curator at the Uffizi Gallery, in Florence. She said one of the docents had passed on my message saying it was urgent. She led me to the same two places. The Accademia Carrara in Bergamo, Italy, and the Pierpont Morgan Library in New York. Both said my description of the Hanged Man tarot card sounded like it might be from one of the fifteenth-century Visconti decks, most likely a deck called the Pierpont-Morgan. Accademia Carrara actually has twenty-six cards from that deck in its collection, and the Pierpont Morgan Library has thirty-five. All known others are in private collections. There is no complete deck anywhere. They took my name and number and said they'd refer my quest to some expert. I figured I wouldn't hear back for a while since, unlike the curator of the Uffizi, they seemed dismissive, but a woman called me back right away. A Madame Luna. Said she is considered the expert on Renaissance tarot decks and she travels back and forth between Italy and the US. She's currently in the US. I explained that we now have a second card, the Tower, and described both cards to her. She asked a few questions, about size and imagery, then said the same thing the museums did, that they sounded fifteenth-century. She asked if she could fly down to see the cards in person. Said it's very hard to verify authenticity from photographs."

"You sent her photographs?"

"No. I was going to, but I couldn't get the film processed. The guy I talked to at Gary's Drugs said, given the upcoming storm and preparation, it could take several days to process the film. Apparently Gary and a few other guys are on the mainland stocking up on supplies. But now, with Madame Luna coming, we don't need photos, at least not right away."

"When can she be here?"

"She's taking the first flight out of New York in the morning. It arrives in Charleston at 9:54 A.M. Since it's the closest, I said I'd meet her at the Charleston airport and escort her here. I figure with traffic and the ferry we'll be back around one P.M. But she also cautioned us not to get too excited, that our cards could be from what she called a 'facsimile' deck. Bottom line, if the cards are the real deal, they could be pretty valuable."

"How valuable?"

"Depends on the buyer, but if there is a full intact deck somewhere and it's in pristine condition, it could be worth thousands, maybe millions, of dollars. Single cards would be worth less, of course, but still a lot. Especially if it's the only one in existence. She said each individual card is a work of art in its own right."

"Why would someone leave such valuable tarot cards at a murder scene?" I asked. "Why not use cards from a deck that isn't that rare?"

"Good question," Colin said.

Maria arrived with our orders. "Discussing the murders?" she asked. "I think the Ghost Women have something to do with them."

The statement surprised me. "You believe in the Ghost Women?"

"I'm from Italy," she said. "Ghosts have lived in my country for centuries. Just walk into an ancient cathedral and tell me you don't feel their presence. And I've lived here long enough to have met many Gullah root doctors. Every now and then, they leave poppets and Mojo bags on my door stoop for my protection. I think they're protecting my food more than me. Do you know Priscilla of Priscilla's Antiques? They call her the Swamp Witch. She loves my cannoli."

"My girls love her shop," Colin said.

"We haven't met," I said.

"By the way," Maria said, "the radio is saying we should be preparing for a hurricane. It's expected to arrive day after tomorrow.

The merchants are all getting together to help nail boards on windows. Gary Berman over at the drugstore went to the mainland with a couple of other men to purchase supplies."

It was the most conversational I'd ever heard Maria be.

"We heard," Colin said. "A bunch of the merchants and guys at the station are planning to help. We're meeting at Joe's tonight around seven for a planning session."

"I guess I'll see you then," she said. "What do you think of the wine?"

"It's amazing," I said.

"Agreed," Colin agreed.

"Good," she said, and walked away.

"Maybe we'll get lucky and the eye will at least hit north of us," I said.

"Maybe," he said between bites. "This mushroom risotto is out of this world."

After another glass of Barolo and Maria's decadent struffoli for dessert, we thanked our hostess and chef and went our separate ways, Colin to help out with hurricane preparations and me to the police station.

"You have a message from Joe," Friday said when I greeted her. "Sorry, I didn't write it down. He said to tell you that no one had come in asking for you. He said you'd know what that meant."

"I do," I said. "Thanks. Why are you manning the phones again? You don't have to do that. We have voicemail."

"I enjoy it," she said. "People are always telling me the most interesting stories. Everyone seems to have their own idea of who's doing these murders. The winner at the moment is the Ghost

Women. No surprise there. Though one women insisted that dead monks have been murdering children right under our noses for generations."

"Dead monks?" I asked. "Did she say why she believes that?"

"She was pretty passionate, and a little crazy, I'd say. She went on and on about it in circles, but what I gleaned from what she was saying is that it dates back to when the monks were burning witches. She said the killings never stopped." She smiled. "Oh, by the way, I left you my tarot cards and a book on tarot in case you want to do some research before Madame Luna comes tomorrow. They're on your desk."

"Thanks," I said. "I didn't know you read Tarot."

"I just play around. I do it with friends. We don't really know what we're doing. Our questions usually have to do with romance. It's actually really fun."

I headed to my office to review my notes and make some additional comments on the Tower fire and my day's interactions. I yawned, closed the notebook, sat back in my chair. It felt like it had already been a long day—being called to a murder scene at three A.M. can do that—but I still needed to find out which students had dormitory rooms facing the Tower. Surely someone had seen something. I doubted Alice would share that information. Maybe I could still catch Esme Li.

I stuck Friday's tarot cards and book in my bag and grabbed my car keys.

When I got to St. Luke's, I parked in the lot outside the administrative offices and took the path that led to Studio Row. Before I paid a visit to Esme, I needed to answer one question: Would it have been possible to see the Tower fire from the studios? The studio closest to the Monastery was situated at the highest point of the hilly terrain. Though the Tower structure was crumbled and shorter now, it appeared its crown and certainly the shooting flames would have been visible from there. I kept walking to the studio farthest from the Monastery, passing Esme's studio as I did. She was sitting at her drawing table seemingly lost in her painting. At the last studio, and the terrain's lowest point, the Tower's crown was no longer visible and the fire itself might have been blocked by the twenty-foot arborvitae trees on either side of the pristine grassy meadow. It was possible, however, that the glow of the fire could have been seen through the trees. If garage doors were open, anyone inside should have been able to smell the fire. They might even have been able to hear the commotion.

I doubled back to Esme's studio and announced myself. She looked up but didn't seem too surprised to see me. "You're working late," she said. "Especially since you started your day in the middle of the night." She noticed my questioning glance. "I saw you," she said. "My room is on the back of the Monastery facing the Tower. The sirens woke me. Was anybody hurt?"

The question was disingenuous. Karla had already known there had been two deaths early this morning. And given Esme's status as class liaison, even if she'd been working in her studio all day, there was no way she didn't know. Why pretend otherwise? Was she still following Alice's now senseless directive to keep the murders secret?

"You haven't heard?" I asked. "Two students were killed."

"I'm so sorry to hear that," she said. The lack of eye contact and monotone delivery wasn't lost on me. Esme was not a good liar. "Though I can't imagine how I can help with your investigation."

"Did you happen to see anyone entering or leaving the Tower earlier, before the fire broke out?" I asked.

"No. But I wasn't really looking. I was here at the studio until pretty late. I forget the time when I'm working."

"Who else's dorm rooms are on that side of the Monastery?" I asked.

"Other than me, the three other Second Years who don't live in a cottage and a First Year. George Archambault, Marcus Jones, Hazel Donovan, and Jeannine Hart. There are only five rooms on that side because they're nicer, bigger rooms with balconies. It was supposed to be all Second Years, but when Pearl won the lottery, Jeannine got her room."

"Why did the Second Years get those rooms and not the Third or Fourth Years? Wouldn't they have seniority?"

"It just worked out that way. We stay in the same rooms all four years, and Fourth Years had the rooms before us. It makes a lot more sense than continually moving the entire student body around every time Fourth Years graduate."

I wondered if the students who didn't get those bigger rooms with balconies felt the same way.

"What about Abel? Dean Landry mentioned he had a room on the main floor?"

"Yes. That room is huge. It has its own private entrance. When Abel moved in with Pearl, we all thought the school would begin using that room as a guest suite again. But they didn't. Officially, it's still Abel's room. Abel got all kinds of special treatment given his father's status."

"I imagine Abel's death was hard on his father," I said. I was fishing.

"I don't know," she said, and started biting a nail. I saw they were bitten to the quick.

"You don't know what?" I asked.

"How Mr. Montague feels about Abel's death. Their relationship was pretty strained."

"How do you know that?"

"Pearl told me. Mr. Montague took her and Abel out to dinner a few times when they first started dating, and after they moved in together, he came to their cottage. Pearl said he was very handsome, but rude and aloof, and pretty cruel to Abel. She said he kept checking her out, and not in a curious-about-the-girl-dating-his-son way. 'Slimy' was the word she used."

"I need your help," I said, trying to appeal to Esme's obvious need to feel important. "I'd like to interview your dormitory floor mates. To see if any of them saw something or someone at the Tower this morning. Could you give me directions to their studios?"

"Is Dean Landry aware of this?"

"Of course," I lied. The two glasses of Barolo were boosting my bravery.

She gave me a suspicious look. I didn't elaborate. It was best to keep lies to as few words as possible. Instead, in an attempt to put her at ease and boost her ego, I smiled widely.

"George's studio is next door to mine away from the Monastery," Esme volunteered. "Then Hazel and Marcus and Pearl. Pearl's studio is last. It's the closest to the wrought iron gate that cuts through the brick wall. It's a pretty convenient trek from her studio to her cottage. Eric Bernard's and Jeannine Hart's studios are on the end closest to the Monastery, along with the rest of the First, Third, and Fourth Years. There are metal nameplates on each mailbox. Marcus is in his studio, I think. I haven't seen Pearl or Hazel yet today, their garage doors aren't open, but Marcus's isn't either, he never has it open, so I guess they could be there."

Esme had already made her way to her sofa and was sketching a map of Studio Row. She finished and handed it to me. "I included whose studio is in which building. You know there's also a map of the entire campus available. It was in our First Year welcome packets. I have no idea where mine is, but you could probably ask Christine for one."

I found it odd that this was the first I was hearing about a campus map. Such a map would have been helpful just for routine police inquiries these past few years, and it would be exceptionally helpful now. "Thank you," I said.

"Good luck. The boys, especially, can be difficult to locate. They aren't nearly as responsible as us girls. They get away with murder."

They get away with murder. "Why is that?" I asked.

She rolled her eyes and said, "Because they're boys. Why do you think?"

After I got back in my car, I called Colin and asked him to locate a few of those campus maps for us. "I doubt Alice will give one to me since she hasn't already, but I figure you can charm her out of a hundred if need be." I sensed his sweet Colin smile.

"A hundred campus maps coming right up," he said. "Or maybe ten."

PEARL

It was Karla's idea to do the Banishment spell. *Banishment spells are not the same as Farewell Ceremonies*, she'd said. *They are only done when a dead person inhabits another person or animal and refuses to leave the earth. Bad spirits especially will do anything they can to stay.*

Karla is convinced that your spirit entered the red-eyed owl we saw on her porch after we did your Farewell Ceremony. She says it isn't unusual for spirits to enter a bird or other animal prior to leaving for good.

"How long will it take for the spell to work?" I ask. I'm not sure I want it to work.

"Anywhere from three to seven days," she says. "It could get weird at night, dangerous even. Lucifer and his demons might try to protect him. Wolves might circle our cottages or studios. To be safe, we should keep fire on hand, line our porches and studio fronts with candles or lanterns until we know he's completely gone."

"Will it be painful for Abel?" I ask.

"You mean for the owl?" she asks. "If Abel is inside it, I sure hope so."

Esme arrives just as we begin setting up. "I have everything," she says. "I was freaking out because Detective Germany showed up."

"What did she want?" Karla asks.

"The names of the students whose dorm rooms face the Tower," Esme responds. "Thank god I'd already put the stuff for the spell in my backpack."

It feels odd with just the three of us. Neither Karla nor Esme have mentioned inviting Hazel. I assume Karla doesn't want to upset me, given your and Hazel's relationship, but I'm not sure why Esme hasn't. I'm happy no one invited her, but for an entirely different reason. I haven't told anyone, even Karla, about the Revenge spell I did when I found out about you and Hazel. I stuck the black-tipped pins into your hearts to break the two of you apart. But when you died, I thought I must have gotten some part of the spell wrong. And now there have been two more murders. What if Hazel is one of them?

Karla lights the candles; then the three of us don the blood robes, circle our eyes with black chalk, and hold hands. Over and over, we chant, "Stop the dead man's interference. Cleanse him, take him, hasten his journey." And somewhere between the second and third chant, I see your molecules spinning, swirling faster and faster like a funnel cloud, and then your face emerges and you look directly at me and I see great pain and sadness in your eyes and I want so badly to comfort you, but the cloud swallows you. I feel tears running down my cheeks as the three of us utter the spell's final words. Together we thank the Great Priestess and cross our hearts. Then Karla lights a match, tosses it into the cauldron, and we watch you burn.

LOLA

I flashed my badge when he opened the door to his studio. I had knocked on a few other doors, but he was the only one who'd answered. "Are you Mr. Marcus Jones?" I asked.

"I am," he said. "But you can ditch the 'Mr. Jones' part. 'Marcus' is good."

"My name is Detective Lola Germany. I'm looking into the death of Abel Montague and last night's fire at the Tower. Is this a good time?"

"Sure." He stepped back, opened the door wider.

I walked past him into the studio. The walls of the space were covered with huge abstract not-quite paintings. They were comprised of keys, photographs, clock faces, compasses, antique watches, portions of old balusters, letterpress letters, a broken hammerhead, antique chess pieces, and so much more.

"They're fascinating," I said. "I love the palette and the found objects, the industrial simplicity but complicated arrangement. What do you call them? They're not really paintings."

"Assemblages," he said. "Sorry about the mess. I don't get guests very often. Here, let me move these books." There were stacks everywhere. Old and new, hardbacks and paperbacks, open and closed. Underneath the stack in question was a wooden bench. I sat while he grabbed an old crate and sat on it. "Can I get you something to drink? I have sodas and beer." He checked his watch. "It's getting close to that time, I guess."

"No, I'm fine," I said.

"Just so you know, I'm not supposed to speak to you."

"Why not?"

"Alice in Wonderland," he said. I was flattered he'd used Alice's nickname. None of the girls had. "It's not just you," he continued. "We need permission before we speak to anyone outside the school. There are so many rules here. Believe me, if I didn't want the payoff in the end, I would have quit after the first week."

"Payoff?"

"Fame and fortune," he said. His smile lit up his face. He was handsome. Did I imagine that his chiseled features matched the hard yet contoured edges of his art?

"I can leave, if you'd prefer. I don't want to place you in an uncomfortable position."

"You aren't," he said. "Really. I imagine you're here to talk about Abel Montague?"

"Yes, how well did you know him?"

"As well as any of us, I guess. It's a small school. The school and all the instructors considered him the best artist here."

"Did you consider him the best?"

"Joseph Covington was by far the best artist at St. Luke's. But since he disappeared, I guess some might say Abel was."

"Joseph Covington?"

"He was a Fourth Year when my class were First Years. All the instructors said he was the best artist St. Luke's had ever seen. But then, lucky for Abel, Joseph quit and moved to Italy. Nobody understood why. He was set to graduate and had already signed with a gallery. But I kind of understood. Fame isn't for everyone. Sometimes you find yourself going down a road you never intended to."

He was smiling when I glanced up from my notes. He cocked his head. Looked to the side as if thinking. "You asked about Abel. May I be honest?"

"Please," I said.

"Abel Montague was an asshole. Rich, entitled, chauvinistic, drank and partied continually. Everyone knew he slipped drugs into women's drinks so he could have sex with them. Sometimes he forgot the drugs and just pushed himself on them. Where I come from, we call that rape. Here, they call it an overactive libido. He thought everything and everyone belonged to him to do with as he pleased. But we learn here to separate the art from the artist. Was he the best? In my opinion, his paintings were among the best, but art is so subjective. And there's an amazing wealth of talent at St. Luke's."

Marcus's candor was refreshing. "I appreciate your honesty. What about his girlfriend? Pearl Calhoun?"

"Are you asking if I consider Pearl the best?"

"I was just asking what you think of her. But since you brought it up, what do you think of her talent?"

"Let me put it this way: If Pearl wasn't a girl, the entire school would think she was the best. We're kind of chauvinistic around here. I'm obviously no better. I honestly didn't even think of her when you first asked the question, but I should have. I consider Pearl a friend. Her studio is right next door. I know Abel's death has been hard on her, but she'd never tell me or anyone how she really is."

The comment felt more genuine than anything I'd heard about Pearl from the Weird Sisters. Marcus obviously cared for Pearl.

"Why do you think Pearl was with Abel?"

"We can't always help who we are attracted to. In Pearl's defense, Abel was a con artist. He was good at reading people and figuring out how to pull them in. I don't really know why she continued to stay with him. Maybe he just never stopped conning her, or maybe she denied what she knew. We all do that."

Was he talking from experience, or was he keenly perceptive? I was noticing that many of St. Luke's students exhibited insight and perception beyond their years.

"It seems Abel might have been seeing someone on the side, a First Year named Jeannine Hart." I'd purposefully dropped the name.

"Jeannine Hart? That girl was after Abel, not the other way around."

"Abel wasn't sleeping with her?"

"I didn't say that. He probably was. But he wasn't *into* her."

"Do you know of someone else he may have been seeing?"

"Not for certain, but I did overhear him telling George Archambault in the cafeteria a week or two ago that he was into Hazel."

Pearl had already mentioned that Abel and Hazel were seeing each other, but Marcus's statement confirmed that others knew as well.

"What was he saying? In the cafeteria, I mean."

"Basically, that he was interested in her. But that he didn't want to just use her. Which surprised me. But also made me angry."

"Why angry?"

"Because of Pearl."

"Did he mention Pearl?"

"He said he'd been trying to figure out how to let Pearl down easy. Pretty much since they moved in together. That he'd only moved in with her because she got the cottage. He hated the dorm. Said it was below his station. That's the word he used, 'station.' Even though he had the best room. That room is like a suite."

While I had a feeling Abel had an ulterior motive for being with Hazel, I doubted it was because of the cottage. “How do you think he got that room?”

“Just like he got everything else none of the rest of us got. His dad is chair of the board and one of the school’s founders. Believe me, Alice in Wonderland does nothing around here without Monty Montague’s permission.”

“Did Pearl know that? That he was considering leaving her?”

“I sure didn’t tell her.”

“I don’t understand,” I said. “I mean, it’s one thing to sleep around, not that I’m excusing that, but if he was actually interested in someone else, why not just break up with Pearl?”

“He figured if he treated her like shit, she’d dump him. Guys do that all the time. Think about it. If he broke it off with Pearl, especially if he was interested in someone else, like Hazel, her good friend, then he’d be the bad guy. Here’s the thing: Abel was a total narcissist, maybe even a sociopath. People like that don’t care about anyone but themselves. He was fine with Pearl as long as she worshipped him, but I’m betting once he started living with her, some of her worshipping wore off. And then there was Hazel, or someone like her, a new worshipper. It fed him.”

I felt myself involuntarily shudder. We had studied narcissists, sociopaths, and psychopaths at the police academy, but I also had personal knowledge of their behavioral characteristics.

“You mentioned Abel’s paintings being among the best. I saw Karla’s and Esme’s and now yours. I find it interesting that in all cases, the art feels like an extension of the artist. Do you think that was the case with Abel’s paintings?”

He smiled. “That’s perceptive. It’s so weird, but I’ve been thinking about that since I heard about his murder. Wondering whether Abel would be at peace with where he left his work or, if there’s such a thing as an afterlife, if he feels cheated out of finishing what he was exploring. But you're asking about style, right?"

He didn't wait for me to respond.

"First of all, his paintings were huge. Well, I guess I should say *are* huge. He might be dead, but his paintings are still alive. Stylistically, some might call it color-field painting. You might even say it's derivative of the abstract expressionists of the '50s. Mark Rothko especially." He laughed. "Abel would hate me calling his work derivative. Large areas of black and gray with minimal areas of primary color. Red, yellow, blue. From a distance, they appear simply as space and form. But if you look closer at the achromatic areas, you see layers and layers of paint and hidden color inside the black. Deep blues and browns and even white. The first time I saw one of his paintings, I expected all those layers to feel coarse and rough to the touch. But they weren't, they were smooth. Luscious even. He called them *Contradictions*. What's weird is that if his paintings were, as you say, an extension of Abel, then his art would say he knew that about himself and was studying it, maybe even fighting who he knew he was. It's fascinating if you think about it. The artist was a total asshole, but his paintings were exquisite. If that's not a contradiction, I don't know what is."

The explanation intrigued me. I tried to record as much of what Marcus was saying about Abel's work as I could so I could study it later. It was rare for a victim to leave something so tangible behind, something that could provide clues to who he was and potentially why he was murdered.

"I just have a few more questions," I said to Marcus.

"Shoot."

"Are you aware of these claims that the ghosts of the women burned at the stake in the fifteenth century still roam St. Luke's?"

"Everybody's aware of those stories," he said. "The Fourth Years hold bonfires down at the beach where they reenact the burnings. It's a tradition. Something the graduating Fourth Years pass on to the incoming Fourth Years. They stuff women's clothes to look like people, tie the dummies to stakes, and light them on fire. 'Witch dummies,' they call them. I don't go. I think it's sick."

"Do you believe the spirits of the dead witches roam St. Luke's?"

"I don't know. I wouldn't be surprised. If I'd been so brutally murdered, I might be inclined to wander the grounds of the place where it happened. What's that got to do with Abel's murder?"

"I suppose it's more to do with where we found his body. Hanging from the Ghost Tree. Do you know anything about the fire at the Tower early this morning? I understand your dorm room at the Monastery overlooks it."

"I overheard someone talking about it when I went out for a smoke earlier, but I don't know that much about it. I slept here at the studio last night. I do that most nights." He pointed at a cot with a rumpled blanket in the back.

"You didn't hear or see it?"

"The Tower is pretty far from here. And you're the first person that's knocked on my door. I did sit by George at dinner last night. He said he was going up there to hang out with 'some chick.' His words. You might want to ask him about it."

"Do you mean George Archambault?" I asked. "Do you think he went?"

"I have no idea. He's a big talker. Abel and George were tight, you know. And Eric Bernard. He's a Third Year. Cohorts in crime. They chased girls together. Covered for each other."

I wrote down Eric Bernard's name.

"Do you have any idea who the girl was, the one George Archambault was going to meet?"

"He didn't say. At least while I was there. I left before they did."

"'They'?"

"Eric was there too, and some other guys. Sorry, I thought I mentioned that."

"How would he have gotten into the Tower?" I asked. "I thought it was kept locked?"

"That means nothing around here. Alice in Wonderland keeps the keys in her desk, but she leaves the drawers unlocked. Everyone knows that."

It was time to drop the hammer and note his reaction. "Two students died in the fire."

His face registered surprise. "Oh wow. Who? Was it an accident?" Recognition dawned on his face. "Geez. Was George one of them?"

"We haven't identified the victims yet."

Unlike Esme, he seemed genuinely surprised.

"You didn't answer my question, so you must think they were murdered," he said. "Should I be worried? Should we all be worried?"

"I think you all should be cautious," I said.

"So someone is killing St. Luke's students?" he asked. "Wow. Do you have any idea who?"

I gave him my standard response. "We are following all leads."

"Guess I need to start locking my doors at night," he said sarcastically. "Oh, that's right. There are no locks at St. Luke's."

I stood. "Thank you, Marcus. You've been most helpful. Do you happen to know where Jeannine Hart's studio is?"

"Two from the end closest to the Monastery, but I doubt she's there right now."

"Why is that?"

"It's Art Sunday."

"Art Sunday?"

"There's a social gathering at the Monastery every Sunday night at eight. Lasts most of the night. Sunday is the only day that Alice in Wonderland can't keep tabs on us. No classes. No critiques. So she created Art Sunday."

I checked my watch. It was ten minutes to. "Sorry, I didn't mean to keep you. I had no idea it was this late."

"I don't attend. Total waste of time. Alice in Wonderland gives a stupid pep talk about how famous we all will be, and everyone walks around and praises each other's work, even though our work isn't even there and no one really has any idea what everyone else is currently exploring. I'm betting there will be no mention of a killer on the loose. No one talks about bad things or things that make any sense around here. Everything is Mad Hatters and talking caterpillars."

And secrets, I thought.

PEARL

I am sitting alone in the dark on Karla's front porch holding a sharp kitchen knife for protection and listening to the sounds of wolves howling, owls hooting, and the occasional growl of a bear. She and Esme left for Art Sunday right after the spell. I said I wasn't feeling well. But the truth was the Banishment spell unsettled me. I've sat on Karla's porch many times in the dark, but tonight it's different. Something very bad is going to happen. Though I can't yet see it, I *feel* it. It is as if the spell opened up some sort of portal to the underworld.

I hear the tap-tap of footsteps in the distance. Someone on the cobblestone path. My body stiffens. It's too early for Karla's return. A shadow is making its way down the walk, veering off toward the forest's east entrance. The figure is slight, carries a satchel, and wears a hooded cape. She looks in my direction. *Hazel.*

For a moment, it feels like I've seen a ghost. My heart pounds. I'm relieved that my spell didn't kill her. That she didn't die in the Tower fire. But where is she going? I nearly call out but stop myself as she slips through the trees, the cape billowing behind her. I recall the painting she just finished, another one of her creepy elongated-figure fairy-tale paintings, Little Red Riding Hood tromping through the forest with teeth-bared wolves on her tail. She always dresses like the characters in her paintings when she's working on them. Thus the red cape, I take it. Lately, she's been experimenting with expanding the flat painted characters of her canvases to theatrical tableaux vivants. She sews the costumes, buys the fabric at a place in town called Flora's Fabrics, and pays First Years to model. Hazel's family is super rich. The productions and props add a level of disturbance that her paintings lack. Sweet fairy-tale characters juxtaposed with their frightening and evil counterparts. Big, scary bears with spread claws bending over a crouched Goldilocks. Cinderella's stepsisters holding pitchforks and caught mid-stride as they chase her. The old witch preparing to light the oven where Hansel and Gretel crouch. It's the motionless pose of the actors and the stilled terror on their faces that makes them so intriguing, the sense that they've been caught just before the tragedy occurs. They're promising. Perhaps this new direction will give her the confidence that to date she's lacked. I think sometimes you have to be fully immersed in an environment before you find your place inside it.

Just then, the sharp sound of dishes hitting the floor draws my attention to our cottage. I jump. My tea set? I look toward the cottage. Through the window on our porch, I see the beam of a flashlight playing across the walls. Someone is inside. What are they looking for? How did they enter the cottage without me seeing them? The beam is now on the wall above my sideboard. My stomach drops. What if whoever it is finds the tarot cards? What if whoever it is took the five missing cards and has come back for more?

Then I hear another set of footsteps on the cobblestone path. These more purposeful. Karla. Thank god. I breathe a sigh of relief. I can't let her see me or she might call out. I slip off the rocker and crouch behind it. She trots up the porch steps.

"Pearl," she says. "Is that you? What are doing back there?"

"Shh. Someone is in my cottage." I point at the flashlight beam.

Her eyes follow my finger. "Who is that?" she whispers, obviously alarmed. "Let's go inside. We can watch from the window while we think what to do."

I hold my breath as she opens the screen door, hear the squeak of the hinges. I sneak a peek at our cottage. No change in the beam. We walk inside. And then it happens. Karla lets go of the door. The clap of the door hitting the frame echoes in the night air. We both freeze.

"Maybe they didn't hear it," Karla whispers.

The beam of the flashlight goes dark. A full minute goes by before we hear the squawk and swoop of a large bird coming toward us. A great horned owl lands on the railing of Karla's porch and stares straight at us. We gasp in unison. Because instead of yellow, its eyes glow bright red in the night sky.

LOLA

I radioed Colin as soon as I got into my car. "I just met with Marcus Jones. He said George Archambault was going to the Tower last night."

"Rebecca just called to say she got the files from St. Luke's and identified the bodies. The male is George Archambault and the female is Jeannine Hart."

"Jeannine Hart? Is she certain?" When Hazel Donovan didn't show for our meeting at Joe's, I'd jumped to the conclusion the female was her.

"She verified both victims against dental and medical records," Colin said. "George Archambault lost his front teeth playing hockey in high school. Jeannine Hart had a large mole removed from her back when she was a kid. Location matches the scar Rebecca found on the female victim's back."

"Has Alice Landry been informed?" I asked.

"I'm heading to the Monastery now," he said. "Christine mentioned she was at some sort of student function in the Worship Room."

"Okay, good." It was better that Colin be the one to deliver the news to Alice. Perhaps he could convince her we were dealing with a murderer. She wouldn't doubt the word of a man. "Let me know if you need me."

"Will do. What are you up to?"

"Since Karla Gardyn and Pearl Calhoun are likely at that same function, I think I'll head back to Pearl's cottage to do some sleuthing. I have a hunch."

I decided to take the trail that ran along the south side of the forest so I'd be on the back side of Karla's and Pearl's cottages. The overcast skies made for a dark run. The sounds of scurrying animals were enough to test my nerves, but at one point I swore I heard footsteps. I shined my flashlight in their direction. Nothing. Took a few steps forward and heard them again. "Is anyone there?" I called. Now my heart was pounding. There was a murderer loose. What had I been thinking to set off on such a rarely used trail at this time of night? Since I was too far into my journey, turning back made no sense, so I kept moving, taking care to continually check the surroundings. Finally, I saw the two cottages maybe fifty feet ahead. Both were pitch-dark. Good, the girls had gone to Art Sunday. I remembered seeing stairs in Pearl's kitchen when I interviewed her. I had assumed they led to a cellar. But I found myself standing before the back of a walk-out basement complete with a ground-level door and window. I peeked inside—completely dark—and then turned the door handle. It was locked or stuck. After wriggling it a few times, I decided to try the window. It opened. I crawled inside, turned on the flashlight, and shined it through the space. A few cardboard boxes were stacked in one corner, one filled with random gadgets, high school yearbooks, *Playboy* magazines, and a baseball glove, and another with an armless Raggedy Ann doll, a broken teapot, a Betty and Veronica comic book, and several art books with library envelopes still inside the front covers. I hadn't taken Pearl for a book thief, but the thought of it brought a smile to my face, as I'd been known to pilfer library books as well, especially when the books were out of print. I headed upstairs, rummaged through kitchen drawers and cabinets, dresser drawers, under the bed, and inside the closet. And then something odd occurred. I found myself inextricably drawn to the blank wall behind the Mies van der Rohe chairs. I was certain there had been a large painting on the wall the last time I was there. I remembered a forest, the figure of a woman. I had wanted to look at it more closely, but Pearl hadn't invited me to. Where had the painting gone? I ran my flashlight along the wall, saw a light line of paint in the shape of a large rectangle. Rubbed my fingers over it and looked at their tips. Green. Held the fingers to my nose. Turpentine.

A sharp crash behind me. I jumped. Turned. Pearl's tea service had fallen off the coffee table. I hadn't touched it. I was nowhere near it. I expected there to be shards splattered across the floor, but it appeared totally intact. I waited for a good minute before I peeked out the window closest to the front door. Nothing. I shined my flashlight on the wall perpendicular to the window. I'd completely forgotten about the altar. I set down the flashlight, removed the covering and candles. A solid top and deep front and sides, but oddly there were no drawers. I felt under the bottom. There was something there. A latch. I worked at it.

A loud clap drew my attention to Karla's cottage. The screen door.

Shit.

I turned off the flashlight, quickly returned the covering and candles to the sideboard's top, ran back downstairs, opened the basement door, and intended to run back down the path. But there, not even three feet before me, blocking my way, was a great horned owl with large piercing red eyes that were staring directly at me. It had to be the same owl I'd seen on Karla's porch the night I saw the girls chanting and wearing the red robes. I was keenly aware that I was alone with a creature that could sever my spine. I wasn't sure how long we stood there staring at one another. Terror has a way of slowing time. And then, for no obvious reason, the owl decided to end our game of dare. It swiveled its head, spread its wings, which had to be four feet across, and flew around the corner of the cottage.

I ran and didn't stop until I got home.

PEARL

The owl is perched on Karla's porch rail, its red eyes staring at us through her window. It came from the direction of the walking path behind our cottage, the one that leads to the beach. It is huge, around two feet tall and stocky, with mottled grayish-brown coloring on the majority of its body, white plumage on its chin, tall feather tufts on the top of its head that resemble horns or ears, a hooked black bill, and white halos circling its red pupils. I have never seen such a beast of an owl, at least this close up. It's not just the eyes that remind me of you. It's the stoic posture and piercing focus. I feel a flutter in my stomach. The same nervous flutter I felt the first time you looked at me.

"What is it doing here?" Karla asks. "And that sound he made when he flew toward us just now, he sure seems angry."

I see you? I silently say.

Who-who-whoo-whoo-who.

"He's staring right at you," Karla says. "Be careful. He might rip through the screen on the door. Their talons can kill."

"I don't think he wants to hurt us," I say. "I think he's here to warn us."

The full force of my words bears down on me, and I open the screen door, and as if it is trying to tell me something, the owl's eyes meet mine; then it spreads its wings and flies into the air, and I follow. "Where are you going?" I hear Karla say behind me. But I don't look back. Periodically, it flies in circles, waiting for me to catch up. Then we are at the gate that breaches the brick wall surrounding St. Luke's, the one that leads to Studio Row. I key in the code and follow the owl to my studio. The owl alights on a nearby post. Our eyes meet as I open the studio's side door and walk in. And there, leaning against that same stack of freshly stretched canvases, is a new painting, still wet and smelling strongly of turpentine. A lone skeleton stands holding a crooked staff with a white fabric ribbon fluttering from its tip. Trump 13, Death, one of the five tarot cards that went missing from my special deck. Like the Hanged Man and the Tower, I have no memory of painting it.

And I know I have been right to be frightened. Because now, I don't only *feel* that something bad is going to happen. I *know* that someone is going to die tonight.

PART THREE

Death

Death and the corresponding transience of life were never far from the minds of the Renaissance Italians . . . The skull became the focus of this preoccupation. It was what remained once the body has decayed.

—HELEN FARLEY,
A CULTURAL HISTORY OF TAROT

Day 4

Three Days After the Autumnal Equinox
Monday, September 25, 1972

LOLA

The first time I checked the time, it was around two A.M. I closed my eyes, hoping sleep would come, praying the phone wouldn't ring with the announcement of another murder. The minutes ticked by. My mind vacillated between wondering whether I was doing all I could to find the murderer and a deep sense of fear and foreboding. I had never been particularly psychic, but I knew whoever was doing this wasn't done. At around three A.M., about the same time as I'd risen the morning before, I decided to quit chasing sleep. I put on my running clothes and headed to my tree. It was still dark when I arrived, so I sat with my back against it, closed my eyes, listened to the sounds of the forest and its creatures. I woke just before daybreak. The thin orange line had already formed into a sphere and was rising into the sky. And for a moment, thoughts of the murders were replaced by that familiar tingling sensation. For me, watching the sunrise was a religious experience, the closest I ever felt to the supreme force many referred to as God. And so I stood there, basking in the new sun's light, for as long as I could.

But as always, by the time I got to the station, the feeling had left.

"Colin called twice," Friday said. She handed me the messages. I proceeded to my office, got situated, and read. The first said, *At airport waiting on Madame Luna's plane.* The second said, *Madame Luna's plane delayed two hours. Maintenance issue.*

My phone buzzed just as I finished reading. "Yes?" I said to Friday.

"A Karla Gardyn is on the phone? She sounds upset."

"Put her through." I hung up the phone, waited for the buzz, and answered.

"Detective Germany?" She sounded alarmed and out of breath. "It's Karla Gardyn. Mr. Bones is on the veranda."

"Mr. Bones?"

"Our school skeleton. We use him in anatomy class. To learn the bones and muscles for figure drawing. It's mostly a First Year class."

I was confused why this news had warranted a breathless call to me. "I don't understand. Is the class meeting on the veranda?"

"No. It's just him. He's always popping up around campus. It's kind of a thing, but this is different. I mean, I thought that's what it was at first, but then I saw the roses and the blood and the position of his head and the card."

"Wait, did you say 'blood'?"

"Yes, and the tarot card. Death. Trump 13."

Death? "Where are you now?" I asked.

"At school. I'm calling from the main office. Dean Landry isn't here."

"I'll be right there," I said. "Meet you on the veranda?"

I slammed down the phone, hurried to my cruiser, and drove to St. Luke's.

KARLA

"Why am I the one who keeps finding bodies?" I asked as Detective Germany inspected the scene on the veranda outside the Monastery. "Well, I suppose a skeleton isn't a body exactly, but it's weird, don't you think? What with the Death card and all? And I can't find Pearl."

"What do you mean, you can't find Pearl?"

"She ran off last night after this huge owl with red eyes that she thinks is Abel. When I saw she hadn't returned this morning, I was going to go looking for her, but I had my monthly meeting with my advisor, Miss Blumenthal. That's when I first saw Mr. Bones sitting there, but I was running late, and I honestly didn't think much of it. As I mentioned, Mr. Bones is always showing up in random places. Though I admit I did find those black roses odd, eerie, actually. Anyway, I figured I'd go look for Pearl at her studio as soon as my meeting was over, but then, when I came back out and took a closer look at Mr. Bones, I saw that the roses were *painted* black. Then I saw what looked like smears of blood on his skull, so I followed it down his arms to the teacup, and I'm like, why a *china* teacup, and why a *teacup*, for that matter, and there it was. The tarot card. I immediately went down to Dean Landry's office, but she wasn't there and neither was Christine, so I looked up the station's number on Christine's Rolodex and called you. Sorry, I know I'm babbling. I do that when I'm nervous or weirded out. My mum and aunts always say I'm the girl who fills silent spaces. A lot of people find it irritating, I know, so I have been working on these not-talking and talking-only-when-talked-to exercises. Though I pretty much fail miserably. Anyway, I never got to Pearl's studio."

"I'm sure Pearl is fine," she said. "Are you the only student who saw this? I'm just wondering why no one else reported it."

"A bunch of students had to have seen it. A few walked by while I was examining it. They even talked and laughed about it. It's what I said about him always showing up in weird places. I guess for the most part we're used to him, so no one looks that close anymore."

"And yet you did," she said.

"Maybe I overreacted? It could just be a practical joke, I guess. What with all the murders, some of the students, the boys mostly, are acting all tough and making sick stupid jokes about it all."

"You did the right thing to call me." She bent over the table, took a closer look at the Death card.

"Were the Hanged Man and Tower cards old too?" I asked. The truth was the card looked similar to the ones Pearl found in the sideboard she got at Priscilla's Antiques, which worried me. But then again Priscilla sold lots of tarot decks. She could have others that looked like Pearl's, couldn't she?

Detective Germany shot back up and looked into my eyes. "How did you know tarot cards were found at those other murder scenes?"

"Esme told me." I immediately regretted saying it.

She shook her head as if she was exasperated. "Who else knows?"

"No one," I said. She didn't appear to believe me. "I promise I just learned about the tarot cards last night. At Art Sunday. Esme told me. She said I couldn't tell anyone. She'll get in trouble if Dean Landry finds out she told anyone."

"What about Hazel? Does she know about the tarot cards?"

"I don't know," I said. "We haven't seen much of Hazel. She's been busy preparing for her advisor meeting." It was a lie. Well, it could be true, but the real reason was we'd been ignoring her because Abel was cheating on Pearl with Hazel.

"What makes you think this card is old?" she asked.

"It just looks old, I guess," I said, then added, "There's this store down on Marsh Road called Priscilla's Antiques. The owner knows a lot about Tarot and all kinds of occult and spiritual practices. She's a rootworker, you know, practices hoodoo. She's really cool. Her family has lived on the island for generations. Maybe she could help with the age of the cards."

Detective Germany was writing something down on her notepad. I couldn't tell whether she'd heard me or not. She backed up, assessed the scene from a distance. There was that look on her face again, the one that meant her mind was working. I'd seen it a few times now. When she went into thinking mode, she raised her chin and squinted.

"You said Mr. Bones is kept in the anatomy room?" she asked. "Can you take me there?"

LOLA

I followed Karla through the hallways. There were students carrying huge black portfolios. A memory popped into my mind of the one and only visual art course I took at Juilliard. It was a windy day, and I had just walked outside carrying a similarly large portfolio when a gust of wind grabbed ahold of it, pulling both of us sideways. One of my instructors, who also danced for the New York City Ballet, saw me struggling and grabbed the portfolio before it took me with it into the sky. That instructor later became my husband.

"Here it is," Karla said. "The anatomy classroom."

At first, I thought it looked and smelled like any other art classroom—drawing horses, charcoal pieces and paint splotches on the floor, mild scent of fear and sweat—but then I caught a whiff of some sort of astringent. Bleach? Ammonia? Perhaps the floor was recently mopped? The charcoal pieces said otherwise. I could almost hear the instructor shouting words of judgment to some and promise to the select few he or she had decided were worthwhile. It was the nature of all the arts. No different in my dance classes. The talent hierarchy was established on the very first day. The instructor, all instructors, chose whom they would support and whom they would shame until the student quit. The instructor's excuse? Better that students learn early on that they don't have what it takes. But who was to say the bias of the instructor didn't enter into that equation? We, all artists, were drawn to a particular aesthetic. To a student's appearance. To our own idea of what constituted art.

"Where does the skeleton normally stand?" I asked.

"On that stage," Karla said while pointing to a raised wood platform roughly eight feet square and six inches off the floor. "But Mr. Bones is not always the subject. Sometimes there are live models."

"Where is he kept when he's not the model?"

"That closet." Karla pointed to a door at the back of the room. She began walking toward it. I followed her. The closer I got, the stronger the smell of bleach and ammonia. I felt a familiar dread.

"What is that smell?" Karla asked.

I turned the knob.

A body was slumped on the floor. The scene was grotesque. I immediately wondered how the murderer was able to overpower and carry out the crime given the victim's size. He was large and muscular with white-blond hair. His blue eyes were open, pupils clouded, facial skin scorched bright red, the texture in some places resembling uncooked hamburger meat, lips nearly burned off. It appeared whoever did this had poured a caustic liquid down his throat until he drowned. Something white was peeking through the blood atop his head.

His skull.

Then I saw the poppet. I had been so focused on his face and head, I didn't see it at first. Handmade, burlap, with a black pearl–tipped pin stuck in its heart.

I felt faint and nauseated. I wondered if I'd ever get over this reaction to a dead body, though arguably the last three had been particularly repulsive. I turned to look at Karla as I leaned against the wall to steady myself. Her eyes were wide, her shock and fear palpable. I was the detective here. I had to maintain composure.

"I need to sit," she said, and all but dropped into a nearby drawing horse. "I feel like I might throw up." Her face was white.

"Bend down," I said. "Put your head between your knees. Deep breaths."

She did as I said.

"I know him," she said in between breaths. "It's Eric Bernard. He is—I mean he was—in my class. A Third Year. I just saw him last night at Art Sunday."

I remembered writing the name in my notepad after Marcus Jones mentioned it. *Cohorts in crime*, Marcus had said of him, Abel Montague, and George Archambault. *They chased girls together. Covered for each other.*

"I need to use the phone," I said. "To call for an ambulance and the medical examiner. Are you okay to stay here alone?"

"I'll be fine," she said.

On my way to the office, I considered Karla's reaction to the murder. She was either a very good actress or she had nothing to do with Eric Bernard's death. She was also right: Both doors, the one to the main office and the one to Alice's office, were wide open, and neither Christine nor Alice were at their desks. I grabbed Christine's phone, dialed.

"I'm at the Monastery," I said when Friday answered. "There's another body. Do me a favor and call Rebecca Beach and Barney Cougar, would you? And if Colin happens to call back in, let him know?"

"Oh my gosh, that's awful. Of course," she said, and rang off.

"Can I help you?" I heard a woman's voice say.

I looked up to see Christine. "Sorry. I needed to use the phone. There's been another murder."

"Oh my," Christine said.

"Where's the closest bathroom?" I asked her.

"Just down the hall to the right," she said.

When I got there, I went into one of the stalls and just sat. Attempted to center myself. Slow, deep breaths. I kept seeing Eric Bernard's face. These murders were vicious and hateful, the victims stripped of all dignity. Abel Monague was not just hanged. He was hanged upside down in the manner of a traitor. George Archambault and Jeannine Hart were burned beyond recognition. And now Eric Bernard's face was also burned off, but with bleach instead of fire. Why? Why so brutal? As if the murderer had wanted to burn away their identities, erase them. I paused. *Burned*, I thought. Just like the accused witches back in the fifteenth century. *Is there a connection?*

And why the poppets? Why those in addition to the tarot cards? On the surface, it appeared the murders were part of some sort of ritual connected to the Ghost Women. And then there was art itself, the "paintings in space" Karla had mentioned. I thought about the poppets on the Unmarked Tombstone in the Garden of Angels. Did the killer want us to believe the Gullah were somehow involved? Or their magic? But that didn't make sense. They were known to be highly spiritual and superstitious, but not dangerous. Could the poppets be a ruse, meant to throw us off track?

Both Karla and Pearl had mentioned the same store on Marsh Road. Maria and Colin knew of it too. What was it called? I flipped through my notes. Priscilla's Antiques. *The owner knows a lot about Tarot and all kinds of occult and spiritual practices. She's a rootworker, you know, practices hoodoo*, Karla had said. I flipped back to my interview with Pearl. *I got it at Priscilla's*, she said when referring to her sideboard. *She's an expert on the witch trials and burnings that took place on the island.*

A memory came to me of tagging along with my father once when he went to see a woman who practiced rootwork and conjure. She had one blue eye and one brown eye. I was just a child, but I remembered being mesmerized by the flickering candles, the thin dancing swirl of the incense smoke, and the tools of her trade that were spread across the table. A Mojo bag filled with conjure oils and herbs, sparkling crystals, bones and seashells, and a small pile of dirt. I had specifically asked her what the dirt was for. "It's from your mother's grave," she'd said. "It will help us connect to her spirit."

I needed to pay Priscilla's a visit.

PEARL

The envelope that was pushed under my door is definitely from Hazel. The flowery cursive of my name and the abundance of heart and star stickers are a dead giveaway. Letters are a total Hazel thing. If she's involved in even the mildest disagreement, she writes a letter of apology. If she reads an article that she thinks someone might like, she clips and tapes it to a letter. All the Weird Sisters have been recipients of envelopes sporting heart and star stickers. When I first met Hazel, her breezy femininity and ease with fake sweetness and kindness had immediately reminded me of some of the mean girls at the orphanage and made me distrust her. Later I questioned that distrust, chastised my prejudice, but then I saw her with Abel. I've been staring at the envelope ever since I found it under my door. Waffling on whether to read it or burn it.

An earnest knock at my front door. "Pearl, are you in there?"

I rise, stick the envelope under one of the cushions of the green leather sofa, and open the door. Karla rushes in and plops down right where I put the envelope. “Oh, thank god, I was worried about you. Where were you?”

“In my studio,” I say. “I fell asleep.”

“Something horrible happened,” she says. “Eric Bernard is dead. I was at the Monastery. I had my monthly critique with Miss Blumenthal.” She proceeds to tell me about finding Mr. Bones, the Death card, the teacup, the painted black rose, and the poppet, then calling my ballerina detective and finding Eric Bernard’s body. “The poppet looked just like the one I saw at the Ghost Tree when Abel was murdered. Actually, it looked kind of like the ones you make, but I didn’t really look that close. Because later when I saw Eric’s face—oh my god. Someone had poured bleach and something else on it. The skin was burnt and blistered so bad I hardly recognized him. His eyes. Pearl, they were so cloudy you could barely tell they were blue. And I could see his skull through his head. I will never get that image out of my mind. By the way, are you missing a teacup? The one there sure looked a lot like one of yours. Little pink roses on white. Same pattern.”

“Not that I know of,” I say. We head to the kitchen and count all the teacups and saucers. “There are seven cups and eight saucers,” I say.

“How many did you have?” Karla asks.

“Eight of each.”

“Why would someone steal one of your teacups?” Karla asks. “And come to think of it, is your tarot deck missing any cards?”

My stomach drops. I feel caught. I can't lie to Karla. She was with me when I found the tarot deck in the sideboard, the day she helped me bring it into the cottage. Karla had suggested we celebrate the purchase by reading the cards with the Weird Sisters later that night. I had wanted to show off my find, but even while doing the reading, it had felt wrong. As if I were betraying something so much larger than me, something sacred. I had painstakingly cleaned them to get rid of everyone else's energy. I never invited them or anyone to read the cards again. But the size and gilding are hard to forget. And in that moment, I realize that one of the Weird Sisters, whether purposefully or inadvertently, must have betrayed me, and I don't even say that to Karla because I can't be sure it wasn't her.

"It's missing five cards," I finally say. "I only discovered they were gone the night we did Abel's Farewell Ceremony."

"Which cards are missing, Pearl?" Karla asks. It sounds like an accusation.

I lean back, close my eyes, take a deep breath. "The Hanged Man, the Tower, Death, the Fool, and the Devil."

"What?" Karla asks, her voice rising. "Those are the same ones that have been showing up at the murder scenes. Could they be yours? Why didn't you say something?"

"You were passed out," I say. "We'd had a lot of wine, remember? I decided to do a reading. I didn't realize the cards were missing until after the reading. And then I saw the fire out the kitchen window, and I left the cottage and ran to the Tower. At the time, only Abel was dead, and I didn't know someone was leaving cards at the scenes until you told me Esme had told you." I realize I sound frantic, which equates to guilt. And then I remember something Karla said. "Wait, didn't you say Mr. Bones was sitting? In my deck, the skeleton is standing. What about the card you found? Was the skeleton standing?" What I don't tell her is that the skeleton is also standing in the painting I found in my studio. Which is weird because the other paintings exactly match the cards. But I had already decided not to tell her about the paintings. If I tell Karla about the combination of the missing cards and the paintings I don't remember painting, she won't be able to help but wonder about my guilt. Anyone would wonder.

"I can't remember for sure," Karla says. "But I think so. That is weird. You haven't told anyone else about your cards, have you?"

"No. No one."

"Well, don't." She pauses. I see recognition dawning on her face. When she looks at me, her eyes are huge. "Oh my god."

"What?" I ask.

"I told Detective Germany she should go talk to Priscilla because she knows about Tarot. Did Priscilla know the cards were in the sideboard?"

"I don't know," I say.

Karla and I look at each other. I see compassion on her face. She reaches for me, hugs me. "It's going to be okay," she says. "We'll figure it out."

LOLA

Rebecca and Friday were helping me inspect and photograph the scene. Colin hadn't returned with Madame Luna yet. I'd asked one of my guys to drive Karla back to her cottage. A few others had cordoned off the room with yellow crime scene tape and were standing guard outside the open door. Given the strong chemical scent, I'd provided strict instructions to leave the door to the room open but not allow anyone but police and crime scene investigators in. This included Alice and her Lackeys. Unfortunately, there were no windows in the room. Rebecca had passed out surgical masks, but they did nothing to safeguard our stinging, watery eyes. For me, it was the most brutal crime scene I had worked yet, both in terms of chemical discomfort and my intimate inspection of the boy's gruesome body. Thanks to Colin, I had been spared close inspection of the Tower victims' bodies.

Rebecca turned to me and said, "You were right. Someone drowned him in bleach. But the damage to the face is from more than bleach. It's acid. That's why the eyes look the way do, as if they've been partially burned away. The left eye is disconnected. If we don't gauze and tape it, it will likely fall out when we move the body."

The language of murder had begun to feel normal to me. "What about that spot on the top of the head?" I asked. "The—um—skull."

"Someone hit him with a blunt instrument. Repeatedly, by the looks of it. Maybe to knock him out at first. I'm betting he was also drugged like the others. There doesn't appear to have been a struggle. Given his size, the killer would have waited to pour the bleach and acid until the victim was incapacitated. I can't say much more about the circumstances until I get him on my table. Whoever is doing these murders is a heartless SOB. You know, I remember reading in one of my medical books that the Renaissance Italians considered the skull to be the symbol of death because it was what remained after the body decayed. Makes you wonder if the murderer might have had that in mind. Sure looks like he intended to expose the skull. You should get going. You look wiped. I've got this. Where's Colin, by the way?"

"On the ferry." I looked at my watch. "It should be docking right about now. He left early this morning to collect a Tarot historian from the Charleston airport. We thought we'd share the cards we've found at the scenes with her. See if she might shed some light."

"A Tarot historian?" Rebecca asked. "I didn't know there was such a thing." She lowered her voice. "Do you know if Alice has called the parents of the Tower victims yet? I moved them to refrigeration."

"She left a message on my machine saying she hadn't been able to get ahold of them. Apparently, she told the students that the Tower murders were an accident. These students need to know the truth so they understand they might be in danger. What about Abel Montague?"

"His father sent a man named Percy Lamb to claim the body as soon as I finished his autopsy," Rebecca said. "Geez, that feels like eons ago now. I thought I saw him here with Alice before your guys escorted everyone out of the room. Odd-looking guy wearing a purple suit coat and green shoes."

I had noticed Alice with the same guy. He was hard to miss. I thought he was a *friend* of hers.

Rebecca backed away from the body, shook her head. "Who knows. Maybe Alice is downplaying all this to protect the students. But she certainly can't claim this poor kid's death was an accident. It appears we have a serial killer on our hands."

LOLA

The three cards were laid out on the table of our small conference room in the order of the murders. The Hanged Man, the Tower, and Death. Madame Luna sat opposite Colin and me. She was an attractive and enigmatic woman with a chic, no-nonsense elegance. Fiftyish, slim, with sharp features and dark shoulder-length hair. She wore black pumps and a tailored black suit over a cream silk blouse and carried a worn but obviously expensive leather briefcase. She spoke fluent English with an Italian accent. She appeared totally unassuming but endlessly knowledgeable. There was nothing hesitant or apologetic in her presentation. She knew her subject inside and out.

"On first assessment, your cards appear similar to the fifteenth-century packs known as the Visconti-Sforza decks. Like those decks, the images on your cards appear to be reproductions of actual paintings rendered by an artist of the Renaissance period. It is important to note that though individual cards from all three Visconti-Sforza packs are currently in museum collections, no complete set of any of the three currently exists. There is some disagreement among historians as to which pack came first—the Brera, the Cary-Yale, or the

Pierpont-Morgan—or even the exact dates each deck was created. There is general agreement that all three decks were created around the mid-fifteenth century. Often such cards were commissioned to honor special events. For instance, some say the Cary-Yale pack was painted for the marriage of Filippo Visconti to Maria de Savoy, whereas the Brera pack is said to have been a wedding gift to Bianca Maria Visconti and Francesco Sforza. The Pierpont-Morgan pack may have been a tenth-anniversary present to Bianca from Francesco. Theirs was a matched marriage between two wealthy aristocratic families of the Italian Renaissance. Bianca was promised to Francesco when she was only five years old. He was twenty-two years her senior. But while your cards appear to be an aesthetic match to the Visconti-Sforza decks, I can say that the images themselves are not exact matches to their existing counterparts."

"What do you mean by 'aesthetic match'?" Colin asked.

"The cards are the same weight and size, and the images on them share similar composition, coloration, and general painting style. There is, however, enough difference in style to suggest they were painted by different artists. But now let's consider the images themselves. Remember I said that your cards *appear* similar. Like the Pierpont-Morgan, your Trump 12, the Hanged Man, hangs upside down wearing green tights and a white shirt with billowy sleeves, a common wardrobe for the time. But in your card, the man's hair is straight, not curly, and there's a green pouch and silver pieces in the bottom left corner. Your Trump 13, Death, and the one in the Pierpont-Morgan, is standing, while in the Brera he's sitting on a horse. The background is different in your card as well. But given the overall similarity of the cards, it's my assessment that if your cards are authentic, they come from a sister pack."

"Sister pack?" I asked.

"A fourth pack. One of which to date we've been unaware."

"Is there any significance to our three cards in terms of witchcraft, sorcery, or divination practices?" I asked.

"The use of the Tarot for divination purposes wasn't popularized until the eighteenth century. It is widely believed that the early packs were used to play a game called Tarocchi. Some say it was the inspiration for the game bridge."

"What about the position of the bodies?" Colin asked. "Our murderer appears to be replicating the images on these cards. Is it possible the use of religious iconography is also intentional? Could the killer be some kind of religious fanatic?"

"I agree your Hanged Man appears to be an obvious reference to the disciple Judas's betrayal of Jesus Christ, but without all the other major arcana cards in this particular deck, it is difficult to ascertain the extent to which religion plays a role."

"But why tarot cards, and especially cards from the Renaissance?" I asked.

"Good question." Madame Luna opened her briefcase, pulled out a manuscript filled with pictures of various tarot decks through the ages, and flipped the pages until she arrived at a section called "The Renaissance."

"This text provides a detailed overview of the history and evolution of the Tarot. It can get dry and academic at times, but it's worth a read. As you can see, the early packs were influenced by traditional playing cards. Tarocchi itself was a favorite pastime of wealthy, bored aristocrats. These families also collected works of art and fraternized with famous and highly respected artists, such as Leonardo da Vinci. *The Last Supper* was actually commissioned by Bianca and Francesco's son, Ludovico Maria Sforza. If there is any connection between your murders and the Renaissance Tarot, I believe it is art itself. Colin indicated on our ferry ride here that this is an art school, correct? A prestigious, secret art school located in a monastery where witch trials once took place. Perhaps the killer holds a grudge against the school or particular artists in the school? What better way to denigrate art or the learning of art than to essentially kill with art?"

I was reminded of what Karla had said about Abel Montague's murder scene feeling staged and theatrical. She'd called it a "painting in space," a phrase she said Pearl often used.

I had been concentrating on the divinatory aspects of tarot cards in general, not on the fact that the murderer was using a specific deck, which, if authentic, dated to the Italian Renaissance, a time when artists and painters were revered for their talent, and their works were collected by the aristocracy as testament to their wealth and good taste. This wasn't so different from the practices at St. Luke's. Even the name of the school itself was chosen because Saint Luke is the patron saint of painting. But what did all this have to do with our murders? For that matter, what did this particular tarot deck have to do with our murders?

"May I borrow the manuscript?" I asked.

"Consider it a gift." She closed the book and handed it to me.

"Thank you," I said. "Where do we go from here?"

"If at all possible, I would like to take the three cards back to New York with me and gather a group of curators from there and Italy to establish provenance. I understand you may need them for forensic purposes, but I won't be able to help you until I at least have agreement that the cards are worth further study. To ease your concerns, you should know that we are curators and scientists. We will leave the cards in your forensic coverings, and if we do need to take them out, which I imagine we might, we will do so in dust-free environments while wearing conservator's gloves and the proper clothing. If they are legitimate, we will, of course, want to begin discussions on adding them to a museum collection. But ultimately that will be your decision."

"I need to verify with our forensic expert that we have what we need from the cards before I pass them to you," I said. "When were you planning to leave?"

"My flight leaves at eleven A.M. tomorrow."

"That should work," I said. "But we do need to ensure we get you out of here as early as possible. We are expecting some bad weather tomorrow evening. Where are you staying?"

"I have a reservation at Tania's Bed-and-Breakfast. I understand it overlooks the water?"

"Yes," I said. "It was once a turn-of-the-century grand hotel. It still maintains its original color palette, white with light blue shutters. Lovely and quaint. The light blue color is called haint blue. It is particular to the Lowcountry and Sea Islands."

Colin jumped in. "A haint is a type of ghost or evil spirit. A colloquialism for 'haunt.' According to local hoodoo folklore, that particular shade of blue was originally chosen for protection because it resembled water, and evil spirits couldn't pass through water. My wife insisted on painting the exterior of our house haint blue. If you look around, you'll see that the color has become kind of a signature here. By the way, Tania's scones are out of this world. They've won awards."

"Colin's right," I said. "They're amazing."

"Well, I must certainly try them," Madame Luna said. "If you wouldn't mind, I'd like to see the murder sites. Just for context."

"Of course," I said. "And I'd love to buy you dinner."

Madame Luna smiled. "Dinner sounds wonderful, but it's on me."

"I insist," I said. "Dinner is a small price to pay for a discussion on art, music, and culture."

PEARL

Karla is busy pulling hemlock from her garden. I'm rocking on her porch. Aunt Matilda and two other Ghost Women hover around her. They travel in threes. The Ghost Women believe that threes unlock the secrets of the divine. Body, mind, and spirit. Birth, life, and death. Wisdom, knowledge, and understanding. I assume, like me, they're here to offer Karla moral support. Though she would never admit it, seeing the grotesqueness of Eric Bernard's body has unsettled her, even more than Abel's body had. *It was his face*, she said. *It looked like ground meat.* There is something so heartbreaking about seeing someone like Karla, who is always the strong one, now in need of caretaking herself.

"Why are you pulling hemlock?" I ask.

"I overheard someone at Eric Bernard's murder scene say that all the victims had been drugged with hemlock before they were murdered. I decided to grow it because it's pretty. I mean, I knew it could be poisonous if ingested, but I never imagined someone might actually use it to *kill* people. I realized I don't want something in my garden that kills people." She stops, grabs the rake she brought out earlier, and gathers all the plant parts into a pile on the stone walkway. Then she puts down the rake, grabs a pack of matches from her pocket, and sets the pile on fire. "Seems only fitting it should be burned, don't you think?"

Just then, the red-eyed owl alights on her railing.

She walks up the porch steps, sits on the other rocker beside me, lights the pipe, breathes in, and passes it to me. "You were an asshole, Abel," she says to the owl. "Why weren't you burned like George, Jeannine, and Eric?" The owl's eyes slowly close and open.

I take a toke and pass the pipe back.

"He *was* an asshole, you know," she says. "He might be a gentle and protective owl now, but you and I both know that when he was alive, he was a total dick. Pearl, please don't be one of those women that deny what you know." She passes the pipe. "The kind of woman who forgets what an asshole her partner was after they've gone. It wasn't you, Pearl. It was never you. You are a good person. I know you don't believe that right now, but trust me, you are."

I pass the pipe while thinking that Karla has no idea who I am and what I've done. She and I have never discussed my ability to hurt people with my mind. I don't want her to know the awful things I did at the orphanage. I don't want her to know I merely had to imagine someone falling and they would, or someone's arm breaking and it did. Karla doesn't know I stuck black pearl–tipped pins in the poppets I made of you and Hazel. Did I want to kill you? Kill Hazel? I don't know. Maybe not. But what I do know is that I wanted to hurt you both as much or more than you hurt me. When I saw the two of you together, it was like my entire body took over. It was way beyond my mind. Beyond calculation. I felt my whole being spiraling and I couldn't stop it. Karla is wrong. I am not a good person.

She passes me the pipe. "Do you remember Joseph Covington?" she asks.

I feel immediately uncomfortable. "He was a Fourth Year."

"What do you remember about him?"

I'm not certain how much I should say. "He was preparing for his one-man exhibit in New York."

Karla puts down the pipe. "Yes. I was a Second Year. Everyone thought he was the best artist that had ever come through St. Luke's. But he was more than that. Rarely do students, even St. Luke's students, receive critical reviews in major art periodicals prior to graduation. Joseph was lauded in every respected art magazine, and the art and culture sections of newspapers. *Art in America* called him 'the modern-day Michelangelo.' *Art News* said his talent was unsurpassed. GQ said that only once in a generation did an artist with Joseph Covington's talent emerge. He made everything look easy. Art, life, kindness. Then a jealous and entitled person destroyed him. Abel Montague."

"You don't know that."

"There," Karla says. "That's what I mean. You're still sticking up for him. I know you know Abel had something to do with his demise because you told me."

"What did I tell you?" I ask.

"You were a new First Year then," she says. "Earlier, I had been assigned to show you around. We were friendly after that but not really friends yet, so I was surprised when you showed up at my cottage. But also flattered because you'd chosen me to confide in. We shared more than one bottle of wine and we smoked this very pipe and sat on these chairs, like we're doing now. Do you remember what you were upset about?"

"Someone had gone into Joseph's studio and slashed all his paintings," I say. And then my body gets cold and I feel the same fear I felt then.

"At one point, you blurted out, 'Abel didn't do it.' Why would you have said that? I hadn't even asked."

I don't remember telling Karla that. I don't even remember discussing Joseph Covington with her. Obviously, I'd drunk and smoked too much. I wonder what she'd said that caused me to lie to protect you. Lie to her. Lie to myself. We were so new. I was so in love with you. What I didn't tell her or anyone then was that I knew you destroyed Joseph Covington's canvases because I *saw* it. Not with my eyes. With my mind. I saw you pulling out your hunting knife, ripping the canvases from their stretchers, and slashing them one by one. And I felt your anger as you did it. It scared me. What I also didn't tell Karla was that you had become obsessed with Joseph Covington. That after those reviews came out, you were seething. Pacing and yelling and throwing and breaking things and calling him names. "Fraud" and "kiss-up" and "loser." You kept mentioning Mr. Alabaster. Saying the only reason Joseph got those reviews was because Mr. Alabaster had paved the way for his fame. Mr. Alabaster was Joseph's advisor, but he was also a famous and well-respected art critic for several art magazines and books, and he spoke all over the world. He was considered the most desirable instructor and advisor at St. Luke's. Everyone wanted him, but he was very selective. He'd only agreed to advise two students.

I take a deep breath and then another, try to calm myself. I never told anyone all this, still haven't. All this time I've carried your secret. And even still, I can't tell Karla what I know. But one thing is different: I've finally admitted it to myself.

"It was awful," Karla says. "We were all terrified there was a mad person loose. Joseph's paintings were set to be transferred to a prestigious New York gallery that very afternoon. With no paintings to exhibit, the gallery had no choice but to cancel the show. Worse, Joseph wasn't allowed to graduate. Monty Montague, Abel's father, said the board voted that it wouldn't be fair to the rest of us to allow a student who didn't fulfill all the graduation requirements to graduate. It was stunning. He *had* fulfilled all the requirements. It wasn't his fault that someone had destroyed all his paintings. Everyone—students and faculty—thought he should be allowed to graduate. Everyone was angry that the school would do such a thing. Many of us complained. But the school was twisting it all, even lying. Alice in Wonderland especially. And Abel was bullying all the boys into taking the school's side. But here's the thing: If there was ever anyone St. Luke's should have gotten behind, it was

Joseph Covington. He was the school's ticket to fame. It wouldn't have taken him long to create more paintings. They could have delayed the exhibit. The galleries were willing to juggle some exhibitions around to accommodate Joseph. But fucking Monty Montague put his foot down. We were all devastated for Joseph. And then Joseph disappeared into thin air."

"What do you mean, 'disappeared'?" I ask. "I thought he had some sort of breakdown and moved to Italy."

"Who told you that?" Karla asks. "It was Abel. Wasn't it? And you believed him? People, especially talented artists on their way to fame and fortune, don't choose to disappear. They fight back. They pick themselves up."

I think about how happy you were when you told me. I can still see your gloating smile.

"Don't you remember the investigation?" Karla asks. "That his belongings remained in his dorm room and his art supplies remained in his studio. Three days after his disappearance, a load of wet clothes was found in one of the laundry room dryers. The maintenance man who found the clothes said that when he opened the dryer door, he had to cover his nose because the damp, stale odor was so strong. But there was one piece of clothing that wasn't found in the dryer or Joseph's dormitory room. Everyone knew about his expensive red silk designer shirt. His 'lucky shirt,' he called it. He wore it to every important school function. Do you remember any of this?"

I squirm in my seat. "I remember."

What I don't tell Karla is that remembering and knowing are two different things. There were things about you that I just didn't want to know. I didn't want to know that Joseph hadn't chosen to leave. I didn't want to know that the "favor" you asked your father, and Joseph supposedly quitting St. Luke's, were connected. I didn't want to know that you casually asking your father not to let Joseph graduate would lead to his demise. Why didn't I say anything to you when you gloated? Why wasn't I brave? I was never brave where it came to you. I was enamored, smitten. I thought I was in love.

"You do remember, don't you?" Karla says.

"His mother insisted that Joseph would never have left the shirt behind," I finally say, my voice barely above a whisper.

"His parents reported him missing to the police," Karla said. "The investigation went on for several weeks. The police deduced he'd had an accident and declared him dead. Accident? Seriously? Yeah, like a shark ate him? Why wasn't there a body? Mr. Alabaster was very upset. Do you remember what he said when he delivered the eulogy at Joseph's remembrance ceremony? He called what happened a cautionary tale. 'A reminder of the hubris of artistic bravado,' he said. The thing was, some people thought he was speaking about Joseph when he said those words, but that wasn't true. He was speaking about Abel."

"How do you know that?" I ask.

"Because Mr. Alabaster told me," Karla says. "Mr. Alabaster was my advisor too."

"You were the second student Mr. Alabaster chose to work with?" I ask.

"Yes," Karla says. "I was so honored when he chose me. But after all that happened with Joseph, he quit and returned to teaching at Yale University and writing for *Art in America*, and I was reassigned to Miss Blumenthal. She was hired to replace Mr. Alabaster. From the most prestigious advisor to the greenest. I remember Mr. Alabaster telling me I should quit too and follow him to Yale. He said he'd already talked to the department head and he was more than happy to have me. Yale would even cover all my expenses and aid with whatever else I might need to smooth my transition. Believe me, I thought about it. I wasn't above wanting fame and fortune. Who wouldn't want that? But art was not the only reason I had come to St. Luke's. There was Aunt Matilda and my loyalty to my matriarchy. And I naively believed what happened to Joseph Covington was an isolated incident. Until these murders, that is. What I saw today, Eric Bernard's burned-off face, brought what happened to Joseph Covington back. I mean, the desecration of his body was far worse than Abel's. All of the victims' murders were far worse than Abel's. This school is no stranger to violent crime. There's something going on here that has to be exposed. And with the help of the Ghost Women, I'm going to do that. Are you with me, Pearl? This is important. I need you. And you need to get on the right side of all this."

"Yes." I pause, look down.

"What's wrong?" Karla asks.

"There's something else. Something I should have told you back then. It wasn't too long after Joseph Covington disappeared that Abel told me he wanted to show me something. He said it was a special witch dummy burning. Better than the ones the Fourth Years do. I've never really liked those fake burnings, but I agreed. We walked quite a ways along the beach until we came to a tall cross, taller and sturdier than the crosses the Fourth Years build. Three figures were wearing animal masks and red robes—'blood robes,' Abel had called them, like the ones I later found in the antique sideboard. They were standing before the cross carrying lit staffs and chanting in a foreign language. Italian, I think. I could tell by their voices they weren't Fourth Years. They were grown men. One looked in our direction and briefly nodded. It was Abel's father. Kindling made of sticks and leaves formed a substantial mound at the base of the cross. The men kept repeating the same chant over and over. I remember thinking it was a much more dramatic performance than the one the Fourth Years put on. It was strange and hypnotic and beguiling. The reflection of the fire on the water. The empty beach. The red robes. The animal masks. I couldn't take my eyes off of it. They continued chanting as they stepped toward the witch dummy. When they were a staff length away from it, they lit the kindling at the base of the cross. Almost immediately, the fire engulfed the witch dummy. But the flames were different. They were crackling and bursting into the sky, and there was this awful smell, putrid and nauseating, like rotting meat, and I realized it wasn't a dummy at all. When I gasped, Abel put his arm around me and told me not to worry, that *he* was already dead. I remember looking at Abel's face, seeing the satisfaction on it, and then *knowing*."

"Knowing what?" Karla asks.

"This is going to sound crazy, but I *knew* it was Joseph Covington. I *saw* it. And so I told Abel that."

"What did he say?" Karla asks.

"He flattered me for being so perceptive, but then he said it wasn't Joseph. 'It was just some corpse from the morgue'—those were his exact words. And I remember wanting to believe I was wrong about it being Joseph but also wondering why his father would do such a thing. Burn a real person, alive or dead. I always wanted to believe Abel. But then, just recently, before I'd seen him with Hazel, I went to his studio looking for him because he didn't come home. He'd been working later than usual a lot, but he'd never been gone the whole night. I expected to find him there, but the studio was empty, so I went to the bathroom, and there on the back of the door was a red silk shirt. Remember it had that paint stain on the pocket? I wasn't going to ask him about it because I already knew the answer and I didn't want to hear the lie, but then, when he came home the next morning, I smelled sex on him, and instead of asking him who he had sex with, I asked him about the shirt. He got really angry and asked me what I was doing in his studio when he wasn't there. He never did say where he got the shirt. Later that day, I saw him leaving Joe's with Hazel. All I had wanted was for him to tell me the truth. Even if it wasn't what I wanted to hear, I would at least have known he was redeemable."

"That was a big step, Pearl," Karla says. "How did you know one of the men burning Joseph's body was Abel's father?"

"I recognized his blue eyes. Not a light blue like mine. A deep blue like the ocean when the moon shines on it. The same color as Abel's."

Whoo-who-who-whoo-whoo. You, the owl, land on the rail of Karla's porch. Your eyes fix on mine.

Is your showing up like this your way of making amends? I silently ask. *Or are you still to be feared, your talons ready to dig into anyone who dares challenge you?*

LOLA

Madame Luna, Colin, and I were at Rebecca's. Eric Bernard's body was on her table.

"It was as we thought," Rebecca said, primarily to me. "The victim was drowned with bleach. It burned his throat, esophagus, intestines, and stomach. Acid was poured over his face."

"He's a big guy," Colin said. "It would take someone pretty strong, or large themselves, to overtake him."

"That was my initial thought, but if you look here, you'll see that the top of his head was hit with a heavy blunt object. Detective Germany and I discussed this at the scene. Hard to say what happened for certain, but the killer might have been trying to slow him down. They may not have planned for his size, which could imply the killer didn't know him. There was also hemlock in his system. And a large amount of benzodiazepine."

"What's that?" Colin asked.

"Antidepressive or anxiety meds," she said. "They can slow someone down. It could have been added to the hemlock as a kind of fail-safe. It seems this killer is either getting sloppy or cocky. They might hope we will assume that the victim took the drug himself.

Due to the high stress of school or some such. Which could be true, but you might want to check into anyone who may have had a prescription for Valium or something similar."

"I'll run that down," Colin said. "I've also been trying to locate anyone that may have been in the building during the night. Janitor, students, faculty. Someone that may have seen something. So far, I've come up short."

As with the others, Rebecca showed us the victim's organs. She indicated that he had no birthmarks, caps on his teeth, or anything similar that a medical examiner could use to identify him. "It's true that Karla Gardyn recognized him, but we still need physical verification. Poor guy. I believe he knew what was happening to him. This was a brutal, sick murder. Whoever is doing these seems to be getting more comfortable with killing. Maybe even enjoying it."

Colin drove us to the Monastery after we left Rebecca's.

"These murders are just awful," Madame Luna said as we parked. She had been very quiet while Rebecca presented her findings. The look of shock on her face led me to believe it was her first autopsy. It was impressive that she hadn't fainted. "Did the victims know each other?"

"They were classmates," Colin said. "The two young men were buddies of Abel Montague's. We've heard that they hurt girls. Abel had a live-in girlfriend whom he treated poorly. Her friends didn't like him. But that's as much as we know. The students here are very close-lipped. It's the school culture."

I was impressed with Colin's careful choice of words. *A live-in girlfriend whom he treated poorly. Her friends didn't like him.*

"Who is this girlfriend?" Madame Luna asked.

"She's part of a group of girls who call themselves a coven," I said. "They practice all manner of divinatory arts, including Tarot."

"Witches?" Madame Luna asked. "I would love to talk to them. Perhaps I will be able to read them. I do have some powers of my own."

"I might be able to make that happen," I said.

We arrived at the veranda. Two Lackeys stood watch. The yellow crime scene tape still surrounded the wrought iron table. With the exception of the Death card, I'd directed my guys and the Lackeys to leave the scene intact so Madame Luna could see it. She studied the pose, the black roses, and the teacup.

"The student who found the skeleton here said it was known to travel around campus?" Madame Luna asked.

"Yes," I said. "Karla Gardyn. But she said it was always meant as a practical joke."

"What time was the skeleton found?"

"She first saw it around nine A.M., before a scheduled critique with her advisor," I said. "She said she didn't think much of it at first, but she checked again an hour later, after the critique was over. That's when she called me."

"And students were coming and going all that time and no one other than this one student saw the card? Is she one of the witches?"

"Yes," I said. "How did you know that?"

"Her energy is still here." Madame Luna closed her eyes. "I feel another young woman as well. She is special, this one. She has the gift of sight. Yes, I believe I should meet these witches." She opened her eyes. "Colin," she said, "I'm sorry to say you cannot join us. It has been a pleasure."

If Colin had found the statement blunt, he didn't indicate so. "I've got plenty of work to do," he said. "I'll walk back to the station so you can have the car."

"Are you sure?" I asked.

"Yes. It's not that far. I could use the exercise." He handed me the keys and addressed Madame Luna. "I'll pick you up in the morning?"

"Thank you," she said.

She waited while Colin walked away, then said, "He is a lovely young man. You are lucky to have him."

"I am," I said.

"I hope I didn't offend him, but there is something else I saw," she said. "He is not a believer, which could interfere with the energy. There is an owl. A troubled owl. The spirit of your first victim is inside it. We will have to be cautious around it, but I believe that as long as I am there it won't bother us."

"Colin isn't the only nonbeliever," I said. "I'm not much of one myself."

Madame Luna flashed me a smile that looked very similar to Karla's. A *knowing* smile. "The seer is expecting us," she said. "Shall we?"

PEARL

I know they are coming, my ballerina detective and the Tarot witch. I am looking out Karla's window. You, the owl, are perched on the porch railing. Your red eyes stare back at me. They have been following me everywhere I go. Like me, you are aware they are coming. Karla isn't. She is a green witch and a believer, not a seer. I haven't told her because I don't want to answer a litany of questions. I fear their arrival. The Tarot witch will *see* me. She is arrogant about her power, boasts of it with pride. I am the opposite. I hide it. I worry she won't respect my privacy, that she will announce it in front of my ballerina detective. Even Karla doesn't know the extent of my powers. I feel the rage returning. The rage I try so hard to resist.

The worst incident was when Pretty Paula Lovelace fell off the swing. I remember watching her swing higher and higher. She wasn't really doing or saying anything more or less than any of them had said or done in the past. She just kept repeating "Pathetic Pearl" over and over, but there was just something about the way she kept stretching that word, "*paaaaathetic*," like it was taffy, while the girl on the other swing laughed. I imagined it first. *Saw* her reaching the highest point. *Saw* her hands slip from the swing's ropes. *Saw* the fear on her face. And then it happened, just as I had seen it. Pretty Paula Lovelace fell and broke her arm and ankle and, worse, cut and scraped her face against the dirt and stones. She needed fourteen stitches on her cheek. She was no longer as pretty as she used to be.

I feel the Tarot witch before I hear her. It is not an actual hearing, not like two people talking and listening; it is a silent hearing. A kind of telepathy. The first fellow witch I knew was Sister Winnifred. Though I didn't know then what she was, what we were, she knew. That was why she took such interest in me. I see now that our connection was a thread back then, a thread she honored. I was too early in my journey. I wasn't ready to know what I was. It was really through you that I learned to fully control it. It sounds sappy to say love saved me, but it did. Yet not in the way you might think. It was my love for you that fueled my anger, that caused me to recognize the connection between it and my actions. Witches are not alone in their disconnection from their true selves. All people deny what they don't want to know or see. But disconnection for a witch is dangerous. I would have hurt you if love hadn't stopped me.

Your red eyes burn into me. There is envy and anger behind them. Envy of life. Anger at death. I wonder how much longer you will be here. And for a moment, I feel sad. Where you, the owl, are concerned, my emotions rise and fall.

They're getting closer. I see them in my mind, feel them in my throat. That's where I feel all my powers first. It's like a dryness, an inability to breathe too deep without coughing. Now I *actually* see them. Approaching Karla's cottage from the top of the walk. Closer. They reach the porch steps. My ballerina detective stares at you. I see her fear.

LOLA

I saw the owl from a distance, the one with the red eyes, perched on Karla's porch railing. My body tensed. My father had called owls highly intelligent creatures, noting their air of mystery, stoic stature, and wisdom. While he had espoused these qualities in a positive light, I found these same qualities suspect. I'd seen them suddenly leave their perch on a branch, swoop, and dig their talons into unsuspecting prey. Generally, I made a point not to look directly at them, but in that moment, curiosity got the better of me. Its eyes met mine and slowly blinked as if acknowledging my presence.

Madame Luna noticed me shudder. "Owls are bewitching creatures," she said. "Do you know the fairy tale of the enchanted owl princess?"

"No," I said.

"A king had three sons that he felt were ready for marriage. So he told them to shoot their arrows out of the castle's magical window and that wherever the arrows landed, they must trust that was where they would find happiness, but only one son would rule his father's kingdom, the one who encountered a difficult or painful quest but, trusting in his father's words, would persevere. The arrows from the first two sons' bows landed near beautiful young women, whom they each fell in love with and married. The arrow of the third son hit deep into a tree. When he climbed the tree to dislodge the arrow, an owl flew out of a hollow and dug its talons into his shoulder. The more he fought the owl's talons, the more they dug in. His first inclination was to kill the owl with his knife, but remembering his father's words, he decided to return to the kingdom with the owl still attached. As he embarked on his return journey, six more owls fluttered out of the hollow and flew alongside him and the first owl all the way back to his father's palace. So tired was he when he finally returned that he went straight to bed. And when he awoke the next morning, the owl that stuck to him had turned into a beautiful princess, and the six accompanying owls were her maidens. And so this prince became king, and he and his queen ruled the kingdom with his kindness and her wisdom for the rest of their lives. So you see, the owl's wisdom and talons ultimately brought good."

The door to Karla's cottage was already opening when I raised my hand to knock on it.

"Detective Germany," Karla said. "What a nice surprise. Please come in, both of you." Then, to Madame Luna, "Hello, I'm Karla."

"I'm Madame Luna. It's a pleasure."

"I would say we should sit on the porch, but that owl has been there all morning. It's quite unsettling."

Just then, Pearl emerged. "Get," she said to the owl. It flapped its wings and flew into the forest.

"The porch sounds lovely," Madame Luna said. "You must be Pearl."

"Madame Luna is visiting from New York," I said. "She's a scholar in fifteenth-century Italian Tarot." I didn't want to say much more than that.

"How interesting," Karla said. "Isn't that interesting, Pearl?"

Pearl didn't attempt to hide her irritation at the two of us showing up uninvited. "I'll get some extra chairs," she said.

"Detective, why don't you and Madame Luna take the rockers?" Karla asked. "It's a lovely evening. We can watch the sunset. Are you hungry? I made a huge pot of vegetable chili. From my garden. I can easily warm it up. Or I can make tea?"

Pearl returned with the chairs.

"Tea is perfect," I said.

"Yes, jasmine sounds lovely," Madame Luna said.

Karla cocked her head. "That's exactly what I was thinking. I'll be right back."

I sat, attempted not to rock. I needed to be on my game. I saw that Pearl was looking at Madame Luna, her expression hard to decipher. Was it curiosity? Distrust?

Karla arrived with our tea, set it on the table in front of our chairs. "It's hard to believe a hurricane is on its way," she said.

"It will bring fury and damage," Madame Luna said. "But everyone will be safe."

"Pearl was just saying the exact same thing right before you arrived, weren't you, Pearl? That everyone would be safe."

"Is that your cottage?" Madame Luna asked Pearl. "There's a lovely view of the water from your kitchen window, isn't there?"

She didn't wait for Pearl's response, but rather immediately blurted more questions that I assumed Pearl would find invasive. "I understand your boyfriend was the first victim. Abel, wasn't it? I suppose the polite thing to say is that I'm sorry for your loss. But I'm actually not. I imagine you aren't anymore either. You did a spell, right? To banish him? Not to worry, his spirit has already realigned. It merely took time for him to embrace his greater purpose."

"How did you know that?" Karla asked, while Pearl glared.

"I understand you were an orphan?" Madame Luna asked, ignoring Karla's question and obviously not bothered by Pearl's distrustful demeanor. "A journey such as yours adds perspective."

I tensed. I hadn't told Madame Luna that Pearl was an orphan. I looked at Pearl to gauge her reaction to Madame Luna's directness.

Karla interrupted. "I don't think we should be talking about sad things. Pearl is vulnerable right now."

I was getting very uncomfortable with the direction of the conversation. I could feel Pearl's irritation.

"I'm fine, Karla," Pearl said without taking her eyes off Madame Luna.

"I've heard your paintings are exquisite," Madame Luna continued. "They are set in the forest, aren't they? And you have a recurring subject?"

I also hadn't said anything to Madame Luna about Pearl's paintings. I hadn't even seen them myself. It felt like I was at a shooting range without a gun.

"I do," she said. "A woman."

Madame Luna's lips curled into a knowing smile. "How about you, Karla? Do you have a specific subject?"

"Sort of," Karla said. "I paint bad men."

"Well, you won't be running out of subjects any time soon, then," Madame Luna said.

Karla laughed. "True. What exactly does a fifteenth-century Tarot scholar do? Are you associated with a museum?"

Good, I thought. The conversation was taking a positive turn. I felt my body relax.

"Actually, I am what you'd call a consultant. My clients keep renewing my contract. Tarot cards of the Italian Renaissance are my specialty. Mostly, I provide expertise on identification and provenance."

"That's so interesting," Karla said.

"Detective Germany asked me here to share anything I might know about the cards they found at the murder scenes. They're hoping this information will help them find the killer."

"So you believe the owner of the cards is also the killer?" Karla asked, while looking at me.

"It stands to reason," I said.

"Not necessarily," Karla said.

Pearl interrupted. "Madame Luna, did Detective Germany tell you that they used to burn witches on the island? Karla actually has an ancestor who was burned at the stake on this island, don't you, Karla?"

"Yes," Karla said. "My aunt Matilda."

"How did you find this out?" Madame Luna asked.

"I inherited a genealogy of my mum and female ancestors. We're a matriarchy. One of the reasons I chose to come to St. Luke's was to—um—feel closer to Aunt Matilda."

"By 'matriarchy,' do you mean your entire family is women? No men?" Madame Luna asked.

"Yes," Karla said.

"Fascinating," Madame Luna said. "How did you find your way here, Karla? I understand it's a secret school. It seems quite synchronistic that the school recruited you given your aunt Matilda's unfortunate history."

"Synchronicity had nothing to do with it," Karla said. "Given Aunt Matilda's fate and the Ghost Tree, we had always been aware of the island, including the school, when it came to be. I've known since I was a very little girl that I was destined to come here and seek revenge."

"That's quite a destiny," Madame Luna said. "But given the secrecy and prestige of St. Luke's Institute of the Arts, did you ever worry that attendance here might be wishful thinking?"

"No," Karla said, and flashed Madame Luna a condescending smile. It was the first time I'd ever seen Karla not try to mask her irritation. "As I said, it was a foregone conclusion. You see, every year on the autumnal equinox, since St. Luke's opened, of course, all living members of our matriarchy would gather and call to the spirits of those of us who had passed, and for one week practice green magic rituals and spells meant to attract the school's attention, and one day Dean Landry showed up on my mum's and my doorstep."

"This time of year is powerful, isn't it?" Madame Luna said. "The autumnal equinox having just passed, I imagine the forest is alive with spirits. What about you, Pearl? How did you come to be at St. Luke's?"

She didn't answer right away. She took a long sip of tea. "My situation isn't as interesting as Karla's," she finally said. "I was called into Mother Superior's office and introduced to Dean Landry. She said she had been following my art and asked if I'd like to attend St. Luke's."

"Where was your home?"

"I didn't really have a home. I was raised mostly by nuns in a Catholic convent not too far from here."

"You were never adopted?" Madame Luna asked Pearl.

"Twice," Pearl said. "But neither placement worked out."

Madame Luna cocked her head. "I believe there was more to your recruitment," she said to Pearl. "There is a darkness at this school. It will take the strength of all three of you to fight it."

"Do you mean our coven?" Karla asked. "There are four of us."

"I mean the three of you sitting here right now. You have a similar affinity to the island, don't you, Lola?"

I stood. I wasn't about to discuss my connection to the island with Karla and Pearl. And even doing so with Madame Luna felt invasive. "Thank you for the tea, Karla," I said. "We've had a long day. I need to get Madame Luna some dinner. I'll be in touch."

"It's been a pleasure," Madame Luna said. She reached into her briefcase, pulled out two business cards, and handed them to Pearl and Karla. "Here is my contact information. Both in New York and Milan. Perhaps you will visit me sometime. If we don't connect in person before, I'll be sure to attend both of your first major exhibits in New York. Ciao."

When we were halfway up the walk and out of earshot, Madame Luna said, "Karla's ancestor, Aunt Matilda, was on the porch with us, along with two other spirits. Did you notice?"

"No," I said.

"A lovely young woman. A healer like Karla. A bad man who was once the abbot of a nascent monastery sealed her fate. It's so awful. Mark my word, there is a reckoning coming. And by the way, you will."

"I will what?" I asked.

"See the Ghost Women."

"I'm not really a believer in the Ghost Women."

"And yet you regularly talk to a woman whom you believe lives in a tree," she said.

I was stunned, and somewhat embarrassed. How did Madame Luna know about my tree goddess? I kept her my secret for a reason.

PEARL

You, the owl, immediately returned after my ballerina detective and Madame Luna left. I'm getting used to your piercing red eyes always staring at me. The shell of the owl you wear is as still as a statue. Sometimes I forget you are there. It was the same when you were in the shell of a young man and we lived together. While at first it felt exciting and unusual, over time there was a sameness that I found comforting. Something I had never felt before. Something I easily fell into.

Karla is talking away. "She was interesting, don't you think? How did she know so much about you? And that stuff about there being a darkness here, that was intriguing."

I am trying not to listen. I'm unwinding my tightly wound defenses. Trying to restore my energy. I was wrong about Madame Luna *seeing* me. Perhaps she could see parts of me, but definitely not all. I felt her sneaking around in my psyche, like an ant looking for crumbs. Initially, I worried about the extent of her powers, especially when she started discussing the subject of my paintings. Karla knows that my ballerina detective is the woman in my paintings, the woman who talks to trees, but I don't want my ballerina detective to know that. At least not yet. Nor do I want anyone else to know, especially a know-it-all, loose-lipped glorified Tarot scholar. But I honestly don't think she knew for sure. She might have suspected, or intuited, but I don't think she *saw* it. And yet, even though she saw Aunt Matilda and the other Ghost Women on the porch with us, she'd kept this knowledge to herself. Perhaps it was out of respect for Karla. Or perhaps, like me, she keeps knowledge close as a means to maintain power both personally and professionally. But unlike me, throughout the meeting, she had sought and probed as if it were a game. A true seer would never outwardly seek and probe. A true seer would never challenge another seer or casually share what she sees. There is a code.

And what about my tarot cards? Though I haven't seen the ones left at the scene of the murders, I know they are mine. Madame Luna's visit to Waverly Island is proof that my ballerina detective and her sidekick are trying to find out not only the source of the cards, but also why the murderer is leaving cards from a particular deck. A unique and ancient deck. I would like to know that too. Why *my* cards? Is someone trying to incriminate me? I feel fear beginning to creep through my body, not the kind of fear I get when I'm scared, a different kind of fear. It's like someone is chasing me and they're right on my heels and I'm both desperate and afraid to turn around and confront my pursuer. Because what if it's me? After all, everything points to me. The paintings I don't remember painting. The tarot cards I might have pulled from the deck myself. What if I'm the one leaving them at the murder scenes? What if I'm the murderer?

LOLA

Maria's was empty except for Madame Luna and me. Everyone else was preparing for the hurricane. Hurricanes were a fact of life on the island. While they invoked fear, they also brought the islanders together. We boarded up one another's homes and businesses. When I was very young, I remember folks waiting hurricanes out in the church basement, where cots and blankets had been set up. The children, often oblivious to the severity of the threat, played games like Twister, red rover, or jump rope. I was six years old when a major hurricane hit. We lost most of the town's structures and many residents that day. The only building left completely untouched was the church, a fact the townsfolk insisted was a sign that the good Lord himself had blessed us. As a result of that storm, many of the island's buildings were rebuilt to withstand major hurricanes. But not my house. Rather than wait for government contractors, my stubborn father insisted on doing all the repairs himself. Perhaps I was being cavalier, but I wasn't worried about this storm or my house. I felt grounded, as if I was part of something greater than me. A community. People who knew me and would be there for me. Even the murders at St. Luke's hadn't shaken that sense of affinity.

Maria and Madame Luna were talking about Italy. While they chatted, I enjoyed my arancini di riso, Maria's famous deep-fried Sicilian rice balls, and yet another exceptional Barolo, and moved on to my salad—I still couldn't get used to the Italian tradition of serving salad at the end of the meal—when Madame Luna finally had a chance to take her first bite.

"Oh my," she said, "this arancini is the best I've ever had. What's your secret?"

"No secret," Maria said "Same as I always make it. A little butter, a little onion, fresh herbs, generous portions of lemon zest and white wine, and only the best mozzarella." Knowing Maria, I suspected the list of ingredients she'd disclosed to Madame Luna was incomplete. A secret ingredient was just that, a *secret*.

"The lemon zest," Madame Luna said. "That's what I taste. It's divine."

Maria addressed me. "I made fresh cannoli. I can bring it now while Madame is finishing up. And I have a lovely Vin Santo dessert wine."

"Yes to both," I said. As far as I was concerned, Maria's cannoli was not only perfection; it was comfort food. I sometimes got it takeout. And no one in their right mind passed up a glass of Vin Santo.

Madame Luna finished up her salad and joined me in wine and dessert. Maria left us after apologizing that she had to get started on tomorrow night's dinner. Obviously she wasn't worried about the impending hurricane.

We were enjoying our second glass of Vin Santo when Madame Luna said, "I saw you dance."

"What?" I immediately felt trapped.

"In New York," she said.

"You did?" I asked, while trying to ignore my racing heartbeat.

I felt hot, sweat oozing from my pores. Though it had been only six years since I danced, it felt like another lifetime. *Does she know?*

"Twice, actually. When the New York City Ballet still performed at City Center. You were an angel. One of the best prima ballerinas I've ever seen. Your absence is quite a loss to New York and the dance world." She paused, looked away, bit her bottom lip. "I hope I'm not prying, but I want you to know I understand what happened."

So she did know. I immediately felt fear. Stiffened.

"In my opinion, and I believe the opinion of most, he got what he deserved. I followed the trial. What he did to you. It was awful, evil. You are lucky you lived. I'm sorry you had to go through that."

Now I was nauseous. With the exception of my defense attorney, I hadn't talked with one living soul about what happened that night and during the months that followed. The lengthy trial. The other dancers spilling every secret I'd shared with them about my relationship with Jeffrey Villanova. About his extracurricular activities. I knew one day someone would recognize me. But I hadn't expected one day to be today. The trial was on the front page of the *Times*, *Journal*, and *Post*. I saw myself on the cover of all the seedy tabloids as I stood in line at the grocery. I wore baseball hats and sunglasses for a year straight. I switched careers. At the time, I told myself that I chose to be a police officer because the academy was the perfect place to blend in. I was a woman in a man's field, yes, but not one of those men followed the dance world or, for that matter, read the arts section of the newspaper or tabloids. And even if they had, I don't think it would have mattered. They were just average guys, mostly good, who watched sports and drooled over *Sports Illustrated* models, and who always acted as if I was one of them. But over time, I came to understand that the real reason I chose to be a detective was because of, not in spite of, my father. I grew up around the badge. I knew how to use a gun. I knew the work and the life. Dance, I reasoned, had taught me focus, strength, and agility. But most of all, being a detective, especially in the town where I grew up, felt like a safe harbor from the most volatile waters I'd ever experienced. It felt like the only place I could survive.

It happened six years ago, after the last dance of the season. It was the best performance I'd ever given. There was an after-party. Pretty dresses, fancy tuxedoes, lots of champagne. I was in a state of bliss. The press was clamoring to interview me, praising me, saying I was brilliant, the best prima ballerina the company had ever seen. I watched the danseur, who was also my husband, out of the corner of my eye. He didn't like it when I received more attention than he did. When you're married to an abusive man, you learn to watch for the signs. The incident my defense attorney called self-defense and the prosecutor called murder happened after we got home. "They were husband and wife," the prosecutor had shouted to the jury. "It was a well-known fact that their relationship was, shall I say, *frisky*." He painted me as extremely jealous, crazy, and irrational. "They had to handcuff her to the hospital bed." He didn't mention the statement I gave to the police, downplayed the brutality of my injuries, and repeatedly referred to me as "a woman scorned."

"Thank you," I said to Madame Luna. I couldn't think what else to say.

"It must have been so frightening and upsetting, but why did you stop dancing?"

"It wasn't my choice," I told her. "The company was kind, understanding even, but they felt the publicity wouldn't be good." I held back tears. "Their prima ballerina and danseur, well, it was a scandal. They wanted a clean slate."

"For one thing, none of it was your fault. I am very disappointed in the Ballet. At some point, I may just give them a piece of my mind. And going home seems the right choice. Are your parents still here? It's nice to have extended family around you when you're going through a trauma."

I hoped she wouldn't give them a piece of her mind. It was the last thing I needed or wanted. I preferred that no one knew what had become of me. I wasn't done hiding and wasn't certain I ever would be.

"My mother died when I was a baby. My father raised me. He passed while I was at Juilliard. Cancer. I live in the same house I lived in as a child." I hoped Madame Luna wouldn't ask me to elaborate on my mother's death.

"Everyone knew Jeffrey Villanova was a shit," Madame Luna said. "A friend of a friend dated him for a while. She said he had extreme anger issues. Alcohol- and drug-induced, yes. But he was also known to be arrogant and entitled."

I felt myself unintentionally squirm.

"I'm so sorry to bring this all up," Madame Luna said. "Just know you have a friend in me."

She changed the subject to the tarot cards then. Shared more of what she knew about their origin and how they verify authenticity. I only heard half of it, but I nodded and smiled when I was supposed to.

I dropped her back at the bed-and-breakfast. She said she'd be in touch soon and reiterated what she'd said earlier about believing the hurricane wouldn't do too much damage. "Not to worry, Waverly Island will be spared the worst of the storm."

"Colin will pick you up in the morning," I said. "It was a pleasure."

"Yes," she said. "It's not every day I meet such a strong and interesting woman."

I watched her walk into the B and B and then drove home.

I parked under my house, a common practice with stilt houses, and walked up the stairs. My heart quickened when I saw the burlap poppet perched upright against the front door. It looked just like the ones at the Garden of Angels, Pearl's altar, and the crime scenes, with two exceptions. Its red heart was larger, and it was pierced with a blue-pearled pin. I went inside, locked and bolted my door. Then I poured myself a huge glass of bourbon. It wasn't just the memories I was trying to kill. It was the demon that began eating my soul all those years ago, the one I thought I had conquered, but it was obviously still inside me. I had merely paused it.

It went by the name Jeffrey Villanova.

Day 5

FOUR DAYS AFTER THE AUTUMNAL EQUINOX
TUESDAY, SEPTEMBER 26, 1972

LOLA

My alarm went off at the usual time. The bourbon had helped me sleep through the night. The first thing I did upon leaving my house for my morning run was smell the air. Salt water. Listened. Waves softly rolling in. Then, even though it was still dark out, I looked at the sky. Stars. According to the meteorologists, the hurricane they were tracking was due to make landfall later that afternoon or early that evening. They were still uncertain exactly where it would make landfall. Hopefully, Waverly Island would escape a direct hit. My property extended all the way to the ocean. The front yard was a wide swath of sand that bled into the sea. Like many of the homes that perched on stilts, it was more susceptible to hurricanes, but when I was a child and there was a hurricane scare, I never considered that it might get flattened. Instead, I imagined the house swirling through the air, then slamming to the ground in one piece.

On a witch, I mused.

I slipped the blue pearl–pinned poppet left on my porch into the inside pocket of my running shorts, walked down the stairs toward the beach, stretched, and began my run. There was something about the rhythmic slapping of rubber soles that helped release tension and unwanted thoughts. A kind of ticking, of time running out before the bomb went off. Last night's conversation with Madame Luna was still on my mind. I felt exposed, as if they were putting the handcuffs on my wrists all over again. I felt myself coming to, a police officer shaking me awake.

"Ma'am," he was saying, "can you tell us what happened?"

I couldn't.

"Ma'am," he repeated, "what happened here?" Shaking my shoulders as if I had merely been in a deep sleep, as if I weren't a sloppy, woozy drunk with a killer hangover.

The slow dawn of the waking mind as it tries to make sense of the scene before it. The bronze statue on the ground. A reproduction of *Little Dancer*, by Degas. Blood everywhere. The pain excruciating. My head throbbing so loud I started to scream. Later I would discover that there was a large lump and lesion on my forehead. That I'd gotten stitches. That I would spend months in the hospital handcuffed to bed rails. I would learn what a trickster memory was. How fear seeps into your pores. How killing someone kills a part of yourself. And the endless questions: Did he deserve to die? Were everyone's eyes on me? Would I ever dance again?

"Ma'am," the officer repeated.

"Stop badgering her," a female officer said. "She's lucky she's alive."

Was I?

Ticking. Ticking. Rhythmic slapping of rubber against pavement.

Since I moved back to Waverly Island, I had been going along just fine, living in obscurity. Doing my job. Surrounded by people who weren't aware of my past, who didn't know the real me. The accused murderess. What if Colin found out? Or Rebecca? Or Joe or Reggie or Maria? What if they lost respect for me? What if island residents whispered when I walked by?

Ticking. Ticking. Rhythmic slapping of rubber against pavement.

I'd changed my surname back to the one I was born with. The name I was given on this very island, a place where the earth was a mixture of sand, rock, and water. Where I crabbed in the marsh and fished in the ocean when I still wore diapers. Where my father was a policeman. Where I took ballet classes in the church basement. Performed in recitals. Where I was first told I was exceptional. Where the forest felt like home. Where dance and the New York City Ballet became a shadow, an experience that happened to another girl. But sometimes, especially when I was tired, it resurfaced and I tried to break it down, dissect it.

"You look better with your hair down," he'd said.

Such a seemingly innocent comment. I remember wondering why it made me feel uncomfortable. Not *Your hair looks nice that way.* But I was being silly and unfair, I thought. He was older, already established. He'd mentored me. I owed him so much. Would I have even been hired by the company if not for him? Would I have become the prima ballerina? He insisted on going shopping with me, choosing my clothes. Commented on my weight. And then came the affairs, or maybe I was only then discovering them. Even now, I doubted myself. Was it really as bad as I thought? One day, during practice, he lifted me into the air, twirled me, and dropped me. We'd successfully accomplished the same move a million times before. Was it an accident? But then, lying on the floor, before the pain hit, I saw the look in his eyes. Anger. No apology, just this: "Jesus, Lola, are you kidding me? You're heavy as hell." By that time, I was nearly anorexic. The first time he hit me, I was coming out of the shower. The second time, he pulled me by the hair out of bed and slapped me across the face. The third time, he punched me hard enough to cause a welt and a large bruise. I started wearing makeup. I receded.

"What are the lengths to which a woman will go when shunned by a man she loves?" the prosecutor had asked the jury in his closing statement at the murder trial. "What is her breaking point?"

Ticking. Ticking. Rhythmic slapping of rubber against pavement.

Self-defense, the jury concluded. But just because the legal system found you innocent, there was no guarantee the world would. I enrolled at the police academy.

While searching the jobs board after graduation, one caught my eye. Some might think it was a coincidence that Waverly Island, the island I grew up on, was looking for a lead detective. A coincidence that it was the only advertisement posted on the board that day. A coincidence that it was added to the board the very day I passed my detective exam. But for me, these were signs from the universe that everything was going to be just fine. And it was.

Until last night. Until Madame Luna recognized me.

My footsteps slowed when I reached the Garden of Angels. I opened the heavy wrought iron door, headed to my parents' graves, fell to my knees, and wailed. Cried as I hadn't since the events of that day. Cried for the death of the girl I once was, so filled with thoughts of that girl's beauty and promise, so grateful for the elegant flow of her body and mind. Cried for these last six years of self-pity and shame. Then I picked myself up and thanked the gods who protected me, and I beseeched them to watch over all little girls and women on earth and beyond who have and will come face-to-face with the devil.

I continued to the Unmarked Tombstone. The two poppets I saw a few days earlier were no longer there. I reached into the pocket of my running shorts, pulled out the blue-pinned poppet, and placed it in the same spot where I'd seen the others.

"Please help me solve these murders?" I asked the hoodoo root doctor said to be buried there.

I heard a squawk. The resident black raven was flying overhead, a faint orange glow in the sky behind it. I needed to get to my tree. I no longer heard the slap of my feet as I continued the journey through the Garden of Angels and the gate that crossed into the forest. Instead, it was the sounds of the waking birds and the pitter-patter of the forest creatures that surrounded me. I felt a soft breeze and a kind of euphoria, as if a great weight had been lifted, as I approached my tree. Then I was before her. My goddess. I put my hands on my hips, bent over to catch my breath, straightened, and walked to the edge of the cliff. There they all were, standing below me on the edge of the sea. The watchers of the sunrise. Creatures large and small. Crawlers and fliers. Then complete silence from the gallery as, together, we watched the orange sphere rise high into the sky. I stood, stretched, and began my run home.

As I neared the east entrance to the forest, I saw one of the officers Colin had posted. We'd beefed up security on the island, assigned officers to monitor the cottages, St. Luke's campus, the student dorms, Studio Row, and the three murder scenes in the event the killer returned. Instructed them to be invisible.

"Everything was quiet last night," he said to me. "That owl's pretty creepy though. Hung there all night."

"Thanks," I said.

Everything appeared normal at Karla's cottage, but Pearl's was a different story. The owl was perched on her railing, its red eyes staring out at the world, as alert as a guard dog. I stood still lest it see me. The front door opened. Pearl was carrying a large backpack. She greeted the owl, trotted down her front steps, and headed in my direction. I only had a moment to consider my next move. I darted off the path, barely made it to a thicket of trees, and ducked out of sight. I watched as she walked by me, waited until she was far enough ahead that she couldn't hear my footsteps. At the fork, she took a left toward the Ghost Tree. Was she going to the scene of the crime? No, she passed by it. She veered off the path. The trees and overgrowth got thicker and thicker. I couldn't remember ever traversing this area of the forest. My shoe hit a branch. The sound of the crack seemed to echo through the air. I stopped. Slipped behind a wide tree. Held my breath. "Hello?" Pearl called out. "Is someone there?" My heart beating. The sound of leaves crunching beneath her feet. I waited until I was certain she was far enough ahead of me that she wouldn't see or hear me following. When I stepped out of my hiding place, she was nowhere in sight. She couldn't have gotten far. I started jogging. At this point, I didn't care if she discovered me. It was more important I catch her in whatever act she was engaging in. I changed directions. Nothing. And again. Nothing. I was running in circles. I heard a hoot. The owl was above me, flying down at me. Then it was on me, its talons digging into my scalp. I fell to the ground, crouched, and covered my head with my arms as it shrieked, its wings wildly fluttering against my neck and ears. Then I heard a loud squawk. The raven from the Garden of Angels. The owl pulled in its talons and flew away.

"Thank you," I said to the raven.

Shaken, I rose and felt my scalp. It was wet. I looked at my fingertips. Blood.

PEARL

I'm staring at Hazel's letter. She's been hiding in the dark and shallow dungeon below St. Luke's for the past three nights, a fact I find hard to imagine. I considered burning the letter, like any tragic heroine would. I even imagined myself reciting some sort of passionate soliloquy right out of *Othello* as I watched it burn. But then I told myself, why not read the letter, *then* burn it?

Dear Pearl,

I need your help. I imagine I'm the last person you'd want to help. I know I don't deserve it, but I have nowhere else to turn. First off, I'm sorry. There is no excuse for stealing someone's boyfriend, especially a friend's. All I can say is that I am weak and insecure and I was only thinking about myself. You should know that the night Abel died, he told me that you were the only person who ever surprised him. That you loved him in spite of who he was and what they *did. He didn't say who* they *were or what they did. Only that initially you were supposed to be his "cover"—he used that exact word—but that he'd had an epiphany. He wanted to change, to be a better man, to be with you forever. There were tears in his eyes. Then he started mumbling about the school and his dad, but I didn't really understand any of it. Maybe because I was in shock, since he had just told me he loved you? Or maybe because the psychedelic I gave him had started to take effect? Only now I'm not so sure it was a psychedelic.*

I think it's best I say the rest in person. I'm paranoid someone might see me if I go to your cottage again. Can you meet me here? I have been hiding in the dungeon for the past three nights. Do you remember when Karla took you, me, and Esme here when we were First Years? It was the same time she took us to see the Ghost Tree and told us about her aunt Matilda and the witch trials. I know what you're thinking. Hazel Donovan is the last person you'd expect to be hiding in such a dark and creepy place where there are bats and rats. That's why I chose it. I figured no one would look for me here. And I don't have a choice. Someone wants me dead.

Your fellow witch,
Hazel

I was still angry after I read the letter the first time, and even the next few times, but now guilt has set in. And worry. Hazel *is* the last person I want to help, but I also don't want to be responsible for something awful happening to her. If what she said is true, that she is in danger, I can't just leave her there. I look at my watch. I have a class at ten. If I am going to go,

I need to do it now. She didn't say anything about needing supplies or food, but she must be hungry. I gather some crackers and peanut butter, a bottle of wine, a thermos of water, a flashlight, two packs of batteries, and a sweatshirt and baggy sweatpants, and make my way to the dungeon.

LOLA

Friday was studying a document when I walked into the office. Colin had been giving her research assignments. “Good morning,” she said before she looked up. “Oh my, what happened?” she added when she saw the bandages on my forehead and neck.

“I had a run-in with an owl,” I said.

“Ouch,” Friday said. “Was your hair in a ponytail? A friend of mine got attacked by an owl once when her hair was in a ponytail.”

I always ran with my hair in a ponytail. I could respond that I believed Abel the owl had attacked me because he was protecting Pearl, but that would require further explanation.

“Yes,” I said.

“You have three messages, two from Colin and one from Alice Landry. Colin wanted you to make sure to read his messages as soon as you got in. Something about showing a Polaroid picture around on the off chance someone might recognize one of them. He didn’t say who.”

“Thanks,” I said, and headed to my office.

The message from Alice was her wondering if we could get together for breakfast at Helen’s Greasy Spoon, “whatever time works for you." I really didn't feel like having breakfast with Alice. I always tended to drag my feet getting to wherever she suggested we meet. The first message from Colin was him reminding me he was taking Madame Luna to the airport. On the second, Friday had written, *Colin at airport on pay phone. Jerry, the ferry driver, recognized one of the girls in the Polaroid picture. He should be back around 10.*

I looked at my watch. It was 8:52. Just over an hour until his return.

I buzzed Friday. "Did Colin mention the name of the girl Jerry recognized? It's not on the note."

"No, sorry," Friday said.

"Okay, thanks." It wasn't like Colin not to leave the name. Maybe he figured that would have left me with even more questions. I mentally ran my interviews with each girl through my mind. I'd interviewed Pearl once, and both Karla and Esme at least twice, and none of them had mentioned a recent ride on the ferry. Maybe it was Hazel Donovan? That would explain why she didn't show for our appointment at Joe's. I realized my foot was shaking. A nervous habit I'd had my entire life. I decided to kill two birds with one stone, so to say.

I picked up the phone and returned Alice Landry's call.

PEARL

I'm still thinking about my visit to the tunnel when I get to my Modern and Contemporary Art History class. You were supposed to be in this class, but you never went. *Art history is boring and has nothing to do with what's happening now*, you always said.

Mr. Smith loves art history. He's jumping around excitedly, his arms flailing every which way, telling us all about the New York School, which had its beginnings in the '40s and '50s, gave birth to a movement known as abstract expressionism, and includes the likes of Jackson Pollock, Willem de Kooning, Mark Rothko, and other artists working in Manhattan after the Second World War. "Why is it considered the most influential modern art movement?" he asks the class.

No one responds.

Esme, who is sitting next to me, whispers, "Have you seen Hazel? Dean Landry has been looking for her."

"No," I lie. I promised I wouldn't tell anyone where she was. She'd asked me several times. Said it was a life-and-death situation, which seemed somewhat melodramatic. She didn't tell me why she'd been hiding in the tunnels. She said it was safer for both of us if I didn't know.

"Think, people," Mr. Smith says. He looks around as if trying to figure out who to call on. I pretend I'm invisible.

A Fourth Year named Roberta Little raises her hand. I like her work. She sews her canvases together so they look like quilts.

"She's such a kiss-up," Esme whispers.

"Roberta," Mr. Smith says.

"Because it helped New York replace Paris as the center for avant-garde art."

"That's right," Mr. Smith says. "Who coined the phrase?" He scans the class, sets his eyes on me. Dang. "Pearl?"

"Robert Motherwell," I say.

"That's right." He flips through several slides. Stops on a painting by Willem de Kooning, one of his nudes, completed in 1953, called *Woman III*.

Like all abstract expressionist paintings, it is gestural in application. According to Mr. Smith, like all de Kooning women, it is comprised "mostly of geometric and biomorphic shapes." *Woman III*'s standing body, or perhaps she's supine, takes up the entire canvas. Her face is basically a triangle. Her breasts are large circles. An upside-down triangle points at her pubic area. The painting itself is very "painterly," and the palette mostly shades of black and gray with spots of yellow and orange. It dawns on me that it was Mr. Smith who suggested I title and number the individual paintings in my body of work in a similar manner. *Fairy Painting No. 1*, *Fairy Painting No. 2*, and so on. He suggested the use of the abbreviated word for number and actual numbers instead of roman numerals. "That way it's your own."

My mind wanders to you calling my titles *derivative*. Were you ever in the art history lecture hall? Surely you were. But just in case you weren't, which actually wouldn't surprise me since you rarely showed to classes, the art history lecture hall is basically a small theater. A large screen is at the bottom of a set of stairs. Entry to the room is at the top of these stairs, where the instructor's lectern is. Generally, art history instructors instruct at the lectern, behind students, but not Mr. Smith. He likes to be part of the show. The seating is also theater style. Black Naugahyde armrests divide seats. Puffy burgundy cushions with scratchy fabric pop up when you stand. I always leave class with big red spots on the backs of my thighs.

Mr. Smith's voice brings me back. "Your assignment for next week is to write a paper on this significance," he says. "Between ten and fifteen pages. Class dismissed."

Sounds of shuffling and chairs popping shut as students file out of the class.

"Miss Calhoun," Mr. Smith says, "may I see you for a moment?" I look around to see if anyone finds it strange that he's calling me up to the lectern again. He's been doing this more often. If anyone finds out what's going on in my studio, unlike him, I could get expelled. It's one of the many double standards at St. Luke's that we girls have to delicately maneuver. Male teachers can have sex with their female students, but female students can't have sex with their male teachers.

"Good luck," Esme says as she steps over me. Her smile is conspiratorial. *Does she know?* I haven't even told Karla.

"I'm worried about you," he says when I reach the lectern. "With this hurricane coming, I hope you're taking steps to ensure your safety."

"I am," I say. I try my best to keep non-art-related discussions to a minimum with Mr. Smith. I have to exercise some control where he is concerned.

"And then there's these murders," he continues. "I expect you check to make sure who is outside before you open your studio or cottage doors to visitors?" I think to myself that this would be a good time to mention the recklessness of St. Luke's no-locks-on-doors policy, but I keep my mouth shut.

"I do," I say.

"Good," he says. "That's my girl. By the way, Hazel Donovan is a friend of yours, right? Will you tell her I want to see her? Art history is a mandatory class. She's already on thin ice."

"I will," I lie.

"All righty, then," he says. "I'll see you next week?"

"Yes, see you next week *at class*," I say. I walk at as normal a pace as I can out of the room, being that I feel his eyes checking out those red spots on the backs of my thighs.

ALICE IN WONDERLAND

I arrived at Helen's Greasy Spoon before Lola, which was not in the least unusual. Good thing patience was one of my virtues. Believe me, my job required it. When the waitress popped over, a new girl who looked as if she could be in grade school, I ordered my coffee, Lola's tea, and fresh cherry turnovers. "Don't bring the tea and turnovers until my friend arrives," I said. Then I pulled the cellophane strip from the Virginia Slims I'd just gotten from the cigarette machine, tapped the end until one popped up, lit it, smoked it down to the butt, and lit another. It was obviously my lucky day. I'd never seen Virginia Slims in that machine before. "You've come a long way, baby," I said to the cigarette, and smiled at my wit.

What was taking Lola so long? I had a board meeting to prepare for, a rescheduled meeting that was initially supposed to have taken place the morning Abel's body was found and had been delayed for the second time. "Prepare" was a somewhat loose term. We followed the same exact agenda every single meeting, and the same group of rich, arrogant assholes attempted to talk over one another, some more forceful than others, as they vied for position, advantage, and the respect they thought they rightly deserved. Especially the women. I supposed it made sense that all that jockeying to find their place in the male-dominated art world would turn them into complete bitches, but that didn't mean they had to direct that behavior at me. I ran an entire school of *younger* arrogant assholes. It seemed to me they would at least try to identify with what I had to put up with every single day.

The board consisted of two membership levels: wealthy donors and famous artists. Neither had any say in school management or decision-making. Board meetings were ceremonial at best but could literally go on for hours. We discussed the art world at large, current trends, innovative or popular artists, or our ongoing list of potential candidates for St. Luke's. I provided general progress reports on the school itself and its students. For the privilege of aiding in the identification of the future famous artists of the world and enjoying unique prestige in art, gallery, and museum circles, the twelve wealthy donors contributed an initial substantial financial gift, and similarly substantial yearly dues. A financial gift was not required of the famous artists. Their job was primarily to elevate the school's prestige and ensure its graduates were automatically revered. Neither category was privy to the school's finances or had any say or control over how their gifts were spent or how the recruitment process and the school itself was managed. Still, upon admittance to the board, all members signed nondisclosure agreements. According to the agreement, their major responsibility was to aid in the final selection of students. I said "aid in" because Monty Montague maintained right of first refusal over all selections. He was St. Luke's owner, director, founder, and chairman of the board. He selected the board members, approved the talent scouts, and ran the school. He knew where every penny went. He was king, and I was his lowly scribe and periodic concubine. Although I'd indicated to Lola that I was keeping the board apprised of the recent murders, that was a lie. The only person I was keeping apprised was Monty Montague. What he did with that information was solely at his discretion.

When I first became dean, I knew nothing about the workings of the school. I was surprised at the level of secrecy that surrounded it. I was even more surprised by the lengthy nondisclosure agreements signed by parents or guardians and students. Parent or guardian visits to campus were allowed but limited and had to be preapproved. Student visits home required preapproval and were capped at twice per year, unless there were extenuating circumstances. For their discretion and adherence to the "guidelines" set forth in contracts and NDAs, parents or guardians received both monetary and nonmonetary benefits. Nonmonetary benefits were assigned on a case-by-case basis and could potentially include such things as guarantees of good jobs, release from or avoidance of incarceration, the best possible doctors and drugs available for ailments, memberships to exclusive clubs, vacations to exotic locales, and "realization of lifelong dreams," a vague category that demanded passionate appeals and which was rarely granted. Some of these benefits were agreed to prior to parents signing the nondisclosure agreements, while others were considered individually at the "discretion of the board." But of course that meant Monty Montague.

I met Monty Montague when I was twenty-four years old. I had no plans to enter the art world. A girlfriend and I were attending a pop art exhibit at the Guggenheim. We were both working as secretaries at Bendix Corporation, a manufacturing and engineering company in Stevensville, Michigan, a small town on Lake Michigan, and got an itch to see the Big Apple. We went to Broadway plays and museums, saw the Statue of Liberty, rode in yellow cabs, all very grand and touristy. The exhibit was my friend's idea. It was Abel who initially caught my attention, a boy dressed in an adult-looking suit, shadowing a handsome older man dressed nearly the same. The man saw me staring, walked over to my friend and me, leaving the boy to stand alone.

"I'm Monty Montague," he said. "And you are . . . ?"

It was obvious he meant me. His eyes were brazenly ogling my entire body, which I admit wasn't too hard to imagine through my skimpy and stretchy red dress.

"Alice Landry," I said.

In addition to handsome, Monty Montague was charming, filthy rich, and extremely pompous. There were no men like Monty Montague where I grew up. He immediately told me how important he was, and that he and the exhibiting artists were friends. This turned out to be an understatement. After the exhibit, my girlfriend and I went out with Monty; his son, who I would later find out was ten years old; and a few of the exhibit artists, including Robert Rauschenberg, Jasper Johns, and Andy Warhol, and the art critic Harold Rosenberg. The discussion was way over my head, centering primarily on how the theories of the psychoanalyst Carl Jung, including ideas about myth, archetypes, and the collective unconscious, had influenced their work. I had no idea my life was about to change. Monty and the artists started talking about some art school located on an island somewhere down South. They were throwing around words like "nondisclosure agreement," arguing over some sort of selection process, and lamenting that a chick named Monique had just been fired or quit. I was already well on my way to drunk. But even if I hadn't been, nothing they were discussing would either have made sense or mattered to a small-town secretary whose idea of art was either rock and roll posters or velvet paintings of dogs playing poker. Monty kept running his hand up my skirt and kissing me while the room got more and more wavy. I woke up in a hotel room. I had no memory of getting separated from my girlfriend. Funny, I can't even remember her name now. Monty ordered room service. A cornucopia of fruits, pastries, eggs, sausages, and lots of champagne. And after we had sex again, he put on one of those fluffy white hotel robes, sat on the sofa, and, in a totally businesslike voice, said, "I'd like you to be my mistress. But it comes with strings. I need a new dean at a secret art academy that's located on an island off the coast of Charleston, South Carolina. You'll be very well paid. We'll also pay for an apartment and car of your choosing. But you must agree to being both my mistress *and* school dean, or the deal's off, and I need your answer and contact information right now. My son and I have a plane to catch." He paused, his eyes briefly wandering to a plush sofa in front of the large floor-to-ceiling window overlooking the city. I followed his eyes and saw that the boy, still wearing his suit, was asleep on one of the sofa's ends. I was horrified. How much did he hear and see? What kind of man would have sex with a woman while his son was in the same room, asleep or not? Obviously not a model parent, or for that matter a model human being. But I was seduced by Monty Montague's charisma and wealth, and a job offer so incredible it felt like I was living inside a fairy tale. When Monty's eyes returned to me, he added, "You also might want to consider that given how much you overheard last night, and what I'm telling you now, if you don't accept the position, I might have to kill you." He smiled.

I took the position. We fucked on and off while he proceeded to divorce two wives and marry a third, who delivered twin baby boys four months after they married, which made it clear that though he'd dangled the marriage apple before me the entire time, he never had any intention of following through. It was true that in the beginning I had fantasized about being the next Mrs. Monty Montague, but that changed when I met the one true love of my life.

Everything about my life was perfect. I was rich, drove a Mercedes, and had a gorgeous waterfront home. Perfect, that was, until three weeks ago, when I found the envelope. I was cleaning out files in one of the filing cabinets, a task I had put off since I'd arrived at St. Luke's ten years earlier, just like I'd put off hiring someone to clean out the tunnels below campus. But that was a whole other story. The drawer had gotten off track. I had to take it completely off to fit it properly back into the grooves, but it kept getting stuck on something. That was when I saw that someone had taped an oversized and sealed manila envelope under the drawer. I worked at the seal, being careful not rip it. Inside was a nondisclosure agreement for a woman named Monique Chevalier. *Monique*, I thought to myself. It was a hard name to forget. She was the woman discussed at that fancy New York dinner the night I met Monty all those years ago. The woman who used to have my job. I looked closer at the agreement. It appeared to be exactly the same as mine. Same job title, same responsibilities, same benefit package, same language noting that she served at the pleasure of Monty Montague. I flipped to the signature page. Miss Chevalier had signed the agreement six years before I became dean. Though I did find the fact that she appeared to have hidden the envelope odd, I wanted to believe she was merely some kind of paranoid privacy freak. I decided to return the agreement to the envelope for the moment and think about it later. But when I attempted to do so, the envelope wouldn't push all the way in. Something was in the way. I pulled it back out and fished inside. There at the bottom of the bottom were three documents: Monique Chevalier's driver's license, social security card, and passport, and a brief handwritten note that read: *To the finder of these documents, please be aware that your life is in danger. RUN!* She had signed and dated the note March 12, 1963, three days before Monty offered me her job. No matter how many times I tried to convince myself that Monique Chevalier's note and documents meant nothing, I couldn't shake my suspicion. I knew what Monty Montague was capable of.

I stuck everything in my briefcase. When I got home that night, I hid it under my mattress until I had time to think through and plot my next move.

"There you are," I heard someone say. I looked up to see Lola Germany. She slid into the booth across from me. "I need to be back to the office in an hour. Important meeting. Does that give us enough time?"

She was fifteen minutes late, and *she* needed to get back to the office?

"That's fine," I said. "It's so good to see you. Have I told you how grateful the board is that you're handling all these, well, *incidents* so professionally. Any leads?"

"If by 'incidents,' you mean the murders, we don't have any official leads yet. You do know that the town is on edge and students are really scared. Their classmates are dying and they don't know why or, god forbid, whether they'll be next. They tell me that there are no locks on their dorm room doors. Is that in the process of being rectified?"

"Unfortunately, the local locksmith is busy helping with hurricane preparations, but I'm sure he'll get to it as soon as the storm has passed. You seemed stressed."

"I'm just trying to make sure no one else dies."

Poor Lola. So married to her job. I hadn't known her to have a man in her life since she moved to the island. It was surprising really. She was a smart, attractive woman. More than attractive, actually. Lola Germany was one of the most beautiful women I'd ever met. There was an innate grace about her, an elegance. I was envious of her height, thick chestnut hair, and taut runner's body from the moment I met her. Where a lover or, for that matter, any man you want for yourself was concerned, Lola Germany was the type of woman you kept close and secretly undermined.

"How's it going on your end?" Lola asked. "With the parents?"

I proceeded to lie. What else could I do? "I called Eric's parents yesterday," I said. "And I'm in the process of scheduling his, and George's and Jeannine's, transportation off the island. All the helicopter companies are grounded due to the hurricane. So I've made reservations for tomorrow. Hopefully, by then, everything will be back to normal, and we won't all be dead. Due to the storm, I mean."

Lola smiled. I also hated her sweet smile, full lips, perfect white teeth, and olive skin tone. I'd studied her face many times and hadn't noted one line, which was astounding, given we were nearly the same age. "Thank you for doing that," she said. "I imagine it's difficult delivering that sort of news."

"Oh my gosh, no need to thank me. I'm here to help. And nothing I do can possibly be as hard as what you do," I said, using a technique called mirroring that I'd learned in secretarial training way back at Bendix. The class was called How to Please Your Boss. A better, more accurate title might have been How to Kiss Up to Your Boss. The technique had come in handier than I would ever have imagined. I use it on Monty Montague regularly. "I heard you were trying to meet with Hazel Donovan. Did you ever find her?"

"How did you hear that?"

"I can't remember. I think it was at Art Sunday." Another lie. Esme provided me with daily reports. All the class liaisons were my little spies.

"I haven't been able to meet with her yet," Lola said. "I'm hoping to catch up with her today."

"If you'd like, I can coordinate a time for the two of you to meet." I had no intention of setting up any more meetings between Lola and St. Luke's students. Especially that little bitch Hazel.

"Thanks, but I'll figure it out on my own. I know you're busy."

Just then, the child-waitress delivered Lola's tea and our cherry turnovers. "More coffee?" she asked me.

"Sure," I said.

And Lola and I preceded to do what girlfriends who aren't really girlfriends do. Engage in niceties and pretense. And avoid the truth.

PEARL

You have been following me. I see you perched in trees, on Karla's or my porch railing, and now you perch atop a bicycle rack across from my studio, the sun shining on your feathers. It's a nice day out, my garage door is open, and there's a warm breeze off the ocean. No high winds, no rain. It's hard to believe there's a hurricane coming. Karla is hanging at my studio while I try to paint. I point you, the owl, out to her.

"He'll be gone soon," she says. "Dead like that asshole inside him. Good riddance as far as I'm concerned. Abel Montague deserved to die. He treated you like shit. He was a chauvinist pig."

"I believe he's trying to make amends," I say. "Everyone deserves a second chance. Don't you think?"

"*Second* chance? I'd say he was up to the triple digits as far as chances go. Speaking of things he did to you, have you heard anything from Hazel yet?"

I want to tell her about visiting Hazel in the dungeon, but Hazel asked me not to. *No one can know*, she said. *It's too dangerous.*

"No," I lie.

"Well, I may be mad at her, but there is a hurricane coming. Last I heard, it's supposed to make landfall between five and six tonight. Everybody at school is talking about it. The islanders are planning to gather in the church basement. They say it's the safest place on the island. Esme says Alice in Wonderland wants us to meet at the Monastery. Yeah right. The last person I want to die with is Alice in Wonderland. Hey, why don't we hang out at my cottage? We can do a séance. Or, better yet, we could open that Ouija board my mum sent. Did you know that 'Ouija' means 'good luck'? Apparently, some medium was leading a séance back in 1890 and she asked the board what it wanted to be named and it spelled out *O-U-I-J-A*. And then she asked what that meant, and the board spelled out *G-O-O-D-L-U-C-K*."

"How do you know this stuff?" I ask.

She shrugs her shoulders. "I guess I'll get going so you can paint. But don't be too long, okay?" She pauses. "Aren't you scared? Not of the storm. Well, that too, but someone is murdering St. Luke's students, and it doesn't seem like anyone's scared. Or is wondering who's next. And Alice in Wonderland expects us to act like nothing whatsoever is different."

"I think everyone is scared," I say. "I've heard people whispering about it. They're just afraid to say too much publicly because of what you said about Alice in Wonderland. I have noticed that more students seem to be skipping classes. It's as if they're holing up in their dorm rooms, cottages, or studios."

I want to tell Karla about the paintings that keep showing up in my studio, the ones I can't remember painting. But I can't because even though she is my biggest supporter, she won't be able to help but be suspicious of me. Yet another secret. But this one is for *my* protection. No one would believe I was painting murders before they occurred unless I was involved in them. And not only that, the paintings seem to show not only when but how the murders will happen.

"It's pretty crazy when you're afraid you'll get in trouble or expelled if you talk about being afraid of getting murdered. But you're right, I have noticed that people are skipping class," Karla says. "My art theory class was nearly empty this morning. Maybe you should just plan on staying at my cottage until all this is over. Neither of us should be alone. I see those cops Detective Germany posted at the entrance to the forest watching our cottages. So that's comforting. They're really friendly. I've been taking them tea and water." She pauses. "We'll be fine. I'm going to go, okay? Don't be too long."

She doesn't wait for me to respond. After Karla leaves, I study my *Fairy Painting No. 6*. My ballerina detective is standing before the tree again, her sheer white gown caught by a loud, strong wind. But still she talks to the tree. That's what she does. That's how I know what happened to her. That she was accused of killing her husband, but the jury said it was self-defense. That he used to hurt her when he got drunk or angry. I am amazed at her physical and emotional strength. Like always, I'm trying to capture that strength as well as her mysterious elegance in this painting. She's looking up through its branches, her hands in prayer, her long chestnut hair and white gown blowing sideways. The forest creatures are gone. They've taken refuge from the impending storm. She stands in wait, ready to fight. But there is another storm brewing. One that began a long time ago. I *know* because I *saw* it. A hazy vision of an old crumbling brick monastery and a young woman in white tied to a cross while three blood-robed men set her on fire. My ballerina detective can't stop what was set in motion centuries ago. At least not alone. She will require the ongoing magic of the Great Priestess and the Ghost Women, the knowledge contained inside the pages of a black velvet book, and the interference of a scorned wife, a swamp witch, and *you*, a red-eyed owl.

LOLA

Colin sat across from me, took out the picture, and pointed to Esme Li. "Jerry said he saw her on the ferry back in July. To and from Charleston. Two weeks apart. Wouldn't she have needed permission to leave school that long? He gave me the exact dates. Here, I wrote them down."

"Esme Li?" I asked. "Was he certain?"

"Yep," Colin said.

I felt my hopes slide. I had wanted it to be Hazel Donovan. I was convinced Hazel contacted me because she knew something. But someone or something had stopped her from entering Joe's that day.

"What does that have to do with our murders?" I asked.

"Jerry said she was throwing up the whole way to the mainland. Made a huge mess that he had to clean up. Said it would be hard to forget the girl, given his clean-up effort. I said maybe she had the flu and he said he didn't think so. That she kept caressing her belly. Said his wife used to do that when she was pregnant. Jerry's a pretty sensitive guy, so it made me think. And I remembered Jody doing the same thing when she was pregnant. So I thought I should check it out. I called in a favor from a good friend at Charleston PD whose wife, Maggie, is a maternity doctor in North Charleston. Maggie is a strong proponent of abortion reform, but also part of a doctors' advocacy group that keeps tabs on backdoor clinics."

"Go on," I said.

"Anyway, Kevin—that's my buddy—asked Maggie to check whether any of her colleagues knew of a nineteen-year-old Asian girl who had a successful procedure or was checked into a hospital with complications around the time Jerry says he saw her on the ferry. I figured Esme wouldn't use her real name, and I was right. A Jane Doe fitting Esme's description was rushed to the Medical University of South Carolina after a botched procedure. According to Maggie, she nearly died. She spent the remainder of the two weeks in the hospital recuperating. Bad news, she won't be having any more kids."

"Wow." I was dumbfounded. "Poor thing."

"Yep. One more thing. It looks like Esme was raped."

"Raped? Were they sure?"

"Esme didn't deny it when one of the nurses asked. The hospital could tell because the uterus was damaged and there was lots of internal bruising. It seems before the rape, Esme was a virgin. And so then my brain is going crazy and I start wondering if Abel Montague got her pregnant because there seems to be a pattern here. I mean, it's not really a leap, given his reputation. And to some, that just might be a good enough reason to kill him."

I sat back in my chair and closed my eyes, took a deep breath and then another.

"You okay, boss?"

"I'm fine. It's just so awful."

"Yep. Sounds like we might need to talk with Esme."

I felt guilty. I had pegged Esme as controlling and wanting to be in charge. But how unfair I had been. None of us knows what's really going on with anyone else, what their life has been. I could see now that her behavior and choices could easily be attributed to a need to control *something* in her life. I, of all people, knew that one. I felt the need to take Esme into my arms and hold her until she let it all out, hug her tight as she screamed and cried at a culture that allowed boys like Abel Montague to hurt girls. Is that why he was murdered? Who else had Abel hurt? I knew about Karla Gardyn. Were there more? And what about the other murders? Could they all be about revenge? But why Tarot? Why cards from the fifteenth century? Why stage the bodies to represent specific cards?

What am I missing?

Esme's paintings came to my mind. The dripping blood. The exquisite fury. I had totally underestimated the rage that was building at St. Luke's. And for a moment, I felt what would come. Whatever was going on here wasn't finished.

"Yes," I said to Colin. "Let's go visit Esme Li."

ESME

I was sitting at my drawing table in my studio when I heard my name.

"Hi, Esme."

I looked up to see Detective Germany and a man in a suit standing at the edge of my garage door where everyone could see them. I always left my garage door open. Part of my position as class liaison was to be a role model, and open garage doors promoted camaraderie among all the students. "This is my partner, Detective Colin Pierce. We apologize for interrupting your process, but we have some questions."

"Can it wait?" I asked, not even attempting to hide my irritation. "I have a critique with my advisor in an hour, and I wanted to get this gilding right. It's the sort of thing that has to be done immediately and I just applied it."

"I'm afraid not," she said. "It's an official visit. We'd actually prefer you come to the station with us."

"Why?" I asked.

"We want to talk without interruption. You can call your advisor from there to tell him or her you'll be late. We'll drive you back."

"Her," I said. I found it odd that she didn't know my advisor was Alice in Wonderland. She was the advisor for all class liaisons. That didn't seem like very good detecting on Detective Germany's part.

I knew why they were here as soon as Detective Germany mentioned it was an "official visit." I didn't plan for the so-called doctor who did the abortion not to be a medical doctor. As soon as the cab had stopped in front the broken-down house in a seedy area of town, I knew I might be in trouble, but what choice did I have? I was there. I'd made up my mind. So I paid the driver and knocked on the door. I could tell the first time Detective Germany interviewed me that she was circumspect. Perhaps all detectives were. I lied a few times during that interview. Like I talked up Pearl, said what a good and innocent person she was. The Weird Sisters all agreed to say that so no one would suspect her of killing Abel. But Pearl wasn't innocent. She was self-centered and oblivious. She had no idea whatsoever that her boyfriend had raped me, and if she did, she obviously didn't care. And then there was our good friend Hazel fucking Abel on the side. How did neither of them see that he was an asshole and a rapist? What he took from me I would never get back. As far as I was concerned, he deserved to die. Couldn't Pearl at least see what a mess I was? Couldn't any of them? How sick I was? I was with the three of them doing those stupid spells, and more than once I had to excuse myself to run to the bathroom and throw up. And then there was Mr. Smith. Pearl was his class pet. Always praising her perceptions in art history and her drawings and paintings in studio classes. Saying how talented she was, that she'd be "the Next Big Thing." Right in front of the whole class. As if the rest of us weren't thirsty for that coveted title. One time, he even said that the art world had been waiting for her "to step into the scene for a long time." I always wondered what Abel thought about that. Did it piss him off? He thought he was the best. Or was that what attracted him to her? *Was* he attracted to her? I would swear he didn't give a shit about her. I could never figure the two of them out.

I paused, thought about how unfair and self-destructive it was to blame Pearl or Karla or Hazel. What happened to me wasn't their fault. I could have told them I was pregnant. Why hadn't I? Wouldn't they have kept my secret? Helped me? As Karla always said, we girls needed to stick together. Infighting would be our downfall. If we stuck together, we would be unbeatable.

But now I had to lie again, say I found the run-down house and the so-called doctor on my own. If I told the truth, that it was actually Alice in Wonderland who set it all up, I'd get expelled. She didn't do anything for altruistic reasons. She wanted something in return. *St. Luke's doesn't give you girls a free ride just for you to get pregnant*, she'd said. *We are breeding famous artists here, not babies. Giving back to the school is part of the contract. But nobody has to know about this unfortunate situation, do they?*

I looked down at my painting. I hadn't begun the series until after what happened. I had been experimenting with miniatures and a jewel-toned palette reminiscent of the Renaissance, but in terms of subject matter, all I'd settled on were things with wings. Birds and butterflies and angels. Sweet things. It was when I was in the hospital that I decided on the penises. They were perfect. So tiny they'd be hard to identify at first. I liked the idea of the viewer being shocked once they looked closer. I liked that in my paintings, at least, I had total control over them. I could make them fly and crash, make them wander aimlessly, make them bleed. The irony was I'd never seen a penis in person. I barely remembered anything from that night. I used pictures from one of my art history books, *Gardner's Art Through the Ages*, to get them right. Naked men with idealized penises abound in drawings, paintings, and sculptures from the Renaissance period, like Michelangelo's *The Vitruvian Man* and *Da-*

vid, not to mention their abundance on the ceiling of the Sistine Chapel. But interestingly, it seemed only male artists painted them. Some sort of self-idealization? I wondered what Sigmund Freud would have thought about that. I was certain a girl painting penises would raise more than a few eyebrows, and I was right. The first time I showed them to Mr. Smith, his demeanor toward me changed, and from then on, he looked at me differently, even asked my opinion during class. But what no one knew was that the paintings weren't meant to be the entirety of my thesis exhibit. I had a secret weapon up my sleeve. Upon graduation, on my opening night, I was going to throw every painting, one by one, into Karla's witch's cauldron and light them on fire. I planned to film the whole thing so it also became performance art. Castration by fire.

I rose, grabbed my jean jacket and backpack. Outside, I pulled down the garage door and closed the side door. There were no locks on the studios or dorm room doors. St. Luke's wanted access to every part of our lives. St. Luke's had seduced us with promises of fame and fortune, and now they owned us. The Weird Sisters all felt this way. We'd downed many bottles of wine over discussions at Karla's about how to access our power. We knew we were the stronger sex, at least at St. Luke's and, it stood to reason, beyond. The boys didn't work nearly as hard. Everything came easy to them, but it wouldn't always be easy out in the big art world, would it? While they were busy jockeying for position with other male painters, we women would be slowly but surely growing our wings, and one day, when the time was perfect, we would soar right past them.

I didn't talk on the way to the station, and neither did Detective Germany or her sidekick. Even though they'd left the window between the front and back seats open, I felt like a caged criminal.

They took me into a conference room once we got there. Asked me if I wanted anything to drink. "Tea, coffee, Coke?"

"Do you have water?" I asked.

"One water coming up," the male detective said. He sounded like a cheerful sort.

He returned with my water. What was his name again? Colin something. But what did names matter anyway? What did anything matter? He proceeded to tell me about the ferry driver seeing me this past July. Then came the hammer. He'd done some detecting, like a good detective did. He seemed pretty proud of himself for finding out about the abortion. That was when Detective Germany joined the conversation.

"I'm so sorry, Esme," she said. "It's not fair what you've been through. I'm so sorry for your loss."

Was she? Really? She wasn't sorry for screwing up my painting. Or my time. Or the challenges I faced in my role as class liaison. Everyone saw them come to my studio. Everyone saw me pathetically following them. Everyone saw me not in control.

"Loss?" I asked. "I didn't want the fucking baby. It came from a rapist."

"I'm sorry for that too," she said. "But I meant about the operation going wrong. About losing your ability to have children in the future."

That was what she had? That was how she'd planned to break me down and turn me into a sniveling idiot?

"I'm fine," I said. And for the most part, I was, but I was also afraid. I wasn't sleeping. Alice in Wonderland had been watching me. And there was something else. A feeling of impending doom.

"I'd be angry too," Detective Germany said. "It must have been so painful, so scary." Her voice cracked.

I looked at her eyes. There were tears in them. For a brief moment, I felt her sadness and I wished I could tell her about St. Luke's unwritten rules, overt sexism, male chauvinism, and culture of unwanted sex. Maybe then she would better understand my choice. I felt my face getting red. I swallowed, pushed the sadness away. But I couldn't tell her. I couldn't tell her anything bad about St. Luke's. There was too much at stake. And the truth was, I was luckier than most. I didn't get kicked out when I got pregnant, which was what I thought was going to happen when Alice in Wonderland figured it out. Like the ferry driver, she saw me throw up. But at least that time, I'd made it to the bathroom. But instead of kicking me out, she'd actually saved me. She set up and paid for the whole thing. And even though I knew what that meant, that she'd expect something in return, I figured I could handle whatever it was.

I was wrong.

Pull yourself together, Esme. "I'm not angry," I said. "I'm grateful."

"How so?" Detective Colin asked.

"I'm grateful I can fuck all I want in the future and not get pregnant."

He looked offended. Poor man.

"Esme," Detective Germany said, "who raped you?"

"Does it matter?" I asked.

"He should be punished."

Did she think I was stupid? That I didn't know she was trying to trap me? "He was already punished," I said.

"Were you the one who punished him?" she asked.

I hunched my shoulders.

"I think he deserved to die," Detective Colin said.

Psychology. Identifying with the victim. How naive did they think I was? Not to mention condescending. How could *he* identify with me?

"Me too," I said.

"Esme." Detective Germany again. Using my name was an interview tactic. I knew because I used to watch those TV detective shows with my parents and grandfather back in San Francisco. *Hawaii Five-O*, *Dragnet*, and *Mannix*. "Can you tell us who did this to you. Whose baby it was?"

I considered my options. Should I tell? Should I not tell? I felt myself smiling in spite of myself. I was done with the lies and deceit, done with the sexist environment St. Luke's bred, done with Alice in Wonderland's threats, done with obeying, done with being a sweet little girl. What was it she'd said to me when she told me I should get the abortion? Oh yes. *Don't throw the baby out with the bathwater.* Well, I was done with that too.

"I can tell you who did it, but not whose baby it was," I said.

Detective Germany cocked her head. Was it confusion I saw on her face? Sadness? Worry? "Who?" she asked.

"The three dead men," I said. "Abel Montague, George Archambault, and Eric Bernard."

LOLA

“There was a party at the Monastery,” Esme said. “They were drunk. I’d had one glass of wine. But I wasn’t feeling well. I felt woozy. Abel offered to walk me up to my room. He came in. Then the other two were there. I don’t remember all of it. They probably put something in my drink. I’d heard they were doing that. When I woke up, there was blood on the sheets, and I was bruised and sore down there, so I knew what had happened. They never bothered me again, so I figured it was some sort of rite of passage. Six weeks later, my breasts got sore and then I started throwing up.”

“So Dean Landry gave you the name of the abortion clinic?” I asked.

“No.” She avoided my eyes.

I could tell she was lying. I understood why. If Alice found out Esme had told anyone, especially the police, there would be consequences. She might get expelled. The question was, why did Alice help her? Was she more compassionate than I gave her credit for? Did she want something in return?

“Then how did you find the clinic?”

"I read about it in the classifieds," she said. "In a newspaper someone left in the library."

I was pretty certain illegal abortion clinics weren't listed in the classifieds.

"Who else knows this happened?" I asked. "The other witches?"

She started laughing. "Other witches? That's funny. I'm supposed to monitor them."

"Monitor?" Colin asked.

"I'm class liaison. It's my job to keep tabs on what everyone is doing. For Dean Landry. The three of them are harmless really."

"Do you tell Dean Landry everything?" I asked. "If you knew who was responsible for these murders, would you tell her that?"

Again she avoided my eyes. "I tell her anything she asks me."

The words were carefully chosen. *Anything she asks me.* Meaning, not everything?

Her eyes met mine. They were defiant.

It was clear to me that Esme was in a lot more pain than she was letting on. I wondered whether it was fear of repercussion that was holding her together or if she had mentally shut down. I believed she needed to talk with someone. A professional. A safe space where she was allowed to feel her pain. I'd felt the same way about Pearl when I interviewed her, even though I had yet to fully understand the extent of Abel's abuse. There is a silk thread that connects all women. A shared knowledge of our own vulnerability. No matter how alert we are or how many self-defense classes we've taken, we are all keenly aware it just takes one moment, one blind spot, one unexpected circumstance.

After we drove back to the Monastery, we insisted on walking Esme to her studio. Alice was leaving the building just as Colin parked. A stern look of disapproval crossed her face.

"You didn't show up for your appointment," she said to Esme.

"It's my fault," I said. It hadn't entered my mind that Alice was Esme's advisor.

Without saying another word, Alice got into her car and drove away.

Back at the station, we reviewed where we were on the case. "Abel Montague, George Archambault, and Eric Bernard," Colin said. "It can't be a coincidence. Do you think Esme had something to do with their murders? Poor kid, not sure I'd blame her."

"I don't know," I said. "But she can't be their only victim."

"What about Jeannine Hart?" he asked.

"Wrong place, wrong time maybe?"

"Where does that kind of violence come from?" he asked. "Peer pressure? Or were these boys inherently bad? Surely that sort of thing lives with you forever. I mean, I have three daughters, and the thought of that happening to one of them—well, I'm not sure I could hold my anger. It's pretty obvious that someone wanted these three boys dead. The question is who?"

"Actually," I said, "I'm beginning to think the question is, who didn't?"

HAZEL

I've been trying to find Detective Germany alone ever since I was supposed to meet her at Joe's. I know she goes to the forest every morning really early—Pearl, or was it Karla, mentioned that—but I never seem to make it out of the tunnels before sunrise, when the light peeks through a crack in the hatch. Right now, I'm watching the station from a bench across the street. I'm wearing sunglasses and a baseball cap so no one recognizes me.

Detective Germany's police car drives up. She gets out of the car. I nearly call out to her, but then I see she's with her sidekick guy and someone else. *Esme*. No way I can let Esme see me. She's Alice in Wonderland's spy. And the whole game thing started with her. The three of them go inside.

Esme had showed up at my studio the day before the autumnal equinox. "A group of us are playing a performance art game," she said. "It's very selective. Only the best artists. Are you interested? It'll be fun."

Only the best artists? "What kind of performance art game?"

"It's kind of a chain. I left a black velvet book under your bed in your dorm room. You don't need to read the whole thing, just the section I marked with the envelope. The rules of the Game, the name of your subject, and directions on how to administer the psychedelic are inside the envelope."

"Psychedelic? I don't use drugs."

"I know," she said. "We're sisters, remember? It's for your subject, not you. And it's harmless. Trust me. It'll just make your subject drowsy. You must complete your task tonight. If you don't, you'll break the chain. Don't share the book or the contents of the envelope with anyone, including your subject. If you do, you'll break the chain. After you've completed your task, burn the envelope and place the book back under your bed. I'll retrieve it and pass it on to the next player."

"Who are the other players?" I asked. "Are Pearl and Karla playing?"

"Part of the fun is that you won't know the identities of the other players until the Game is over. But just between you and me, no, Pearl and Karla aren't playing. We don't have to do everything with them, do we? Afterward, all the players and subjects will meet at the Monastery for a party and recap. Very exclusive. It's cool, don't you think? Total performance art. So are you in?"

I felt special, especially because Pearl and Karla weren't invited, and so I said yes. Then I returned to my dorm room, found the book, and opened the envelope. My subject was Abel.

Nearly an hour passes before the three of them exit the station, get back in the police car, and drive away. I consider waiting until Detective Germany returns, but the wind is picking up. When Pearl came to see me this morning, she said there was a hurricane coming.

I look around, don't see anyone leaving or entering the station, so I cross the street and try the door. It's unlocked. I hear voices coming from somewhere in another part of the building, but I don't have a choice. I can't wait another day to get the book to Detective Germany. I tiptoe through the building, barely breathing, while I check out the names on the doors. Finally, I see her nameplate. I go inside, reach into my backpack, retrieve the black velvet book, set it on her desk, and hightail it out of the building.

Should I have left a note? What is there to say? When she reads the book, she'll understand.

PEARL

It is around three P.M. when I see my ballerina detective and her partner take Esme away with them. I'm still in my studio painting, but I'm watching the clock more than I normally would because of the hurricane. It's supposed to hit between five and six. I'm worried about Hazel. When we asked Karla whether the tunnels were safe when she took us down there last year, she said they'd stood for centuries. *The walls and ceiling are made of the same rocks that stand between St. Luke's and the ocean*, she added. But I'm not just worried about the walls, there are all kinds of creepy crawlers down there. Who knows whether any of them are poisonous. Hazel's show of bravery when I saw her yesterday made her appear even more lonely and scared. Should I go get her? I'm still angry but also torn. Stealing a sister's boyfriend is a pretty awful thing to do. But she's one of us. The Weird Sisters.

I stand back, assess my progress. It has been a good painting day. Good days are rare. I love this part of the process, when the ébauche, the underpainting, is on the canvas, when the composition is established, when white space still intermittently shines through color. It's the layering I love best, the strokes of the brush, some thick and dense, impasto, others dry or flat washes or scumbling or stippling. My ballerina detective's gown is many shades of white. The light plays across it, enhancing the contrast between it and the raw umber, burnt sienna, yellow ocher, and mars black of the tree trunk. But I need to stop for the day. It'll take at least a half hour to clean my brushes.

I notice the wind is picking up when I finish with the brushes. I walk over and close the garage door, start to do the same with the side door when I see my ballerina detective and her partner escorting Esme to her studio. Slowly, I slip back inside and watch through a crack in the door. After a short while, they leave. I grab my raincoat and boots, bundle up, and head into the wind.

Out of the corner of my eye, I notice someone standing in the field. Her back is to me, her dark hair and black skirt blowing sideways like mine. It's Esme. Why is she standing there? I call to her, but she doesn't appear to hear me. She's pouring something out of a container. Dots of color. Pieces of one of her canvases. I've seen her do this before. She cuts her canvases into tiny pieces when they don't meet her high expectations. As they fall, the particles are caught by the wind. They swirl around her, wrapping her body like moths spinning a silk cocoon. Around and around. Denser and denser. Faster and faster. Then I see *them*, the Ghost Women. Swooping in from all directions, the forest and the ocean and the school. They join the particles in circling Esme. Wispy white translucent scarves flowing and winding through and around the particles and her. A dance. A dance of gentle, sensuous warriors. I've never seen the Ghost Women do anything like this before. It is dazzling. Enchanting. Bewitching.

"Esme," I call again, but now I can't even hear myself, my voice no match for the roar of the wind. And then the vision comes to me and I *see* what you, George, and Eric did to her and I know why she left for those two weeks and I feel a deep sadness for Esme and her lost child. And guilt that I didn't see what she was going through then, that I wasn't there for her. Tears come to my eyes as I wrestle with my emotions. I should hate you, but I don't. I shouldn't love you, but I still do.

What is wrong with me?

Then it stops. The wind dies. Complete stillness. Eerie, unnatural. The particles fall to the ground, like colorful sprinkles dusting a cake. The Ghost Women dissolve into the air. In the distance, perched in a tree, I see you, the owl. *Why did you do it? Why would you do that to Esme? She is my friend. Why would you do that to anyone? What is wrong with you?*

Your glowing red eyes merely stare.

"Esme," I call again, "you need to come inside. There's a hurricane coming. The wind will pick back up soon."

She turns, looks at me, her eyes wide as if she's in a trance. I go to her, take her hand, walk her back to her studio. Tell her to sit.

"Can I get you anything?" I ask.

"I'm fine," she says. "What was that? It felt like time stopped. I felt so safe. As if I was inside an angel's arms. You saw it, right? It was beautiful, wasn't it?"

"Yes," I say.

"Those detectives were here," she says. "They don't know anything. They were just fishing. And they pissed me off. It was their fault I had to cut up my painting. That Detective Germany is just like every other non-artist. No respect for the artistic process. Her sidekick seemed okay though."

I want to tell Esme that Detective Germany is an artist in her own right, that she was once a famous prima ballerina. But I don't.

My knowledge of her will always be sacred.

"We need to leave," I say. "The storm is coming. Do you want to go to Karla's with me? We can walk together."

"Dean Landry wants all the class liaisons to shelter in the Monastery. I'm sorry, by the way, for everything. Please tell everyone how sorry I am, okay? Tell them I know I should have been stronger."

"There's nothing for you to be sorry for," I say.

"Just tell them," she says. She rises, hugs me. It has been a long while since the two of us held each other. I forgot how thin and frail she is. I taste a salty tear but don't know whether it's hers or mine. I promise myself I will make it up to her, that I will do whatever it takes to rebuild the friendship I let slip away.

We leave her studio together but go our separate ways, Esme toward the Monastery, me toward Hazel and the forest. The storm is getting angrier. The garage doors rattling. Trees bending sideways. Loose leaves floating through the sky. I am pushing my way through the wind when I have the urge to turn and look back at Esme. All I can see is the outline of her fragile body fading into the storm.

LOLA

I dropped Colin off at his house.

"Are you sure you don't want to spend the hurricane with us? Jody and I are telling the girls we're camping. Unrolling sleeping bags, filling backpacks with valuables and a cooler with water. We've got this hurricane thing down. I worry about your house. The older houses on pylons are more vulnerable than other structures on the island."

"I'll be fine," I said. "I'm a stone's throw from the forest. The trees will protect me. Kiss the girls for me."

"Will do," he said. "And be safe, okay?"

"You too," I said.

I had intended to go back to the station, but the wind was getting stronger. My house was situated far enough from the water to easily avoid high tide, but hurricane surge was different. Already, the tide was so high the water was covering the road in places, causing my wheels to slide. As I passed the marina, I saw the waves crashing against the docks. It would be a wonder if they survived. We replaced them after nearly every hurricane. Some of the boats were still moored, banging back and forth against the wood posts. Surely, they would get damaged or their ties would break and they'd blow out to the sea. Probably their owners didn't live full-time on the island. Soon the water would start crashing against the stone cliffs that both St. Luke's grounds and my tree goddess overlooked. There was nothing I could physically do to save my tree or the motley crew that watched the sunrise with me. Except pray.

I turned into the long driveway that led to my house. Even from a distance, the house looked like a fort in a World War II movie. The Waverly Island Hurricane Fighters, a group of local do-gooders, including fire department officials and police officers, had boarded up my windows and built a wall of sandbags. It was the third time I'd been through this drill since I moved back to the island.

Inside, I took a shower, put on sweatpants and a sweatshirt, closed the fireplace dampers, poured myself a glass of pinot (courtesy of Maria), and turned on the TV. News reporters wearing slick black raincoats stood in White Point Garden overlooking the Charleston Harbor. They were struggling to remain upright against the storm surge. Outside my house on Waverly Island, the wind whistled and the rain pounded. Doors and windows shook. Periodically came the sound of loud bangs. Loose objects hitting the sandbags or roof. I was alert but not scared. I'd been through this drill many times as both a child and an adult. Surrendering was the trick. I was no match for Mother Nature. I nestled beneath my quilt on the sofa and studied the victim and potential perpetrator maps I'd created, zeroed in on the photograph of the four girls Alice Landry had given me.

"At least one of you knows more than you're saying," I said aloud to the picture. "Maybe you all do."

Madame Luna had called Pearl a seer. A seer, according to her, was a person who possessed the ability to see or foresee future events but also had extraordinary insight or knowledge into the past or present. The Weird Sisters called themselves witches. In my dictionary, "witch" had two distinct definitions: "a person, especially a woman, having supernatural powers as by a compact with the devil or evil spirits" and "a practitioner or follower of white magic." I wondered which applied. Perhaps a bit of both? I reviewed my notes. Alice Landry had called the witchery of the four girls harmless. *They light candles and incense, smoke pot, read cards.* Madame Luna had called Karla a green witch, a healer. And what of the tarot cards found at the scenes? Were they from a fourth, yet-to-be-discovered Visconti-Sforza pack, the earliest tarot packs in existence? A loud thud on the roof. I stiffened. Slowly breathed in through my nose and out my mouth. Waited. Brought the wineglass to my lips and took a sip. I returned my attention to the maps. Something was missing. Why did the killer leave tarot cards at the scenes? Why from a fifteenth-century deck? Madame Luna had said that tarot cards weren't used for divination until the eighteenth century. Prior to that, they were used to play a game called Tarocchi. What did that game have to do with St. Luke's Institute of the Arts? Wait. I wasn't thinking about this correctly. It wasn't always St. Luke's. Centuries earlier, it was an abbey, a practicing monastery. Were the three cards left at the murder scenes part of a tarot pack that originally belonged to the monks? If so, what did the monks do with the cards? I had meant to get to the store on Marsh Road that both Karla and Pearl had mentioned, Priscilla's Antiques, to see if she could answer some of these questions. I also still needed to find and interview Hazel Donovan. She was the only Weird Sister I had yet to meet in person. Why hadn't she shown for our rendezvous at Joe's? Too many days had gone by for her absence to be unintentional. I was more and more convinced that Hazel Donovan was the key.

My concentration was interrupted by a chipper talking head on the news. He was standing to the right of a blown-up map of the southeastern United States. "It looks like the worst of the storm has passed over Florida, Georgia, and the Carolinas, and is heading up the coast," he said.

I poured myself another glass of wine, muted the volume, listened to the dying wind, and continued staring at the victim map. "I'm close," I said to them. "I'm sorry I didn't catch your murderer before it was too late for you, but I'm going to do my best to catch whoever it is before they can hurt anyone else."

I leaned back, closed my eyes. I was so tired. I hadn't been sleeping well. I felt my body relaxing, and then wavy, scattered images were floating through my mind. Tarot cards and the Ghost Tree and the poppets at the murder scenes and the Unmarked Tombstone and Pearl's altar and the four dead bodies. Abel Montague hanging upside down. George Archambault and Jeannine Hart diving to their deaths. Eric Bernard's exposed skull. Each of the bodies deliberately posed to resemble a certain tarot card. I woke. Shook my shoulders and head. Realized I might be thinking about the murders all wrong. Could the murders themselves, like the cards they represented, be part of a game?

I reached for the phone book, looked up the number for Priscilla's Antiques, picked up the phone. I intended to leave a message, thinking she wouldn't be at her shop on the heels of a hurricane, but to my surprise, a voice said, "Priscilla's Antiques."

"Hello," I said. "My name is Detective Lola Germany. I apologize for calling you at such an inopportune moment, and I hope you weathered the storm okay, but I was wondering if perhaps we could meet. I have some questions about Waverly Island's history, specifically the monastery and the witch burnings, and your name came up."

"I have been waiting for you," she said.

Why is she waiting for me?

"Is there a time tomorrow that is convenient for you?" I asked.

"I will be here. My shop is on Marsh Road behind my house. Try both doors."

"What is your address?"

"There is no address. Just look for the bottle tree."

PEARL

I can't see more than two feet in any direction. The temperature has dropped several degrees. I'm fighting against a moving wall of wind and rain, digging my shoes into the wet ground to stay upright, my skirt whipping my legs as my fists hold my jacket closed, my hair slapping my face, choking my nose and mouth. But I keep moving. Finally, I see Karla's cottage. Sandbags piled to the top of the porch railing, leaving only a narrow path through the steps. A window shutter slapping open and shut. A figure standing in the doorway. Karla. She appears to be shouting, but I can't make out what she's saying.

"What?" I say as I climb.

"The school hired the Waverly Island Hurricane Fighters to stack the sandbags and nail the shutters closed, but this one keeps flying open," she says. "Your cottage looks fine, but we need to try to lock this one, and we need to move the rocking chairs and tables off the front porch so they don't become projectiles. I tried to get them through the door, but they were too big. I already took the smaller stuff inside."

"Okay," I say.

We decide to drag the chairs and table into the forest and lay them on their sides against trees, hoping that might stop them from flying too far away. Then we close and latch the shutters. We are drenched when we finally get inside. Karla heads to the bathroom to get towels. We dry ourselves off as best we can, grab the Afghans her mum and generations of aunts made, and huddle into a corner. The cottage rocks. The wind blows and rumbles so loud it sounds like a train is on top of us. The shutter we secured flies open again. We watch in awe as the trees in the forest bend sideways in perfect unison like tall grasses in a large open field. At some point, I see you perched on the porch rail of our cottage, the lids of your red eyes closing and opening against the rain as you attempt to hold on but then slip and disappear. Your scream hurts my stomach. I think about what Hazel said in her letter about your feelings for me. Maybe you weren't always the boy you became. Maybe what you became wasn't your fault. Maybe you were shaped by your distant, cruel father. A man whose eyes you witnessed wandering over your girlfriend's body. A man who owns everything and everyone he comes across. The man who rules St. Luke's. Or maybe the culture at St. Luke's had unleashed dormant deviant desires you hadn't known existed and had neither the strength nor the modeling to fight. But so you know, while others might have questioned its existence, I did see good in you. I witnessed your suffering, heard the screams from your nightmares, lived your self-destructiveness. Wouldn't a boy who felt destruction all around him seek to destroy? You hated that I saw this.

In many ways, we were alike, you and I. Two unseen souls both fearing and desperately wanting to be seen. Two empty vessels seeking at all costs to be filled. The notion of being loved as alien to either of us as it is expected by others. And so we held on to this thing called relationship as if it were a slippery life raft in a brutal storm.

And in that moment, inside the chaos and fury of this real live storm, a portal in my mind opens, and I *see something* and *someone* I completely missed. Me, a seer who has been blind to all things you. What was it Hazel said in her letter? That I had loved you in spite of what *they* did. That initially, I was just supposed to be your *cover.* What had she meant by that word, "cover"? And I remember you had said something similar during that last fight we had. That I was supposed to be your "cover." And I see the distant past and the future. I see an evil abbot. I see wailings and rapes. Young women, women younger than me, tied to crosses and burned. I see an infant child hanging from a tree. The abbot admiring himself in a cloudy mirror. I see centuries pass. More burnings. A monastery crumbling, its grounds wilting. Then a rebuilding. Bricks upon bricks with seeping mortar. Classrooms with drawing horses. Theater seating facing a large screen. Students from throughout the world converging inside a high brick wall. More burnings. And finally, I see you and I see the sequence of events that led to your murder, which, in turn, led to other murders. I see all five of my tarot paintings standing side by side. And I understand that I was always meant to be in this place at this time, that my powers, my ability to see and my mind's ability to hurt, can help stop the horrific chain of events that began centuries earlier. And just as the storm inside me calms, so does the one outside. And Karla and I look at each other, our eyes so big, our hearts so wide, and I know what we must do. For we are sisters, Weird Sisters, and it has always been our destiny to right these wrongs.

"You *saw* something, didn't you?" she says.

"Yes," I say. But I don't tell her what I saw. Because I now understand what Hazel meant about not telling me more. I understand that anyone who knows what I just saw will be in danger.

HAZEL

I curl inside my sleeping bag, my hands pressed against my ears, as the wind howls and rumbles. Thank god the original monks had built the walls, ceiling, and floor out of stone, but I swear the place still shakes. My heart pounds, throat hoarse from screaming, the sleeves of my blouse soaked with my tears and snot. Now and then the thud of a fallen limb, like a soldier lost in battle. Rats and mice and very large bugs, obviously as frightened as me, scurry in circles. Two bats hang upside down, struggling to stay attached to the wall opposite my cage. I wonder if they are a couple, a random thought, but it makes me happy they have each other. My flashlight is almost dead from continually shining it on whatever new noise I hear. Surely Pearl will come to check on me after the storm. The thought keeps me sane. But what if she doesn't come? What if something happens to her? What if *they* find me first? What if I'm wrong about them thinking this is the last place someone like me would hide?

It *is* the last place I would choose to hide. No way I would be inside this horrible, inhumane dungeon, had I not seen and heard something I wasn't supposed to see and hear. Something so scary and shocking, it stopped my heart. Four of my classmates are dead, and there is no doubt in my mind that I'm next. That's why I risked sneaking into Detective Germany's office and leaving the black velvet book on her desk. Because until she knows the whole truth, no one is safe.

It's scary enough down here, but now, with the storm, it is terrifying. I am not a brave person. I know I could die here. I know the ceiling could cave in or my hair could turn white and my heart just stop from fright. I've seen that in horror movies. What if I don't die? Then what do I do? Everyone hates me. I've done awful things, but I want to change. I want to do something selfless. No matter the consequences, I want to tell Detective Germany everything.

I open my satchel, take out my sketchbook and a pen, replace the batteries in my flashlight, and write.

To: Detective Lola Germany
Date: September 26, 1972
Subject: The Game

My name is Hazel Donovan. I am a Second Year student at St. Luke's Institute of the Arts. I'm writing this letter in the event I am unable to share its contents with you personally. I have information that I believe will help solve a series of murders that have taken place over the past several days on Waverly Island. The following is my best recollection of the events surrounding the murders of Abel Montague, George Archambault, and Jeannine Hart. I do not have personal knowledge of the murder of Eric Bernard.

Earlier today, before the storm, I left a black velvet book on your desk that further explains the contents of this letter. I had hoped to give you the book and share what I know in person, but then I saw you drive up with Esme Li, which concerned me because I believe she is involved in these murders. On September 21, 1972, Esme Li invited me to participate in a "performance art game." She said the participants had been chosen because they were the best artists at the school and then proceeded to tell me she had left a black velvet book under my bed in my dorm room that included an envelope containing directions for how to play the Game, as well as the name of my subject and a small baggie containing a white powder that she called a "psychedelic." I was to administer this powder to my subject without their knowledge, then return the book where I'd found it under my bed and she would retrieve it. On checking the envelope's contents, I discovered my subject was Abel Montague. I followed the directions exactly. The next morning, Abel's body was found in the forest hanging from the Ghost Tree.

The next day, September 23, I left a message at your office asking you to meet me at Joe's the following morning. I planned to tell you everything and give you the black velvet book. That evening, as planned, Esme and I walked to Karla Gardyn's cottage to do a Farewell Ceremony for Abel. On our walk, she wasn't acting like the Esme I knew. She was tense and jumpy, and when I brought up Abel's death, the only thing she said was that he deserved to die. When I got back to my dorm room that night, I angled a chairback under my doorknob to secure it.

The next morning, September 24, I headed to Joe's to meet you. When I got there, I looked through the window and saw you inside. I was holding the doorknob when I heard a man's voice behind me. He told me not to turn around. He warned me not to go inside and said he would kill me if I told you about the Game. I waited until I heard his footsteps retreating and snuck a look behind me. I'd never seen this man before. He was of average height with salt-and-pepper hair. But what mostly caught my attention was the clownish way he was dressed. He was wearing a purple suit coat and green shoes. I ran back to my dorm room, angled the chairback under my doorknob again, and hid in my dorm room the rest of the day. Esme knocked on my door at one point asking me about the black velvet book. When I didn't answer she tried the door several times but finally gave up. Right before she left, she said, "I hear you had a scare at Joe's today. So if you need a minute, fine, but George Archambault will be coming by tonight to get the black velvet book and you need to give it to him, okay? If you don't, you'll break the chain, and you can't do that. Do you understand? If you break the chain, you'll be in danger." I had every intention of staying awake all night, but must have fallen asleep, because around ten, I woke to someone knocking at my door. It was George Archambault. "Esme said you have a book for me," he said. "I know you're there because I can see the light under your door. Jeannine Hart and I are going to hang at the Tower. I got this secret invitation to play a game and was supposed to bring only you and some book, but Jeannine wanted to tag along. Way too many stupid rules around here. Esme said you wouldn't want to come but that I'm supposed to make you, whatever that means. We've got some good weed and booze. Just bring the book, okay? Esme will get pissed if you don't. And you know how she is. She'll tattle to Alice in Wonderland and we'll both get expelled." Then he said, "We're going to drink to Abel." I had no idea those would be the last words he ever said to me. I lay there trying to figure out what to do. I must have fallen back to sleep because I woke to a commotion outside my door. I checked the time on my alarm clock. Half past 3 AM. Then I looked out my window and saw the Tower was on fire. I got out of bed and ran downstairs to the veranda. A crowd of students had already gathered, and there were fire trucks and police cars and ambulances. That's when I saw the boys loading two bodies onto stretchers. I could hardly breathe I was so scared. What George had said to me about going to the Tower with Jeannine kept running through my mind. I was supposed to be dead, not Jeannine. I grabbed some clothes and a flashlight, and the black velvet book, and stuffed it all into my satchel, then I threw on my red wool cape, left out the Monastery's front door so no one would see me, and ran. I had no idea where to go. All I could think about was getting as far away as I could. I don't know how far I ran before I got a stitch in my side. I stopped to rub it out and catch my breath. When I checked the surroundings, I saw I was on a part of the beach I'd never been to before. I had no idea how I ended up there. It was as if I lost time. In the distance, I saw a ring of fire on the sand. Then I heard chanting. Curious, I kept walking until I was mere yards from the ring. Three men wore animal masks and the same blood robes that the Weird Sisters wear when we do spells. They were standing with their backs to me before a wooden cross with a witch dummy tied to it, a more realistic witch dummy than the Fourth Years make for their reenactments. They were chanting, their deep voices rhythmic above the sound of the angry waves. Then, in unison, they stepped forward and lit the debris at the base of the cross. It felt like I'd been transported to an ancient world where fire ruled. I stood in the shadows, the Tower burning behind me, the witch dummy burning before me. But the dummy wasn't burning as fast as the ones we stuffed, and it didn't smell like burning leaves. It took me a while to make sense of what I was witnessing, and then the horror of the scene became clear. The chanting stopped, and the waves must have calmed, because I could clearly hear one single deep voice say these words: "Sono davanti a te, mio Principe delle Tenebre, e ti offro l'anima del mio figlio primogento." *The others repeated the words over and over. I knew what the words meant. I went to prep school, so I speak fluent French and Italian.* I stand before you, my Prince of Darkness, and offer you the soul of my firstborn son.

I felt a combination of fear and confusion. It felt otherworldly, like maybe I wasn't there. Like I had been transported back in time or was inside a bad dream. Questions floated through my mind. What was this ceremony? Who were these men? Was the person tied to the cross really someone's son? I felt faint, nauseated, and lightheaded. I lost my balance and fell to the ground. By now, the sun was starting to rise over the water, so when the man with the deep voice pulled down his mask and looked in my direction, I could see that his eyes were a brilliant blue. I scrambled to my feet and ran until I was inside the forest. That's when I heard the hoot of an owl. I stopped, looked around, saw I was standing before the Ghost Tree, the tree where Abel's dead body had hung two days earlier. An owl was perched on one of its branches staring straight at me. I was startled, not because it was huge, which it was, just like the one that landed on Karla's railing during the Farewell Ceremony, but because of its eyes. They were red. Usually a creature like that would terrify me. I can't say why, but it didn't. It spread its wings, hooted again, and flew ahead. I followed. It landed on a tree stump not too far in the distance, and I recognized the stump. It was the same one Karla had taken the Weird Sisters to when she was a Second Year and we were First Years. She said it led to St. Luke's underground tunnels and the dank, dark dungeon where her aunt Matilda was imprisoned before she was burned at the stake. Like she had, I used my foot to push aside forest debris, exposing a hatch, bent down, and pulled on the corroded brass handle. The door was heavy, but I was determined, and the hatch finally opened. Then I climbed down the metal rungs.

It is now September 26. A Tuesday. I have been hiding in this dungeon for two nights and three days, but it feels like it's been much longer. There are bugs and mice and bats. Other than dropping off the black velvet book at your office earlier today, trying to find you two other times, and slipping a message under Pearl's door, I haven't left this tunnel since the night of the Tower fire. This morning, Pearl brought me some clothes and supplies and told me Eric Bernard had been murdered. She also mentioned that a hurricane is heading toward the island. It is my intent to deliver this letter to you as soon as the hurricane is over. That is, if I live through it. I know there are people looking for me. Bad people. But if I do make it out, I will elaborate on the information in this letter as there are some things I'd prefer to tell you in person. And if I don't, well, I can only hope you, or some good soul, will at least find this letter.

Yours,
Hazel Donovan

I stop writing, sign my name. Rip the pages from my sketchbook, fold them, and put them in the front zipper section of my satchel. I hunker back into my sleeping bag and pray the storm will end. It is during that weird place between wake and sleep when memories and imaginings mix that I hear those words again: *I stand before you, my Prince of Darkness, and offer you the soul of my firstborn son.* I follow the words to the man saying them and see his piercing *blue* eyes. The same color as Abel's. Then his eyes become Abel's and Abel's become his, and though I don't want to believe it, I fear that the burning body was Abel.

PEARL

"I don't know about you, but I need a drink," Karla says, and heads inside.

It was after midnight by the time Karla and I decided to sit down on her porch to rest. We had spent several hours inspecting and cleaning up the damage caused by the storm. There was debris everywhere. Twigs and branches and roof slats, a steering wheel that must have come from one of the boats down by the docks, and, weirdly, a blue sneaker that didn't belong to either of us. Some trees on the forest's edge were down. Others had splintered. But those inside the edge were remarkably intact. We were able to find Karla's rocking chairs, the chairs we now sit on, in the field behind my cottage. We dragged them, broken and scarred, back onto the porch. There was no sign of the table.

Karla emerges, hands me a cup of hot black tea. "It's spiked with whiskey," she says. "The best medicine right now."

I hear squawking sounds. "What was that?"

"Look, there's that owl," Karla says while pointing at the sky. You are soaring toward us. You perch on the rail. Your red eyes penetrate me, and then you fly in the direction of Studio Row.

"Something's wrong," I say. "I think Abel wants us to follow him." Then someone is calling our names. I look up to see Marcus Jones running down the walk. He's out of breath, wild-eyed, and disheveled. Marcus is normally Mr. Cool. He bends at the waist, puts his hands on his knees, tries to catch his breath, and stands upright again.

"It's Esme," he says. "I went to her studio to check on her." His voice cracks as he wipes tears from his eyes. "Jesus, someone murdered her. The spineless bastard suspended her body from the metal rafters of the sunroof. He left one of those tarot cards. The Fool."

PART FOUR

The Fool

[The Fool] functions in the game as a sort of wild card which can be played at any time, excusing the player from the obligation to follow suit or play a trump.

—MICHAEL DUMMETT,
THE VISCONTI-SFORZA TAROT CARDS

Day 6

Five Days After the Autumnal Equinox
Wednesday, September 27, 1972

LOLA

One of my guys was manning the door to Esme's studio. Several students stood behind the crime scene tape that was stretched across the garage and side doors. I saw Pearl, Karla, and Marcus among them. Many held lit candles in tribute. They flickered in the night sky. I removed and replaced the tape when I entered. The first thing I noticed was the strong astringent odor. Just like the closet where we'd found Eric Bernard's body. The murderer had obviously used bleach or something similar to clean the space. It was spotless, the floor shiny, all the tools of the artist neatly stacked and organized. I saw Colin talking to one of the crime scene investigators and our station's photographer. It appeared as if they'd just arrived. Two of my officers were manning points of egress. I wasn't sure if others hadn't arrived yet or if Colin had limited attendance out of respect for Esme. I'd been touched by how kind and understanding he was when we interviewed her. Was it because he was the father of three girls or was it Esme herself who had brought that out in him?

Esme's body was suspended from the crisscrossed metal braces of the sunroof. Trump 0, the Fool, was on the floor directly beneath her body along with a burlap poppet. The poppet was different from the others left at the murder scenes. A *pink* pearl–tipped pin pierced its red heart. Why pink? The killer had dressed Esme to resemble the figure in the card. Bleached blond hair. Yellow robe over white shirt. White feathers extending from her hair. As if she were going on a journey, a staff with a stuffed pouch tied to the end was positioned over her left shoulder. Of all the murder scenes I'd visited in the last several days, this one upset me the most. Probably because I knew Esme, but also because the murderer had garishly painted her face to resemble a centuries-past courtesan. It felt like a violation. *A rape.* Was that intentional? Meant to expose what had happened to her? There was so much hatred and callous cruelty behind these murders. Each was perverse and sadistic in both method and visual effect. But Esme's painted face and the suspension of her slight body were distinctively theatrical. The term "painting in space" especially applied to the scene before me.

I heard someone say my name, turned to see Alice. "How can I help?" she asked.

"You can't," I said. "And I'd prefer that you and anyone else associated with the school leave. I don't want any evidence destroyed."

"I promise I'll be careful," Alice said. "I cared for Esme, you know."

Since when did Alice care for anyone?

"Colin," I said. He was standing close by. "Can you please escort Ms. Landry outside, along with anyone else that isn't necessary to the investigation?"

"Follow me," he said to Alice, who huffed loudly but didn't argue.

A picture on Esme's drawing table caught my attention. Birds, not penises, flew through a bright sky. Was it an older painting, done before her recent images? I touched it lightly with my gloved finger. It was completely dry.

"Are you busy?" I asked one of the crime scene investigators. "Can you see if you can get any fingerprints off this picture?"

"Will do," she said.

"Have you dusted everything? The floor, the walls, her portfolios, the brushes?" I knew I sounded curt, but anger owned me.

"Still working on it," she said. "There are only the two of us right now. There's backup coming."

I searched the studio for Esme's current paintings. The only ones I found were in an unzipped black Naugahyde portfolio, and none of them featured flying penises. Only various species of birds. Did the murderer take her most recent paintings? If so, why? Were they somehow a clue to the murderer's identity?

I called Colin over, relayed my thoughts.

"I'll make sure to have the inside of the portfolio tested for prints," he said. "Staging this body would have made a mess. I noticed when we were here yesterday that she kept an orderly space, but this is like a museum."

Colin was right. It wasn't just the pristine floor. Papers were stacked. Paint tubes lined up. Brushes cleaned and set in a row. That pretty painting on the drawing table. Murder was messy. But like Esme, our killer had been meticulous. There was no sign of a struggle. It must have taken hours to undress and redress her, paint her face, hang the body just so, then restraighten and clean the space.

Extra crime scene investigators arrived and went to work searching for clues and fingerprints as the photographer snapped pictures. I stood in the center of the studio watching, my body spinning like a hub in a wheel, my mind mesmerized by the flash of the photographer's light bulb and the various discussions going on in the space. I felt cold, lightheaded, dizzy.

"You okay, boss?" I heard Colin ask from somewhere far away.

His voice woke me. I saw he was holding my arm. "Your face is white. Why don't you sit for a minute?"

"I'm fine," I said. "I'm not sure what happened."

"It's been a rough few days," he said as he guided me onto Esme's sofa.

After a while, a man in a maintenance uniform came in holding a ladder.

"I hear you're in charge?" he said to me. "Here to cut down the body."

"Her name was Esme," I snapped.

"Sorry, ma'am," he said. "I meant no disrespect."

"Just be careful with her," I said.

"Sure thing," he said, and began setting up the ladder.

"Shit," I heard someone say a few minutes later. I looked toward the man who was now on the top rung of the ladder. He was attempting to balance the staff in Esme's hand. I watched in what felt like slow motion as the pouch slipped off the staff and fell to the ground. A cracking sound when it hit and opened. And there on the floor was a naked and partly shattered porcelain baby doll. I rose, went back to the drawing table to take a second look at the painting atop it. That was when I realized that the birds weren't generic. They were storks. Who knew Esme had been pregnant?

I was still staring at it in shock when I heard Colin calling my name. "You need to see this," he said.

He was standing before the wooden flat file near the front of the studio. I walked over. "I found this in the bottom drawer," he said while holding up what looked like another tarot card.

Trump 15, the Devil.

PEARL

It is the first murder scene I've been to. The three of us—Marcus, Karla, and me—have been standing on the lawn outside Esme's studio for over an hour. Our candles will soon reach the end of their life. Since we arrived, the crowd has gotten dense with students and instructors. Now many candles flicker in the dark, so beautiful. I believe Esme would have liked them. Their ritual. Like the Weird Sisters' spells. I see Alice in Wonderland and Mr. Smith, who appears to be flirting with the new female instructor. Good, I think. Maybe he'll lose interest in me. Everyone is deep in conversation, whispering. *Stop talking about her*, I want to scream. She was a person. Not a curiosity. She didn't deserve to die.

I feel the anger rising in me and with anger comes my sight. I see someone, a shadow, taking off Esme's clothes, studying her body. Then I am inside Esme, watching my murderer. She or he wears a black hood over their face. They are undressing me slowly. They keep me naked as they take me to the sink and wet my hair, gently wash it and my body. Then, using the same gentle care, my murderer lays me on the floor and paints my face. Dresses me. Ties a rope around me. Carries me up a ladder and attaches the rope to the sunroof rafter. Places a long staff in my right hand, balances it over my left shoulder. Pulls a long syringe from their pocket and puts it in my arm. Then my vision goes dark. *No, please come back. Show yourself to me!*

Quietly, so no one will notice, I slip inside the studio. Just like in my vision, Esme floats in the air, her eyes still open, staring down at me. *Help me*, they say. I know by the way she is dressed what tarot card she is meant to represent. The painting of her face is a departure from the card. It is vulgar, clownish, as if the killer was trying to cheapen her. But why the open eyes? And then I know why I had the vision. Why it stopped after the syringe went into her arm. Because the killer paralyzed her body, but not her eyes. She was present as he or she washed her, painted her face, and hung her from the rafter. She watched everything being done to her. Death coming only when the killer was through with the ritual. It was about control. The killer got off on taking control. On turning Esme into a living doll.

A younger officer approaches me, asks me to leave. I don't argue. I've *seen* enough. I need to be alone. I need to paint. I head to my studio. Once safely inside, I position a chairback under the doorknob, turn, then stop.

Because there, in front of the stack of stretched canvases that line the wall, are two new paintings. The Fool and the Devil.

HAZEL

A slim ray of light streams through the hatch in the ceiling. I crawl out of my sleeping bag, stand, and stretch. Pearl never said she would come to get me before the storm, but I thought she might. It would be like her. She has a soft and forgiving heart. How else could she have stayed with Abel? I hope she's okay. Probably she got caught in the hurricane and is planning to come soon. Whatever the case, I don't want to wait anymore. I need to get Detective Germany the letter I wrote her. I especially need to tell her what I saw on the beach that day.

We all knew about the witch burnings that took place on the island centuries ago. We treated them as cool legends, fodder for ghost stories, and witch dummy reenactments at drunken midnight beach parties. We poked fun at the horrors of those times. But what I witnessed that night on the beach wasn't fun at all. Even this dungeon, with its bats and roaches and rats, with its weird sounds and the screams I heard in my nightmares—even it isn't as terrifying as the ritual I saw on the beach that night. The chanting, the staffs of fire, the blood robes, the animal masks, the deep male voices repeating their monotone Italian chants, their advance toward the witch dummy, the lighting of the debris, the witch dummy going up in flames.

Abel, not a witch dummy.

I open the letter I wrote the night before. Wrote as the storm swirled around me and I was all but certain I would die. Read it. To the best of my knowledge, everything in it is true, but it's what I don't say that plagues me. What I don't want to admit even to myself.

The night before Abel's body was found hanging from the Ghost Tree, I went to his studio. He and I had already planned to meet up before Esme invited me to play the Game. Before I learned that he was my subject. The moment I saw his face, I knew he was done with me. The desire that was once in his eyes had been replaced by lack of eye contact, evasiveness, and an impersonal tone. He said he almost called off our date, but I deserved to hear what he had to say in person. He seemed proud of himself for that, as if he considered the act noble. While he cleaned his brushes, I opened the bottle of wine I'd brought along, poured each of us a glass, made sure he wasn't looking, and mixed the white powder—the "harmless psychedelic"—into his glass. He finished up, put his brush in a glass filled with turpentine, sat down, and then, as if he thought I would totally understand and would just smile sweetly and go away, he proceeded to tell me that though we'd had "fun"—*fun*—we could no longer see each other in "that way." That we could be friends, of course, that in fact he really wanted to be friends, that he'd "had a blast" with me. He said those last words as if all that we'd done together, all that I thought we'd meant to each other, was to him as meaningless as going bowling or playing miniature golf. Then he dropped the final bomb. He told me he'd realized that he loved Pearl. And, as if I were his friend and confidant, he began asking my advice, talking about her, wondering how he could make up for everything he'd done to her, whether he should bring her something when he professed his love. Flowers? Chocolates? Jewelry? "I've been awful to her," he said. "And still she loves me. What kind of man throws away someone like Pearl?" I could feel the tears coming to my eyes, tried to stop them, but they rolled down my cheeks. He didn't seem to notice. I remember wondering why I wasn't stomping out or throwing something at him. I remember thinking I was pathetic. Why was I sitting there so nicely listening to his questions? How awkward it was going to be to face Pearl. How unlikely it was that either of us would bring up my *fling* with Abel—over time wouldn't that be all it was? Never discussing it would always leave it floating in the air between us. Would she and I ever get beyond it? The entire time, he'd been sipping on his wine. He asked me to pass him the bottle, refilled his glass, and then he just stopped, set the bottle down.

"It's hot in here, don't you think?" he asked while wiping perspiration from his forehead.

He untucked his shirt, tried to stand. The wineglass dropped from his hand. I watched the glass fall as if it were traveling in slow motion, heard the sharp ping and shatter when it hit the hard concrete floor. Abel fell to the side, rolled off the sofa, his head making a thudding sound. He started shaking and jerking, his mouth foaming, blood slowly oozing from his head where it hit the hard concrete, his eyes wide open. I rose and bent down next to him, tried to stop the blood. I was panicking. I didn't know what else to do. It had happened so fast. Stupidly, I asked him if he was okay. But of course he wasn't. I watched as life slowly left his eyes.

I don't know how long I sat there. Long enough to know he was dead. Long enough for my mind to try to wrap itself around what had just happened, to understand that though I hadn't meant to kill him, I had. Because isn't that what everyone would believe? I was covered in his blood.

I remember wondering if that was Esme's intent. The Game's intent. That Abel would die and I would go to prison. And then it dawned on me: *I won't go to prison because she means for the Game to kill me too.*

I washed what blood I could off my hands in the sink in his studio. Watched it flow and trickle down the sink drain. Went back to my dorm room and waited for the police to come, but they never did. The next morning, Abel's body was found hanging from the Ghost Tree. I wondered if the police had even checked his studio for evidence. And then it dawned on me that someone had probably followed me. They would have seen me enter and leave his studio. Were they just waiting to clean it and move his body to the forest? Were they following me from the moment Esme invited me to play the Game? Was it Green Shoes? Was it Esme?

Now, with my sleeping bag and backpack in tow, I head toward the hatch, climb up the slippery rungs, hold my breath as I try to open it. Will it open? Did a tree fall on it during the storm? Is it my punishment to be trapped down here? To die a slow death? Push. It opens. I sit on the stump and inspect the storm's damage. It's remarkable, actually. Broken branches and twigs and leaves and a multitude of wildflower petals are strewn about the ground, a colorful carpet, but nearly all the trees still stand sturdy and tall.

A movement in a nearby tree catches my attention. That same red-eyed owl that led me to the tunnel. Do I imagine its eyes are filled with compassion? Six nights and five days have passed since I killed Abel Montague. Though it feels like forever ago, it was only yesterday that I left the black velvet book on Detective Germany's desk.

The owl hoots, flaps its wings, and flies into the sky.

LOLA

The sun rose into one of the clearest and bluest skies I'd seen in a long while. A rainbow stretched across the ocean. The angriest of weather giving way to the sweetest. Was it a good omen or the calm before another murder? The Devil card weighed on me. Its presence had to be significant. Questions ran through my mind. Why was it tucked away in the bottom drawer of Esme's flat file? Was it intended for a future murder? Was Esme involved in the other murders?

I got to my tree a bit earlier than usual. I was worried about the creatures that had always shared the sunrise with me. But luckily, when I stood on the precipice that overlooks the ocean, it appeared they were all still there. Wildlife knew how to survive in a storm. After the orange line bled into the rising sun, I stood before my tree and began to update her on the case. I heard a familiar sound. *Whoo-whoo-who-who-whoo.* Looked up. There was the red-eyed owl perched in *my* tree. It flapped its wings and circled above me. I crouched, covered my head with my hands. It landed back in the tree. *Whoo-whoo-who-who-whoo.* Again it flapped its wings and circled, only this time it landed in a tree up the way and hooted loudly.

"Do you want me to follow you?" I asked.

It spread its wings and flew from tree to tree as I followed. Finally, it stopped. I found myself standing before the Ghost Tree.

"Why am I here?" I asked the owl.

But of course it didn't respond. It merely stared. Then it did something even more unusual. It flew to the ground, hooted again, then took a few steps. And I saw why it had brought me here. There on the ground was a wet cigarette butt. I bent to pick it up, noticed another partially buried in the dirt. And then another. All three were soggy, limp, and dirt-stained. If they had been there when we found Abel's body, why hadn't we seen them?

"Did the storm move the dirt and leaves that were covering them?" I asked.

Whoo-whoo-who-who-whoo.

"Thank you," I said. And with that the owl flew away. *Utter craziness.* Now I wasn't only talking to trees, I was talking to owls. In case there were still any fingerprints, I used the tail of my running shirt to put them in my pocket. I carefully placed the cigarette butts in an envelope when I got home; then I showered and dressed for work. On my way into the station, I stopped at Rebecca's. Knocked. She wasn't in yet. I slid a note and the envelope containing the cigarette butts into her mail slot.

"Good morning, Friday," I said when I arrived at the station.

"Good morning, Detective Germany," she said. She was forever chipper. "How did you fare from the storm?"

"Pretty well, considering," I said. "How about you?"

"Same," she said. "Colin told me about the new murder. It's just awful. And so scary to think someone on the island could be doing these. How are you? Is there anything I can get you?"

"No, thanks," I said. "I'm fine."

"Oh," she said. "Someone left a book on your desk."

"A book?" I asked.

"Yes. A black velvet one. It looks really old. I hope you don't mind, but I paged through it. I wore gloves, of course. I thought maybe someone had left a note. There's an envelope inside it with the name 'Hazel' on it."

"'Hazel Donovan'?"

"Just 'Hazel,'" Friday said.

"Thank you, I'll take a look."

The book did indeed look old. Black velvet, with no title. I reached into my desk for a set of crime scene gloves. Opened it. Though the end boards were tattered around the edges and the velvet smelled of mildew, it appeared to be in good condition. The edges of the parchment pages had browned, but there were no signs of brittleness or disintegration. The pages were highly decorative. Mineral-derived paints, gold leaf, and silverpoint were used to create a variety of scrolls, patterns, and images. The words were written by quill in black ink in Old Latin. Letters and words were distinguished by flourishes and loops making them appear highly stylistic. Below each line, someone had neatly translated the original Latin into English, an act that would certainly have diminished the book's value. It was hard to say when the translation had occurred, but it didn't appear to be recent.

The envelope inside the book was, as Friday had said, addressed to Hazel. The only thing inside it was a small empty plastic baggie that contained residue of a white substance. I bagged the envelope and its contents and inspected the book. Then I began reading.

The seventy-eight illustrations in this book represent facsimiles of a Tarocchi pack I created on my journey from Italy to Waverly Abbey. The pack was to the best of my memory re-created from a deck I completed in Italy, which my teacher falsely claimed as his own creation, an act I could never have imagined from a man of God. Though the images are not exact replications of the ones I painted in Italy, as an artist can never precisely duplicate a previous painting, I have reproduced them to the best of my memory. This record and its attribution are done not out of vanity, but to ensure no individual can claim artistic authorship of these re-created cards or the images in this book.

The book's author was listed as Scribe Francesco. Below the name was an impression that read *Property of the Order of Waverly Monks, 1436*.

I opened to the first page and introduction.

In summary, Scribe Francesco presented himself as a student artist of the official court artist for a powerful noble family in Florence. Scribe Francesco claimed he had invented a game called Tarocchi, which consisted of seventy-eight cards, including twenty-two major arcana and fifty-six minor arcana, or pips. Each card included a unique painted image that had specific meaning within the game's larger context. Once completed, he had presented his creation to the Church for its blessing, then shared it with his teacher, the court artist, who, rather than praise its artistic and intellectual inventiveness or discuss options for improvement, criticized it. Shortly thereafter, the court artist claimed to both the noble family and the Church that it was he who had created the game and that Francesco, his student, had falsely claimed authorship. Francesco was arrested for thievery, a crime punishable by death. The royal family backed that punishment, as suggested by the court artist, but the Church, suspicious of the court artist's claim, and in a show of mercy, gave Francesco a choice. He could either be sentenced to death by hanging or banished to a faraway abbey located on an island off the southern coast of a "wild and untamed land." He knew little of Waverly Abbey or its location but reasoned that continuing to serve God was more devout than sacrificing his life out of pride. It would take several months for Francesco to arrive at his new home, as travel by ship was a long and tedious affair. He spent the journey re-creating the Tarocchi pack the court artist had stolen from him.

I stopped reading. Could the cards that had been showing up at our murder scenes be from the Tarocchi pack Scribe Francesco re-created?

What followed were seventy-eight original paintings, each representing a card from what Scribe Francesco said comprised a full Tarocchi pack. At the time, no such pack existed, so both the pack itself, the number of its cards, and the images were completely original. I took time to study each. They were stunning, ornate, and intricate, the images on the twenty-two major arcana cards drawn and painted with the brush of an exceptional artist. Beneath each card was a brief description of its meaning. A stray thought came to my mind. The banishment of Francesco was not only a loss for him. It was a great loss for Italy and the art world at large.

And again, I found myself wondering who had dropped off the black velvet book, why, and whether there was a direct connection between it and our murders. It did appear that the five cards we'd found at the murder scenes were painted by this Scribe Francesco. But was that all that was going on here? A lesson on the history of Tarot and the Waverly Island witch burnings?

I flipped past the card illustrations to the back of the book. There was a detailed list of names categorized under the following headers: *Name*, *Date of Trial*, *Reason for Arrest*, *Sentence*, *Execution Date and Method*, and *Time of Death*. While most if not all Waverly Island residents knew of the witch burnings and the Ghost Tree, seeing an actual list of names made it feel so much more real. I was surprised to learn that not all the accused witches were burned alive. Some were hanged or stoned to death, then burned. According to the text, burning was intended to purify their souls and protect against post-mortem sorcery. I looked at the names of the victims. One stood out. A woman listed as Matilda, with no surname, was burned at the stake in 1437, the same year Karla said her aunt Matilda was. Two reasons for her arrest were listed: *Maker of Devil's Brew* and *Seductress.* Most of the crimes of the other accused witches were frightening in their mundanity. *Practiced medicine. Grew suspicious herbs. Unmarried. Barren. Flushed pregnancy. Disagreeable. Contrary. Smart-tongued. Proud.* This had to be Karla's Aunt Matilda. I paused. If the information contained in the black velvet book was correct, that the monks and the village were here as early as 1437, that would mean that the island that became Waverly Island was inhabited decades before the Europeans settled in mainland North America.

I had nearly closed the book when I saw the bookmark. It had slid down into the crease. The chapter header it marked read *The Game of Death.* It began with a notation by Scribe Francesco that the game was something he devised to aid in determining the fate of the women charged as witches. I looked closer at the bookmark. The name *Priscilla's Antiques* was stamped on it.

A knock on my office door.

"Ma'am," Friday said, "Colin is on the phone. I buzzed, but you didn't pick up. Should I forward the call?"

I must have been so engrossed in my reading I didn't hear it. "Thank you, Friday. Put him through."

I waited for the buzz, answered, then put the call on speaker phone.

"Lola. It's Colin. I'm at Rebecca's. Thought you might want to know that there was hemlock in Esme's system, but there was also a neuromuscular blocking agent in her system. And there's something else: The remains of the last three bodies are missing."

"Missing? What do you mean?"

"Rebecca checked refrigeration for them this morning, but they weren't there."

"Where are they?"

I heard Rebecca asking for the phone. "Hi, Lola," she said. "I'm still finishing up on Esme. But yes, it looks like the bodies were stolen, which makes no sense. Why steal dead bodies?"

"Very little about these murders makes sense," I said. "Does Alice know they're missing?"

"I haven't told her."

"Don't," I said. "I'd like to see her reaction firsthand."

"Got it," Rebecca said.

"And what's this about a neuromuscular blocking agent? Is it deadly?"

"It can be. These drugs can lead to respiratory arrest, permanent harm, or even death. But I don't think that's what the killer was going for. He or she had the hemlock for that. I think the killer wanted Esme to watch what was being done to her. All of it, but paralysis wouldn't allow her to fight back. The killer undressed her, washed and dyed her hair, and redressed her. She was naked much of that time. Who knows what else was done to her. Esme couldn't fight back."

I took a deep breath, tried to calm myself. "This killer is a sick fuck."

"Yep," Colin said.

"Did you get the cigarette butts I dropped off?" I asked.

"I did," Rebecca said. "Sorry I wasn't here when you dropped them off. I got a late start this morning. Can you head over in about an hour? I should be done with Esme by then."

"I'll be there," I said.

I hung up the phone and returned to the black velvet book. I still didn't understand why our killer chose to leave these particular cards at the scenes. Were they random? I flipped back to the chapter that included the Tarocchi paintings and read the descriptive explanations of the five cards left at our murder scenes and the Devil.

The Hanged Man: Betrayal and sacrifice. Abel Montague betrayed everyone, especially Pearl.

The Tower: Destruction and ruin. Abel Montague, George Archambault, and Eric Bernard drugged and raped girls.

Death: Endings and transformation. Symbol of the skull. Eric Bernard's skull was exposed.

The Fool: Capricious. Unpredictable. Wild card. Was Esme wearing two faces?

The Devil: Violence. Malice. Evil intent. Who was the devil?

It was hard to believe that these connections weren't intentional, but at the same time, I didn't buy that it was the only reason the victims were chosen. There was something more sinister going on here. Each of these victims had either posed a threat to the killer, or at least in the killer's mind, deserved their revenge. Why? And why had the killer not only left Tarocchi cards at the murder scenes, but cards from this particular pack? A pack that Scribe Francesco claimed was the first ever created.

I continued reading. According to the book, witch hunts were well underway in Scribe Francesco's new home when he arrived in 1436. The following was a direct quote from Part III: The Introduction to the Game.

The screams are my first memory of arriving at my new home.

When the boat docked, there on the shore were two young

women who had been tied to tall wooden crosses. I watched as men wearing vestments the color of blood lit a long staff on fire and proceeded to use it to light the debris gathered below the stakes. The women wailed in pain. The monk who greeted me, seeing the shock on my face, told me that the women had been tried earlier that day and were found to be guilty of witchery. Somewhat later, I witnessed such a trial. Five of my peers, fellow monks, sat before another young woman, this one proclaiming her innocence between sobs. One of the monks suggested she choose one of three upside-down cups. If she were to choose the one with a gold piece under it, she could go free. I was taken aback by their casual indifference. As the official Scribe for my new Order, I was made to bear witness to several witch trials. These arbitrary practices of determining a young woman's fate by choosing a cup or flipping a coin or checking the sky for a puffy cloud were what prompted me to consider using my Tarocchi pack to save some of them. I explained to my fellow monks that the pack had been blessed by the Church. This, I reasoned, was a minor untruth given that my original pack had received such a blessing. Then I suggested that during the trial of each accused witch, she would blindly select one card from the pack, and if any card other than the Hanged Man, the Tower, Death, or the Fool was pulled, the accused witch in question would go free. They readily agreed to this suggestion without asking why I had suggested these particular cards. The truth was, I had chosen them entirely at random.

I stopped, reread that last paragraph. So, it was Scribe Francesco, not our Tarocchi killer, who had chosen these particular cards? Chosen them centuries ago as a means to save women. But how did Scribe Francesco's attempt at something virtuous lead to the presence of those same cards at the horrific murders on Waverly Island?

I read on, and then my heart quickened. In a later chapter, Scribe Francesco said that, unbeknownst to him, some of his fellow monks had created a different game using a deck of playing cards but had pasted amateurish copies of his Hanged Man, Tower, Death, and Fool cards over four of the cards. The game, entitled the "The Game of Death," became a favorite among the monks. Up to eight players were recommended. All players had to toss an agreed-upon amount of coins into the center of play. The first player shuffled the deck and passed out all the cards. The player who got the Hanged Man was removed from play. The player tossed his remaining cards into the center and any accumulated coins into the cauldron. The removed player would then shuffle the deck and distribute the cards. The player who got the Tower card was removed from play and so on until the player who got the Fool card was removed. The game could be played over and over, and the coins in the center of play would continue to increase until a player got a card that had been painted entirely black. This they called the Devil card. That player won all the coins in the cauldron. In Scribe Francesco's words, "The Devil killed the game."

The Devil killed the game.

I found the choice of the word "kill" interesting. Was it possible that the Devil card Colin found in Esme's flat file was the last card meant to be played? That its sole purpose was to end the Tarocchi Murders?

I closed the book, took a deep breath and then another, leaned back in my chair, and watched a spider crawl across the ceiling. I was trying to wrap my mind around the seemingly unlikely and disparate series of events that led to our murders. Was someone on Waverly Island playing the Game of Death? Was that what the person who left this book on my desk was trying to tell me?

I remembered the cigarette butts, checked the time, quarter past the hour. I had told Priscilla that I'd be coming to see her, but her directions had been less than helpful. I buzzed Friday. I figured if anyone would know exactly how to get to Priscilla's Antiques, she would.

"Yes?" she said, her voice upbeat. Friday was forever pleasant. I'd never once seen her frustrated or in a bad mood.

"Do you know anything about an establishment called Priscilla's Antiques on Marsh Road? The only directions I was given were something about a bottle tree."

"Oh, I love that place," Friday said. "Priscilla is so cool. People call her the Swamp Witch. The store itself is divine. It smells of candles and incense and is chock-full of native antiques and collectibles. It's one of those floating houses. About a mile or so after you turn onto Marsh Road. Actually, the shop is behind her home. You can't see either from the road, but there's a large wooden sculpture of some ancient goddess right across the street. And yes, there's a bottle tree at the edge of her property. You know, empty blue bottles hanging off the tree's branches?"

I was embarrassed I had to ask but did. "Do you know what those are for?"

"The bottles? They trap and capture evil spirits so the sun can destroy them. By the way, you'll need to park on the shoulder of the road somewhere near the ancient goddess. The shoulder is much wider there. Then walk across the street and take the foot bridge over the marsh. You'll come to her house first, but if you veer to the left past the house, you'll see the shop behind it. Do you want me to call Priscilla and tell her you're coming?"

“She’s expecting me,” I said.

I switched off the intercom and called Rebecca. “Change of plans,” I said. “I need to make a stop at a place called Priscilla’s Antiques before I come your way. It shouldn’t take longer than an hour.”

“That’s fine,” she said. “That place is amazing, by the way.”

PEARL

I am packing some supplies for Hazel when Karla bursts through my door. "Alice in Wonderland has called an emergency meeting of the student body in the Monastery," she says. "Why are you packing all that?"

"I thought I might go for a hike," I lie. I hate to hike.

"That's a first," Karla says.

The room is practically full when we arrive. Alice in Wonderland proceeds to give Esme a eulogy that elevates her to saint status. Rather than make me sad, the words make me angry. They feel false and empty. I keep seeing Esme standing in that vast grassy field that fronts Studio Row with those pieces of her painting and the Ghost Women swirling around her, and I can't get the last words she said to me out of my mind. *Please tell everyone how sorry I am, okay? Tell them I know I should have been stronger.* Why did she ask me to tell everyone that? Did she know she was going to die? It is the image of her small body disappearing into the storm after she said those words that most haunts me. Could I have done something? Why didn't I *see* her death?

And it is in that moment, inside my feelings of regret for Esme, that I decide to give Hazel a second chance, to search for common ground. Everyone sees Hazel as a pretty little rich girl, entitled and superficial, with her expensive clothes and designer handbags. The other girls at the orphanages where I grew up saw me as the scrawny, funny-looking girl with Martian eyes. Easy fodder for dismissal and meanness. I know it's no excuse for my behavior, but maybe if just one of those girls had attempted to befriend me, I wouldn't have hurt them with my mind. Mr. Smith once said that when a painting has lost its freshness, sometimes you need to throw paint all over it and start over. So maybe that's what I need to do with Hazel. Start all over. I lost Abel and now I've lost Esme. I am not about to lose another friend.

While Karla is busy talking to some of the other Third Years, I sneak out of the room and head to my studio. I pull out the five paintings I've been hiding—the Hanged Man, the Tower, Death, the Fool, and the Devil—rip them off their stretchers, roll them up, slip them into a vinyl tube, and secure all the edges with packing tape. I'm not certain why or when I painted them, but I've decided not to destroy them. One day in the future they will serve as a record of an awful time in both Waverly Island's and St. Luke's histories. In the meantime, the tube can act as a time capsule, a container that's buried and resurrected months or years in the future. And so, with the tube in hand, I head to the hatch that leads to the dungeon. When I arrive at the tree stump, I face east and count to twenty-one, the number of steps from the stump to the hatch. Over the years, moss had grown over the hatch, which helped it blend in with the surroundings. But now the hurricane has left the hatch entirely exposed. I bend down, grab the wrought iron handle, and pull.

Who-who-whoo-whoo-who. I recognize your hoot now, just as I always recognized the sound of your breath as you slept and your gait as you approached, and just as it was when you were alive, my heart skips a beat. There you are in the tree nearest me. Your red eyes stare.

"Will you watch this tube for me?" I ask. "It's important, so don't let anyone take it, okay?"

Who-who-whoo-whoo-who.

"Thank you," I say. Then I take the flashlight from my overfull backpack, turn it on, no light, shake it, still no light, smack it. There it goes. I put it in my mouth so I can leave my hands free while I feel for the first rung, climb down a few, reach back up to close the hatch behind me, and keep descending. Darkness and moisture greet me. A few inches of water sit on the dirt floor. I can't imagine anyone sleeping down here. It's disgusting and claustrophobic. There are mice swimming through the water and bats hanging on the ceiling and walls. Even I, who have lived in some pretty repugnant orphanages over the years, am not sure I could have endured this squalor. I aim the flashlight at the ground so as not to trip. Slog through. I don't have too far to walk.

"Hazel," I call, her name echoing in the darkness. No answer. "Hazel," I call again. "It's Pearl." Still no answer. She must be sleeping.

I stop and shine the flashlight into the cage, the same cage where Karla's aunt Matilda was kept before she was burned alive by the man who impregnated her. A long time ago, when Karla first told me about her aunt Matilda, I *saw* the selfish, evil man who fucked her for months, who killed her and one of the twins he fathered. I saw the new child who was growing in her belly, a result of him fucking her in the dungeon while she awaited her death. Didn't he ever think about the fact that burning her was burning a part of himself? That is where it all began, with the burnings. I've seen them. I've felt the women's fear and pain. I've watched their spirits rise from their burned bodies and join those who came before them. Sight is both a gift and a curse. But the longer I live with it, the more I learn how to manage it, the better I get at feeling its wonder instead of its pain.

I arrive at Hazel's cage, focus the flashlight on a wet, rumpled blanket. Move in closer. Both the blanket and cage are empty.

I try not to worry, climb back up to the surface, cover the hatch with debris, retrieve the tube I left with you, and make my way to the Ghost Tree to bury it.

LOLA

On a sunny day, Marsh Road was a packed dirt trail just wide enough to accommodate one car. But today, given its location inside the edges of the forest and the lack of direct sunlight, the hurricane had left it a mud pool that could easily take several days to completely dry. As a longtime resident, I knew to take the police department's jeep and wear a raincoat and mukluks. The ride was bumpy due to occasional potholes, and the open vehicle did little to shield me from splashing water. Magnolia trees lined parts of the road. The tall sculpture Friday had mentioned was hard to miss, a carved wooden likeness of an ancient African woman, her torso long, belly round, legs short and thick, breasts large. A memory came to me of driving this road as a child and asking my father about the statue. "Your mother called it a fertility goddess," he said. When I'd looked back at him, there were tears in his eyes. I slowed down, checked the other side of the street. As Friday had indicated, there stood the bottle tree. I veered onto the narrow shoulder, making sure there was as much space as possible for other vehicles to get by, got out of the jeep, and headed to the wooden bridge. Drooping branches festooned with the Spanish moss typical of live oak trees formed a canopy over the narrow and creaky bridge. I grabbed onto the rope handles and slowly crossed, trying to avoid too much swaying and a slippery fall into the marsh. The house itself was made of weathered gray shingles. The front door and porch ceiling were painted haint blue. I briefly wondered how a house that appeared so fragile had outlived so many hurricanes over the years. Priscilla opened the door before I even had a chance to knock. She was lovely, older than I'd imagined, with smooth caramel-colored skin, and casually dressed in a sleeveless batik dress and wrapped head scarf. But it was her eyes that drew my attention, one brown and one blue.

One brown eye and one blue. I was taken aback. Priscilla was the rootworker my father and I had gone to see all those years ago. Immediately, a memory of the visit came back to me. The flickering candle, Mojo bag filled with conjure oils and herbs and sparkling crystals, and the small pile of dirt from my mother's grave. "It will help us connect with her spirit," she had said.

Now she smiled and said, "I see you remember me. I am much older now, but I have been told my eyes are hard to forget. The pagans believe mismatched eyes are the sign of a witch."

"It was a long time ago," I said.

"And I've been waiting for you for a long while, Detective," Priscilla said.

A long while?

"Come in. This is my home. I'm not sure we visited my shop when you were last here with your father. I did most of my readings and rootwork in my home back then. But even if we did, I doubt you'd remember. You couldn't have been much older than four or five. It has a separate entrance, the bridge wraps around, but we can also get to it through the house. That way we can avoid the slick wood."

She held the door open for me. "Anna, your mother, had the gift, you know. Sometimes a gift as powerful as hers is difficult to bear. I imagine, other than your visit here, your father rarely spoke of her. It was hard for him. They were very much in love. Perhaps, once this case is over, you will come visit and I will tell you about her. But this is not the time. We have much to talk about."

"I would like that," I said. I was always hungry for information about my mother.

Her house was that of a collector. Ancient artifacts, wooden masks, quilts, and baskets hung on the walls. Beautiful textiles adorned curtains and pillows. Chairs and tables were constructed of blond wood. The sweet smell of berries mingled with that of lit candles and incense. I saw a large pot on the stove. "I'm making a batch of jam," she said. "I found a spot in the forest where raspberries grow wild." We proceeded through a back room and a screen door, crossed another short floating bridge, and entered the shop. It was stuffed with antique furnishings, crafts, books, and unique sculptures, wooden and otherwise. Paintings and ancient masks lined the walls. Crystals and rocks, fine and antique jewelry, and objets d'art filled glass cases. One entire case held packs of tarot cards. I stopped to peruse it. Some of the cards were obviously old but not as ancient as the Tarocchi cards found at the murder scenes. A basket atop the case caught my attention. It was filled with poppets of various sizes and shapes. Some were made of burlap like the one I saw at Pearl's cottage and the ones left at the murder scenes, at the Unmarked Tombstone, and on my front porch.

"Pearl Calhoun makes them," Priscilla said. *Pearl Calhoun makes them?* "They sell very well. Tourists especially buy them by the numbers to keep as souvenirs of their visit to the shop of the Swamp Witch. They find me and my rickety house on the marsh exotic. I can see you are wondering how my house and shop continue to survive hurricanes. The trees surrounding it help, but the Great Priestess has something to do with it as well." She smiled.

"Are tourists your primary clientele?" I asked.

"They make for a steady stream, but my primary clientele are collectors from all over the world. A room in my house serves as my boxing, crating, and mailing center. Of course I also serve local residents. I have quite a few regulars from the mainland and islands. I keep busy."

She led me to a sitting area toward the back of the shop. A pink velvet sofa, circa 1930s, and two batik easy chairs surrounded a large steamer trunk with a tea service atop it. I touched one of the chairs. "The fabric is lovely," I said.

"It's called adire," she said. "The dyeing technique is native to the Dogon region of Mali. It dates back to the eleventh century. Sit. Would you like a cup of my homemade brew? I assume that your young coven has spoken of witch's brew, though they probably call it tea. A generalized term used primarily to ease the wariness of non-witches. There's a pot on the stove made in honor of your arrival." Without waiting for my response, she poured us each a cup.

"How did you know when I'd arrive?"

She smiled knowingly. It was the same knowing, somewhat condescending smile Madame Luna and Karla Gardyn had given me on a few occasions. An eye roll without the actual eye roll, as if to say, *I am witch, therefore I know.*

"It's a family recipe. Neroli, orange blossom, rose, lavender, essential oils, and a touch of gin."

"Gin?" I asked.

"Just a touch. How is my dear Pearl? I am very fond of her. She is an exceptional witch. A seer. She is yet to realize her full power, but it will come in time, once she builds confidence. She has nothing to do with your murders. I sense you've wondered about that. That's understandable, given she has questioned it herself. Sometimes, when young witches do angry or hurtful spells, they mistakenly believe they cause *real* harm, but aside from minor mishaps perhaps, they do not. Spells that cause actual death must be specific and intentional, and they must include demonic forces. But her gift of sight is very special. You would be wise to consult her on these murders because they come from very dark places. Places she can *see*. She had an exceptional mentor when she was a child, someone I believe you know." The knowing smile again.

"Someone *I* know? I doubt that."

"In time, you will understand," she said. "But you came here for a reason. To talk about the murders?"

"Yes. I was hoping you might know something about a specific pack of Tarocchi cards and a black velvet book that was left on my desk. It's quite old, written in 1436. It includes exact duplications of the cards found at our murder scenes. The author was a scribe at the monastery that's now St. Luke's Institute of the Arts."

"The book came from my store," she said. "The cards did too."

"I don't understand. Are you saying *you* left the book on my desk?"

"Oh, no. The book went missing. It was in my possession for years, part of an estate sale purchase, but then it was stolen. Isn't that interesting that it found its way to you?"

"Stolen? By whom?"

"I have my suspicions. But we can get to that later. What do you want to know about it?"

"Did you read it? It was written in Latin, but someone had translated it."

"Yes, many years ago, when I first came into its possession, I sent it to a reputable translator and friend at a monastery in Italy. As soon as I felt the book's energy, I knew the words in it held clues to a mystery that has plagued Waverly Island for centuries. But I believe it's necessary to discuss the Tarocchi represented in the book first. Because there is a story here, one that has been trying to be told for some time, and which will not rest until it is fully known. Will you bear with me?"

Trying to be told for some time. Will not rest until it is fully known. As if a story were a person with a heart and mind. The words had nearly slipped by me. Was I starting to believe?

I nodded.

"Some might say I found the cards by accident, but there are no accidents. I was meant to find them, and Pearl Calhoun was meant to keep them safe. They were found along with four blood robes inside an antique sideboard that came from the dungeon area of the tunnels below the Tower. I was overjoyed, of course. I had been looking for the cards ever since I found the book. They were exquisite, and as I said, I believed they held the key to a mystery. A mystery that, if solved, could heal a very unfortunate past. As I'm sure you know, the Tower is where they held the witch trials. A few years ago, Dean Alice Landry of St. Luke's Institute of the Arts showed up at my shop and asked if I could manage a cleanup effort in the tunnels. She said she wanted nothing to do with anything I found. To 'just toss it all.' The sideboard and its contents were among my findings. Pearl Calhoun came into the shop sometime after it had been in my possession and was immediately drawn to it. Which was unusual in itself, given that I had all but hid it in the furthest corner of the shop. While she was opening drawers, she came upon the four blood robes, the vestments the monks wore during ceremonies, including the witch trials. She became noticeably uncomfortable when she first touched them. I remember she paused, closed her eyes, and silently moved her lips in prayer. 'Can you light a white candle?' she asked, and so I did. 'It'll be okay now,' she finally said. There was a trapdoor, a hidden compartment under the sideboard where I was keeping the cards. After the loss of the black velvet book, I knew the cards were at risk, so I'd left them and the robes in the sideboard for safekeeping. I went as far as to leave the sideboard dirty and dusty so no one would be attracted to it. I took the cards out every day to allow them to breathe and to feel their energy. But I didn't tell Pearl this. Instead, when I saw her admiring the sideboard, I said it had just arrived, and I offered it to her without mentioning the cards. I knew those who sought them wouldn't expect them to be in her possession. I also knew once she found them, she would guard them."

"I believe the four cards left at our murder scenes may have been part of this pack," I say. "So she couldn't have guarded them well."

"Ahh, but you must step back to *see*. The entire circumstance was destined. Dean Landry requesting the cleanup effort, the sideboard being found with the robes and cards, Pearl being the lone soul attracted to the sideboard. The *five* cards going missing—"

I interrupted. "How did you know there were five cards?" I hadn't told anyone other than Colin about the fifth card.

"There have always been five cards. The fifth one, the Devil, represents the killer or orchestrator. It's like the book says. 'The Devil killed the game.'"

I shifted in my seat. I was beginning to get very frustrated with Priscilla's mysterious tone.

"I do apologize," Priscilla said. "I forget you aren't a witch. At least not yet. You see, Pearl was always supposed to be the keeper of the cards and the conduit between the past and the present. It was *her* destiny. You were always supposed to return to the island to lead this investigation. It was *your* destiny."

"*My* destiny?"

"Yes, of course. Why else would I know you would call?"

"What about the Game?" I asked. "Are you saying you knew students would be killed? And you didn't stop it?"

"I can't stop what is destined any more than you can. May I tell you a story?"

All I could do was nod.

"The story Scribe Francesco tells in the black velvet book is one of fear, envy, and greed. It is a story as old as time. But it isn't an isolated story. In Scribe Francesco's story, a Florentine court artist, the pet artist of a wealthy and powerful noble family, witnesses one of his young students create something so beautiful and divine, so peerless, he is forced to come face-to-face with his own mediocrity, a realization he cannot abide. Fear, envy, and greed torment him. Fear of exposure. Envy of his student's talent. Greed for fame. He decides he must destroy the perceived destroyer. Thus he creates a false story. He claims the student actually stole *his* creation. The student is arrested for thievery and the creation seized. But while the high court proclaims that the student should be hanged, the Church shows pity. The student is banished to a monastery in a distant land to live a simple and sacrificial monk's life. And now we come to the second story of fear, envy, and greed. But is it a separate story?"

She looks at my empty cup, pauses, is already filling it when she asks, "More brew?"

She continues. "Far, far away, a similar story is taking place. It is the story of an abbot and a young girl. By virtue of his role, an abbot is to set an example for the monks of his monastery by living a solitary life of service and prayer. But this abbot yearns for a different life, one of pleasure and adventure. To indulge these yearnings, he institutes a doctrine directing all the monks of the abbey to use the tunnels beneath the monastery for all transit between buildings, the same tunnels that house the dungeon where criminals are held. This doctrine allows the abbot to walk anywhere aboveground he desires without risk of discovery or report to his prior, the bishop in charge of his diocese, or the pope. Soon he stretches his walks beyond the abbey to a small nearby village, where he comes upon an outdoor market. There he partakes of fruits and vegetables and cakes. Foods of pleasure rarely served within the walls of the abbey. It is at this market that he first sees the fair Matilda. She is but a ten-year-old child at the time, and he has been sworn to celibacy, so he fights his desire for her. After four years of watching her grow into a fetching young maiden, he gives in to his desire. He commands two of his henchmen to bring the maiden to his chambers, and there she stays and services him until he notices her belly becoming large and round. He suspects she is with child, and realizing that a child born at the monastery will expose the truth of his indiscretion, he has the henchmen return Matilda to the house of her mother and keep watch on her activities. A few months later, the men report back to the abbot that the maiden has given birth to twin boys. The next morning two of the village's female spiritual leaders show up at the monastery and threaten to expose the abbot's deeds. The abbot promises to repent for his deeds and support Matilda and the infants."

She pauses, looks into my eyes.

"Here is where our stories intersect," she says. "The abbot like the court artist is consumed by fear, envy, and greed. Fear the spiritual leaders will expose him to the Church. Envy for those who are free to roam as they please. Greed for youth, wealth, and the pleasures of the flesh. And so he commands his henchmen to arrest Matilda and the spiritual leaders for practicing witchcraft, and to take the babes to a midwife in the village while he considers their fate. That night he prays to God for forgiveness, but God recognizes his prayer is insincere, so God takes from the vain abbot that which he cherishes most: his youth. The next morning, when the abbot looks in the mirror, he sees an old, tired man. In a fit of despair, he begs God not for forgiveness but for the return of his youth, but instead it is Lucifer who answers his prayer. Lucifer who promises him youth, longevity, and prosperity, but he must sacrifice his firstborn son and raise the other in the ways of the Prince of Darkness. Now the abbot has become aware of the young scribe from a faraway land and the magical Tarocchi cards he created. Cards that have the unique ability to judge the innocence or guilt of a women arrested for witchcraft, and thus whether she will live or die. So he lies and says that he drew the four cards when determining the fate of Matilda, her firstborn son, and the spiritual leaders. He has his firstborn son hanged, Matilda burned at the stake, and the two spiritual leaders dressed to resemble the Death and Fool cards and then burned at the stake. The morning after the four murders, the abbot sees a younger, more vital man in his mirror and a carrier pigeon arrives to apprise him of a large inheritance. And so the Game of Death is born."

She pauses, looks into my eyes. "Do you understand?"

"Yes, but it seems rather fantastical."

"But is it?" she asks. "Here are the questions you must ask yourself: In the two stories, who are the original victims, who are the perpetrators, and why did the perpetrators do what they did?"

I sit back, wrap myself inside my detective skin. "Scribe Francesco and Matilda were the victims," I say. "The court artist and the abbot were the perpetrators. The court artist believed if the young student's talent was discovered, he would be destroyed. The abbot believed if Matilda's pregnancy and sons were discovered, he would lose his position and thus be destroyed."

"Ahh, yes, *belief*," she says. "And belief is a powerful tonic, is it not? One that can last generations?"

"I suppose," I said. "But what does this story have to do with the current murders at St. Luke's Institute of the Arts?"

"The abbot's surname was Montague."

LOLA

I was still in a daze on my drive to Rebecca's. The story Priscilla had told me was, after all, just that. *A story.* Was it really possible that Monty Montague was a descendant of the abbot in Priscilla's story? And if so, was she saying these murders had been going on for centuries? I kept hearing her words. *Belief is a powerful tonic.* I arrived at Rebecca's garage but sat in her driveway for a while. I needed to digest. Pulled out my notepad. I had been so immersed in Priscilla's story I had only recorded bits and pieces. *I knew the cards were at risk, so I'd left them in the sideboard for safekeeping*, Priscilla had said. *I offered it to her without mentioning the cards*—"her" meaning Pearl. *I knew those who sought them wouldn't expect them to be in her possession. I also knew once she found them, she would guard them.* Who sought them? I felt myself getting paranoid. Who other than Priscilla knew about this part of the island's history? Did Colin? Rebecca? The other Weird Sisters? *The abbot's surname was Montague.* I got out of the jeep and went inside. Colin and Rebecca sat at one of the tall, now bodiless tables discussing the case. They saw me and stopped talking.

"Let me get my notepad," Rebecca said, and stood.

"How was Priscilla's?" Colin asked. "That place is wild, isn't it?"

"It was, well . . . it was enlightening and confusing." I briefly filled him in on what I'd learned and asked him to find Monty Montague. "If he's on the island, bring him in for questioning."

Rebecca returned and launched right in on the results of Esme's autopsy. "With the exception of the murder method, the rest is the same," she said. "Hemlock in her system. A tarot card that was wiped clean. But your cigarettes are a different story. I wish we would have found them earlier. They were soaked and muddy, so I wasn't able to capture any saliva or fingerprints. But I can tell you I think your smoker is a woman. There's lipstick residue on them, and they're definitely slimmer than regular brands. I'm guessing they're Virginia Slims."

"Virginia Slims?" I asked. "How do you know that?"

"Mostly the slimmer profile, but also the butts are white, not brown. It's distinctive. Does that mean anything to you?"

"Alice Landry smokes Virginia Slims," I said.

HAZEL

The receptionist is on the phone when I walk into the Waverly Island Police Station. I attempt to sneak past her and head straight to Detective Germany's office. "Hold on," she says to the person on the phone. "Can I help you?" she asks me. She looks suspicious. I imagine I look pretty scruffy. I haven't showered in days.

"I'm here to see Detective Germany," I say.

"She's not in right now. Do you have an appointment?"

"No," I say. "But I have something to tell her that I'm sure she'll want to hear. It's about the murders."

"Give me a second." She finishes her phone call, hangs up the phone, and looks at me. "What's your name?"

"Hazel Donovan."

"Hazel?" she asks. "The Hazel from the black velvet book? Did you leave it on Detective Germany's desk?"

Should I admit that? "Yes."

Just then, Detective Germany comes through the station's front door, walks past me, and addresses the receptionist. "Any messages?"

"There's someone here to see you," the receptionist says. "This is Hazel Donovan. The girl that left the black velvet book?"

Detective Germany turns to face me. "I'm very happy to see you, Hazel Donovan. Follow me."

When we get to her office, she motions me toward one of two chairs that face her desk, and rather than sit behind her desk, she takes the other.

"You look like you've been through a war," she observes in the tone of a chastising but supportive mother, something I never had. "How are you?"

"I was in the tunnels," I say.

"During the hurricane?"

"Yes."

Her eyes narrow. "Why?"

"Someone wants to kill me," I say.

"Who?"

"I don't know for certain." I start wringing my hands.

She sits back in her chair, stares at me, as if waiting for me to say more. Which I don't, because I'm starting to think that maybe I should have just gotten on the ferry and run.

"Let's start over," she says. "I can tell you're scared. You can trust me, okay?"

Can I? "Okay."

"Is it all right if I ask you a few questions? If you are uncomfortable answering them, just tell me, okay?" Her voice is reassuring, her eyes compassionate.

I nod.

"Why did you have the book?" she asks. "Where did you get it?"

"From Esme," I say.

"Do you know why Esme had it? Or who she got it from?"

"She didn't say. You should ask her."

"Esme is dead," she says. "She was found in her studio late last night."

“What?” I ask. My heart starts pounding. I feel faint, nauseous. The newfound strength I felt after the hurricane turns back to fear. “Do you have a restroom?”

“Right across the hall,” she says.

I run from her office, head straight to a toilet, and throw up. She’s waiting for me by the sink after I flush and leave the stall. She hands me a wet, warm washcloth and a glass of water. I wipe my face, drink some of the water, swish it around in my mouth, and spit it out. She walks me back into her office and closes the door. “You must have had a very difficult time in those tunnels,” she says. “I can’t imagine what you went through. But you were brave, weren’t you?”

“I didn’t feel brave,” I say.

“Well, you were.”

And in that moment, I decide to tell her everything, the entire truth, even if it means I might go to jail. About sleeping with Abel even though I knew he was with Pearl. About Esme and the Game. About going to Abel’s studio because he was my subject. About him breaking up with me. About putting the supposed psychedelic in his wineglass and watching him die. About contacting her to meet me at Joe’s. About George knocking on my door and inviting me to go with him and Jeannine to the Tower. About seeing her waiting for me inside Joe’s but not going in because Green Shoes threatened me. About the men in blood robes and animal masks burning a dead body on a remote beach, describing as well as I could where it was and what they were chanting. About going to her house once to find her and leaving one of Pearl’s poppets so it would protect her. About the terror of the hurricane. About writing letters to Pearl and her. About Pearl coming to the tunnel but not telling her about what happened for fear it would put her in danger. The detective listens intently, lets me ramble on without interruption. By the end of it, tears are rolling down my cheeks and my nose is running. She hands me a tissue, but I've already wiped my nose with my sleeve. I unzip the front of my satchel and give her the letter I wrote. "It's all in there," I manage to say. "Except the part about killing Abel. I couldn't bring myself to put that in writing."

She rises, hugs me. "Thank you. I'm going to have my colleague—her name is Friday—take you to my house. You can take a shower or a bath or just sleep in a warm bed, whatever you want. I have a guest room. There's plenty of food in the fridge. You can stay as long as you want. I promise you'll be safe. Friday will stay with you until I can get there. She's a badass. Does that work?"

I nod yes, because by now I'm crying so hard I'm hiccuping, and I can't talk.

LOLA

The image of Hazel Donovan I'd had in my mind didn't match the slight, frightened girl who just left my office with Friday. I checked my notes. "Shapely in all the right places" was how Joe had described the girl he'd seen having coffee with Abel Montague on occasion. *All lovey-dovey, the two of them were.* She was definitely pretty, but not what I would consider the kind of shapely Joe meant. But if it wasn't Hazel, who was it? I thought about the cigarettes I found at the Ghost Tree. Alice Landry had dark hair, youthful features and energy, and she was definitely shapely. Perhaps Joe could have mistaken her for a St. Luke's student? I radioed Colin. "Any luck on finding Monty Montague?"

"I don't think Montague is on the island," he said.

"Add Alice Landry to that," I said. Then I told him everything Hazel told me, including what she saw on the beach.

"Do you want me to put Alice Landry in holding?" he asked.

"Maybe just the conference room for now. But make sure you or someone else stays with her and she doesn't leave. I'd like to try to see if we can get her to tell us about her involvement in all this. If we arrest her, she might shut down. Just say we need her help or something like that. Make her feel important. And I guess just keep looking for Monty Montague."

"Was she sure it was him on the beach with the others burning the body?" he asks. "And how did she know it was Abel Montague they were burning or what they were chanting? Didn't you say it was in Italian?"

"She said she couldn't be absolutely certain on all those counts except for the blue eyes and the chanting. Apparently, Hazel went to a fancy boarding school with a study-abroad program. She speaks fluent Italian. Can you send some of our guys to check that area of the beach for signs of recent fires or burnings? It's pretty remote there, not an area that gets a lot of traffic, so we might get lucky. But just be careful, okay? I think this is much bigger than we thought."

PEARL

The sun is setting when *you*, the owl, and I emerge from the forest. I look in the direction of Karla's cottage. Her lights are off. Where is she? I need to tell her about Hazel hiding in the dungeon, about going to see her once, about her not being there now. Even though Karla asked me not to, I should have told her earlier. I climb her porch stairs, knock on the door. "Karla, are you in there?" No sound, which confuses me, and I don't feel her. I always feel her when she walks into a room before she says even one word. "Karla," I call again. "Are you there?" I put my hand on the knob, but it's already turning. The door opens.

"Hello, Pearl," Alice in Wonderland says. She looks different. Her face is tight, lips pursed, body stiff. Her eyes aren't right. Her normal ditzy demeanor is gone. There is no gibberish, no Wonderland banter.

"Where's Karla?" I ask while trying not to sound worried.

"I have no idea," she says. "She was supposed to meet me here." I look around the cottage, see that furniture has been moved, drawers and bookshelves emptied. I'm trying to make sense of what I see when she asks, "Would you mind making us a cup of coffee while we wait for Karla to return? Karla's coffee is always so good." Karla didn't say anything about Alice in Wonderland meeting her here. And she never makes coffee.

"I don't know how to make coffee," I say.

"Well, tea, then," she huffs.

"What kind of tea?" I'm stalling, trying to figure out what to do. Something is *very* wrong with her eyes. The pupils are big and dark. The sockets look empty. My body feels the fear before my mind registers it.

"I don't care what kind of tea. Something black, I guess."

I feel my eyes expanding and my body shrinking. A memory pops into my mind. *I am eight years old, back at the orphanage, standing in the middle of a circle of girls. "Weird, weird Martian girl," they are chanting.*

"The tea?" she asks.

"Yes, sorry." On the way to the kitchen, I check the porch to see if *you* are there, but you aren't. Hopefully you're in a nearby tree. I look back at Alice in Wonderland. She's staring at me.

"Are you afraid, Martian girl?" Their laughter echoes.

I have no idea which jar in Karla's pantry holds plain black tea. I only helped with the tea mixtures that once. I check all the labels, see one that reads *Morning Tea Blend.* I grab it and take it into the kitchen. The teakettle sits on the counter beside the stove. I fill it with water and turn on the burner. My hand trembles as I reach for two of Karla's and my handmade cups, put the leaves into the tea infuser, and balance it on the lip of the teapot. Where is Karla? Something is very wrong. Why can't I *see* it? Fear has taken my sight before. I need to calm myself, push the fear away. Finally, the teapot whistles. I pour it. Now I have to wait for the tea to steep. It's all taking so long. My heart beats loud and fast. I wonder if Alice in Wonderland can hear it. *Deep breaths, Pearl*, I tell myself.

"Weird, weird Martian Girl," the girls chant. My eyes scan the circle they've made as I look for exits.

I pour the tea into the cups, carry them to the living area, and put them on the crate that serves as Karla's coffee table.

"Thank you, dear," Alice in Wonderland says. "Would you mind getting me some sugar? I have a sweet tooth." She smiles. A normal Alice in Wonderland smile. Perhaps I just imagined her earlier sinister appearance.

I head back to the kitchen, grab the sugar bowl and a spoon. I note that she puts less than a quarter teaspoon in the tea. The sound of the spoon scraping the inside of the cup as she stirs. The clock ticking. Her high heels scraping against the floor as she moves.

"Thank you, Pearl," she says. "How are your paintings coming along? The board is very proud of you."

"Was Karla expecting you?" I ask, deflecting.

"Yes. We had a critique scheduled."

Miss Blumenthal does Karla's critiques. The only critiques Alice in Wonderland does are with the class liaisons'. I try to stop my face from showing emotion.

The circle of girls is so tight there is no exit. I focus my eyes on the leader, Anita Long. Make my pupils into laser rays that can penetrate her body.

I notice Karla's bedroom door is closed. Why didn't I notice that before? Karla never closes that door. Her canvases always lean against the frame. I look back at Alice in Wonderland. She's smiling. I paint a smile of my face. Years of being an orphan taught me how to pretend. I need to get us outside. Where *you*, the owl, will see us.

"You aren't drinking your tea. It's very good." She stares at me over her cup's rim.

I take a few sips while trying to figure out what to do. It tastes weird. And then I realize she must have put something in it when I went to get the sugar. "Do you want to go sit on the front porch?" I ask. "The rockers got a little banged up in the storm, but they still work, and it's so nice out. Karla and I always drink tea on the porch."

"Are you okay, Pearl?" she asks. "You look pale."

"I'm fine," I say. "Just a little tired. I took a long walk in the forest."

"You were going to see Hazel, weren't you?" she says. "Oh my. That dungeon is a bit cold and dirty for our Hazel, don't you think?" She notes the surprise on my face. "Percy followed you." *Who's Percy?* "We've been looking everywhere for Hazel. Thank you for leading him to her. He's been following you and Karla and that stupid bitch Lola for days thinking one of you would lead him to Hazel. I figured one of you was helping her, but I must admit I was surprised it was you after what she did to you. Stealing a friend's boyfriend is a deal-breaker as far as I'm concerned. Hazel tried to steal Abel from me too." She pauses, sips her tea. "But only you accomplished that, didn't you?" She sounds angry. "That wasn't part of the plan. How did you do it? Did you put a spell on him?" She narrows her eyes. "I mean, look at you and look at me."

I set down the cup. She can't make me drink it. I only had a few sips. Hopefully that's not enough to poison me. My heart is pounding. *Is Karla dead?* I try not look at the bedroom door. She'll see that I know. She's watching my every move. "I'm going outside," I say, and rise.

"Sit," she commands, and waits for me to do so. Then she leans back in her chair. "You are going to listen to me. You owe me that. I did you a favor by bringing you to St. Luke's. You see, Abel was the love of my life, and he felt the same way about me. But his father wouldn't have approved. I've actually been Monty's mistress off and on for years. So Abel and I had to find a girl for him to keep his father off our scent. Someone his father might not find attractive, at least his kind of attractive, but who would intrigue him. I knew as soon as I met you at the orphanage that you were our perfect cover."

There was that word Hazel had used, "cover." Surely Alice in Wonderland can hear my heart pounding.

"Your talent was just a plus," Alice in Wonderland said. "We planned to leave together as soon as Abel graduated and got his money. But then I found that envelope with Monique Chevalier's driver's license, passport, and social security card, and a note warning whoever found it to run. I showed it all to Abel, told him I was scared, that we needed to leave, that if Monty killed Monique Chevalier, he might kill me. He looked worried."

Even though I don't want them to move, my eyes wander to Karla's closed bedroom door. She follows them.

"She could be dead by now. I'm not exactly sure how long hemlock takes. But Karla isn't important. It's *you* that needs to hear what *I* have to say. Because you're the reason Abel had to die. It was that look on his face after I told him about Monique Chevalier. I thought he was worried about *me*, but it turned out it was about *you*. He said he was going to confront his father. I begged him not to. I said telling his father would put us in danger. I said we should just leave, go somewhere and hide, that we'd be fine without his graduation money, that I had plenty of money. I've been embezzling money from the school for years. And do you know what he said? He said he didn't want to leave or hide. He wanted to graduate. He wanted fame. And then he started talking about you. He said your talent awed him. That you were the real deal. I mean, we had just had sex when he told me all this. I reminded him that you were a fake girlfriend. So his father wouldn't discover he and I were together. We used to laugh about how naive you were. But then he started squirming, and finally, he got to the actual point of why he didn't want to leave St. Luke's or run away with me. He said he didn't want to have sex with me anymore, that we were finished, that he loved you and wanted to be with you. That he didn't know when it happened, but that it just had. He said he was going to buy you a ring. A fucking ring. And then he asked me if we could still be friends. *Friends?* Was he clueless? After all the support I'd given him. All the years I'd given up for him. My entire youth. I practically raised him. And he wanted to marry *you*?" She noticeably tried to calm herself down. "Jealousy is an all-consuming emotion, isn't it? You understand because you were jealous of Hazel, weren't you? And then he left. So I called Monty and I lied. I told him Abel was threatening to expose the Game. He already knew that Abel, George, and Eric were raping girls, and that Esme had an abortion. And can you believe it? He was okay with that, boys will be boys and all that. But Abel threatening to expose the Game, well, I immediately heard the concern in his voice. He asked what I meant, and I told him Abel had been sleeping with Hazel. I said he'd told her all about the Game and I was worried she might say something, which was a lie, of course. But I was angry. I felt betrayed. I wanted to get back at Abel. I wanted Monty to forbid Abel to leave. Then I whined—that always works with Monty, I said I needed his help, that I had tried to handle it on my own, but that Abel could be uncontrollable. Which of course he already knew. Then I fed his ego and his fear simultaneously. I told him that I missed him, that even though he looked older, he was still handsome. Well, that did the trick. Monty is very vain. He said he was sending Percy, his fixer. He said we needed to use the book and play the Game." She paused, looked at me. "Did Abel ever tell you about the Game?"

I shook my head no. Or at least I think I did. I was woozy.

"The Montagues have been playing the Game for generations. Ever since the fifteenth-century witch burnings. Always during the autumnal equinox. Always the same five tarot cards. But only a firstborn son could be the Hanged Man, and if there's a secondborn son, he must be raised in the ways of the Prince of Darkness, like he'd been doing with Abel. Well, when Monty said that about playing the Game, I didn't think he meant Abel. But then he specifically mentioned Abel being the firstborn. I told him I was confused, that Abel's twin brother, who drowned on the island when the boys were just four years old, was the firstborn, not Abel. Monty said yes, but he'd died before his eighteenth birthday, which made Abel the firstborn. I was stunned. Because of course he knew that I knew that wasn't how the Game was supposed to work. I argued with him, said Abel had already passed eighteen, that he was nearing twenty, that I didn't think Lucifer would appreciate him altering the rules of the sacrifice. When I realized that he really meant to kill Abel, I begged him not to. I said I cared about Abel and, surely, he did too. I did everything but come right out and tell him I loved Abel. But he got angry and threatened me. Told me his mind was made up and either I helped organize the Game or I'd be done at St. Luke's. And all I could think about was Monique Chevalier, so I immediately changed my tune and said I was there to help. Then he gave me the names and the order of the victims. Except for poor Jeannine, it went down the way it was supposed to. Hazel, that bitch, was supposed to be in the Tower, not Jeannine. Esme was Monty's idea. We needed a student to help set up the other students. I said I wasn't sure about her. But he said she would be pliable, that she owed the school for helping her with the abortion, that all we had to do was threaten to tell her parents, "*that she would rather die than endure their shame.*" She took a sip of her tea, cocked her head, and then went on as if she were ruminating to herself rather than talking to me. "You know, I've come to see that murder is really quite easy. Percy handled all the gore and heavy lifting, so I didn't have to deal with any of that. But I came up with the choreography and costumes. I think I did quite a good job. Even Monty said so. It's too bad about Esme, but it couldn't be helped. In the beginning, she was such a sweet little helper. It was her idea to leave your poppets at the scenes as red herrings. She stole them from your cottage the same day she took the five cards. I was actually considering having another student play the Fool, but in the end, I was right about her. She told me she didn't want to be part of the Game anymore, that she was going to tell Lola what had been going on. Stupid girl."

She looks into my eyes. "By now, Percy has killed Hazel and hopefully found the black velvet book. And so, this Game is complete. The next one will have to wait until the autumnal equinox of 1987, when Monty's eldest twin with his new wife turns eighteen. Generally, a Montague man leads only one Game in his lifetime, but Monty plans to break that rule as well. He's aged very quickly these past few years. And I might just stay and help. With Abel gone, there's nothing else out there for me." She stops, gloats. "Cat got your tongue?"

"I'm not feeling well," I say.

"It's the hemlock," she says. She cocks her head, makes a pouting face. "You poor thing. You're scared, aren't you? I want you to know I feel bad about all this. If Abel had just left with me, none of this would have had to happen."

Anita Long laughs. "Look at her," she says. "The way she's staring. As if she thinks she can scare me. You are pathetic, Pearl Calhoun."

Alice in Wonderland laughs. Loud. Like a hyena. The skin on her face is melting off the bones of her skull, her eyes all but gone. I have to get out of this cottage. "I need some air." I'm not sure if I said it out loud. I do my best to stand, but I'm wobbly. I hold on to the chair next to the doorframe. I reach for the door handle. It's wavy like water. Push my hand into the water. Feel something round and hard. Turn it. Fresh air. *You*, the owl, are perched on the rail. I climb down the steps. Head toward the forest. You follow.

"You won't get far," I hear Alice in Wonderland say.

I focus my laser eyes on Anita Long. She wobbles, puts her arms out to steady herself; then she falls forward and hits her head on the cold, hard tile floor.

It's what I do. I hurt people with my mind. I look behind me. Alice in Wonderland stands on the edge of the porch. I will her to fall. She loses her balance, topples down the wooden stairs. You fly on top of her, your wings flapping wildly as you dig your talons into her. She screams, her arms flailing as she tries to push you away, but you dig in further, screech loud and shrill. My vision blurs as I fall to the ground and the world goes dark.

LOLA

"We've checked everywhere," Colin said. We were talking on our handheld radios. "No Monty Montague. No Landry. I left a couple of guys at her office just in case she shows up."

"Did you check Studio Row?" I asked.

"Yes," he said. "No luck."

"I meant for Pearl."

"No Pearl either."

"Okay," I said. "I'm almost to her cottage. Keep me updated."

I parked my cruiser in the lot nearest the east entrance, got out. There was a commotion. Someone screaming. *Pearl?* I ran. Saw the screams were coming from the direction of the red-eyed owl, its talons pressed into a woman's chest. I recognized Alice's signature pencil skirt. Her blouse was ripped and hanging. There was blood everywhere. She wasn't moving. "Stop," I said to the owl. It pulled in its talons but didn't move. That was when I saw Pearl. She was lying on the ground between the cottage and forest. She wasn't moving. I checked her pulse. She was alive. "Pearl, can you hear me?" No response.

I grabbed my radio, called Colin again. "Call Barney Cougar. Tell him it's an emergency. We need two stretchers at Karla Gardyn's cottage."

"Will do," Colin said.

I ran into the cottage. Karla's bedroom door was closed. The large easel that had filled the doorway was nowhere in sight. I called her name. Slowly, I opened the door. Saw that the easel had fallen to the floor. Paint tubes spread across the room and the bed. Karla was lying on the bed. I felt for her pulse. It was barely there. There was nothing I could do until Barney Cougar and his grandsons arrived. I raced back outside, sat next to Pearl. Pushed the hair out of her face, rubbed her arm. I radioed Colin again. "I found Karla on her bed. She's alive but barely. Did you get ahold of Barney?"

"He's on his way. I'm about three minutes from you."

"Tell him to put on his light and siren and get his butt over here. Now. I don't want to lose these girls."

The owl was standing nearby, its red eyes focused, body still, a soldier standing guard.

"You might want to fly into a tree," I said to it. Its eyes met mine for a moment, then returned to Pearl. Pearl believed the owl was Abel. In that moment, I thought it just might be. I thought the same when it attacked me in the forest as I was following Pearl. I'd never seen an owl attack like that. As if its anger were personal. As if it were protecting her. "Get," I said to it. "You need to leave. I'll watch her. If they see you here, they'll kill you." Its eyes on me again. It spread its wings and flew into the forest.

I heard two sets of sirens in the distance. Colin's police cruiser. Barney Cougar's ambulance. They'd be here soon. I went to Pearl, fell on my knees, prayed to the God I hadn't prayed to in years. The God I'd replaced with my tree goddess.

"Please spare her," I said.

I heard footsteps. Barney Cougar's grandsons were running down the path holding two stretchers. Colin was right behind them.

Two of the grandsons bent over Alice's body, checked her wrist for a pulse. "She's still alive," one said.

I made the decision on the spot. I didn't care about the consequences. "No, don't. Take the girls first." I pointed to Pearl. "There's another girl in the cottage. You can come back for this one." I watched as the grandsons put Pearl on the stretcher and carried her to the station wagon. And then something magical occurred. A white mist formed above her, and accompanied her all the way to the ambulance. And when she was safely inside, the mist turned into three translucent white scarves that floated in and around and through one another. And finally drifted into the sky.

PART FIVE

The Devil

Those whom he dragged down to Hell were usually seen as immoral and deserving of their fate.

—HELEN FARLEY,
A CULTURAL HISTORY OF TAROT

Day 7

Six Days After the Autumnal Equinox

Thursday, September 28, 1972

LOLA

I spent the night in a leisure chair in Pearl's hospital room. I didn't sleep. I was wired and worried. The hospital had given the girls fluids and used activated charcoal and other methods to cleanse the toxins from their systems. "It was touch-and-go there for a while," the nurse had said. "Especially with Miss Gardyn. But it looks like they're both going to make it. They're tough girls, both of them."

Or the Ghost Women protected them.

The Ghost Women. When had I started to believe? Was it the black velvet book? Was it the shock I felt when reading the long list of innocent women burned at the stake right here on Waverly Island, *my* island, *my* home, back in the fifteenth century? Was it listening to Priscilla's story about the abbot? About how it all started and why, about Karla's Aunt Mathilda? Was it the abbot's surname, Montague? Was it the murders of five young students at St. Luke's Institute of the Arts? Or Hazel telling me about the Game and the burning ritual she had witnessed on the beach? Or was it actually seeing the Ghost Women with my own eyes?

There was a story my father used to tell me when I was child. It was about a morning he went hunting in Dead Witch Forest. He was walking through the trees with his bow and arrow, waiting to come across a deer. It was a few hours before he saw one, a magnificent buck with an eight-point rack. He stilled himself, pulled back the bow, and aimed. Just then, a fluttering mist came down from the sky and blocked his sight of the deer. Soon the mist dispersed, and he realized it wasn't a mist at all; it was a group of ethereal beings. By then, of course, the buck had disappeared, but my father said he didn't care because he had seen my mother that day.

"I see her in the forest sometimes," he said. "Especially when I'm with you."

"Why don't I see her?" I'd asked.

"You will," he said.

It wasn't too long after he told me that story of the poor man's daughter who chose to become a tree rather than marry the rich, fat mayor. Why had I dismissed what my father had told me about seeing my mother inside a fluttering mist yet believed the story of a young woman fusing herself into a tree? Perhaps because in my mind those ethereal beings had taken my mother from me. Perhaps the story of the poor man's daughter choosing to be a tree had given my mother back to me.

Yesterday, when I saw Pearl lying on the ground close to death, I was so frightened I would lose her. But then I saw that white mist floating above her, and I felt a sense of relief and trust I hadn't in years. That was the first time I saw the Ghost Women. It would not be the last.

PEARL

She is asleep in an easy chair when I wake. I wonder how long she has been there. I like watching her sleep. She looks so peaceful. Even in repose, she exudes elegance. I am reminded of watching her dance. How her toe shoes appeared to flutter on a cloud. How her arms stretched to the sky. I remember wondering if she was aware how much the surety of her movements, the pureness of her grace, touched someone like me. Someone who had spent her life surrounded by loudness and chaos, whose dark thoughts became hurtful actions. Who chose to fight her battles with acts of ugliness instead of shows of dignity. I have a choice. When she wakes, I can tell her the full story of what I know about the St. Luke's murders, the one that will clear my conscience. Or I can tell her an edited story. One where I hadn't kept secret my discovery of the missing tarot cards and the paintings that showed up in front of my newly stretched canvases. Where I didn't suspect that the cards found at the murder scenes were from my deck. Where I didn't even confess after I realized the murders were staged to exactly match those five cards.

I hear a small sound, a soft hum of breath. Look at my ballerina detective. She is waking. And in a split second, I *see* our future together. She is a big sister to me. We walk in the woods. Pray to her tree. Watch the sunset. She comes to my graduation. Attends my first opening exhibit and those after that. She stands with pride before my paintings of her. Photographers snap photos of the two of us. We are featured on the covers of *Art News* and *Art in America*. "The Artist and Her Inspiration," one caption reads. And as I see all of this, my heart is full. Because she is *my* sister, *my* family. Because she and I were always meant to be.

Her eyes are open when I look back in her direction. And I am no longer able to hide from her.

"I was eight years old," I say. "An orphan. You were the prettiest thing I ever saw, so graceful. A fairy princess. I'd never seen anything so perfect as you. Sister Winnifred snuck me out of the convent and took me to a touring performance of the New York City Ballet in Charleston. She said her childhood friend was the prima ballerina. That you and she had taken dance lessons together when you were young. After the ballet, we went backstage to meet you. You were so patient and kind. I was certain your eyes really *saw* me, as if my feelings mattered, as if I were the only little girl in the whole world. And when you smiled, I felt such warmth that it was as if the sun itself was washing its rays over me. I never forgot you. And then, one day, my prayers were answered. I saw you here, in the forest by the overlook. Even in your running clothes, I recognized you immediately. It was dawn. I was looking for a perfect spot to sketch the sunrise, and there you were, Lola Villanova, the ballerina from my youth. You stood looking up through the branches of one of the tallest and proudest trees in the forest. And I felt the wisdom of the Great Priestess. She alone had led me to you. You and your tree were always meant to be the subject of my body of work. Every morning from that day forward, I hid nearby and sketched you talking to that tree. More than once, I tripped on a nearby branch or ran if I thought you might discover me. I feared you might forbid me to sketch you. That first day after Abel died, when you came to my cottage, my *Fairy Painting No. 1* was hanging on the wall right behind you. So close I thought for sure you would see it, but you didn't, and so I decided that meant it wasn't time. That your being my secret subject would give the paintings the quality of mysteriousness I sought." I pause. "You probably don't remember me from the ballet."

"I do," she says. "Our company was on a southern United States tour. I remember Winnie bringing one of her orphans with her to the performance. I was so excited to see her again. I remember you were very slight, had the biggest and most beautiful blue eyes, that those eyes looked right into mine with a fearlessness that made you larger than life. I admit when I came to your cottage that first time that there was *something*. And now, thinking about that day, I remember thinking the exact same thing, that you were fearless."

"You took dance lessons with Sister Winnifred?"

"Yes. Winnifred Darling and I began taking classes at Debra's Dance Studio together here on the island when we were five years old. We were fast friends. Debra, the owner of the studio, had danced for a company in Canada before retiring to the island. She saw that the two of us were more committed than the other students, and even though neither of us could afford private lessons, she taught us anyway. Winnie was an amazing dancer. We always talked about dancing onstage together one day. I was so sad and disappointed when she went in another direction, but she told me her faith was calling her, just like dance was calling me. I see it now. Understand that it was Winnie who taught you island magic. She used to try to teach me, but I fought it. My father once mentioned that my mother was a believer. But I was so angry my mother had died that I wanted nothing to do with anything that might have contributed to her death."

"Do you still keep in touch?" I asked. "I missed her so when she left."

"We do," she said. "She's at a convent in Virginia now. We send each other letters. She told me about you, you know. Back then. Before she brought you to the ballet. About what a gifted child you were. About your art. She adored you. I'll write and tell her we found each other again. I'm positive she will want to see you as well. She will be so proud to see who you've become."

And in that moment, I feel her grace enter me. It spreads throughout my entire body, a kind of fire, nearly frightening me with its intensity, and then something odd occurs. The fire dissipates and a part of me rises above myself and I feel a lightness I have never felt before, and I think of the Ghost Women and what they must have felt when their spirits escaped the fire of the stakes, when they rose into the air and flew to the forest, and I wonder if, like I do now, they felt they were coming home after a long time away, and I tell her this and she smiles, a sweet fairy smile, and I swear I see the air around her sparkling. And in this space, I opt to tell her everything, from that first day that I saw *you* in that drawing class to the final day I found Alice in Wonderland in

Karla's cottage. About you, I tell her the ugly and the good, because there was good in you. About Alice in Wonderland, I tell her about your affair, that the Tarocchi Murders had been occurring on the island for generations, and that she was involved in the most recent ones. I tell her about Esme's part in the Game, including her stealing the five cards from my deck and my sadness that she is gone. I tell her about my helping out Hazel in the tunnels, and that I now *see* and understand why Hazel did what she did. That it was actually herself she was trying to steal, not *you*. I tell her that sometimes those of us with less-than-loving pasts desperately seek love wherever we can find it, and it is inside that moment when we see our worst selves that we are given the choice to instead claim our best selves. I tell her that although I have forgiven Hazel, I realize I didn't need to. She needed to forgive herself.

But there is one thing I don't tell my ballerina detective. I don't tell her what Alice in Wonderland said about *you* choosing me. About you loving me, wanting to buy me a ring and spend the rest of your life with me. It seems braggy and selfish to say that, and I'm trying my best to be a more generous and magnanimous person (like Karla) and a less vengeful and vindictive person (like the old me, the one who hurts people with her mind). But on top of that, I would rather keep that knowledge close to my heart. For it to be ours alone. Yours and mine.

My ballerina detective hugs me then. She says she has work to do, a case to solve. She says she'll be back in the evening to check on me, and I know she will. And after she leaves and I am alone, I allow myself to feel you, all of you. To imagine what our future might have been. Would we have had children? Lived happily ever after? Would two artists, each striving for their own success, have had room to selflessly support the success of the other? Would our love have lasted?

Then I try to wipe these thoughts from my mind because I know that's what you would tell me to do. You would say I should stop trying to imagine a future that can never be. You would say, *Be real, Pearl. Stop being so melodramatic and get on with your life.*

My life. Thank you, by the way, for saving it. And Karla's and Hazel's and my ballerina detective's. I wish you'd reconsider leaving this earth. I believe the world is a better place with you in it. You, the owl. And just so you know, I have no doubt that if you do choose to stay, and that involves some kind of showdown, that no crazed, demented, and tyrannical creature with horns and a pitchfork will have a snowball's chance in, well, hell, against the likes of Abel Montague.

One Year Later

THE AUTUMNAL EQUINOX
SUNDAY, SEPTEMBER 23, 1973

LOLA

There was a peace in talking to trees. A quiet. Life could be so loud. But here, standing before *my* tree, I could say nothing and she would still hear me.

One year had passed since I saw Abel Montague's body hanging from the Ghost Tree. Nearly every day since, I had stood on this mound and looked out at the gathering of disparate creatures that shared the sunrise with me. And each time, I marveled at how this motley crew, some bitter enemies, were able to get past their differences in service to a shared wonder. Now here I was yet again. Watching and waiting. Anticipating the end of darkness and the beginning of light.

The Tarocchi Murders would always steal a part of my light. Five students at St. Luke's Institute of the Arts had lost their lives in such horrific and gruesome ways. Perhaps it went with the job, but I couldn't help but wonder if I could have done something differently. If I should have understood from the beginning that Abel Montague would not be the last. If I should have seen past Alice Landry's lies.

Alice didn't survive the owl attack, but we had the black velvet book. And her confession to Pearl that Montague men had been playing the Game of Death for centuries, that she and Monty Montague were this iteration's architects, that Esme Li had helped them carry it out, and that a man named Percy Lamb, a.k.a. Green Shoes, who had since disappeared, had done the heavy lifting. We arrested Monty and charged him with committing a series of ritualistic murders. His high-powered New York attorney argued that Monty had no knowledge of a black velvet book or the so-called Game of Death, adding that even if two students did see someone with blue eyes burning what looked like dead bodies on the beach, how could they prove these so-called bodies were the corpses of actual people? Wasn't it true that students themselves engaged in fake witch burnings? Not to mention that 27 percent of the US population had blue eyes.

A search of the island by a reputable archeologist found no remains or bone fragments. It was their assessment that if corpse desecration had taken place, any evidence of such was probably somewhere in the middle of the ocean.

St. Luke's Institute of the Arts remained open and operational, but Monty Montague's third wife was now listed as founder and chairman of the board. It seemed sometime after his trial and exoneration, Monty, like Percy Lamb, had disappeared into thin air. There was also a new dean, a Miss Wanda Dorchester, who apparently had served with Melissa Montague on the board of the Association of Junior Leagues International. Pearl and Hazel were now Third Years, and Karla was a Fourth Year. Everyone was looking forward to Karla's one-woman graduate exhibition at a prestigious gallery in SoHo. The title of her exhibit was, fittingly, *Bad Men*.

Pearl was doing well. She seemed happy and at peace. We'd gotten close. For me, she was the best thing that came out of the case. A little sister. A great friend. She and I had gone to visit my old friend Winnie, now Sister Winnifred.

Madame Luna verified the authenticity of the tarot cards found at the murder scenes. She asked Pearl, as the pack's owner, to donate them to a museum, promising she would enjoy a hefty tax write-off. Alternatively, she knew of a benefactor willing to pay her a substantial price. But Pearl wanted the cards, not the money. She said anyone who would "give up something so extraordinary for something as fleeting as money or stick them in a glass case never to be touched or read again didn't respect their prescience or power." The black velvet book was safely back in Priscilla's possession. She said she was certain it was Alice Landry who had stolen it because she was in the shop the day the book went missing. Priscilla said, though she thought she'd been being cautious, that Alice must have seen her pull the book from its hiding place under the register to compare its renderings to a new tarot pack she'd gotten from an estate sale. I was getting to know Priscilla, learning all I could about my mother and her powers, and about how much my father had loved my mother. I found it hopeful that I had been conceived from a loving relationship. "Such a love will be yours one day," Priscilla told me.

A few weeks ago, we were in her shop, sharing a pot of her special gin-spiked tea, when she surprised me by saying this: "It's good you have forgiven yourself. Now you can start anew."

"Forgiven myself?" I'd asked.

"The prosecutor's words," she said. "'*What are the lengths to which a woman will go when shunned by a man she loves? What is her breaking point?*'"

I'd wanted to ask how she knew what the prosecutor at my murder trial had said all those years ago but then realized it was a foolish question. Priscilla, like Pearl, had the sight.

"You know, bad men have accidents every day," she added, and curled her lips into one of her signature sly smiles. Then she proceeded to tell me two stories.

"On a two-hundred-twenty-foot mega-yacht somewhere on the French Riviera, a wealthy man who got away with the murders of young students, including his own son, was hosting a group of the world's most famous artists, art critics, and philanthropists. One night, his third wife, the mother of his second set of twin boys, saw him kissing in the moonlight a younger woman, whom she knew would soon be his fourth wife. She imagined how easy it would be for him to fall overboard. How simple it would be to explain to the other passengers that he'd had to leave the ship early to attend to an important matter and then to act devastated when he never returned home."

Priscilla had paused for a moment and said what she always did: "Do you understand?" I'd nodded, but she was already sharing the next story.

"Perched in a tree on an island off the coast of South Carolina, a red-eyed owl watched and waited. The boy inside it had chosen this vessel for its strength, insight, and intelligence, characteristics he didn't previously value. One morning, the owl saw a man wearing green shoes attempt to enter the hatch that led to the dungeon where accused witches were once held while they awaited burning, and where now a girl, a friend of the girl he loved, was hiding. He didn't have to imagine how easy it would be to attack and kill the man because doing so was within the owl's nature. Later the Swamp Witch, who monitored the owl's movements, would come to retrieve the body and bury it in the marsh beneath her floating house. Then she would thank the boy inside the owl. And the owl would slowly close and open its eyes to show how pleasurable performing this deed had been."

Again she paused, but this time her eyes stared deep into mine when she spoke. "You do understand, don't you? Because you have your own story."

And she was right. I did.

In a ballroom somewhere in New York City, a famous danseur and his wife, a prima ballerina, were celebrating the season's closing performance with the company. The prima ballerina was being hailed by the media for giving the most brilliant performance of her career. Reporters were vying for her attention while cameras flashed and champagne corks popped. She knew all too well that when attention was directed at her, her husband would feel slighted. He would get drunk, become angry and abusive. She imagined how easy it would be to put a sleeping pill in his champagne glass when they returned to their apartment that night, how pleasurable it would be to hit him over the head with his prized reproduction bronze sculpture, *Little Dancer*, by Degas. How painful and yet ultimately how freeing it would be to hit and cut herself, drink the entire bottle of champagne, pass out, and when woken by the police, due to a call from a nosy neighbor, a regular occurrence after one of their many violent fights, how easy it would be to act disoriented and claim no memory of the incident.

"But there are some stories that are best kept secret, aren't there?" Priscilla had asked, then curled her lips into her signature mischievous smile. This time she'd waited for my response.

"Yes," I said.

And so this morning, exactly one year since I saw Abel Montague's body hanging from the Ghost Tree, I stood on the mound beneath *my* tree looking over the cliff edge at the ocean below. The motley crew of disparate creatures was gathering on the beach. I heard a cooing sound, peeked up through the branches at my daily greeter. The red-eyed owl. "Good morning, Abel," I said, and looked out to the sea. There was the slim orange line forming above the horizon. The motley crew paused its chatter. The forest stilled. I watched as the line formed into a glorious sphere. Then I stretched and began my run to Karla's front porch with the owl on my tail.

And there, in the distance, I saw them. Pearl and Karla and Hazel and Priscilla stood at the base of Karla's cottage, while a multitude of Ghost Women streamed from the forest and circled the sky. And as I made my way through them, one smiled and nodded. For a moment, I imagined her glowing face resembled the only photograph I had of my mother. But just as I began to dismiss the thought, I heard a sweet whisper. *I'm proud of you*, it said. Tears came to my eyes and it was through them that I first saw the flickering light of the five white candles on Karla's porch rail. When I got closer, I saw that Karla had fashioned a firepit on the ground and inside it were the canvases Pearl had painted of the five murders. The *Hanged Man*, the *Tower*, *Death*, the *Fool*, and the *Devil*.

The owl alighted on the porch rail.

"We have been waiting for you," Karla said to me, and smiled.

We all held hands, and she recited these words: "O Great Priestess, we are here to honor the loss of our classmates who died so viciously one year ago during the autumnal equinox. Especially our sister Esme Li. We ask that you bless her and the others and continue to watch over all the women of St. Luke's, Waverly Island, and beyond, including Aunt Matilda and her fellow Ghost Women." Pearl cleared her throat. "And I guess Abel too," Karla reluctantly added.

Then she lit a match and threw it into the pit. And we all watched as the Tarocchi Murders went up in flames.

Acknowledgments

Heartfelt thanks to my agent, Miriam Altshuler, for your endless knowledge, unwavering support, and continuous cheerleading throughout the realization of this novel. Thank you especially for always being there when I need advice or just an ear. Your energy is infectious, and your knowledge of the publishing world invaluable.

Thank you to my amazing editor, Maya Ziv. I mean, wow, I am so grateful to you. You were beside me every step of the way while I was writing this novel, especially during the times when I felt a bit out of my comfort zone. I mean, red-eyed owls and a magical ghost tree! I can't say enough about your tough but gentle editorial touch and your seeming ability to offer just the right insight when it's most needed. No way would this novel be what it is without your patience, grace, and unparalleled dedication and expertise.

Much thanks to all the folks at Dutton, Penguin Random House, who had a hand in making this novel a reality, including John Parsley, Mary Beth Constant, Sarah Thegeby, Hannah Poole, Diamond Bridges, Melissa Solis, Alice Dalrymple, Sabila Khan, Jillian Fata, Ella Kurki, and Justina Vasquez.

I am forever grateful to my husband, David, and my daughter, Madi. To David, thank you for being the best husband anyone, and especially any writer, could ever want. You are patient and funny and so supportive and, in most ways, perfect. You get one strike for making me move so much, but I suppose that could be looked at as a plus. We have lived in some really cool cities, and along the way experienced so many distinct cultures and landscapes, from mountains to oceans to lakes. To Madi, you are the best thing that ever happened to me. For many years, it was just the two of us. You and me against the world. You were, and always will be, my most fulfilling journey and greatest adventure. It makes me so happy that you are living your dream as an art curator. Thank you also to my best friend, Brutus. You are the pup of all pups. You totally win the cuteness award, and the sit-by-my-side-as-I-write award. And, well, any other furry, four-legged award.

To my mother, Helen, thank you for taking me to the library as a child and introducing me to the joy of reading. I remember walking out of the library every other week with a stack of new books I could barely carry, reading late into the night with a flashlight under the covers, and wishing I didn't have to return them. Love you.

Gratitude to all the ladies of the Houston Bunco Walking Club for your friendship and support over these past few years. Not just for listening to me talk about this novel, but also for adding many moments of levity to our walks, great food and comradery to games, and so many moments of pure silliness and laughter. And to all the attendees at my bookstore and book club talks and readings.

To all my MFA writing instructors at the University of Washington, and to every workshop leader I had at the Wildacres Writers Workshop, Bread Loaf Writers' Conference, Tin House Summer Workshop, and the Spannocchia Writers' Workshop in Siena, Italy, thank you for sharing your insights, for graciously giving your time, and for your ongoing support of my writing journey.

To the town of South Haven, Michigan, you are the best! Your support of my writing and my novels is beyond appreciated. That phrase "you can't go home again" is so untrue when it comes to all of you. I look forward to all things South Haven, including friends, family, the beach and blue waters of Lake Michigan, the shop owners, and the blueberry festival.

To the Library of Michigan, thank you for supporting Michigan authors through your yearly Notable Books awards, and for all the Michigan libraries that so graciously welcomed me into their communities when I was blessed to win one.

This novel could not have come to fruition without in-depth research into Tarot, witchcraft, the burgeoning feminist revolution and art scene of the '70s, Lowcountry magic, religion, and witch hunts. While I did a lot of research online, I also found and read quite a few books. Thank you to all the authors of the books I mention in the following paragraphs. I am amazed at the depth and detail of your research.

Tarot. I have been reading divination Tarot since college—including such decks as the Tarot de Marseille (1789), considered the first divinatory deck, and the Rider-Waite (1909), considered the model for all future divinatory decks—but I wasn't as familiar with what are considered the very first tarot decks. These decks, which were named for the wealthy and aristocratic Visconti and Sforza families of fifteenth-century Milan, include the Cary-Yale Visconti-Sforza deck, Pierpont-Morgan Bergamo Visconti-Sforza deck, and Brera-Brambilla Visconti-Sforza deck. Rather than divination, the decks were used to play a card game called Tarocchi. Surprisingly, there is a wealth of information pertaining to these early decks on the internet. I was also able to locate one book currently in print and two others on used and rare book sites that go into great detail on both the appearance of the cards and the mechanics of the Tarocchi game. These include *A Cultural History of Tarot* by Helen Farley (2009), *The Visconti-Sforza Tarot Cards* by Michael Dummett (1986), and *The Tarot Cards Painted by Bonifacio Bembo* by Gertrude Moakley (1966). In addition to books, I sought out rare facsimile decks so I could describe them firsthand and was excited to find two older used decks that illustrate the characteristics I describe in the novel, such as a much larger format than today's decks, intricate design and coloration, and the stunning application of gold leaf.

Setting. I chose to set the novel on an island off the coast of South Carolina for several reasons. I lived on one of the South Carolina Sea Islands for a few years. It remains one of my favorite places. There is a sultry, mysterious, and magical beauty to Charleston and the Lowcountry that I wanted to capture in the novel. Ghost tours, ancient gravestones, hoodoo culture, historic buildings, and thick heat make it a perfect setting for a story that centers around a series of art student murders. In addition to my personal experience, for Charleston-specific divinatory folklore, I reviewed books like *Lowcountry Voodoo* by Terrance Zepke (2009), *Haunted Charleston* by Ed Macy and Geordie Buxton (2004), *Haunted Charleston* by Sara Pitzer (2013), *Charleston's Ghosts* by James Caskey (2014), *Ghosts and Legends of Charleston, South Carolina* by Denise Roffe (2020), and an amazing cookbook that includes Sea Island history and culture called *Gullah Geechee Home Cooking* by Emily Meggett (2022), the matriarch of Edisto Island. For Southern-specific divinatory folklore, I reviewed *Witch Queens, Voodoo Spirits & Hoodoo Saints* by Denise Alvarado (2022), *The Hoodoo Bible* by Mama Marie (2021), *Hoodoo Herb and Root Magic* by Catherine Yronwode (2002), and *Sticks, Stones, Roots & Bones* by Stephanie Rose Bird (2004).

The 1970s. I chose to set the novel in the seventies because more than any other decade it marked a specific intersection between the feminist movement and witchcraft. This intersection created a unique reclamation and reinterpretation of the "witch" figure as a symbol of female power, resistance, and alternative knowledge. I saw the "Weird Sisters" as "every girls" who were seeking to claim their agency and power inside a male-dominated art world and male-centric art school through Tarot, magic spells, and green witchery. Books like *The Modern Guide to Witchcraft* by Skye Alexander (2014) and *The Green Witch's Garden* by Arin Murphy-Hiscock (2021), and *Power Through Witchcraft* by Louise Huebner (1969), which is considered "a psychedelic, postmodern grimoire" and "the 1960s witchcraft cult classic," were great resources.

Art School and Ancient Monastery. Holding a BFA and MFA in painting, design, and art history, and having attended parochial school, I am familiar with both worlds, but more importantly, both felt like the perfect setting for a series of "visual" murders, or "paintings in space." For further information on fifteenth-century monasteries and monasticism, I located a Legare Street Press reprint of *A Short History of Monks and Monasteries* by Alfred Wesley Wishart (1902).

Timeline. While historians agree that the very first Tarocchi deck was created in northern Italy between 1430 and 1450, there are varying opinions on the timing and heritage of America's first settlers. Although this is a work of fiction, I wanted to ensure its feasibility.

And, finally and most importantly, thank you to all you readers, book advocates, booksellers, librarians, bloggers, reviewers, and others who support and spread the word about reading and books. I appreciate and am so grateful for all of you!

About the Author

Jennifer Murphy holds an MFA in painting and art history from the University of Denver and an MFA in creative writing from the University of Washington. She is the recipient of the 2013 Loren D. Milliman Fellowship for creative writing and was a contributor at the Bread Loaf Writers' Conference from 2008 through 2012. The author of *I Love You More* and *Scarlet in Blue*, a Michigan Notable Book, as well as the winner of the Nancy Pearl Book Award for Fiction, she lives in Alexandria, Virginia.